Thoroughly Captivated

Book 3 of the Aldbey Park series

Chantry Dawes

ARE YOU SIGNED UP FOR DRAGONBLADE'S BLOG?

You'll get the latest news and information on exclusive giveaways, exclusive excerpts, coming releases, sales, free books, cover reveals and more.

Check out our complete list of authors, too!

No spam, no junk. That's a promise!

Sign Up Here

www.dragonbladepublishing.com

Dearest Reader;

Thank you for your support of a small press. At Dragonblade Publishing, we strive to bring you the highest quality Historical Romance from some of the best authors in the business. Without your support, there is no 'us', so we sincerely hope you adore these stories and find some new favorite authors along the way.

Happy Reading!

CEO, Dragonblade Publishing

Additional Dragonblade books by Author Chantry Dawes

The Aldbey Park Series
Thoroughly in Love (Book 1)
Thoroughly Besotted (Book 2)
Thoroughly Captivated (Book 3)

PROLOGUE

1809
Battlefield of the Combined Frontier Force
of the British and Persian Army
somewhere near Erivan within the Russian
and Ottoman Empire

"I AM NOT leaving them!" Captain Warwick de Walton's voice thundered over his shoulder to his commander who had just sounded the retreat.

"It is too dangerous," his commander shouted back through the acrid smoke and the booming of cannons that lit up the darkness of twilight over the battlefield. "You will be killed, you fool. I ordered a retreat. Leave them! Anything still out there is dead!"

The huge man called War stopped as the smoke swirled around him. He turned to the commander with fire in his eyes and anger in his clenched fists. *"I will not leave them. I will bring them out of that hell. My word is truth."*

With those words, he disappeared back into the smoke-filled darkness before his commander could issue another order that he would have to disobey.

War's breath roared in his lungs as he ran back toward the fire and the noise and the chaos of the battlefield. He jumped over the bodies lying on the ground that were staring sightlessly up at the night sky with blank, dead eyes. War knew that it was too late to help them.

The boom of the enemy cannons shook the ground as he ran on, ducking as the eerie, high-pitched hissing of the iron balls sailed over his head and landed somewhere behind him.

Still, he ran back into the fires of hell while behind him his battalion fled the field of battle.

He willingly ran toward the fire, toward the smoke, toward the guns and cannons, *toward the enemy*.

He kept his head low, scanning the figures laying on the ground as he got closer to where the front of his battalion's line had been.

He saw a red coat amongst the mud and debris. It was one of his men lying on the ground. He rushed to the soldier's side and knelt down, relieved to see that this man was alive. He helped his soldier to sit up, noting that the man had not suffered any injuries that he could see. He knew the blast from a nearby shell could knock a man out and cause a severe headache if it did not kill him.

"Good God and bloody hell, here you are, having a nap on the battlefield like a lazy bounder!" War clasped the man on the shoulder and smiled with his white teeth showing starkly against the dirt and blood and soot on his face. "You must get up! The battalion is in retreat! Get yourself out of here!" he bellowed.

The man nodded his aching head. "Thank you for coming for me," he said on a ragged breath.

War shook his head and smiled again, a wolfish smile. "I did not come back just to rescue your pretty face. There are others."

A screaming hiss of a shrapnel shot went over their heads. War threw himself on top of the man, protecting him from any metal projectiles within the exploding shot that may hit them.

The shot went wide.

War hauled the man to his feet. "Go!" he roared. "Those eight sisters of yours are depending on your return!" He shoved the man in the direction of his battalion and watched as he quickly stumbled away from the battlefield.

War turned back and steeled his jaw as he looked left and right, peering through the smoke and fire for any other red coats while once again listening.

He went forward. He would not let his men die or let the enemy take them.

He saw the dark shapes ahead of him in the hellish orange glow of the fires.

They were screaming. Calling out with such agony and terror as fire raged around them.

He pulled off his red coat as he ran faster now, oblivious to the freezing cold. The scarlet of that uniform was too easy to see, even in this hell.

Dread sank heavy in his chest at what he feared he would find.

He burst through a cloud of heavy smoke and stopped.

His breath caught in his chest at the sight before him.

The four big horses pulling the wagon of their battalion's last remaining large cannon had been hit by a blast of cannon fire from the enemy.

The wagon was an inferno.

Two of the poor beasts that had been hitched closest to the wagon were lying on the ground dead from the blast, but the two lead horses that he had heard calling out were still in the traces, rearing and screaming in fear as they moved frantically in place, pulling at the weight on the ground behind them. They were still connected to the other horses by the harness and the broken pieces of the wagon shafts. Their tails were burned as were their hind legs and haunches, showing bloody patches here and there where the fire had caught them.

Worse, they were unable to flee.

Fiery embers floated all around them as the burning embers landed on their bodies. Several of the flames from the burning wagon snapped and crackled as the flames moved ever closer over the horses' backs like glowing orange fingers whipping at their coats.

War quickly used his own shirt to smother out any remaining embers still burning the coats and hides of the two horses. He ducked under the flames and cut them loose from the harness and shouted for them to move on. Just then, the two horses let out frightened screams. He quickly ducked and covered his head as he held tight to their reins. Another cannonball landed off to his left. It hit one of their battalion's smaller wagons that had also been left behind in their hasty retreat. The wagon burst apart with the impact, sending splinters of wood flying into the air as that wagon, too, caught fire.

Thankfully no horses were attached to the wagon, it was only this team of horses that had not been accounted for.

He peered through the smoke and fire to see something coming toward him on the ground.

A light cannon rolled slowly toward him. It had come off of its base on the smaller wagon from the blast.

The cannon stopped near his feet and then started to sink in the mud from its weight.

Without thinking, War hefted the short, heavy bronze cannon onto one shoulder and let what felt like three hundred pounds roll and sit against his neck and cheek. The thing was still hot from being used over and over but with the freezing cold air he barely felt it.

He tugged on the reins to the two horses and called to them once again to move on, urging them away from all the death and smoke and fire. The pair were terrified but he spoke to them in his deep, rumbling voice, calmly and gently coaxing them away from the havoc of the battlefield.

He promised the two big horses that if they made it off the battlefield he would see that their burns were cared for.

War also promised them that they would never experience such horrors again in their lifetime.

CHAPTER ONE

North of London on the road east
from Aldbey Park to Graestone Castle.
Winter, just after Boxing Day
1812

S UCCESS IS A *collection of failures and hardships overcome and*
problems solved, Miss Lula Darley thought to herself as she
bounced along in the carriage.

She was going to make a brave attempt at success for herself
since she was no longer marriage material, not after what had
happened to her.

"Oh!"

Lula gritted her teeth as she rubbed at the pain in her head
under her warm, orange and cream velvet bonnet. Her head had
hit the roof of the carriage again. She peered out the window of
the carriage at the bleak, snow and ice-covered landscape and the
road that they were moving slowly over. *She would never make it*
on time. Her heart started beating furiously with panic.

So much for bravery. She had never been brave. She had
never liked going places or being around large groups of people.
She liked her books on medicine. And she liked helping horses.

She began singing nervously as she held tightly to the strap on
the carriage wall above her seat. Humming or singing had

become a habit whenever she was frightened or tense, *or panicking.*

Just then, the carriage rumbled over yet another rut in the road.

The rain mixed with snow from the days before had left the roads in a perilous state for anything with wheels after the snow storm from a few days ago.

She had lost count of how many times she had been bounced and thrown left and right on their family's carriage seat as the wheels of the carriage had lurched and bounced and slammed over the ruts or hit another slush-filled puddle on the wet, bumpy, dirt road.

"Sorry, Miss Lula!" the coachman shouted down to her from the coach box for possibly the hundredth time. "No need to sing, all is under control. I'll have you there in no time, Miss!"

"Never apologize for that which is not your fault, Mr. Smith!" Lula called back to him as she renewed her grip of the strap beside her seat.

She peered out the window again, up into the gloomy, bruised-looking afternoon sky. She thought she saw the outline of an old gothic-looking castle sitting atop a hill but then the gray clouds moved over it and blurred it from her vision.

She continued to look for the austere castle but it did not reappear out of the clouds. She shivered nervously as she moved away from the window with a frown. Settling back against the cushions, she made herself start to sing again to take her mind off of what was ahead of her as she bounced and jostled along.

Another bump of the carriage wheels sent her head crashing painfully into the ceiling of the coach once again, crushing her beautiful bonnet down flat on her brown curls. *What a ninny she had been, thinking she was brave enough to do this,* she thought. She should have waited until her Aunt Eggy was over her bout of sniffles and could come with her as planned, but Aunt Eggy had insisted Lula not miss this appointment and the opportunity it afforded her.

Lula adjusted her favorite winter bonnet on her hair and adjusted some of the curls down over one particular side of her forehead with shaking fingers.

As the carriage dipped and jolted through another deep puddle, a loud crack suddenly came to her ears.

"Mr. Smith!" she called out. "What was that?"

"I fear that something cracked on one of the back wheels. We must stop," he shouted down to her from the coach box.

Lula frowned. "Very well, Mr. Smith," she called back to him.

"I see an inn just ahead of us, Miss. I'll direct the horses to pull in there so that I may inspect it."

Lula looked out the window into the gray, colorless day. "Do as you must, Mr. Smith." She picked up her satchel from the floor of the carriage and then pulled the hood of her warm, velvet green cloak over her bonnet and buttoned the cloak securely at her throat with her gloved hands.

Shortly after, the coach pulled into the yard of an inn.

Mr. Smith climbed down and inspected the wheel.

"It is cracked, Miss Lula. Just as I thought. We cannot go further." He whistled toward the stables where some young grooms were watching them.

A groom hurried out from the stables and seeing that there was no post boy riding the left side horse pulling the carriage, he turned and called for another groom to help unhitch the horses. The two of them led the horses behind the inn to the stables.

Mr. Smith helped Lula down from the coach. They walked across the yard, dodging the slush and mud-filled puddles as best they could as they walked toward the inn.

Suddenly, Mr. Smith slipped on the icy slush. Lula grabbed at his elbow but it was too late. Mr. Smith's face turned white as he groaned loudly.

"My ankle," he uttered with pain.

Lula stared down at his ankle. "Never fear. We shall get you warm and have your ankle tended to."

Lula pushed back the hood of her cloak with one hand to

look up at the sign hanging over the large wooden door just as it was opened for them.

"Graestone Inn," Lula read aloud. "We must be very close to our destination, Mr. Smith," she said as she slowly helped him inside.

With a wary nod and a wide berth around the portly inn-keeper who was holding the door for her, she guided Mr. Smith to a chair by the fireplace. She set down her satchel and pulled off her bonnet and gloves and knelt down beside Mr. Smith's chair. She gently pulled his boot from his foot, ignoring his weak attempt at shooing her away. She felt his ankle with experienced hands.

She turned to the innkeeper who was watching them with great interest. "A large basin of water for Mr. Smith to soak his sprained ankle, if you please?" She turned back to Mr. Smith. "It is not broken but it is sprained. No walking or climbing up on a carriage for you. It is lucky that we are so close to our destination."

She noticed once again that the innkeeper was still staring at her.

She hastily adjusted a few curls over her forehead and then turned away to stretch her hands out to the warmth of the cheery fire with a sigh.

"I am glad to hear that my inn is close to your destination, my lady," the innkeeper said as he came closer. "The roads are not fit to travel on!" The innkeeper cleared his throat and stared curiously at the woman before him who had come inside his inn wearing the most colorful bonnet he had ever seen. She was also wearing an oddly bright green cloak that matched her eyes. *She was a pretty thing,* he thought appreciatively as he ran his thick fingers over the bushy mustache covering his lips and then smoothed his hand over the long strands of gray, greasy hair covering the top of his head. A dog came sniffing at the floor near him. He gave it a kick with his large boot while still managing to keep his eyes on the young woman before him, ignoring the sharp whine of pain from the dog.

Lula took a step back from the innkeeper and held out a hand to stop him. "That is close enough, if you please," she said firmly.

The innkeeper backed away as he stared at her in surprise at her words. "Certainly, er, my lady," he uttered with a frown as he licked his lips again at the sight of her. The young lady had rosy cheeks and lips and a riot of glossy, brown curls piled atop her head that had been hidden under her bonnet. "Where exactly did you say your destination is, my lady?" the innkeeper asked with deepening curiosity as he stared openly at the swell of her bosoms under her cloak.

Mr. Smith turned from draping his heavy coachman's cloak over the chair back to look at the innkeeper. He raised his chin and frowned as he managed to stand with great effort. He leaned on the back of his chair as he stepped partially in front of his mistress. "In fact, she did *not* say, Sir, but Miss Darley is expected at Graestone Castle," he announced with great importance and then sank back down onto the chair with a groan.

The innkeeper pulled his many chins in and scowled back at the coachman before turning to Lula. "I see. Well then, you are only a short walk up to the castle from this inn. Tis a shame this storm came upon us the other day and made the roads so rough, and your driver hurt his ankle." He looked Lula up and down again as his frown deepened. "I best get you something to warm your innards. You'll be needing it where you're going." He made a "tsking" noise as he looked her up and down again, shaking his head and scratching his buttocks through his greasy trousers as he shuffled close to her to walk toward the kitchens.

Lula quickly backed well out of his path as the man brushed past her. She watched as he kicked several skittish dogs out of his way.

"A short walk?" Lula asked after him, but it was too late, the innkeeper had already walked away toward a door where a large woman and several younger ladies were peeking out. Lula assumed they were his wife and daughters. He waved his hand at them to move and went through the door. Lula turned to Mr. Smith. "*A short walk*, the innkeeper said."

"Miss Lula, you cannot be thinking of walking," Mr. Smith said with alarm.

"But indeed, I believe it is the only way since we have a broken wheel on the carriage and you are injured." Lula touched her wildly curling brown hair as she smiled reassuringly at Mr. Smith with her bright blue-green eyes. "The Darley sisters are known to be willful creatures. Did you not know this, Mr. Smith?" she asked with a bravery she knew that she was not truly capable of.

No, this Darley sister was not brave, she thought. Her bravery had been lost last year. She reached up and pulled her curls over the scar on her forehead. The need to cover and hide the scar had become such an automatic reflex that she barely was aware she was doing it. She could hide her scars and pretend they were not there, but she could not make the memories of the day she received them go away.

When the innkeeper returned with two mugs of steaming cider, Lula backed away from him as she asked him the directions to the castle. Once again, he came far too close to her person as he handed her the mug. She took another step back and gratefully cradled the warm mug in her cold hands. "The directions to the castle?" she prompted him.

The innkeeper looked at her with horror. "You cannot be thinking—" But at her severe look, he answered her question. "There's a path just out back of the inn that leads to the village and from the village you'll find another road to the castle, my lady. But it is just as bad as the one you were on, I'd wager. Or you could just continue on the road out front but it does wind its way a bit up to the castle. Either way, you cannot miss Graestone. We have a view of it from the inn, it's that close, it is." He scowled and shuddered. "Best you wait until morning, my lady, to let the roads dry out a bit more."

Lula sipped at her cider and sighed with pleasure as the sweet, hot liquid warmed her from the inside. She shook her head as she took another sip of the hot drink. "I have an appointment that I do not wish to be any later than I already am and unfortunately one of our carriage wheels needs to be seen to. Mr. Smith shall be staying as well to rest his ankle and to see to the repairs, but I can walk. Have no fear!"

"An *appointment?*" the innkeeper scowled. "What kind of an appointment does a *lady* have with him, up in the castle?" he demanded rudely. "That one up to the castle doesn't like visitors," he said belligerently.

Lula watched as his scowl deepened and he made a jerking motion of his thumb, presumably in the direction of "that one, up to the castle".

"I beg your pardon?" she asked as she controlled the instant pounding of her heart. Mr. Smith was with her. She knew she was in no danger from the innkeeper with the big coachman beside her. Even with his injured ankle, he was still a large man. "Certainly you cannot be referring to Baron Warwick de Walton?"

The innkeeper sputtered when the coachman managed to rise from his chair and take a threatening though hobbling step toward him.

"Yes, that one. He's a recluse, he is," the innkeeper said hastily as he looked at Mr. Smith and then back to Lula. "And a frightening giant to boot. He doesn't like visitors is all!" His courage returned as the big coachman stepped away and sat back down with a sigh. He continued, "He is as angry a man as you'll ever meet. Ever since his parents died and his uncle, who has a weak heart but who I say is *touched*," he said pointing to his head, "dumped all the responsibility on him when he came home from the battlefield. Left it all to him, just as the uncle did his father. But this time, he gave him the title as well as the work. He is better known as *War*, that one. And rightfully called that, I'd say," he added. "What business could you have with him?" he asked insolently as he eyed her from head to foot.

"Now see here!" Mr. Smith said indignantly as he started to

rise toward the portly innkeeper once again. He sloshed some of his own cider onto his own tunic and sat heavily back down again with a grimace of pain. He gave the innkeeper a fierce frown. "You have no right to question Miss Darley!"

Lula set her mug firmly down on the table in front of the fireplace, ignoring the innkeeper's description of the baron even though it made her heart beat frantically with fear. The only thing she knew of the baron was that he was a quiet, solitary man. It was a description which she had liked the sound of.

"Never mind that, Mr. Smith," she said hiding her trepidation. "I should leave at once before it gets dark." She scooped up her bonnet from the table with shaking fingers.

"But, Miss—"

She held up one finger to silence her coachman and then placed her vibrant orange and cream velvet bonnet back on her hair and secured it with its wide, parrot green ribbon. "Very well then!"

Her eyes fell on Mr. Smith once again and paused as she looked him over. His skin was still frighteningly pale with the pain of his ankle and the cold of sitting up on the coach box on the way here.

"You cannot go alone, Miss. I can make it, I swear I can," he said as he struggled once again to rise from the chair.

Lula held up her hand to stop him. "You *must* stay here, Mr. Smith and *rest* that ankle. Take this to cover your lodgings and supper." She handed him several coins from a small reticule attached to her gown at her waist, and then thought a bit and gave him some more. "There is enough there to repair the coach wheel, as well." She held up her hand again, as he started to argue once more. "You have faith in my medical knowledge, do you not?" When he nodded his head, she continued, "Then you can trust me when I say that of a certainty *you cannot walk on that ankle.*" Her voice was stern and brooked no argument.

"Very well, Miss Darley," Mr. Smith said reluctantly with a bow of his head.

Lula looked over at the innkeeper and saw his gaze drift down to her hands and, in particular, the scar there. She quickly pulled on her yellow kid gloves that were the color of spring jonquils. The fine leather gloves perfectly matched her yellow kid ankle boots. Their cheery spring color always uplifted her mood, even on dreary winter days like today.

"Just follow the road you say?" she asked brightly with a tight smile as the innkeeper continued to look at her hand until her glove fully covered it.

At his speechless, open mouthed, single nod she said with forced confidence, "Very well then, off I go!"

Lula gathered her satchel, raised the hood of her bright, Pomona green cloak over her precious orange and cream bonnet and walked to the door of the inn.

She heard the innkeeper speaking to Mr. Smith. "Twilight will be coming soon. At least she'll not have to worry about any wolves. She'll frighten them away with all those colors she's wearing."

Lula hesitated with her hand on the latch. She looked down at her clothing. She loved bright colors, but then she realized what else the innkeeper had said. *Wolves?*

She heard Mr. Smith proudly repeating her words to the innkeeper. "The Darley sisters are known to be willful creatures. They are *all* very brave women, indeed! Miss Lula Darley will not be afraid and, besides, there's been no wolves in this area for years!"

She took a calming breath and smiled tightly.

It was not wolves that she was fearful of.

She knew that there was something far more dangerous than wolves.

Men.

Lula took a deep breath. She opened the door of the inn and walked out to the road that would lead her up the hill to Graestone Castle and her appointment with Baron Warwick de Walton.

A man known to be a recluse and from what she had just learned, a giant, angry man.

A man better known as War.

CHAPTER TWO

L ULA STOPPED TO catch her breath after walking up the long and twisting hilly road. She looked down at the hem of her Pomona green cloak and under that to her favorite emerald green dress that she had picked precisely for this day. Her gaze traveled further down to her beautiful yellow kid boots.

She groaned. Her hem and her boots were stained with the mud and the wetness of the leftover slush in the road.

She switched her satchel to her other hand and looked with determination up at the top half of the gray stone castle that could be seen ahead of her just over the trees. She stilled as her heart began to race. It was the same, austere-looking gothic castle she had seen rising out of the fog. It did indeed look to be a very ancient castle. It had four, tall, square towers, one at each corner, as well as a shorter, squat tower in the center capped with a tall, out of place turret. All were grasping up toward the dreary, bruised sky like an ominous, colorless picture from one of her younger sister Birdie's dreadful stories.

From what Lula could see of the castle, it looked as gloomy and lifeless as the dreary, dark gray, overcast sky.

She could not find a single thing that looked warm or welcoming about it.

It appeared that Graestone Castle was as aptly named as its owner.

She could just imagine Birdie going on and on at the sight, making up some dramatic, horrible, terrible tale about the castle and its inhabitants.

Her eldest sister, Julia, would vow to fight anyone within the gray edifice that may do any of her sisters harm.

Lula was the pragmatic and prudent one out of her sisters, however. She was known to be the bookish one and therefore the predisposed intellect. She would not be frightened. She would use reason.

It was simply a very old castle.

With a recluse deemed to be an angry giant living there.

A man that she knew would become even angrier when he found out who she was.

She took a fortifying breath as she continued trudging up the hill. She nervously began singing a happy tune. She found its chorus particularly uplifting when she was frightened or stressed.

"Ben Backstay was a bos'n
He was a jolly boy,
and none as he so merrily
could pipe all hands ahoy.

With a chip, chop! Cherry chop!
Fol de rol, riddle-rop!
Chip, chop! Cherry chop!
Fol de rol ray!
With a chip, chop! Cherry chop!
Fol de rol, riddle-rop!
Chip, chop! Cherry chop!
Fol de rol ray!"

Lula sang the merry little chorus over and over as she rounded the bend in the road. She was about to take a breath to start the second verse when she thought she heard a plaintive sound.

She stopped and looked around.

There it was again!

A soft whining of an animal.

She followed the sound to the edge of the road where it fell off into a steep, muddy ditch.

A dog was lying there in the mud. As she watched it struggled to pull itself from the mud with its front legs in an effort to climb back up the steep bank, exhausted, it lay its weary head back down and whined softly.

"Oh, you poor thing!" Lula cried out softly.

She set her satchel on the driest piece of ground she could find and hoisted up her skirts. No sooner had she taken one single cautious step over the embankment when her yellow boots slipped and slid and she found herself flailing her arms as she tried not to fall backward onto her bottom. Down the slippery embankment she went, landing in the muddy ditch on her backside in her Pomona green velvet cloak and her emerald green gown. She was splattered with mud everywhere. She moaned at the thought of what her backside looked like. She moaned again when she realized that she could not even see her lovely jonquil yellow kid boots anymore for her feet were sunk deep in the muck.

At her side, the dog became frantic. It kept looking over at her as it began struggling valiantly in earnest to free itself and get away from her as it yipped and whined fearfully.

"No, no!" Lula murmured as she reached out a hand to pet the animal. At its quick fearful recoil and high-pitched yelp, she pulled her hand back. "I won't hurt you. I am here to help you," she said gently. "Easy now, easy," she crooned as she slowly reached out once again to lay her hand on the animal's head. It let out a soft whine and dropped its head to the mud as it lay there, exhausted from its efforts and shivering with the cold.

Lula pulled her boots out of the thick, gooey mud and carefully stood up. She slowly leaned down and gently placed her hands around the dog's middle as she crooned reassuring words to it. Instantly, it began struggling forward. But within moments, it collapsed back to the ground, shaking and weak.

Lula tried and tried but she could not pull the dog's back end and feet from the mud. She looked down at the mud, studying all around the exhausted dog quietly. It had to be caught on something that she could not see under the mud. Finally she spotted a mud-covered rope rising out of the muck where the dog's hind end and feet would be. The rope went toward a branch that leaned over the ditch on the opposite embankment.

"Ah, I see. I believe you have caught yourself in a snare," she said softly as she stepped carefully through the mud to the other bank. "One moment, my friend. Keep your courage and do not give up. I shall have you free soon!"

She quickly untied the rope from the overhanging branch and looked down triumphantly at the dog. "You are free!"

The dog just laid there looking at her with misery in its large eyes. Every now and then, a shudder would rack its body.

She trudged carefully back to the dog through the mud, then she bent down and pulled the poor animal forward out of the muck. This time, she was successful in freeing it entirely from the mud. She found and untied the snare from one of its hind legs and stepped back with a smile.

"There now, you are out of the mud and the snare. Run home!"

Still the dog lay there, whining softly.

She reached down and lifted it to its legs but it immediately collapsed to the ground. She tried again, holding it up with her hands. The poor animal's legs shook as it tried to stand with her help.

"I have you. Take your time," she crooned.

She watched as the dog wagged its tail once and took a wobbly step forward and then another and another. It wagged its tail again and then shook its body once. Flecks of mud flew everywhere.

Lula laughed as she closed her eyes and turned her face away from the droplets of thick mud flying through the air. "Very good then," she laughed as she opened her eyes and brushed ineffectively at her cloak. "Your face is less covered in mud but you will do! Make your way home now. I am sure there is a little boy or girl missing you dreadfully." Lula took a few steps up the steep bank before looking back at the dog.

The dog had not moved. It continued to look up at her with its pointed ears pricked forward. It took a few hesitant steps up the bank but slid right back down.

"You cannot make it up the bank, can you?" she asked with her hands on her hips as she stared down at the animal. She went back down and stopped and studied the dog looking up at her so hopefully.

Lula did not hesitate, she scooped the dog up in both arms while managing to grasp a piece of her skirt to lift it out of the way of her feet. She then clambered awkwardly back up the embankment out of the ditch. With a sigh of relief that she had not slid back down, she placed the dog on the road and patted its head. Giving the dog a quick study, she did her best to wipe the remaining mud off of its body and, in particular, its face and eyes. Then she scooped up her satchel just in time, for the dog shook itself again, mightily this time, sending more flecks of mud in every direction.

"Feeling better now with all that mud off of you? There you are then, now run home! I am very late I fear, and must hurry off myself," she said and turned around and began walking.

A sharp whine had her stopping and turning back to look at the dog once again.

The dog was staring at her. Its ears were lowered and it was wagging its tail in hopefulness as it shivered pathetically.

She tilted her head left, and then right as she studied it. Her breath slowed as her heart pumped loudly in her chest. The dog had tall, pointed ears and a long tail. Its fur was a mixture of gray, tan and brown. Its eyes were wide-set. She noticed with a start as the gray light of the afternoon shone on the animal's head in just the right way that one eye was a most curious yellow-green color while the other was blue.

She took a step back as her breath caught. "You are not someone's pet are you?" she whispered and then took several more steps away from the animal.

The animal looked at her and wagged its tail and whined as it took a cautious, uneven step forward to follow her.

Lula quickly lifted her hand. "Stay!" she called out as she hastily backed up.

The animal stopped instantly and whined again, softer this time.

"Sit!" she said hesitantly as she kept her eyes on it.

The animal sat down and thumped its tail as its tongue lolled out of its mouth. It tilted its head as it stared back at her, waiting.

"Perhaps you *were* someone's pet," she whispered as she studied the animal. "What other commands do you know, I wonder?"

She watched in amazement as it lowered itself onto its belly and crawled forward another few inches as it looked at her and whined plaintively.

Lula took a breath. This was not a wolf as she had thought. The sad-looking animal was terribly skinny with patches of fur missing here and there. She could see its ribs and its hip bones. She opened her satchel and felt around inside until she found what she was looking for. She pulled out a small tin of biscuits. She tossed one to the dog who gulped it down without seeming to even chew it. He looked at her hopefully as his tail thumped on the ground. She threw him another biscuit and studied him as he ate this one slower.

She frowned sadly to see that the snare had made one hind leg almost raw. But it was the other leg that she stared at longest. There was an old injury there, perhaps from another snare, or a trap even. The foot was misshapen and above it was a mangled scar. It was long healed over, but still visible. The dog walked with a limp that it seemed accustomed to.

"You must possess great courage to have survived whatever

you have been through before the mud and the snare," she whispered. "I cannot imagine what happened to have caused your body such scars, but you are free now." She heaved a great sigh. "I must go," she said to the dog.

It tilted its head and whined softly.

She shook her head as she turned to go but the dog stood up and looked expectantly at her.

"Go," she commanded with a wave of her hand and then turned around to start walking up to the castle once again.

He followed her of course. Each time she turned to look, he immediately sat down and thumped his tail with his tongue hanging out of his mouth.

"It is because I gave you those biscuits, isn't it?" she said with a shake of her head. She turned around and lifted her mud-stained skirts and continued walking.

The dog continued to follow her.

All the way up the hill, he trailed behind her, until they reached the top where the old gray stone castle sat hovering over the valley, peering through an overgrowth of trees down at the inn and the village which stretched out in the valley behind the old inn.

Lula stopped and looked up at the ancient walled enclosure of the castle. She stared at the old stones with trepidation. In front of her, the road led through a massive wrought iron gate that seemed to be rusted open. She doubted it would ever close again for small trees and shrubs were growing up through it.

The road she had been following led right through the gate and into a massive courtyard overgrown with dried stalks of brown winter grass. The road circled around the courtyard and widened at the entrance to the house. There, she saw wide stone steps leading up to a pair of huge oak doors that stood like tall sentinels, watching over the empty, uncared for courtyard where one could imagine the ghosts of the people that had once populated it roamed.

Lula stood there at the open gates not yet able to summon

enough bravery to cross the expanse of tall, dead winter grass. She stared across the vast courtyard, staring up at the house, or rather, the castle. For it was indeed an old castle.

She felt a damp nudge at her hand and looked down to see the dog staring up at her.

She laid her yellow, mud-stained gloved hand on its head. "Yes, I am frightened," she whispered. "I have not the courage that you have, my friend."

She hummed nervously to herself as she stared up at the castle. In her mind she was lecturing herself over the situation. *What had her mother and Great-aunt Egidia been thinking? To let a young woman venture forward on her own like this? Oh, Aunt Eggy was supposed to have accompanied her but a bout of the sniffles at the last minute had caused her to take to her bed. The wily, tiny, old lady. How foolish had she been to have thought nothing of traveling by herself? To walk away from the broken-down carriage thinking she could walk all the way to the castle. And now, here she was covered in mud with a dog that looked like a starved and injured wolf at her side. If she had not been able to manage her fear over the simple journey to her destination, then how could she manage whatever she may encounter inside Graestone Castle?*

Lula's humming increased in volume as she hugged her cloak tightly to her chin with her free hand. Her satchel was growing heavy in her other hand as she stood there, numbly looking up at the dark, dreary fortress of a castle.

She knew that she had always talked like she was intelligent and brave. She also knew that she was anything but that. If her older sister, Julia, was able to overcome her fear of riding and jumping horses after their father had died coming off his horse, then she could overcome her own fears to do this.

Lula frowned. Julia had had Pasha at her side. Pasha, who was a Prince of Persia with his calmness and his quiet strength, had given Julia her courage back.

Lula, however, was alone. And her fears were very different from her sister's.

She looked down at the dog once again. "You are my inspiration," she said tightly. "You shall be my courage, and that shall also be your name." She took a deep breath as she looked back at those thick, oak doors.

"Come along, Courage," she called softly to the dog. She lifted her chin and began walking across the large courtyard. "*With a chip chop, cherry chop, fol de rol, riddle-rop,*" she sang in a whisper to herself, over and over, all the way to the wide stone steps and up to the front doors of Graestone Castle.

They were expecting her after all.

Or rather, they were expecting someone she was pretending to be.

CHAPTER THREE

L ULA LIFTED THE heavy, round, iron door knocker that hung
from the mouth of a small, cast iron horse's head and banged
it against the door for the third time. She wondered if anyone
could possibly have heard the sound through these ancient, stout
doors. She pressed her ear to the oak and listened for any sounds
from within.

Silence.

She was met with absolute silence.

The castle was as lifeless as it looked. She nervously pulled
her curls over the scar on her forehead as she hummed her song
for the umpteenth time while she stared at the door, wondering
what to do.

Suddenly, something tiny and white flew past her ear and
landed with a small splat on the door.

Lula stared at the white thing. She bent closer.

Could it be-?

Yes, she thought. Indeed, it was a tiny paper spitball.

A small voice came from behind her.

"Your dog is ugly."

She whirled around to look behind her. And then lowered her
eyes to stare down to the bottom of the steps.

"*Your* aim is off," she retorted, looking back and forth from a
small boy of about six years staring up at her to two slightly taller

boys of possibly nine and ten years old who were standing behind him. She looked back at the littlest of the three, thinking that it had been he who had called her dog ugly.

The little boy just stared at the dog with wide eyes.

"Your dog is ugly and my aim was just fine and Jolyon won't talk," one of the larger boys who had dark, curly hair said loudly to her. In his hand, he held a hollow reed which was presumably the agent of the launched spitball. He saw when her eyes landed on the reed he held. He quickly put his hands behind his back, hiding the reed as his face turned bright red.

"Oh?" she asked. "And who might you be?"

The two taller boys looked at each other and grinned and then both turned their grins back to her with an added air of importance as they puffed their young chests out. "We are Machabee and Melchisedec," the one with the dark curly hair said. "I am Machabee." He pointed his thumb proudly into his chest.

"I see," Lula said, "Such very fine names you have."

"We're brothers, all three of us," the other boy, presumably the one named Melchisedec, announced. He was slightly shorter than Machabee and his hair was a bit straighter than and not as dark as his brothers'. "Jolyon is our baby brother. Don't bother talking to him. He won't talk to anyone. Not even to Mack or me."

"Why doesn't he talk? He is certainly old enough to be talking," Lula asked.

Machabee frowned at her. "We didn't say he *doesn't* talk. Like Mel told you, we said he *won't*."

Lula frowned. "I see." But she did not see. She looked down at the silent little boy whose brown hair was in a tussled state. He looked as filthy as she was sure that she was. His clothes were in disarray also, and he had no coat. His skin looked white and she caught him shivering now and then. "He is cold. Perhaps you should take him home to get warm."

The older two boys looked at each other again and rolled

their eyes. They turned back to her with impatient looks on their faces. "We *are* home. We were invited to live here at Graestone with our Uncle War." This was from Machabee, who seemed to be the leader of the trio. "Everyone knows who we are. Well, they don't usually get our names correct. Instead they call us incorrigible." He held up a finger and then another and another as he listed what they were called. "Difficult, impossible, irredeemable, but mostly we are called the wildlings, which makes the most sense of course." He shrugged his shoulders. "We live here. Everyone knows that," he stated with a frown as if she were foolish not to know this.

Lula stared at the boys, taking that all in as she remained silent. She looked back at the door and then again to the boys. "My great-aunt calls our puppies wildlings. She is Scottish, you see." The boys just stared curiously at her. "Well then," she said as she looked at the door again. "I knocked and no one has answered."

It was Melchisedec that spoke this time. "Tuedy takes a long time to open the door." He shrugged indifferently.

"Tuedy?" Lula asked.

"Yes, Tuedy Tweedy, the housekeeper and our cook," Machabee clarified.

She looked back and forth between the two older boys.

Melchisedec just stared back at her and shrugged again as if he had said all that he needed to say.

Machabee looked from his brother to Lula and shrugged as well. "Unless Tuedy sent Todrick Tweedy to open the door. He's the butler. He's supposed to answer the door but no one ever comes so it doesn't matter really. Todrick Tweedy takes even longer and most times gets lost and ends up in another part of the house. Then we must go looking for him and bring him back to Tuedy in the kitchens. Tuedy makes us go find him before he ends up in the dungeons or lost in a secret tunnel."

"Or tries to shoot one of the old cannons up on the battlements," Melchisedec said with enthusiastic relish.

"Goodness," Lula breathed out.

A loud, screeching, grating noise made her spin back around. The dog she had named Courage let out an alarmed, soft bark.

Lula spun around to see that one of the great oak doors was opening.

She heard the boys giggle and turned back to them but they had taken their younger brother's hands and all three had ducked behind some ragged bushes to the side of the stone steps.

Lula whirled back to the door.

A very tall and very thin, elegant man with fine, sharply handsome features and dramatic long sideburns stood there staring at her. He was dressed all in black with his black hair pomaded forward over the front of his head to spill in artful disarray upon his forehead. He continued to stare at Lula with curious, expectant, dark eyes.

"Yes?" he finally asked in a shrill voice as he held the door open just enough to look Lula up and down.

Lula swallowed and once again absentmindedly fussed with the curls over her forehead and the scar there. She felt Courage duck behind her skirts. "I am here to see Baron de Walton," she said in what she thought was a calm, firm tone.

"You are?" the man asked with astonishment as his voice rose higher.

Lula tried again. "You must be Mr. Tweedy, the butler? I believe Baron de Walton is expecting me."

The man stared at Lula, continuing to look her up and down. His eyes widened as they landed momentarily on Lula's muddy yellow boots before looking back up to her face. "I am Tuedy Tweedy, housekeeper and cook. I am not a *Mr.* Tweedy, eh? Since there are two Tweedys in the household, neither of us go by *Mr.* Tweedy. That was our father. He is dead," he explained in a high-pitched tone.

Lula's lips fell open. "Goodness," she whispered. "Do forgive me, I did not know." She tightened her grip on her satchel. "I am here to see—"

Suddenly Tuedy let out a small shriek. "Those little *wildlings* are at it again!" Tuedy's gaze had gone to the door and the spitball still stuck to it. His eyes narrowed. "Probably tried to hit you with that, eh? Well, there'll be no supper for them and not just for wasting his lordship's paper!" His gaze went past her as he looked around the courtyard and said in a louder, shrill voice, "Such a shame that they'll have no supper for it's their favorite meal and pudding I have prepared!"

Lula heard a muffled whispered gasp from somewhere in the bushes beside her. She quickly took a breath and coughed loudly as she reached out to knock the spitball off the door. "I believe that was a tiny bit of biscuit. I was coughing you see. It was caught in my throat. So sorry!" She coughed again, louder this time.

Tuedy Tweedy stared at her with open curiosity and surprise. "Oh, eh?" He looked down at Lula's boots again. "Did you walk here in those fine boots of yours? *Jonquil yellow* I believe. I can see the sunny color under all that mud, eh?"

Lula nodded quickly, happy to change the subject away from the spitball. She looked down at her muddy boots and back up to Tuedy Tweedy with a smile. "Why, yes! Yes, they are jonquil yellow!" She continued to smile at the man until she realized he was waiting for her to explain her muddy boots. "The carriage wheel broke, you see. I had to walk up from the inn to make my appointment in time. The road is terribly muddy." She switched her satchel to her other hand. "I could not have the baron waiting for me so, of course, I walked. Baron de Walton is expecting me, you see."

Tuedy frowned. "Oh, I doubt that. The only person that Baron de Walton is expecting is a gentleman by the name of Mr. Louis or was it Lou? I cannot recall his full name but I do know that the baron would never have more than one guest. He never has any, eh?"

Lula's heart began beating furiously. This was the part that she had been dreading.

"Well, you see, Tuedy, I—" Lula began.

"Tis Tuedy Tweedy, eh?" he said automatically as he continued to look her over judgmentally.

Lula's eyes widened. She ignored his obvious critique of her person and asked, "You like to be called both names?" She shivered slightly. It was starting to get dark outside as twilight settled over the hilltop the castle sat upon. Now that she was just standing here and no longer trudging up the hilly road, she was becoming chilled. Or she was just terrified.

"I do like to be called by my first and last name if I do not know you." Tuedy pointed to her cloak. "You have quite a bit of mud on your person as well as your boots." He circled a finger at her as he pursed his lips and wiggled his lips and nose left and right. "I can barely see that your velvet cloak is Pomona green! A travesty that is!" he said in a disapproving shrill voice as he pointed to her cloak and then down to her hemline.

Lula looked down at herself and sighed as she furrowed her brows. She was indeed a mess.

She sighed loudly again in great disappointment with herself. "I fell you see, I was about to step down an embankment off the side of the road and I slipped. I was trying to free a dog from the mud and—"

Tuedy's eyes opened wide. He let out a loud, indignant screech and then demanded in a loud voice, "You went off the road and down an embankment in your jonquil yellow kid boots and your Pomona green velvet cloak? Never!"

Lula's lips dropped open. "Yes, I realize that it was rash but it was to save a dog, you see, and I felt it was an urgent matter that I do so. I have studied animal medicine, you see, and I knew he was hurt, which is why I am here. For the baron's horses."

Tuedy looked at her with growing confusion in his eyes. He opened the door a bit wider as he turned to look somewhere into the castle behind him. "Toddy!" Tuedy Tweedy called out in his rather high, soprano voice. "Toddy! Come at once!" His voice rose even higher, to a shrill squeak. "*At once!*"

Lula tried to peek into the vastness of the castle behind him, but all she saw was darkness. She heard footsteps echoing as they came closer.

Tuedy looked back at her and fluttered his fingers "My brother is mostly deaf, eh? He gets lost in the castle and one never knows where he may be so one must call out for him. Forgive my shrieking."

"That's not right. I am not deaf, *Tudor!*" came a raspy, hoarse, almost painful-sounding voice. "And I explore the castle and wander about it. How many times do I have to tell you? Bloody hell, when will you accept that those who like to wander about are not always *lost?*"

The door was yanked fully open. There stood a man who looked very much like Tuedy but in a less elegant way. His sideburns were even longer in length than Tuedy's, following the line of his face to start to curl forward toward his chin. The top of his head was bald but the sides were cut short and brushed forward in the current Caesar style that some men espoused. He was somewhat shorter and quite a bit thicker than his brother. He was staring at her with great curiosity and a rather clear bit of hostility. "Who the devil are you?" he asked in a rough, raspy voice as he took a step forward in front of his brother.

Lula stifled the squeak that rose in her throat as she stepped back from the force of his voice and the sharpness of his eyes. She started panicking as her heart pounded in hard thudding beats. "No closer, if you please," she squeaked.

The man just stared at her, however, looking her over as had his brother.

Tuedy pulled his brother back beside him. "Don't mind my brother. It only sounds like he is barking at you, eh? He doesn't mean anything by it," he said in a cajoling tone as he gave his brother a quick scowl.

Lula swallowed and nodded as Tuedy's brother remained silent. He folded his arms across his round, barrel chest and continued to silently and stubbornly study her while Tuedy fidgeted in embarrassment.

Lula took a deep breath and studied him just as he was studying her. This gave her heart a moment to calm. She noted a
distortion and scaring of the right side of his lips. *They were burn
scars.* The scars traveled down to the side of his chin and then
curled under his chin to the center of his throat. *Was this the cause
of his raspy voice?*

Lula looked back at Tuedy. Now that the door was fully
open, she could see all of him. He was missing a finger from his
left hand, and that hand had burn scars as well. He saw where her
eyes had landed and quickly hid his hand behind him.

"My twin brother and I were cannoneers, eh?" Tuedy explained quickly with a nervous flick of his fingers. "We were field
artillery men and then we were with the British Rocket Forces.
We were responsible for firing the Congreve rockets. It has its
dangers, as you can imagine. I was fortunate, I only lost a finger.
Toddy lost most of his voice."

Lula's eyes widened. *Twins?* She looked back at the man
called Toddy, which must be Tuedy's name for his brother. *Tuedy
and Toddy,* she said to herself. Toddy was still studying her.

"I can see that you are surprised to hear we are twins," he said
in a rusty croak. "We are not identical twins, obviously." He
glared at his brother. "And it is *Todrick*," he rasped. He looked
back at Lula. "Now, if you are done being sufficiently horrified
and femininely shocked at our injuries, what is it that you want?"
he barked at her in what sounded like a painful, harsh whisper.

Lula's breath caught at the man's rudeness. She started to
panic slightly but was able to control it, this time. She gathered
her wits about her and shook her head adamantly at the two men.
They were obviously soldiers, even without Tuedy's confession
that they had been field artillery men. They were certainly not
the typical staff found working in the service of a great house,
much less a castle.

She quickly pulled off her right glove and held her hand out,
palm down to show them the back of her hand. Her fingers

trembled slightly as she held her hand still for them to see. Jagged scars stretched across the back of her hand and across her knuckles. "I am not horrified," she said softly. Then she pulled her bonnet off her head and pushed the tangle of light brown curls away from her forehead. Another large, jagged scar stretched from just above her right eyebrow up into her hairline.

Tuedy shrieked again, quieter this time. "Pon rep!" His eyes rose to her face from her hand as he worked to control his expression. He took a breath and then quickly spoke into the silence, "Pon rep! You have jonquil yellow gloves as well, eh?" Then he smiled gently at her with his eyes crinkling at the corners. He winked at her and nudged his brother aside as he waggled his fingers for her to enter. "Come in, you must be freezing out there."

Lula smiled with relief. She turned partway once she had stepped through the door to reveal the dog who had been hiding behind her skirts during the conversation. He was still outside the door, looking wary of entering the castle. The dog wore a very dejected and worried look on his face. "May the dog come in as well?"

Todrick put his hands on his hips and looked down at the animal. "What in the bloody hell happened to him? He is as muddy as you are," he rasped.

Lula lifted her chin. "He was caught in a snare and struggling to free himself from the mud in a roadside ditch. I managed to rescue him. He is cold and exhausted and I imagine very hungry and thirsty."

Tuedy's voice rose to a high pitch as he stared down at the animal, "Oh! His poor foot, and look at all his scars, and his ribs are showing too, eh?" His voice rose impossibly even higher. "Oh, the poor, poor, wretched thing! Bring him in! *Bring him in!*" he said shrilly.

Todrick's gaze slowly lifted to Lula's as he held up his hand either to stop her from calling the dog inside or to make his brother wait. "Rescued this wretched creature, did you? It looks like a small wolf!" he said suspiciously in his ruff, raspy voice.

"*He is a dog*, I assure you. Look at his eyes. No wolf has blue eyes, you see, much less one blue and one green eye and besides, he is very well trained." She looked back at the dog still standing out on the stone steps. "Come along, Courage." The dog immediately thumped his tail, lowered his head and walked slowly to her side where he stood, looking up at her in adoration. "Sit, Courage." The dog instantly slammed his rump down to the floor. His tongue lolled out of his mouth and his tail thumped enthusiastically while he stared happily up at her. "There! You see?"

"Bloody bugger!" Todrick said as he scratched his neck under his chin. He shoved the huge oak door closed and continued to stare at the dog as he shook his head. "I don't care if he can stand on his head if you tell him to. You brought a dog with you. That's not right," he grumbled as his gaze rose from the dog to look at her with assessing eyes. "How'd you get your scars? Ladies do not have scars."

Tuedy squeaked. "Toddy! That's rude, eh?"

Lula blushed and pulled the curls back over her forehead as she looked away from the twins. "I am unfortunately very aware that proper ladies should have a perfect countenance absent from any imperfections, *or scars*, Mr. Todrick." She swallowed past the lump in her throat. "I was attacked in Hyde Park one evening," she added quietly.

They both stared at her in silence for several moments. One kindly, the other with a suspicious look.

Finally, Tuedy broke the awkward silence when he stepped closer to the dog. He smiled reassuringly at him as he calmly reached down and stroked the dog's head with gentle fingers. He then started brushing the patches of dried mud off of the dog's coat that Lula had missed. "We all have scars, eh?" he said quietly to the dog. "Some seen, others unseen, but they are there, nonetheless."

Courage thumped his tail slowly, looking back and forth from the man to Lula.

Todrick grumbled, "Bloody hell," under his breath in a coarse rasp.

"Toddy," Tuedy said as he stroked the dog's head, "the lady is here for an appointment with the baron. I told her the only appointment expected today was with a Mr. Louis."

Todrick did not look away from the dog when he mumbled in his rough voice, "Yes, that is so. A Mr. Louis, or Lou something or other. Why are you here, Miss—er?" he demanded as he started to turn to her from the dog.

Lula smiled. "Miss Darley, Miss *Lula* Darley, and I am here by request of the baron to see him about his horses," she said and waited.

The Tweedy twins stood up like rockets and stared at her with their mouths open.

"Eh?" Tuedy shrieked.

"He'll be bloody furious," Todrick croaked in his raspy voice.

CHAPTER FOUR

T UEDY PURSED HIS lips and moved his nose and lips back and forth as he looked at her. "You realize that he's expecting a man, eh?"

"Yes, I am aware of this." Lula sighed.

"He will not like it, not one bloody bit!" Todrick rasped. "I have never heard of a woman horse practitioner. I've never even heard of a woman doctor. And you brought a dog with you. A bloody stray dog that looks part wolf. That's not right." He shook his head angrily as he stared at the dog and then back at Lula. "You'd best follow us," Todrick croaked as he turned his back to her and started walking with long strides.

Tuedy hurried after his brother with short, quick steps of his long, thin legs. "You do recall, Toddy, that during the wars we used anyone who had the knowledge to look after the artillery horses' injuries and most of those were women in the villages where we stopped to rest, eh, Toddy? The men were all gone, off to fight."

Lula heard Todrick rasp out a yes, though he shook his head and grumbled an expletive of some sort about having women around. Whatever word he had said, it sounded extremely rude as he barreled ahead of them.

Tuedy turned back to Lula with an apologetic wince as he motioned for her to hurry along.

Lula followed the Tweedy twins through a large, dark, cavernous great hall. In the shadowy interior, she could make out several dust-covered suits of armor standing like ancient sentinels frozen in time along the walls. Other suits of armor were draped in dust cloths. There were also large, life-sized portraits hanging above them with barely visible shadowy men and women in ancient clothing staring down at her in the darkness. More dust cloths covered what must be furniture pieces along the walls.

Straight ahead of her, a double staircase curved up from either side of the great hall and met in a grand balcony overlooking the entirety of the hall. A massive, arched window made up of three singular tall, arched windows was the backdrop to the balcony. The windows were shuttered, like the other windows she had spotted in the great hall. The arched windows of the balcony managed to let in an eerie, dull, twilight glow in the arch of the glass that peeked out above the wooden shutters. That light, however, was barely able to penetrate through the dusty, cloudy glass.

Somewhere overhead, she heard the soft sounds of weeping. She paused, looking upward toward the sound.

"Someone is crying," she whispered.

Tuedy fluttered his fingers. "'Tis nothing, eh?"

The twins hurried on. Lula looked up beyond the stairs once again, listening to the quiet, tormented sobs. The twins stopped and motioned to her in agitation. Lula's heart started beating rapidly as she suddenly became quite hot and could not find her breath. She glanced down at Courage with a tremulous smile. The dog whined softly as he looked up at her and wagged his tail with encouragement. "You are telling me to be brave, aren't you?"

The dog only thumped his tail faster as he stared up at her.

She took that as a yes.

Lula started singing in a soft whisper as she hurried to catch up to the Tweedy twins with the dog right at her side.

"With a chip, chop! Cherry chop!

Fol de rol, riddle-rop!
Chip, chop! Cherry chop!
Fol de rol ray!
With a chip, chop! Cherry chop!
Fol de rol, riddle-rop!
Chip, chop! Cherry chop!
Fol de rol ray!"

"Why the bloody hell are you singing?" Todrick rasped out in a harsh whisper as he looked behind him to Lula.

Lula abruptly stopped walking and closed her mouth and then opened it again as she whispered back, "I sing when I am afraid or when I am nervous."

"Well, which is it?" Todrick demanded gruffly as he stopped and turned to stare at her.

She stared wide-eyed back at him in silence.

"Which are you now? Afraid or nervous?" Todrick barked in a rough-sounding whisper.

Lula looked back and forth between the Tweedy twins. "Both," she said simply.

The twins stared at her quietly and then looked away in obvious discomfort.

It was Tuedy who broke the silence. "Well then, quite right, eh? And well you should be, I think," he said with a worried frown and an awkward pat on her shoulder.

Todrick scowled at his brother. "She was singing a sailor's song. For *men* to sing. It's not right." He looked back at Lula. "You are supposed to be a lady, yes? Ladies do not sing those kinds of songs," Todrick rasped with disapproval as if taking note of another mark against her.

Lula could only shrug. "It is a merry ditty nevertheless and it makes me feel better."

Tuedy stared at her a moment longer and then nodded once. He looked at his brother. "I think that is a sensible thing to do when one is afraid, Toddy."

Todrick growled. "It's foolish and silly and not right," he grumbled stubbornly and started walking again. "At the very least, she should pick a different song."

Tuedy hurried after his brother with his long legs taking short, quick steps. "Toddy, that was unkind. She can sing what she likes, eh?"

Lula heard Todrick grumble something about her not staying long so what did it bloody matter as he continued to speed up and walk faster than his taller and longer-legged, twin brother.

The twins led her down a dimly lit side hallway and stopped at a door where orange firelight spilled out of the doorway where it was slightly ajar.

Lula stopped. She stared at the door. This was the moment she had come for and she found that she was absolutely terrified. She wanted to turn around and run all the way back home. *What had she been thinking to come alone? And why had she not insisted that Aunt Eggy be here with her or that they wait until she could be here?*

"Well, go ahead," Todrick rasped impatiently as he motioned for Lula to enter the study. "The sooner you go in, the sooner the baron will send you back out the bloody front door. You and that wolf dog of yours. Go on, get it over with."

"Toddy!" Tuedy admonished his brother in a shrill whisper.

Lula stood there frozen, staring at the door, trying to find her courage. She felt the dog press up against her leg and reached down to curl her fingers in his fur.

Tuedy took a step forward, stepping in front of her to peep beyond the door.

"He is in there as we speak," Tuedy whispered dramatically as he peered through the crack of the door. "Most likely in front of the fire having a whisky, eh? Go in!"

The Tweedy twins backed away as they both shooed her forward.

"Are you not coming? Mustn't you announce me?" Lula whispered to the two of them desperately as she clutched at her cloak.

The twins shook their heads. Tuedy stared at her a moment and then rushed forward to take her bonnet, cloak and her satchel. "Fix your hair," he whispered hastily.

"Goodness," Lula breathed out in alarm as she reached up to tuck her wild curls back into some semblance of order into the orange ribbon holding it all together atop her head. She quickly pulled some curls down onto her forehead, over the scar. "Better?" she whispered back to Tuedy.

Tuedy nodded his head and smiled with encouragement but Todrick shook his head as he stared at Lula's head with a scowl. "There's no help for that mess of hair," he rasped.

Tuedy frowned back at his brother. "Oh, eh? Men will look at all those wild curls and think—well, you know." He turned away from Toddy to give a wink to Lula.

"Bloody hell to that," Todrick said in a raspy whisper. "Have you not had a good look at her, Tudor? She's a right mess!"

Tuedy straightened up and stared down his nose at his brother. "I have had a good look at her and I stand by what I said, eh?"

Lula looked back and forth between the twins who were glaring at one another. She did not have time to ask Tuedy what exactly he meant by what he said about men looking at her and thinking—*well, something*.

"And why'd you bother taking her cloak and bonnet, Tudor?" Todrick mumbled in a harsh whisper as he glared at Lula. "He'll have her out the door as soon as he sees her. Waste of time for her to even take her cloak and bonnet off. Give them back. That way we can be done with her, too. Her and that dog."

"Tweedys? What are you two whispering about out there?" growled a deep, smooth, baritone voice.

Tuedy let out a soft shriek. He threw his hands in the air and spun around and hurried away. Lula watched as he disappeared back into the darkness of the large great hall of the castle.

When Lula looked behind her for Todrick, he had gone in the other direction, down the dark hallway that led to somewhere she did not know.

Lula put her hand back on Courage's head as she slowly pushed the study door open with her other hand.

She walked silently into the room with the dog at her side and stopped. She looked around the darkened room. It was lit by only one candle that sat on a large, mahogany Chippendale desk with several stacks of ledgers and papers piled on top of the desktop. There was a high backed Chesterfield leather chair behind the desk and two simple shield-backed Hepplewhite wooden chairs in front of it.

A large, ornate rug was placed strategically in the center of the room. Lula studied the lovely burgundy and gold and green design of flowers and scroll work. She was surprised, for it was an Axminster carpet by Thomas Witty. It made the space feel inviting and warm.

She continued her quick study of the room. Dark shadows danced along the walls and the ceiling from the light being cast by the flames in the fireplace. Every wall in the room seemed to be covered in mahogany shelves that were full of books. Lula could smell the rich leather and the paper and the ink that made up the books.

She looked around further. A pianoforte stood in another corner with a violin propped up against a lovely rosewood music stand with claw feet next to it.

As she looked over to the fire, her eyes landed on Baron de Walton. He was sitting in one of a pair of high backed, leather Georgian chairs near the fire. A tufted leather Chesterfield sofa sat facing the two chairs.

Lula could see the baron's profile. He had a sharp, straight patrician nose and a jaw that was covered in a dark beard. He also had unruly, dark hair that fell over his collar and muscular shoulders, shoulders that were so wide that they protruded beyond the confines of the chair.

He was writing on a piece of foolscap which rested on a large book in his lap. In his hand, he held a cased graphite pencil. On a table beside him sat a short, cut crystal glass of what looked like whisky and a quire of more foolscap. As she watched, he shifted in his chair as he set his pencil on the table. He picked up the glass of whisky, took a swallow and then stilled as he stared into the fire.

Goodness, Lula thought, *the man was huge.*

"Have you completed your inspection of my person and this room?" his soft baritone rumbled in the darkness.

Lula jumped and cleared her throat. "Baron de Walton?" she stammered.

The man rose up from his chair and turned to her.

His dark brows rose and then furrowed as he stared at her. "*You.*"

Lula's eyes widened. Then widened some more.

"You!" she cried out softly, just before dropping to the rug in a faint.

CHAPTER FIVE

LULA WOKE UP on the leather Chesterfield sofa. She kept her eyes closed for she felt sick and dizzy as the memories of the night in Hyde Park flooded back. It was the same night that she and her sisters had attended the Lansdowne ball. Sometime after the ball, she and her sister, Julia, had been attacked by a group of men. They were supposedly trying to kill Julia and Prince Darius, who was now her sister's husband.

The attackers had thought that it was Lula that was to be the prince's bride and had taken her instead of Julia. Lula had fought valiantly, but the men were brutal with their fists as they hit Lula several times to subdue her so that they could put her up on one of their horses to take her away.

That was all that Lula remembered, and it was a foggy memory at best. She had woken up at her home with her injuries tended to, leaving only the pain and the wretched memories of those brutal men and then eventually the scars on her hand and forehead.

"Miss Darley?" A calm baritone voice came to her ears.

The voice was close. *Too close.*

Lula immediately squeezed her eyes tightly shut. She turned her head away from the voice and shrank into the back of the Chesterfield sofa.

"I vow I will not hurt you," the voice said softly. "Drink this and call off your dog." She felt the gentle pressure of glass against her mouth and then a trickle of whisky seeped between her lips onto her tongue.

From somewhere near her feet, she heard the vibrating, threatening growl of Courage. She slowly opened her eyes to look at the dog standing near the other end of the sofa where her feet were. He took a step toward her and whined before turning back to Baron de Walton and growling again.

"I am fine, Courage. Hush now," she whispered as she reached out for him. The dog came up to her hand and ducked his head under it as he nervously wagged his tail. She tugged him gently forward. The dog spared a distrustful look at the big man across from the sofa and then hesitantly stepped closer and licked her cheek. Lula smiled softly and stroked his head.

"So, he *is* tame? I rather thought he was a young wolf," rumbled the dulcet baritone voice from the baron. She heard him rise from his chair across from the leather sofa. He took a step toward her. Out of the corners of her eyes, she saw him reach out, perhaps to give her another drink of the potent whisky.

Lula did not look at him. "That is close enough, if you please!" she said hastily as she cringed away from him.

Courage growled softly again at the fear he heard in his new mistress' voice.

The baron stopped. After a moment, he stepped backward to ease himself down into the chair once again. Only then did Courage stop growling.

"You need not warn me away from you. The animal would have attacked me by now if he had a mind to," his voice rumbled quietly. "It does not help him when he can sense that you are afraid of me."

Silence.

"How did you happen to come by him? He looks half-starved and injured."

Lula knew the baron was staring at her, not the dog. She could feel his eyes on her. "I believe he is part wolf, but he is tame. He was caught in a snare in some mud. I found him and released him on my way here."

Several seconds passed while Lula petted Courage. She was letting her breathing return to normal. *What was she going to do? The situation was far worse than anything she had feared when she vowed to be brave and daring and go out on her own, away from her home.*

All men made her cautious, but this one was different. She was terrified of the man sitting in front of her.

He was *there*, that night in Hyde Park. She knew this. She remembered something about him being there with those men who had attacked her and her sister.

But his voice, his voice brought a different memory. *What was it?* She tried in vain to remember past the images darting through her mind of men's angry faces and the exploding feel of pain from their fists.

What was his part in that nightmare?

The glass was handed toward her again. "Take another sip, it will help." She heard his voice vibrate through the silence of the room.

She turned her head away and shook it adamantly, not wanting to look at him. "Come no closer!" she said in a quiet, panicked voice.

"Miss Darley, I will not hurt you." His voice lowered to a deep whisper. "My word is truth."

"I am not sure but I think you were there, that night in Hyde Park," she whispered, still without looking at him. She concentrated instead on the dog.

She heard a deep sigh.

"You are not protecting me from the wolf. You are protecting yourself from me."

She did not answer him. She kept her eyes averted as she pulled her curls back down over her forehead.

She heard another sigh.

"Yes, I was there that night," his deep voice rumbled. There was a pause followed by a halting question. "You do not remember?"

She shook her head again, still looking away from him. She continued petting Courage's head.

His voice lowered. "This is the second time you have fainted at the sight of me. What, exactly, do you remember of that night?"

Her hand stilled on Courage's head. "I can only remember fists and fear and pain." She heard Courage whine softly. She closed her eyes as she winced and stopped the memories from rushing in and out of her vision again. Then her eyes shot open when his words struck her, "What do you mean 'the second time I have fainted at the sight of you'?"

The dog thumped his tail once and nudged her palm with his nose. Lula looked into the dog's unusual eyes and resumed her petting as she waited tensely for an explanation.

A deep, rumbling sort of sigh came to her and then he said, "You fainted at the sight of me at the wedding of Prince Darius to your sister, Julia." A long pause followed those words. His voice deepened. "I know I am big and not pretty and women fear me but, still, I saved you from the havoc those men were wreaking," he said in a quiet murmur that seemed to vibrate through the air.

Silence followed his words as Lula's breasts began to rise and fall rapidly as images flew in and out of her mind. And then his soft baritone rumble came again. "You seemed to enjoy my company at the ball when we were studying the paintings and architecture of Lansdowne."

Lula's breath caught. "I do not remember much of the ball. I do remember a kindly, older man named Veyril de Walton. Your uncle, I presume? He was describing the columns and statues and artwork and I was following him so that I could listen and learn about Lansdowne." She added in a rush, "Is your Uncle Veyril here? I would feel better if he were here with us."

She saw the looming, massive shadow of him in the firelight on the wall as he stepped toward the sofa once more.

She closed her eyes and pressed herself back into the sofa as far away from him as she could go. "Stop! That is close enough!"

He scowled and backed up several steps and stood there looking down at her.

"Am I so hideous and frightening?" he asked in a gruff whisper. "Have you no thanks for the man that rescued you from those brutal men?" His voice was tainted with anger and disappointment. "At the very least, do you not remember that it was I that was escorting my uncle around Lansdowne describing the artwork and architecture of the house earlier in the evening, before you were attacked in Hyde Park?"

Lula slowly opened her eyes and finally looked up at the giant of a man who was leaning against the mantel of the fireplace, keeping his distance from her.

His hair was roguishly and unfashionably long. It fell past his collar in waves and curls of rich brown. His eyes were dark with even darker winged brows above them. His cheekbones looked high and sharp and right now appeared tinged red with the anger she read in his eyes. Besides his straight, aristocratic fine nose, the rest of his face—his jaw and chin—were covered in a dark brown beard that also grew down the sides of his jaw onto his neck.

His shoulders were indeed wide and immense and powerful-looking. His muscular torso tapered down to lean hips and then powerful thighs and calves encased in black breeches and tall, black boots. He wore only a loose open white shirt with a silvery gray waistcoat that was partially unbuttoned at the top.

"I do not remember," she whispered. "But I thank you, Baron de Walton, if your words are true, though it costs me nothing to say that," she said haltingly as she glanced away from him, "for I do not recall you rescuing me or that you were at the ball beforehand. Somehow, the sight of you only reminds me of the fear and pain I experienced that night. Thus I have a hard time believing you rescued me. You can say what you will for I have no memory of it and would not know if it was truth or lies. Because of this, you must accept that I will not so easily take your version of that night as the truth." She knew she was rambling with nervousness. She willed the waves of dizziness that were threatening to overtake her from being so near to him. "Where is your uncle?" she asked desperately.

He stared at her with his brows furrowed together and his eyes narrowed at the fact that she had just said that she did not believe his words. He remembered her from that night. All too well. "My word is truth," he said firmly. He paused and stared at her angrily for several moments, shocked at the audacity of this young woman calling him a liar. His eyes narrowed further as he thought beyond this moment. "My Uncle Veyril left this morning to visit your Aunt Egidia Ross. She sent a message to him just yesterday. She said that she would enjoy a visit from him as she was feeling lonely with your sister, Lady Julia, away on her wedding trip and with your younger sister, Miss Birdie, so busy with the new help in the stables. Your great-aunt also expressed her further loneliness in that you and your mother would be away as well." He looked at her with one brow arched as he waited for an explanation. "Which begs the question, why are you *here*? And *alone*, without a chaperone?"

Lula's lips dropped open. "Aunt Eggy wrote asking your uncle to come visit her?" She pushed herself up to a sitting position on the sofa and placed her feet on the floor. She looked up at the huge man staring down at her with such hostility. Her entire body was trembling in fear of this giant of a man glaring down at her. She swallowed past the rising fear in her throat and answered his question. "Aunt Eggy was supposed to have escorted me here, but she came up with a bout of sniffles this very morning and begged off." She clutched her hands together nervously in her lap. "My mother could not come, of course, because she has our new baby brother Alex to look after and Lord Hawke would not want her to leave him or the baby of a certainty. And of course my younger sister, Birdie, would be hopeless as a chaperone. What could I do? I could not miss my appointment with you." She brushed all her curls off her face and then just as quickly pulled some of them back onto the right side of her forehead as nervousness threatened to overtake her. *What had her Aunt Eggy done? Had she left her on her own on purpose?* "Aunt Eggy did say she would follow in a day or so when she felt quite recovered and if our appointment went well and I…I stayed on," she finished weakly.

"What in the blazes are you talking about? What appointment with me?" the baron demanded in a deep rumble. "The only appointment I had for today was with a gentleman named Mr. Louis that my Uncle Veyril had recommended highly…to me," he ended slowly as he looked at her with growing shock in his eyes. *And his uncle was conveniently absent and Miss Darley's Great-aunt Egidia Ross was conveniently laid up at Aldbey Park with a "bout of sniffles", while his uncle visited her.* What havoc had his uncle brought on him?

Lula managed to hastily untangle her skirts from her legs and rise to her feet. She straightened her knees to stop her legs from shaking as she smoothed down the skirts of her soft green gown. She then pushed her curls back from the sides of her face with trembling fingers, noting that the entire mass of tight curls had escaped from her tidy bun and were now hanging down her back. *Who knows where her favorite bright orange ribbon that had held it all together was,* she thought absentmindedly as she yanked a few curls over her scar.

She stuck her right hand out to the baron to shake as she had seen men do. She glanced at her hand, noting that it was shaking visibly. She squeezed her fingers into a fist momentarily and then tried again, turning her hand so that he would not see the scars on the back of it.

"Miss Lula Darley at your service. I have an honorary certificate of Veterinary Arts from the Veterinary College in Lyons as well as the Odiham Agricultural Society in Hampshire." She tried to smile bravely as she kept her hand out for him to shake.

Of course, he was ignoring her as he continued to stare at her aghast.

She swallowed tightly. "Well, to be precise, you see," she said haltingly, "first I studied the books and papers of the Odiham Agricultural Society and it was there that I found that Professor Vial de St. Bel of the Lyons Veterinary College did the autopsy on my family's horse Eclipse many years ago." She took a breath and looked away from his cold eyes. "He wished to see why my family's horse was so fast, you see. Eclipse won every race he ran, as everyone knows. That is, until no one would put their horse up against him any longer, knowing they would of a certainty lose the race. So Professor Vial de St. Bel wanted to look at Eclipse's heart and his lungs when he passed away. He allowed me to observe the autopsy, most fascinating. Well, of course, you see, after he left, I wrote him of my greatest wish to learn all I could of horse science. It was I, you see, that had been treating my family's horses at Aldbey Park's stables, and the village horses, too. When my father was killed, I identified the wound on his horse as a bullet wound." She stared at his impassive face before taking another breath and continuing. "I entreated Professor Vial de St. Bel to send me the college books so that I could learn further. Of course, as a woman, I could only read the material, I could not actually attend the classes, you see. Professor Vial de St. Bel was happy to help as I am a Darley. He also personally approved my taking all the required exams, which I passed, of course. He personally signed my certificate stating I am competent to practice veterinary arts." She finally stopped talking and lowered her hand slowly to her side. It was obvious Baron de Walton was not going to shake it.

"Of course, *I see*." He stared at her, and then continued to stare some more. He had known men that had not the bravery to look him in the eyes as this girl was doing. He reached for his glass as he kept his eyes on her. He took a slow sip of whisky, letting the liquid coat his lips and tongue as he studied her from over the rim with narrowed eyes.

Lula stood there with her stomach fluttering, fighting the panic threatening her. She refused to look away from this man who seemed to be staring her down.

He set the glass down slowly without releasing her eyes from his. "Are you telling me," he gritted out in an angry, soft baritone, "that you are here for the position of practitioner for my horses?" His eyes narrowed. "To care for the injuries of the war horses? To see my mares through foaling?" he asked incredulously. He made a slashing motion with his hand. "No! Tis not done. The idea of it is scandalous and preposterous, for so many reasons. Absolutely preposterous!" he growled loudly.

Lula shifted her weight nervously from foot to foot. Her chin trembled. "It is not preposterous—"

"You are not a practitioner of veterinary arts," Baron de Walton said scathingly. "You are just a girl!" He looked her up and down with his eyes pausing on her unruly hair. "Just a girl who has read *books* on the veterinary arts!" He took an exacerbated breath. "Just a girl with a piece of paper," he gritted out.

Lula sucked in a breath as her body trembled. "Just a girl-?"

"You said yourself that you have an *honorary* signed certificate," he stated flatly.

Lula looked away from him to hide the mist of tears that had formed in her eyes. She did not want him to see her fear, her lack of confidence, her indecision at pursuing this.

She reached into a slit at the side of her skirts where a small, linen purse was attached. With trembling fingers she pulled out several folded papers and thrust them at him, hoping he did not see the shaking of her hand or hear the rattling of the papers that she held out to him.

"These are from Professor Vial de St. Bel," she said, forcing her voice against the tightness in her throat. "In these papers, you will find my test scores and a referral from the professor himself." She added in a shaking voice, "Glowing, I might add." She lifted her chin then, holding it tight to still the trembling there. "He said if I were a man, I would have led the class." When the baron still did not take the papers she thrust them at his chest without coming any closer to him.

He had no choice but to catch them.

She quickly shuffled through the other papers in her hand. "And here are others from the Odiham Agricultural Society referring me. And my test scores from Odiham and here are some written testimonies from several horse owners in nearby villages whose animals I treated or whose foals I helped deliver. Successfully I might add, because all the men have been away fighting. They had no choice but to let me help their animals, you see." She thrust those into his chest as well and then stopped and took a quick step back and looked at him. "I beg you to read them." She paused and then continued. "I know horses and have proven myself over and over. You can do no better, I assure you."

When he did not reply she added, "My services were even required at Tattersalls. To ascertain if a horse is healthy and sound." She lifted her chin with pride. "I am very good at reading soundness in a horse."

He stared at her in silence.

She tilted her head slightly, trying to read the look in his eyes. "To see if a horse is sound means to see if it is lame, or not."

"I know very well what sound means," he said in a quiet growl. "How many horses have you actually looked at to say you are good at reading soundness?" he demanded curtly.

Lula shrugged. "Goodness, hundreds." She stared him in the eyes. She started to grow uncomfortable with his silence. "Indeed, I have never been wrong." She pursed her lips and then her face brightened. "There was a tall gelding at the sale one day. The horse had trouble bending to the right. The men kept looking at his right front hoof but the hoof looked fine. I walked over and looked at the poor creature and saw instantly that he had broken withers, for his right shoulder was dropped and his right pastern was crooked. I asked if the horse had fallen coming off of a jump perhaps and, sure enough, the owner said that the horse had indeed had a spill. The injury to his withers and pastern was obviously precluding the horse from bending in that direction. Unfortunately, the sale did not go through. Obviously." She came to a stop and waited.

"Tattersalls you say?" he demanded incredulously.

Lula's confidence faltered momentarily. "Well, outside of Tattersalls, not inside the actual building, you see. In the courtyard, where the other sale horses congregate. But I have garnered many other stables requiring my expertise as well, from the excellent services that I performed there. Indeed, I have lost count of the number of foals I have delivered."

The baron sighed long and low. "Miss Darley," he whispered in a guttural voice. "Good God and bloody hell and the devil confound it," he mumbled under his breath as he ran one hand over his eyes. "Tis unnatural. You are a woman. Delivering foals? Tis not to be done!" He gave her a scathing look from head to toe. "You are an unmarried young girl from a notable family. You should have no knowledge of birth! This will wreak havoc upon your reputation. It will mark you forever as odd and undesirable. On this, you must know my word is truth." He furrowed his brows as he looked at her. "Have you no desire to marry?" he demanded harshly. "Do not all young women want the fanciful and elusive affectation they call love?"

Lula took a breath and steadied her mind to answer his angry question and accusations. She ignored his question about marriage. It was his other remark that stung. "I know I am undesirable." She clenched her scarred hand and resisted the impulse to pull some curls over the scar on her forehead to hide the mark. A resolve came over her and she let her hand drop. "I am scarred," she said boldly. "No one will want me, this I know of a certainty just by my looks alone." She shrugged. "And then of course, I am *odd* as well. I have always been odd, but horses are my life. I pour my love into them," she said stiffly. "My home of Aldbey Park is centered on breeding and training horses." Her heart thudded hard and painfully in her chest as she watched the anger increase on the baron's face. "For years after my father was murdered, my mother, my sisters and I were left to our own resources, shunned by the very society that we were part of.

Someone had to learn how to care for the horses' injuries and to help them foal." She straightened her spine. "I like to learn— anything, *everything*. And I love horses. It was natural for me to pursue this avenue of learning to help my mother and our estate as well. It made sense for me to earn a diploma showing that I am competent although I am *just* a *woman*. Who do you think took care of our country's horses while all *you men* were away fighting our king's wars? *Women,* that is who. In every village there is a shortage of men and there is always one woman who must see after the health of the injured animals." She finished with her face pink and her bosoms heaving with her passion.

"In villages, yes, and on a farm, the farm women have knowledge. You are neither a villager nor a farm girl," he said in a biting voice.

Lula straightened her spine. "I am a girl who grew up in the stables," she retorted instantly. "No matter that ours is an estate and not a stable in a village or part of a farm. I have the knowledge and the experience. Which you need."

Baron de Walton stared at the girl in front of him. This was the first time she had spoken from her heart, the first time that he had not heard fear in her voice. The only thing that gave her away was the faint trembling of her lush, pink, lower lip. An odd girl, indeed, though trying to be brave.

It did not matter.

It would not matter.

Not to him.

The girl with the wide, blue-green eyes and a mess of riotous, long, curling hair stared back at him silently, waiting.

He looked her up and down. "Your clothing is in shambles and you are in disarray," he growled in a low voice. "How the devil am I supposed to take you on? You look like a naughty child who has been playing in the mud," he seethed quietly. "You do not look like a grown woman ready to take on a man's job." His voice had been harsh. Too harsh, even to his own ears.

Courage looked up at the baron and barked sharply.

The baron spared a glance at the dog before lifting a hand and slashing it toward her muddy hem and boots. "The condition of your mud-stained person stands as testimony."

Lula sucked in a breath at his rude insult. She looked down at herself as she clutched her skirts nervously. She started to shrink back but then scowled and stood still. She placed her hand on Courage's head, winding her fingers in his fur. "The carriage wheel broke. My coachman sprained his ankle." She shrugged. "I walked. Along the road, I heard the whimpering of a dog. I slipped down a muddy embankment rescuing this dog because that is what a good animal practitioner should do, no matter that I may get *dirty*. I *go* to places others won't, I *do* what others won't, *for the good of the animal*," she said passionately in a voice that almost sounded filled with pain.

Baron de Walton looked from the dog who was gazing adoringly up at the girl to stare sharply at Miss Lula Darley herself. He had heard the pain and the passion in her voice. A sharp memory of running back onto the battlefield to rescue the two artillery wagon horses flashed into his mind. The very two draft mares that were in his stables, in foal at this very moment. He wanted the best for them for he had never helped a mare foal.

He stood there with a handful of referrals in his clenched fist.

He did not want this young woman here.

This *girl*.

Disturbing the way of things.

He said in a steel-like, low voice, "And will you be bloody fainting at the sight of my ugly, frightening face every time I pass you in a hallway?" His voice had dropped to an even deeper baritone as he spoke.

Lula drew back and clutched her hands together. "Your face has nothing to do with my memory of that night. I never said your face was ugly or frightening," she said slowly.

He leaned toward her and uttered in a deep, guttural voice, "You have no idea how frightened you should be here at Graestone." He took a step and leaned down, even closer, looking deeply into her wide, blue-green eyes with his mouth in a hard line. "You should know that my face is indeed frightening, I'll tell you that much, and you should pray that you never see for yourself that *my word is truth.*" He nodded his head sharply. "I am no gentleman. Nor am I a man prone to pleasantries or insipid topics such as the weather. I am not an easy man to know."

"Yes, I see, but—"

"Graestone Castle is a harsh place. The stables are not what you are used to. We have *injured* horses from the *war* here, not pretty ponies. I guarantee that you will not like what you see," he grated out as he looked her up and down and then stepped away from her. He turned his back to her and swept up the glass of whisky he had offered her and gulped it down. "You are frightened of me, are you not?" he asked as he poured more whisky, keeping his back to her.

Lula squeezed her hands tightly together as her bright eyes widened further and her long, dark lashes fluttered once, twice. "I am frightened of you, yes. I am also frightened that I will retreat from this challenge because I cannot maintain any semblance of courage, but I must try. I am not sure which scares me the most," she said quietly. "You, or failing to take on this task without trying." She swallowed tightly. "One thing that I am not frightened of is not succeeding. I know I *will* succeed."

At that bold statement, he lowered his glass from his lips and whirled around to look at her. Slowly, those lips bent into a cynical line.

Lula was silent as she hastily stepped back from the force of his angry gaze. Her heart was beating frantically. She went still, like a deer, ready to take flight.

He waited.

Lula's eyes widened as she took another step backward and swallowed tightly as she tried to find the words she wanted to say. She stared at him and then realized this was some sort of a test, or perhaps a game.

A test that she must pass or a game that she must win.

She would not be thwarted. She would not be intimidated. Was she not a woman of knowledge? Of science? She breathed in and out slowly, willing her racing heart and fluttering stomach to calm.

She straightened her shoulders and rocked back on her heels as she lifted her chin. It was a man's stance. A stance to take a blow. It was also a rider's position of balance to move with and control the horse between their legs. An animal over a thousand pounds that she knew she could control. Her chin lifted a notch higher.

"Let me stay," she said quietly. "Let me prove myself to you. I promise that I will do my best to not be frightened away by you. I shall look after your horses to the best of my ability." She looked away from his prying eyes to stare around the study, anywhere but at his intense eyes that seemed to look straight into her, to the coward that she was or rather, *had become.*

Her heart picked up speed once again. "Just, just do not come so close to me." She dared to look at him as she whispered, "Do not crowd me." And then in a stronger voice, she added, "Perhaps tis best you stay away from me, altogether."

Finally, the baron's intent expression changed. Slightly. But she caught that change.

His scowl softened but his eyebrows rose at her words and then lowered as he narrowed his eyes on her. He put his glass down without taking his eyes from her. The cut crystal glass made a sharp noise on the wood table in the strained silence of the room.

"You dare to order me about in my own home?" he finally whispered with his mouth tightening into a hard line.

Lula knew it was not a question.

He looked away from her toward the study door.

"Tweedys!" he called out loudly and then turned back to her. "I do not want you here," the baron said in a low, harsh voice. "This is a man's house, in more ways than you can understand."

Lula's whole body shook but she would not be cowed. "Nevertheless, I must stay," she said quickly in a quiet, firm voice that trembled. She held one hand up to stop his next explosion of anger. "I did not want to have to bring this up but your uncle has already hired me and given me payment." She lowered her shaking hand when he sucked in his breath in anger at that news. "If you command it, I shall return his payment for he said I must have an interview with you first. However, I do not wish to let him or *myself* down." She swallowed again as she clutched her skirts. "*Or you.* I do not want to let you or your horses down. I could not forgive myself then."

She looked over at the door.

Todrick and Tuedy Tweedy were standing in the open door looking nervously back and forth between Lula and Baron de Walton.

"Escort Miss Lula Darley and her *wolf* dog to the room we had prepared for 'Mr. Louis'," he snarled as his eyes remained on Lula. He glanced at the Tweedy twins and said angrily, "It appears that my uncle miscommunicated to me that *Mr. Louis* was actually a young *woman* named *Miss Lula* Darley." He turned his sharp brown eyes back on Lula. "It is too late to return you to Aldbey Park this evening. Dinner is at eight. You will be returned to Aldbey Park in the morning, either by my coachman or yours should your carriage wheel be repaired." He slashed his hand dismissively at her as he stalked back to his chair by the fire.

Tuedy scurried forward to her side and guided her toward the door where Todrick was waiting with a frown on his face for her.

CHAPTER SIX

I T WAS TODRICK who ended up taking her to her bedchamber. Tuedy had hurried back to the kitchens when one of the kitchen boys had met them in the great hall to ask a question. Tuedy had thrown his hands up and started a shrill rant about smoking ovens and burned puddings.

The hall was still dark, with only two of the candles along the walls in the massive space being lit by two house boys carrying a ladder. They stared at her and Courage with open curiosity. Lula smiled at them and then looked again as she tilted her head to study the boys as she walked by. She slowed her steps. The boys noticed her curious glances and hurried away with their ladder. Lula stared after them. One was limping and there was something wrong with the other boy. *Was he holding his arm to his chest?*

Lula and Courage had to hurry after Todrick however when he cleared his throat and uttered something rather rude about "demmed nosey women and their dogs in the castle".

Lula caught up to him, ignoring his mumblings as she looked upward to the vaulted ceiling of the great hall to see what could only be a large chandelier. She could only see parts of it, for it disappeared into the dark recess of the vaulted ceiling high above. It looked like it had not been lit for a very, very long time, for what she could see of it was dark and thick with gray dust. Long cobwebs hung down from it here and there amongst its arching arms. She could not see if it was even glass for it had lost any of its shimmering magnificence long ago.

As she walked on with her head tilted back to stare up at the chandelier, she heard a noise. Somewhere in the house, someone was crying, or rather, *still* crying.

"Todrick?" she called to him, wanting to ask about the crying, but he ignored her and mumbled something else about "minding her own self".

He led her silently up the stairs, along the balcony, past the three tall arched windows with the closed shutters, down another long corridor, and then turned down another, shorter corridor. They passed more house boys who were going back and forth lighting candles in the sconces along the various hallways or carrying armfuls of wood to light the fires in the bedchamber hearths.

Lula stared at these boys as well. Studying each one.

"You are in one of the towers now," Todrick rasped, bringing her attention back to himself. "The ceilings are higher here, if you note. It may be colder in your room but the fireplace is large and has been laid and lit. That is all that shall be done."

He stopped short of the door, handed her the satchel, bonnet and cloak that she had arrived with and then motioned for her to go in as he turned to go.

"Todrick?" she called before he could leave her.

He stopped and turned back with a glowering look on his face.

"Who is crying?" she asked carefully.

Todrick scowled and turned back around to walk down the hallway. "Bloody hell," he grumbled. With his back to her as he continued walking away he added over his shoulder, "You are only here one night. You are leaving in the morning. What goes on in this castle is therefore none of your bloody business."

Lula stared after him. She looked down at Courage. "How very odd." She continued to watch Todrick until he rounded a corner and was out of sight. She looked back down at the dog with a frown. "Such an unusual place." She looked at the large door in front of her. "Well then, let us see our room, shall we?"

She opened the heavy door and stopped with her mouth agape. She was indeed in a tower room in a castle. She stood there staring, looking all around the huge room. The ceilings were the highest she had ever seen and the old walls had glass fitted into the several tall, narrow, ancient arrow slits that looked like they had been widened. She imagined that during the day this room would be filled with wonderful light.

She took a step inside with Courage close beside her. He padded over to the cheery fireplace and laid down with a grunting sigh in front of the warmth of the flames.

Lula stopped in the center of the warm room lit by candles and a glowing fire. She stared around her as she slowly bent down to put her satchel on the floor and laid her cloak and bonnet carefully on top of it. She stood back up as she turned in a circle, marveling at the room.

The lower portion of the walls were covered in wainscot and painted a soft green. Above the wainscot, there was a silk paper of white with intricate scrolling leaves of pale green to dark green all over it. There were several portraits of ladies in ancient attire and paintings of various war scenes with heroic-looking men holding their sabers aloft that were at odds with the feminine feel of the room.

She turned to the bed. It was a massive archaic thing. It was taller than any of the old beds they slept in at Aldbey Park. This one had a bed curtain of rich emerald fabric that matched the bed covering itself. The headboard was a work of art. A tufted fabric of soft green bordered in darker green with several blooms in yellow and gold and green that rose high to disappear into the canopy.

She turned around and realized the whole room was done in these shades of green and gold. The velvet bench at the foot of the bed. The two lady chairs in front of the fire, and the settee of tufted velvet over by one wall. A desk and its dainty, feminine chair in more of the soft green fabric with lovely blossoms dancing all over it just like the chairs in front of the fire and the settee. A massive wardrobe stood in one corner, painted a delicate pale green with little flowering sprigs and vines painted in the corners of its doors and drawers. There was a washstand with a pitcher and bowl in white porcelain with green trailing vines painted all around it. The linens laying over the bowl also had embroidered green vines with golden blossoms.

Even the chamber pot had green vines painted all around the top and inside as well!

She looked down to see that the rug upon which Courage slept was a masterpiece of dark green, almost emerald, with pale greens scrolling all over it intertwined with touches of yellow and gold.

Lula spun around with delight. She smiled and clasped her hands together. Her colors, everywhere, her favorite lovely, green colors! This room felt inviting, as if it had been recently redone. It was not at all like the ancient, foreboding stone castle she had seen from the outside or in the great hall.

She unpacked her comb and hair brush from her satchel along with her favorite lavender soap and placed them on the wash basin. She picked up the lovely pitcher and poured some water into the matching bowl and washed her hands and face with a grateful sigh. Then she attempted to fix her hair, capturing all the curls into some semblance of order after finding and unknotting the bright orange ribbon that was trailing down her back, entangled in some of her curls. She kept glancing at the lovely bowl on the basin as she did so. The pretty green vines reminded her of her own personal bourdaloue.

Lula reached back into the satchel and pulled out a leather case that was somewhat wider and longer than her own hand. From inside the leather case, she pulled out her bourdaloue which was her traveling chamber pot. When traveling long distances, or even at an outing or ball, it was a simple matter of finding a private area to lift one's skirts and relieve oneself into the small, oblong bowl that slightly resembled a bloated gravy bowl.

Lula looked at her bourdaloue and then back at the wash basin items. Hers was indeed painted with the same elegant, scrolling green vines as the bowl and pitcher sitting there on the wash basin that matched everything in the pretty bedchamber. She smiled. Whoever had decorated this room had lovely taste.

She looked through the remaining items next; a spare gown of pale green, two extra chemises, a short corset, some medical instruments and her favorite veterinary book, stockings and her new, pale pink pantaloons. She had purchased the scandalous pantaloons without telling her sisters. The ladies of the *ton* thought they were unseemly and had scorned them. Lula was always cold, however, and thought them a prime idea, particularly knowing she would be caring for horses in chilly stables over the winter.

After all, if Princess Charlotte could wear them, why couldn't she?

Several other items were in her traveling trunk which was still in the carriage down at the inn. In that trunk were her veterinary books and the rest of her treasured medical instruments as well as her totally scandalous breeches of which she had only one pair (and thus the need for the pantaloons). She had also packed her tall boots and a thick, quilted, woolen half pelisse in the military style with a high collar, caped shoulders and a pinched in waist that would be sure to help keep her warm.

The baron had said he was sending her home in the morning. *No need to unpack all the things in my satchel,* she thought with a sigh.

She had been unable to convince Baron de Walton to let her stay.

He was sending her home.

She had never been brave. Never been able to stay strong or to convince others of what she knew was so.

Just like that night that her father had been murdered and his horse had come galloping back to the barn in that awful storm. The saddle had been empty, the stirrups swinging wildly around the terrified, exhausted horse. She had seen the wound on the horse's haunches. She knew that the bloody wound's edges were singed from a passing bullet. No one had believed her. *She was just a girl.* A young girl that did not know what she had been talking about. She had gone quiet. She did not argue her reasoning, nor the fact that with her observations she knew before anyone that her father was dead. She knew that someone must have shot at him and he had fallen off his horse, most likely to his death.

In the end, she had been proven correct.

It did not matter. The evil deed had already been done to her father.

Still, Lula felt guilty. She had failed to believe in herself enough to make the others believe as well.

This evening with the baron she had failed again, before even looking at a single one of his horses.

He was dismissing her.

Because she was a woman. Or in his words—*just a girl* who read books, or *just a girl* with a piece of paper, and to him it was quite clear that having that certificate proved nothing.

She sighed again. A long, disappointed sigh. *If only he had given her a chance*, she thought.

She unpacked and shook out her extra gown and hung it in the beautiful wardrobe along with her Pomona green cloak and orange and cream velvet bonnet and jonquil gloves. Then she went to lay on the bed with one of her veterinary books. She would read until eight o'clock and then suffer through dinner with the angry and stubborn Baron de Walton who thought she was *just a girl.*

CHAPTER SEVEN

L ULA WAS ABOUT to go down the stairs when she heard the mournful sound of weeping again. She walked along the balcony, passing the stairs and began walking down another long hallway. As she turned a corner, she came to an abrupt stop when she met Todrick coming her way. He, too, stopped and glared at her.

"If you are looking for the dining room, you must go *down* the bloody stairs to the great *hall*, Miss Darley. There is nothing for you down this hallway. Bloody nothing," he rasped. "The stairs are that way." He pointed meaningfully behind her down the hallway and waited.

Lula did her best to not react to his rudeness. Instead, she thanked him and turned around. She reached the balcony at the top of the two staircases to the great hall at precisely five minutes to eight o'clock. Courage had stayed in the bedchamber, reluctant to leave his warm spot in front of the fireplace. She had promised to bring him back something to eat as she left the room.

As she descended the stairs, she saw no one about except for a lone house boy carrying an ash bucket through the dark great hall. She asked him to direct her to the dining room. The young boy looked at her oddly but pointed to the left side of the great hall. She looked left, and then her gaze went over to the right side of the cavernous hall. There, she saw a long and very dark hallway lit only by a single candle in a wall sconce. That was the hallway that Tuedy and Todrick had taken to lead her to the baron's study. All the other doors were closed. She rubbed at her arms as she peered into the darkness. It was chilly in this ancient place. Here and there, she could make out shapes covered in dust cloths between the shadows of the old suits of armor along the walls.

She walked to the left side of the hall where a soft bit of candlelight spilled from the doorway. This is where the house boy had pointed. She walked through a pair of open, tall, arched doors. The room was lit solely by an elegant silver candelabra set only at one end of a long dining table. The rest of the room was in shadows. The hearth was unlit and cold.

Lula stopped.

There was only one place set at the table.

She glanced around. No one was there.

She walked up to the table and placed her fingers on it as she tried to look around the dark room beyond the candelabra's light. She stood there uncomfortably as she began singing under her breath,

"Benny he got tipsy.
Quite to his heart's content.
And leaning o'er the starboard side
right overboard he went.
With a chip, chop, cherry chop.
Fol de rol, riddle-rop.
Chip, chop, cherry chop!
Fol de rol ray!
With a chip, chop, cherry chop!
Fol de rol, riddle-rop!
Chip, chop, cherry chop!
Fol de rol ray!"

A house boy suddenly hurried in and stopped abruptly at the sight of her and the words of her soft singing.

Lula stopped singing and smiled at him. She nodded, seeing the taper in his hand. "You are here to light more candles, I hope? I am most grateful to you. Tis very dark in here."

He tilted his head at her without answering, but then began singing in a clear, sweet, soprano voice, as beautiful as a choir boy.

"A shark was on the starboard side
and sharks no man can stand.
For they do gobble up everything
just like the sharks on land.
With a chip, chop, cherry chop!
Fol de rol, riddle-rop!
Chip, chop, cherry chop!
Fol de rol ray!"

He ended the second stanza in a whisper as he stared at her with wide eyes. Then he ducked his head and began lighting the candles in the sconces on the wall. Little by little, the room came to life.

"You know that song?" Lula asked with pleasant surprise.

The boy stopped, stricken, as he fidgeted from foot to foot. He was clasping and unclasping the long taper he was using to light the sconces.

"I do, my lady," he whispered. "That's a sea ditty. We sang it often when I was a powder boy for Captain John Talbot on *HMS Victorious*. I carried the gunpowder from the powder magazine in the ship's hold up to the guns." He saw her questioning look. "We call the cannons on a ship guns, my lady, and the cannon-balls are called shot." He smiled back at her when she tilted her head and smiled. "Seventy-four guns we had! I could run very fast, my lady," he added proudly.

Lula looked down at his tightly clenched hand. "You were

injured?" she asked gently. She had seen part of a scar there before he had closed his fist.

"Yes, my lady," he answered quietly. He looked at her with bright, dark eyes. "The ship was rolling terrible and I couldn't run as fast as I normally do. The French ships like to pick off the powder boys running across the deck before we can get the gunpowder to the guns." His eyes fell from her. "One of their bullets hit my hand. I dropped the gunpowder. I knew I would have been punished for such a clumsy mistake but mostly our ship would suffer the consequences. I got the powder to the artillery crew as quick as I could." He looked down at his hand.

Lula stifled a gasp. The boy was missing three of his fingers.

"Well then!" she exclaimed with a great smile. "I should like to know your name for I think you are very brave and surely a hero! England owes you her thanks for your service. I think I may speak for all and say that we are very proud of you."

The boy smiled shyly at her. "I am Ned, and I thank you, my lady, but I was a failure," he whispered forlornly and turned to walk from the room.

"Nonsense," she called after him. "You *were* a success, for success is a collection of failures and hardships overcome, which you clearly did! You made sure that the gunpowder made it to the crew," she swallowed tightly, "under terrible conditions. I am sure that your family and your entire village are proud of you."

Ned stopped in the doorway and turned to her. "I have no family. That's why I signed on to the *Victorious*. No one knows who I am where I come from."

"I am sorry to hear that," she said quietly. "What village did you come from?"

"From Picklescott, my lady. But I am sure you have never heard of it. Just a tiny village, it is."

"I do believe I have heard of it. In Shropshire?" she asked with an inquiring smile.

"Yes, that's right," he said with a bright smile as he looked at her in surprise.

"If I remember correctly Picklescott is just northeast of Rat-linghope," she said with a nod. "Indeed a small village, though very pleasant."

"Yes, my lady, you are correct!" he said with pleased surprise. "Tis very small." He looked down at his hand with a frown. "No one there would say I was a success. In Picklescott, I was just an orphan beggar." He looked at her shyly. "That is why I wanted to wear the fancy red coat of the army. Those that wear the red coat are truly something! All the ladies love a man in the red coat. But they would not take me." He frowned at the memory of the disappointment and then smiled up at her. "I found my way to the sea instead. Tis the captain of the *Victorious* who had great success, my lady. I was just a powder monkey."

Lula offered him an encouraging smile. "As a powder boy for your captain, you had to have great courage and daring. Can a success really be called such a thing if it was easy and took no bravery to achieve?" she asked softly. She reached into a slit at the side of her skirts and pulled out a tiny jar of ointment that she used on her scars. "Here, take this. It will help the skin of your wound."

His smile grew as he took the jar. He blushed and thanked her and then turned bashfully to take his leave.

Lula quickly stopped him with a question. "Ned, am I the only one dining?" she asked him as she pointed to the single place set at the long table.

"Yes, my lady," he said with surprise as he stopped again and turned back to her.

"Where are the baron and his nephews?" she asked him.

He tilted his head at her and frowned. "They never eat to-gether and none of them eat in here. Captain War takes the evening meal in his study and the wildlings eat earlier."

"The wildlings?" Lula asked as her brows rose.

"Captain War's three young nephews, my lady. Tis what they are called."

"I see," Lula said with a small downward turn of her lips. But she did not see. *They never eat together,* Ned had said. "Thank you, Ned."

He blushed brightly and lifted his chin as a small smile grew on his face. "No need to thank me, my lady. Tis I that should be thanking you." He gave her a nod and hurried from the room.

Lula slowly sat down at her lonely place setting. She was used to her family's boisterous gatherings at the table. They always ate their meals together; her mother, Lord Hawke, Aunt Eggy, Birdie.

Even Julia and her new husband, Pasha, dined with them, at least until the improvements to the newly married couple's nearby estate were completed and ready for them.

Lula stared down the long length of the formal dining table. *How very sad*, she thought.

A young footman entered the room with a delicious-smelling tray of food. He stopped abruptly and looked behind him at a commotion out in the great hall.

Lula heard it as well. Men running, another man who sounded clearly distraught as he was speaking rapidly and saying something unintelligible.

Then she heard the baron's deep voice as he tried to calm the man down.

She rose from her chair and went to stand at the door to the dining room.

She glanced at the footman and the tray he held while he, too, was watching the crowd gathering in the great hall. The tray was rattling in his hands as he listened to the men with growing horror on his face.

"Put the tray on the table please," she said quietly.

Startled, he looked at her and then down at the tray in his hands. He hurried over to the table and quickly placed it near where she had been sitting and then all but ran out of the room to the group gathered in the middle of the hall.

"There is so much blood! I cannot control the horse, Captain War! It's bleeding bad, bad I tell you!" He wiped a hand under his nose as he tried to control his fear as well as the tears unabashedly rolling down his full cheeks. "The wound reopened or the horse tore it on something but it's worse than it was when I brought the poor animal off the battlefield, my lord!"

Lula stepped out into the large hall. She took a breath. "I can see to the horse's injuries," she said into the chaos of voices.

No one noticed her, no one heard her. She looked up to the stairs, wondering if she should go get her cloak and her instruments. Then she looked back at the men. There was no time if the horse was bleeding that badly.

She stopped a house boy rushing past her toward the men. "Which way to the stables?" she asked him urgently.

He pointed to the far end of the great hall underneath the balcony of the stairs.

➤➤➤✕◀◀◀

LULA HOISTED UP her skirts and ran out the back door into an immense brick courtyard. She glanced around as she slowed her steps to look around her as she rubbed her arms against the cold. Here, everything was lit by lanterns. She wondered briefly if when she had first arrived, she had come to the back of the house and that this courtyard was actually meant to be the front entrance. This was a walled-in brick courtyard with working iron gates. One whole side made up the stables which were brightly lit.

She could hear men yelling and a horse screaming in pain. It was an ear-splitting, horrible sound. She did not hesitate but ran the rest of the way across the courtyard and into the stables and slid to a stop.

Two men were there, each holding a rope attached to the halter on a horse's head. The massive horse was rearing in fright, its eyes rolling back in terror as they tried to hold it. The aisle was slippery with dark blood. The big horse had a large, gaping gash on its shoulder. Its entire front leg was dark with the blood.

"Loosen your hold!" she said in a commanding voice to the two men.

They looked over their shoulders at her with shocked eyes that turned to incredulous fury.

"Are you out of your mind?" one of the men hollered as he struggled to control the frantic animal.

"Loosen your hold," she repeated firmly. "You are only making the animal more frightened."

"Ha!" the other round-bellied man wearing a cap spat as he yanked even tighter on the rope. He looked at the other man wrestling with the rope. "What would a woman know, eh Popplewell?"

"Do it. Nothing else you have tried has worked, I'll wager." Lula walked calmly closer with her hand out to the struggling horse. The horse was still throwing its head and trying to rear.

"You must get back! Tis dangerous here, best you leave now!" The man who had been called Popplewell glanced sharply at her from over his shoulder. He had the face of a hound, with his jowls drooping so that he looked like he was always sad or frowning. He had eyes that looked like they had seen more than he had wanted to. His head was bare, with a thin layer of blond hair streaked with white. "Buttercup is a war horse and doesn't like strangers!"

Lula took a breath. She did not know if she should fear these men, but she knew the horse needed her. She took another step and said calmly but firmly, "Stop fighting, you are making the animal's fear worse. Give me the ropes and step away!" She held her hand out for the ropes as she kept her eyes on the huge, chestnut war horse who was still throwing its head against the men trying to pull at it.

The two men looked at one another and nodded. As one, they put their ropes into her hand and hastily stepped back. Then back some more as the horse reared straight up on its hind legs and pawed at the air with front hooves as big as dinner plates.

Lula let the ropes slacken right to the floor as she crooned softly to the terrified and angry horse.

As soon as the pressure was taken off its head, the horse dropped back down to all four feet. It stood there with its head held high as it stared down its nose at her.

"You are a noble one, aren't you? You demand respect first. I see you," Lula whispered, waiting for the horse to show some signs of relaxing. Finally, one of its ears twitched, aiming in her direction.

"Which of these stalls is er...Buttercup's, Mr. Popplewell?" she quietly asked the men as she kept her eyes on the horse.

"The one behind you to your left but the straw is full of blood, Miss," came the hesitant voice of Popplewell. "And tis just Popplewell, Miss."

"Do you have a clean stall that I can lead Buttercup to?" she asked calmly, for the horse's sake, not the men's. She heard them hurrying down the brick aisle behind her. She spared a glance over her shoulder, thinking they were deserting her but they were glancing into the stalls.

"This one, Miss!" Popplewell called to her. "Move away, Bumstead! Buttercup will blow again anytime!"

"Thank you, Popplewell," Lula said calmly. "Both of you please move back." She crooned soft words to the horse again as she moved her hand slowly toward its nose and let it sniff the back of her hand.

The horse lowered its head and sniffed Lula's fingers but startled at a motion behind Lula and took several hasty steps back with its giant hooves clattering on the bricks of the aisle's floor. Lula followed the horse, keeping the rope relaxed with only a gentle tension on the big war horse's head.

"Popplewell? Bring me some oats in a bucket for Buttercup, if you would please," she said as she slowly reached out to the horse once more.

The war horse snorted through its nose and backed up again.

Lula heard the sound of a bucket being set down on the brick floor and footsteps backing away. She bent down while keeping her eyes on the big war horse and grasped the handle of the wooden bucket. She held it out toward the horse.

"Now then, Buttercup, would you like a nibble or two?" she crooned softly as she scooped up a small handful of the oats into her hand and presented it to the horse.

The horse eagerly stepped forward and delicately lipped the oats from her palm. Lula scooped up some more and backed up a step as she offered the oats to the horse again. The big animal followed her several steps but balked in passing its stall.

"I know you do not want to go back in there. Walk on, big Buttercup, here you are," she said as she held her hand out with the oats and took a step away from the offending stall. Lula caught a whiff of the sharp, coppery smell of the blood in the straw within. She knew the horse could smell it far better than she could.

The war horse snorted at the stall and danced sideways but once past the stall door, the horse then followed Lula down the aisle, away from the stall with all the blood.

Lula led Buttercup into the fresh stall and hung the bucket on the wall. She untied one rope from the horse's halter but left the other rope attached. She slowly reached up and looped it over the horse's neck.

She glanced back at Popplewell. "Do you have a kettle of water on for tea in the stable rooms?" At Popplewell's nod, she said, "Bring it to me with plenty of fresh cloths and a clean piece of soap and a large bowl. I will also need scissors, thread and a needle please," she said softly as she stroked the horse's neck over and over again. "Oh, and some whisky if you have it and another lantern. I'll need more light." She glanced at Popplewell who was nodding at her as he stood safely on the other side of the low stall door. "What happened to this horse?"

"Buttercup was injured on the battlefield and stitched up upon arrival here, Miss," Popplewell said quietly as he motioned for Bumstead to gather the items that Lula had requested.

Lula made a humming sound as she let her hand that was stroking the horse's neck drift closer and closer to the gash on its shoulder. "I expect it was a length of time from the initial injury to Buttercup's arrival here and the stitching?" she said softly as she studied the long gash.

"I expect so, Miss. You would be correct about that," Popplewell said quietly. "Maybe a week, even."

Bumstead hurried forward and hung the extra lantern to shine into the stall. Then he placed all the items she had asked for outside the stall door and ran back to get the hot kettle and bowl. Lula gave him a quick smile of thanks as she rolled the sleeves of her gown up past her elbows. She tied the largest of the cloths around her waist. She then poured the water from the tea kettle into the large bowl and took that and the pile of cloths into the stall. She proceeded to gently clean the bloody wound, studying it as she revealed the extent of the injury while, thankfully, the big war horse was content to eat the oats.

"The skin around the wound is necrotic," she murmured as she continued to cleanse and study the injury. "I will need a sharp knife, please, Mr. Bumstead. Pour the whisky on the knife and do not touch the blade," she said quietly as she gently examined the edges of the wound.

"A knife!" Popplewell hissed. "Are you going to cut Buttercup?" he asked far too loudly with shock in his voice.

"The dead skin needs to be cut away and whatever is left of the thread that was used to sew the skin together. It was very likely already starting to rot when the horse arrived. The wound was putrid," Lula explained calmly. "You cannot sew dead, rotting skin together to seal an open wound. It will not heal. It will only worsen. I imagine this horse rubbed its shoulder raw from the pain and tore it open."

"Yes," Popplewell nodded, "Buttercup was always rubbing that shoulder on the wall. It was very swollen and hot."

Lula smiled grimly as she continued her work. "I think perhaps that was very wise of this horse. Buttercup was trying to open the wound. Twas the best thing that could have happened. The seeping blood helped clean out the wound. The hot water cleansed the rest of the infection out. Buttercup is still bleeding some, but that I can rectify most assuredly." She gathered the rope up and handed it to Popplewell. "Hold the rope, please, but loosely. Only tighten the rope if Buttercup tries to swing around to bite me. But a warning first, if you please."

Popplewell nodded and then stared at her in silence with his mouth open as he watched her carefully debride the dead tissue around the wound with the knife. Then she dipped the needle and thread into more hot water fresh from the kettle and began sewing the healthy skin to close the wound once again.

Lula had efficiently cleaned and then carefully debrided the wound and now she took her time as she began to neatly sew the wound closed. She had to keep stretching her hand and her fingers out. The scar on the back of her hand made flexing her fingers painful, but she kept on. Luckily, the horse was exhausted from its earlier battle with the two men and the ropes and seemed to trust Lula. The big war horse was content to stand quietly and nap after eating the oats and seemed so far indifferent to the needle and thread on its shoulder.

Lula had to take a break as she took a step back and painfully stretched her hand over and over as she examined her work so far. She sighed deeply and realized how cold and exhausted she was and how much her fingers hurt. She ran her hands up and down her arms in a brisk manner to try to warm herself.

"Second Lieutenant William Popplewell!" came a loud, brassy voice. "Ensign Bertram Bumstead!"

Lula whirled around at the shout. She heard Popplewell groan and saw Mr. Bumstead shrink back out of the corners of her eyes.

Popplewell snapped into a soldier's stance with his shoulders back and his feet together as he put his hand to the side of his forehead and saluted sharply. Bumstead did the same but in a slow, clumsy way. He dropped his salute and scratched at his immense belly as his double chins wobbled in fear.

Lula faced the older man staring angrily at her. His face was apoplectic as he looked at her from where he stood at a safe distance in the aisleway, away from the huge war horse. There was a group of men standing quietly behind him. All were looking warily at the horse behind her. And all were unwilling to come any closer. She recognized some of the house boys amongst the group.

The older man had very bushy white sideburns down to his chin and an immense mane of white hair tied behind his head in a short queue. He had intensely pale blue eyes under thick, bushy white eyebrows. Those pale blue eyes looked from her to the big horse behind her as his face continued to redden with his growing anger.

"Would one of you *men* care to explain what is going on in here?" he demanded in a loud voice.

Bumstead spoke first as he stammered out his words, "Master, er, Mister Worm—er, Womersly, Sir. Poppy and I were struggling with the horse, Sir. The wound had torn open or the horse rubbed the stitches open," he said meekly as he pointed to the big horse behind him. "The horse needed help," he ended weakly.

"I can see that! Who is this *woman* and what on all the Seven Seas is she *doing in here* with that war horse?" he roared. "That horse is dangerous! It hates everyone but its rider!"

Popplewell and Bumstead looked at one another and then at Lula. Bumstead took off the cap he was wearing and scratched the thinning hair at the top of his head as he looked at Lula.

"She never said her name, Sir," Popplewell stammered with an apologetic glance at Lula who had gone white. "The horse liked her just fine," he mumbled. "Buttercup stood still for her, unlike when—"

"She has no business in my stables or touching that war horse!" the older man railed before Popplewell could finish. "My stitches were sound, they could not have been torn open," he groused. He flashed his angry eyes back to Lula. "Who are you,

Girl?" he demanded angrily.

Lula stood behind the door of the stall staring into the furious pale eyes of the man who had so poorly stitched up the war horse.

"Miss Lula Darley, Sir. I am an animal practitioner. And the horse did indeed tear its stitches out. The wound was putrid. The skin was necrotic, you see. Hence your stitches did not hold."

The man's face turned even redder if possible which was quite alarming against all his white hair. His pale blue eyes opened even wider as his mouth worked while he tried to form words. His hands had been clasped behind his back but now they came forward in tight fists at his sides.

"*Putrid?*" he hissed out as spittle flew into the air.

Lula's brows rose as she fought to remain calm and not let her fear show. "Yes, Sir, *putrid*. Malodorous if you prefer, or perhaps nidorous?" She stared at his bulging eyes as his anger only increased. "Fetid? Rotting?" She sighed as he continued to look confused and furious. "The wound smelled bad, you see?"

He took a step toward her but quickly backed up at a sharp snort from the huge horse staring back at him where its great neck and head arched almost protectively over the girl's head. "I know very well what *putrid* means!" His body vibrated with anger. "*What I see* is that you are *a girl!*" he spat out.

Lula clutched her arms as she began to shake with cold. She suddenly realized she was very, very chilled and that she had hurried out without her warm cloak. She started shaking, whether it was from her fear of this man and his anger or the frigid evening air, she was not sure.

Her teeth began to chatter as she hugged herself tightly and stared back at him. She was suddenly finding it hard to speak. "Yes, I am a girl," she said through stiff lips and chattering teeth. She stood up straighter. "*No.* I am a *woman*, grown and educated," she managed to say.

"*Yes*, you say you are a girl, and then you say *no*, you are a woman! Well, *whichever you are*, girl or woman, *you do not belong in my stables!* You, you..." he seethed as he raised his fists at her.

CHAPTER EIGHT

LULA REELED BACK away from the man and his fist. *"With a chip chop, cherry chop!"* she sang in a quiet, nervous voice. She closed her mouth abruptly, realizing too late that she had sung out loud.

His fist stalled in midair as he looked at her in angry confusion. "Did you say *chop*? Are you threatening me, Girl?" His eyes darted to something off to the side of her.

Lula started to speak but then stopped. She was just about to turn to see what the man was looking at when out of the corner of her vision, she saw a shape walk out of the shadows. It was Tuedy Tweedy, walking down the opposite end of the aisleway of the stables toward her.

She watched as he stopped near the stall that she was standing in. He gave the big war horse a wary glance as he moved a small step away. Then he turned back to face the older man who had all the white hair.

Tuedy spoke up in a clear, high voice, "She was just *singing*, Mr. Womersly. She does that, eh? You frightened her and that is when she sings. A fine solution I think, eh?"

A bald man with long, bushy, red sideburns stepped up beside Womersly. He looked Tuedy up and down with a sneer on his face. "Tis a *ridiculous* solution, is it not Womersly? And *you* Tuedy Tweedy," he scoffed, "why you are a just a pretentious prig! You fop, you—"

Lula gasped at the man. "That is a terrible thing to say! You should not speak to him like that."

Tuedy straightened his shoulders and patted his elegantly styled hair. "Particularly if you like the food I cook for you, Womersly, and *all* of you," he said, fluttering his fingers at the bald man standing beside Womersly and then at those behind him.

Womersly's face turned even redder. "You dare to speak to me? You, you—"

"Stop barking as if you are still on a ship at sea, Womersly," came Baron de Walton's commanding voice in a deep growl.

Lula whirled around to see the baron leaning against a wall at the far end of the aisle in which Tuedy had come from. His arms were crossed casually against his chest and one leg was bent with the bottom of his booted foot placed against the wall. He was staring at Womersly with narrowed eyes.

"And why bother asking what she was doing?" War held up one hand when the old seaman started to argue. "Good God and bloody hell and the devil confound it," he said in a low baritone. *"You were standing there watching her the whole time,* as were all of us." He dropped his arms from his chest and stood up away from the wall. He ran a hand over the beard on his chin as he stared sharply at Womersly and began walking slowly down the aisle toward them. "I realize that you are fairly new here, Womersly. What has it been for you, a week? But there are rules that *all* my men are required to follow if they stay at Graestone." He walked right up to the man and stared down into his face. When it looked like Womersly was about to start to speak again he raised one hand.

Silence ensued.

War lowered his voice. "You will not only treat each man civilly, but talk civilly to each and any of the men here, is that clear? There will be no violence in temper or actions allowed here, no matter the hellish battlefields *each of us* has been through.

These are *my* stables just as it is *my* castle," he growled. He glanced at Tuedy and then back to Womersly. He stared sharply at the bald man beside Womersly until the man hastily backed up. "Do not let me catch you speaking to Mr. Tuedy Tweedy like that again, *ever.*"

The older man nodded once and backed up to stand beside the other man. "Yes, Captain-General de Walton," he said. He pointed to Lula with a shaking finger and added quickly, "But she said she was going to chop me, Captain—General!"

Lula heard a soft growl from the baron. "Just Baron or Captain War, Womersly. Another rule you will learn," he growled, "is never argue or question me. *My word is truth.*" He crossed his arms over his broad chest and widened his stance as he looked down at Womersly. "Tis absurd to accuse *the girl* of attempting to *chop* you. Do you see a weapon in her hand?" he said curtly as he turned to glance at Lula. His eyes slid past her to look at the big horse behind her. He stared sharply at the horse's shoulder and the neat stitches there and then looked back at Womersly.

The old seaman looked confused for a moment, but he shook his head and averted his eyes from the big man towering over them all. "No, I see no weapon, but she did say that she was going to chop me," he repeated weakly. "My head, you know. The injury..." he touched his head gingerly with his gnarled fingers.

War's face softened as he stared at the older seaman.

Todrick Tweedy and several other men walked into the lamplight to stand behind the baron.

"Yes. She did say that," Todrick rasped as he folded his arms across his chest, mimicking the baron's stance. "She threatened him by saying *chip chop,*" Todrick rasped in disdain, but his disdain was aimed at Lula. "I heard her bloody loud and clear."

"There was no threat!" Tuedy said shrilly as he flapped his fingers at his brother. "*It was just a song,* as you *know,* Toddy!"

War's eyes turned to Tuedy. "Explain."

Tuedy squeaked inadvertently. His eyes widened at all the

men staring at him. His face reddened while he tried to form words. "Tis a song," he mumbled. He fluttered his fingers and shook his head as his eyes fell helplessly away from all those men staring at him.

"Thank you, Tuedy, I can answer for myself," Lula said firmly. She turned to the baron. "Yes, it is just a song. I believe a sailor's song. That is all it was, the words of a song."

Ned, the young boy from the dining room pushed forward between the men. "She is correct. It is a sea ditty. I know the words well for we sang it often on the ship. It is just a simple song she was singing. She meant nothing by it, I am sure."

Lula smiled at the young boy in gratitude and he smiled shyly back at her.

A man pushed past Todrick. "Let me through! Forget all this song nonsense! I know the sea ditty as well, you fool Womersly!"

He was clearly distraught as he hurried forward to the stall, brushing past Lula as he entered. He gently touched the fresh, neat stitches that had been started on the horse's shoulder and then threw one arm around the horse's big neck while his other sleeve hung empty. He dropped his arm sheepishly and turned around to face Lula as he wiped a tear from his eyes.

"We none of us wanted to disrupt the horse or even yourself, Miss, when you started sewing Buttercup up." He swiped at his nose with the sleeve of one arm. "Buttercup can be particular, if you know what I mean. Wouldn't let me near the wound, even though this horse and I have been together a long time," he whispered.

Lula nodded. "The horse was in great pain," she said gently. "I have not finished sewing up the wound."

The man glanced back at the big horse. "Yes, yes, and I will let you finish but let me tell you, many hellish battles this horse took me into and got me out safely, Buttercup did. I near died many a time but for this horse. I would have been left for dead when I lost my arm," he said as he lifted his empty sleeve, "but Captain War saw big old Buttercup standing there over me." He swiped at another tear running down his cheek. "Buttercup refused to run away from all the fire and smoke and bullets and cannon fire and stayed with me even though Buttercup hates the smell of blood. Funny thing that for a war horse, we always said." He swiped at another tear and then his nose. "When it was Buttercup that got injured, I made a promise that I would do my best to see my horse right again." He swallowed tightly. "So, will my old horse make it, do you suppose?" he asked quietly.

Lula gave him a tremulous smile. "I believe that this horse is strong and healthy, so yes," she answered him. She hesitated a moment. "You do know that *Buttercup* is a *stallion*, do you not?" she asked softly.

He grinned and shrugged as he nodded. "The name was always Buttercup before the thought had struck me otherwise. I chose him as a yearling when I saw him in a field. Found him with a mouth full of the yellow flowers and that was that."

Lula nodded to him and walked out of the stall, giving him his privacy with his old war horse named Buttercup. At a touch on her shoulder, she turned back to him.

"I don't care who you are or that you're a girl. I am Alton, Alton Ditchburn and I thank you for what you did for old Buttercup," he said softly and then with a blushing face turned back to his horse.

Lula stared at Alton's back a moment and then turned and slowly raised her eyes to look at the baron where he had come to stand next to the stall. She took several steps to distance herself from his stormy face as she wrapped her arms around her waist and shivered. She noticed that he was staring at the bald man beside Womersly. The old seaman still looked angry, though unsure what to make of the situation.

Tuedy Tweedy hurried forward as he started to take off his coat. "Here, Miss Darley! You are blue with cold and shivering, eh?" He was about to hand his thick woolen coat to Lula but stopped when Todrick came forward and shoved his twin's coat back at him.

"It's her own bloody fault for coming out here without putting on her cloak first, Tudor," Todrick rasped in his painful-sounding voice. "You don't need to bloody give her your coat. You will freeze if you do. That is not right. Who runs out into the cold like she did?" Todrick crossed his arms across his chest and glared at Lula. "Or touches a killer war horse like Buttercup?" he rasped.

Tuedy bit his bottom lip. He gave a guilty and apologetic glance at Lula who was visibly shaking as she hugged her arms around herself.

The baron's gaze raked over Lula. He shrugged out of his coat and thrust it at her. "Do not leave the castle without my permission much less go near any of the horses here. Todrick is correct, you could have been hurt or killed. These are not the kind of horses you are used to. They are not ladies' horses, nor are they pleasure horses to be ridden in Hyde Park on a peaceful day." His jaw tightened. "These are war horses, trained to charge through the gates of hell, into cannon fire and pistol shot, into the screams of the dead and dying of men and horses. They are taught to rear and attack and strike and kick out. *They are creatures of war*, Miss Darley, of the greed and vengeance and violence of power-hungry men." He stared at her, his eyes dark with memories.

Lula would not meet his eyes. She clutched the big, heavy, woolen coat and gratefully put it on and hugged it closed around her waist. It dwarfed her figure but she did not care. She glanced up at him. She knew what this big baron meant. She had seen some of what he talked of. Many of the horses from her village had been taken for war. Those that were lucky enough to return were few. So many had been lost to war. She could not bear the pain and suffering that horses went through.

"I could not bear to see them suffer," she whispered aloud to herself.

The baron's gaze whipped to her face. He saw the torment and grief there. He watched as her body trembled violently.

Lula hugged the coat and herself tightly as she closed her eyes against the images his words brought to mind.

She sighed with the grateful relief of the warmth of the baron's heavy coat. It still carried the heat of his big body.

Baron de Walton glanced again at the big war horse, his eyes narrowing on its injury, then back to Lula. He walked into the stall and Alton Ditchburn instantly stepped back so that the baron could inspect the wound for himself.

The baron offered his hand for the big horse to sniff.

Buttercup snorted sharply and took a wary step away. When the baron continued to stand there quietly with his hand out, the war horse came forward with his nose stretched toward the baron's hand. He sniffed it and then blew out a soft sound as he stepped back to him.

Lula heard Baron de Walton crooning soft words to the horse as his big hands moved gently over the wound and the stitches that Lula had so carefully begun to sew there. He gave the horse a final pat as he stepped back out of the stall and looked at Lula.

Without taking his eyes off of her, the baron motioned his chin at the men. "Go back to your duties," he growled.

"Yes, Captain War!" several said and hurried away.

"Very good, Baron!" said the others as they, too, took their leave.

The baron waited for silence to settle in the stables as the men shuffled out at either end. He continued to stare at the girl who had stitched up the huge war horse while he waited for the last of the men to leave. At a movement behind him, he turned to see Popplewell and Bumstead still standing there.

"What do you want, Poppy?" he asked in a deep baritone to the man standing there staring at him uncomfortably. Poppy was facing him while Bumstead cowered behind him. "Don't you two have work to do?"

Poppy frowned, or at least his drooping skin did. "We are on shift here in the stables, Captain War, but I, that is—*we*—Bertie Bumstead and I, wanted to tell you what a truly good job the lady did. Buttercup was out of his mind with fear and pain and the lady here walked right in and calmed him down." He stopped and gulped and looked away from the big baron.

"You mean that neither of you could handle the horse?" The baron sighed harshly when they just stared with wide eyes up at him. "Very well, Poppy, Bumstead. Back to work." The baron watched them gather the bloodied items that were outside the stall.

Alton Ditchburn came slowly out of the stall and stood there between the baron and Lula.

"I know you well, War. We fought many battles together," he said, staring up at the younger man. "You saved my life. But this girl saved my sweet old Buttercup's life. No one can handle this horse but me and there are times Buttercup won't even have naught to do with me." He shook a bony finger up at the big baron. "Don't frighten her any more than you and Womersly already have. She did right by Buttercup and you know it, my friend. Let her finish her stitches." He stared sharply up into the baron's dark, storm-filled eyes for several silent moments. He turned back to Lula and touched his forehead with one finger as if doffing an invisible cap on his head to her and then walked out of the stables with a furtive frown at his angry friend.

The baron watched him go. He sighed and turned his dark gaze back to Lula who immediately shrank back away from him.

She hugged herself tightly as she looked up at him warily. "He called you *War*. Tis fitting for such a man as you."

"Tis my name," he said with his brows furrowed at her. "Where is your cloak?"

Lula stepped back further from him and shook her head as she struggled with her rising fear. She hugged his coat tightly to her body as she looked anywhere but at the huge man glaring at her. "I felt I had to come immediately to help the horse," she said quietly as she absentmindedly tugged her curls over the scar on her forehead. "I ran outside without thinking."

War's frown deepened. "You call yourself a woman grown?

Only a child runs out into the cold dressed improperly." He pointed to the coat she was wearing. "And before you further insult 'such a man as myself', remember that it is my coat that is keeping your body warm at this moment." His eyes narrowed as he took in her form made to look even more delicate and fragile wrapped in his big coat. His eyes returned to her white face and those large, blue-green eyes of hers surrounded by a halo of curls as he waited for a response that did not come. "You ran out here to prove yourself. Do not lie to me or yourself."

She looked up at him and gasped as her eyes flashed with angry indignation.

"Excellent," War said with a hard smile. "When you are angry with me you forget to be frightened of whatever this memory you have where you hold me as the evildoer." He slashed his hand toward the door of the stall. "Finish stitching up the horse's wound."

Lula said nothing. She went back into the stall, regathered her needle and thread and stretched her hand. She was about to resume when the long sleeves of the baron's coat got in her way. With the stiffening of her scar and her cold hands, she found it difficult to roll the sleeves back at her wrists. She tried several times.

Suddenly, he was there beside her, towering over her. "Let me," he said gruffly.

He did not wait for her answer but took the sleeve and quickly folded it back on her wrist. When he touched her scarred hand to fold the sleeve back on that wrist, she quickly pulled her hand away and stepped back. "Do not touch me."

Lula glanced up at him surreptitiously. He did not seem repulsed by her scarred hand but followed her even as she stepped away from him.

"I will only touch the sleeve, not your hand," he growled without looking at her as he continued to fix the sleeve. When he was done folding the sleeve back, he let go and instead of leaving, he stayed where he was. "Your hand is stiffening in the cold. I will hold the wound together. You finish stitching."

"I do not need your help," Lula said stubbornly.

He stared down at her, his face was a mask of confidence and calm. "Put your pride aside, Miss Darley." He arched a brow at her when she did not move but stood there staring back at him with a scowl on her face. "For the horse?"

Lula's scowl fell immediately from her face. "Very well."

They worked together quietly, taking turns crooning softly to the horse to soothe him if he became agitated. At other times, they talked quietly to each other.

"Move your hand down slightly," Lula murmured.

"Here?" his voice rumbled softly.

"Yes, there, just there, that's it."

Moments passed where the only sound was their breathing as Lula concentrated on making small, fine stitches or the occasional dulcet sound of his voice, crooning to the big war horse.

"Down lower now. Hold the skin together, please," she murmured.

"Too tight?" he asked.

"No, that is just enough pressure, thank you."

"You are welcome," he whispered back in a low voice.

"Buttercup is getting restless, I fear," she murmured.

"Easy now, old boy, easy. Let her help you," came his dulcet whisper.

Buttercup settled instantly at his melodic, deep tone. The old war horse had lived long enough to know when someone was helping him versus attacking him.

And much later, War said softly, "Take a break, Miss Darley. Sit down and stretch your hand."

"'Tis fine, I need only a moment," she whispered back to him as she stretched her hand and shook it. She leaned back into the task after that one quick shake and stretch of her hand and fingers.

The entire time, she was cognizant of his large body near hers. He seemed aware of keeping a respectful distance. Though before she had time to realize it, he had moved closer and closer. The size of him, the warmth of him. The deep, lulling, almost melodious sound of his voice when he spoke so gently to the horse also kept her calm. He was close to her, but his help was indeed needed, and it was for the horse. For Buttercup. Whenever panic threatened to overtake her at his nearness, he seemed to know and his voice lowered and softened as if to soothe her, not the horse.

Her curls kept catching in his beard or in his own unruly hair. Each time, she quickly pulled her hair away. It unnerved her. Sometimes her hair had a mind of its own. As they neared the end of the stitching, he moved to stand almost behind her with his arms reaching over her head in a better position to hold the wound closed for her.

She tried, but this new and more intimate closeness she could not tolerate. She stepped away. "No, you are too close. I cannot," she whispered in agitation.

War lowered his arms and stepped back.

"I can finish without your help," she said hastily without looking at him.

"I vow I will not hurt you," he grumbled.

She shook her head nervously and flexed and unflexed her hand. "No. Though I do appreciate your help and Buttercup responds to your voice when you speak that way, but I, I simply cannot work with you standing so close to me. I find it most disturbing and most, most shocking to my senses, you see. I do not appreciate it." She did not look at him but made a shooing motion with her hands for him to move away from her. Without looking at him, she moved back to her stitches while he stepped back, yet she knew he was still there watching, holding the horse for her. She finished as quickly as possible. A knife flashed in front of her face but before she could gasp, he had sliced the end of the thread neatly for her. Her breath shuddered out of her in exhaustion as she looked at her work while rubbing at her hand.

"Go to your bedchamber, Miss Darley, before you fall down

from exhaustion or faint out of this fear you have of me." He watched her stretch her hand painfully again before squeezing it into a fist and hiding it in the deep folds of the large coat. "And do not try to hide your scars from me. I know *where* they are and I am aware of *how* you got them. So would you if you only tried to remember that night, and those men who did this to you."

She reeled back from his rude words as her heart pounded, but then she glanced over at the horse and took a deep, calming breath before looking back to him. "I will not speak of that night. Now then, Buttercup *must* be watched through the night," she said firmly. She frowned and took a deep breath. "And may I add that I find it most telling that you know where my scars are and how I came by them because of course *you were there*." She let out a huff of breath as she stared up at him with furrowed brows.

"Yes, I was there, because I *rescued* you," he said firmly. "*Try* to remember, Miss Darley."

"I *cannot* remember," she said stubbornly. "*War*," she added with a lift of her chin and a quelling look.

When he arched one brow at her, she added as an aside with a faint bow of her head, "Forgive me, I should have said, my *lord, Baron de Walton*." She also added a quick, partial curtsy for dramatic effect. Her little sister, Birdie, would be most proud of her, she thought.

War frowned and spoke gruffly. "I do not appreciate your sarcasm, your incorrect and ungrateful memory of the night we met *or* your pretended attempt at a curtsy." He paused, crossing his arms over his chest as the realization came to him that this slight girl had managed to rile him unlike any of his men. "The horse will be watched over," he added in a calm, smooth baritone.

Lula swallowed tightly and looked away from him toward the horse and then around the stables as she clutched his coat tightly around her. "I will watch him so that I can check on him through the night."

"You will not," he said in a clipped voice.

"But," she began to object, determined to make sure the horse was cared for. "It should be me."

"No." He stared down at her with his lips firm. He offered no other words. He would not argue with this slight girl.

Lula let out a huff of breath as her eyes darted to him and then skittishly away. "I do not understand why you won't—"

War sighed loudly. "Do not question it. Go. Go to your bed-chamber." When she continued to avert her eyes from him, he added, "Your orders are to go to your chamber. You need to rest. *My word is truth.*"

Lula gasped as she faced him, her eyes raising to his as she stepped further away from him. "You cannot just stop a discussion by announcing your word is truth and that is the end of it!"

His lips firmed. "I can. *Now go*. Or do I need to throw you over my shoulder and carry you to your bed?"

"You would not dare!"

With that, War smiled grimly. "Wouldn't I? I have rules here, Miss Darley. My orders are followed *without question* by the men here because they know my word is truth. See that you follow my orders as well." He turned his back on her astonished face without waiting for an answer and began walking back down the aisle of the stables. He stopped to speak with Popplewell and Bumstead who had been watching them quietly.

Poppy gave Lula a small nod and smile before he turned to listen to the quiet, low-voiced orders that the baron was giving him.

Lula returned Poppy's smile with a tremulous one of her own. She then walked out of the stables, across the chilly courtyard and into the castle with her chin high. She missed the assessing eyes of the house boys and footmen that she passed as she walked. Some were warm and welcoming and others hostile. She saw none of them, too weary to even turn her head to look with the effort it took to keep her chin high. She climbed the stairs with heavy legs and walked slowly to her room.

Once there, she leaned her back against the door and closed

her eyes. After several moments, she picked up a candle on the small table beside the bed and glanced around the large room looking for Courage. She finally found him under the bed, lying on top of a worn coverlet in a tight ball. It looked like someone had bathed him and brushed him and he was much affronted. She knelt on her knees and gave him a soft pat. She was happy to see that he turned to her and gave her hand a small lick before snuggling back into a ball on the fabric and closing his eyes.

"No dinner for either of us, I am afraid," she said with a sigh.

Lula stripped down to her chemise and draped her gown over a chair. Then she climbed into the huge bed under the green coverlet. Feeling the chill of the sheets, she pulled Baron *War* de Walton's heavy coat on top of the covers and, finally warm, she drifted off into an exhausted sleep.

"RUN, MY SWEET horse, run!"

She was crying out in her dream as she rode at a frighteningly fast gallop through the dark. Here and there, the golden light from the lamps along the pathways offered some light to the otherwise dark landscape of Hyde Park.

They were chasing her! The assassins were closing in on her on their much larger horses. Her little horse was tiring, it could not outrun those men on their horses. They thought she was her older sister, Julia, the woman rumored to be betrothed to Darius Kir Khan Qujar, the Prince of Persia, who was their enemy.

In her dream, she looked over to see her sister, Julia, galloping in another direction on her horse, her face stark with fear. The men spotted Julia as well. Quickly, Lula pulled her horse up, trotting in circles as she glared at the men, daring them to attack her. She could not let them hurt Julia. She *would not* let any of them hurt her sister.

As one, they turned away from her sister and smiled with evil intent at Lula, the target that was closest to them. They began to surround her with their horses as they took turns trying to grab her up onto one of their horses. She deftly moved her little horse left and right off her leg and crop aid, dancing just out of reach.

Until they closed the circle around her even tighter.

Lula kicked and punched and fought them to buy time for Julia. She knew that Pasha had to be near.

And then they started striking her, trying to subdue her in their effort to take her. She held her hands up to block their blows from her face.

One of them suddenly grabbed her roughly onto his horse, swinging his fist at her head to get her to stop fighting him.

Her sister was somewhere close now. She could hear Julia crying out to her, running on foot toward her.

The assassins were bickering over which of them would carry Lula away on their horses as the fighting continued and other assassins in the group tried to take her from the first assassin who had grabbed her.

In her dream, she heard a loud roar as a huge horse and rider came charging into the fray.

Was that big horse an Aldbey Park carriage horse? Why didn't the rider look small on that big horse?

And then large, gentle hands pulled her away from the bad man who held her. Whoever it was pulled her onto his lap on the big horse. She swung and kicked but her world was growing fuzzy as the pain in her head increased. He was saying something to her, but she could not hear it. His voice seemed to come from far away.

Suddenly a gunshot rang out.

Lula sat straight up in bed with her heart racing frantically as the dream faded away.

She wiped the sleep from her eyes as she looked around the room.

It was a gunshot in her dream that had startled her, causing her to awaken.

But had it?

She had thought that she had heard a gunshot but it had been a loud boom. She knew that she had not dreamed it. She'd had that dream many times recalling that horrid night. This time it was different. The gunshot was wrong. It had been a boom. A thunderous, reverberating *boom*.

The curtains around her ornate bed were still fluttering from the vibrations of the boom and dust was still billowing up from the glowing embers in the fireplace.

What could have made such a loud noise?

She clutched the warm, green bedcovers to her breasts as she looked toward the windows of her room. The barest hint of the gray light of dawn was just seeping in. Perhaps it had just been the rumbling of a winter thunderstorm that she had heard. Perhaps a thunderbolt had struck close by.

Another deafeningly, loud boom rent the air and shook the walls of her room in the tower as her bed curtains fluttered again. Lula jumped and clapped her hands over her ears as she froze. The glowing sparks of embers from the blackened logs in the fireplace suddenly swirled upward into the fireplace's chimney and then settled down once again as the vibrations ceased.

Lula slowly lowered her hands and clutched the covers tightly.

That was not thunder, she thought as she began to shake with fear. Her special tune ran through her mind and she put it to voice in a nervous whisper. *"With a chip chop, cherry chop. Fol de rol, riddle-rop,"* she began to sing softly to herself in a shaking voice as she stared around the tower room.

She stopped singing when a triumphant laugh came to her ears from outside the windows.

She slowly pushed the covers off of her and put her feet on the floor as she listened in tense expectation.

There it came again, another deafening boom that made her cringe as it rang out loud even though she had her hands over her ears. This one, too, was followed by a grating laugh of triumph.

Lula quickly pulled on her morning dress and tied the sash tightly around her waist. She hurried to one of the windows to look outside.

Her room was a large square taking up that level of the left hand tower that faced the courtyard. The first window she went to looked directly down onto the brick courtyard and the stables and the expansive view of the fields beyond. She could not see anything amiss but it was not full light yet and the air was full of swirling mists. She ran to the next window. This one looked out to the old battlements that ran along the top of the wall all the way to the right to the next corner tower. Through the early pale light of the morning fog and mist, she could see a shape moving about out on the battlements. There were some cannons set up in the sawtooth crenellations along the walk. In front of one of the many cannons was Todrick.

She saw the spark of flame through the gray mist just as Todrick set it to the cannon. She quickly jumped back and clapped her hands over her ears as she hunched her shoulders, cringing just as the boom of the cannon shook the walls of her room once again.

Lula quickly slid into her half boots and pulled on the too large but wonderfully warm coat that Baron War had loaned her the evening before. She started to leave the room but stopped and bent down to peer under the bed. Courage had shrunk as far back as he could and was staring at her with worried eyes.

"Come, Courage!" she called softly to the dog.

A soft, plaintive whine answered her urging as the dog scuttled further back under the bed and out of her reach.

"Hmm, I thought you were the brave one of the two of us," she said more to herself. "Very well, I shall go see what Todrick is firing the cannon at with such great humor. Fear not, I have high hopes that naught is wrong and that I shall return shortly, Courage!"

CHAPTER NINE

ONCE LULA LEFT her room she paused. The sound of someone crying came to her again in the dark hallway. She could not tell where it was coming from. Down the hall? Somewhere on the floor below her? Or above her? She shivered at the soft, muted, sorrowful sound. At another boom, she turned and hurried on.

It was easy to find the doorway out to the walkway along the battlements. She opened the big, wooden door and was met with a blast of cold, damp air in the gray light of what was barely morning. She hugged the big coat tightly to her waist as she began walking along the battlements. She walked toward a small group of cannons that protruded from some of the crenellations guarding over the courtyard entrance and to the lands beyond.

"Todrick?" she called out with chattering teeth through the rising morning mist as fog swirled all around the battlements. "What are you doing?"

Todrick had been about to set his firing stick to the cannon fuse but stopped and turned to her. A small smile bloomed on his face.

"Did I bloody wake you then, my lady?" he rasped. "Too bad, that." He laughed and then turned away from her. He was about to set match to fuse when another voice thundered from the other end of the battlements.

"Todrick Tweedy, good God and bloody hell and the devil confound it! What manner of havoc is this?"

Lula looked beyond Todrick to see the baron striding angrily out of the white swirling mists from the opposite tower. He wore only his boots and black breeches, hastily pulled on as they were not fully buttoned at his narrow hips or taut abdomen. He had also thrown on a white shirt that he had not buttoned at all. It billowed out behind him as he strode toward Todrick with his breath leaving white clouds in the air.

Lula blinked once, and then again as she watched the big baron. He looked like an avenging warrior of old emerging out of the mists who was perfectly in place on the battlements walkway of this old castle. He lacked only a giant broadsword held in one of his big fists.

War stopped on the other side of Todrick and glared at him before sparing a passing glance at Lula. She had his coat on over what appeared to be her night dress and the same bright yellow boots as the day before. Her hair was loose, with the burnished curls collecting the cold, morning mists like icy jewels.

"What are the two of you doing?" he demanded in a gruff baritone as he pulled his eyes from her. "'Tis too early in the morning to be firing the cannons. You are waking the entire castle and I expect the village as well," he growled in a low voice as he looked out beyond the courtyard gates to the fields and the road to the village shrouded in the heavy morning mists. His eyes narrowed at the new pockmarks that dotted the landscape made by the cannonballs. He turned back to Todrick with an arched brow as a cold, icy rain began to fall. "Well?"

"That girl and I are not doing anything," Todrick replied in a rasping whisper as he nodded toward Lula with an indifferent shrug. "I was cleaning and practicing the aim of these cannons before *she* interrupted me." He pointed out to the fields beyond the walls of the courtyard. "Look there, Captain War, the last shot blew apart that stone wall by the road. Bloody good cannons, these."

"You are destroying those fields with your cannon shots," War growled as he looked out at the stone wall where a section had indeed been blown completely apart by Todrick. He would have some of the men rebuild it. Just as he had so many times so that Todrick would feel triumphant in blowing it apart once again.

Todrick's mouth fell open. "There are no horses that use those fields, my lord, just like you told me and, besides, tis the road I am covering." He lowered his raspy voice. "You never know who might sneak along those roads someday. My aim must be true." He frowned up at the baron as he fidgeted his feet side to side. "The cannons must be used, Captain War. They need to be taken care of or they will be of no use to you or this castle."

Lula looked at Todrick. "I am quite sure that you are keeping them in good order if ever there is an," she paused and offered a small smile, "an attack on the castle."

Todrick gave an angry glare in Lula's direction. "Women do not belong on the battlefield or around cannon fire." He frowned at the baron and leaned toward him as he rasped in a disgruntled voice, "She should not be up here. That's not right."

War stared at the smaller man for several heartbeats. He sighed silently. "Toddy, no more firing the cannons today." War added in a brief, smooth voice, "It is sleeting. Bad weather is the enemy of all soldiers on the battlefield and the equipment as well. Time to go in now." His voice was calm and kind though direct.

Todrick snapped to attention. "Yes, Sir, Captain War," he croaked with a quick salute. "Of course, Sir. Not good for the artillery." With that, he marched past Lula with a fleeting angry look.

Lula watched him go and then turned to the baron with a question in her eyes.

War was watching Todrick with a thoughtful, almost sad frown. He blinked and looked away, suddenly aware that Lula was watching him. He turned fully to stare at her.

"Go inside." His voice was a gruff baritone.

Lula found herself thunderstruck for the first time ever in her life. She was breathlessly silent as she studied him, unaware of his order. The man was getting wet in the freezing rain but he seemed not to notice. It was as if he were some mythical man whom the elements had no bearing on. Lula's eyes traveled slowly over his face with his dark brown eyes and his long, black lashes tipped with glistening drops of icy rain to lips that looked sensuously sinful. Those lips niggled at a memory buried deep within her but she brushed the thought away as she continued her leisurely perusal.

She noted his square jaw, outlined in a dark beard, and his straight nose with the ghost of a scar that showed he was a mortal man, after all, for his nose had been broken at one time. Her eyes traveled further to a strong throat and corded neck also covered in beard hair. Through his wet shirt she saw something. *Were those scars she saw, there where his neck met his shoulders?* Her gaze passed over them and moved down further, down to the skin revealed by the wide "v" of his open shirt. His chest was almost completely laid bare and what she saw was glistening with raindrops. Her gaze drifted to his peaked nipples. She paused as her breath caught at the sight and her eyes widened before traveling down even further to his taut, ridged abdomen before all that captivating skin disappeared from her eyes, hidden by his breeches that showed off trim, narrow hips.

"Once again, I find that you are inspecting my person," he said in a soft, deep whisper. "Perhaps you like what you see?" The corner of his lips lifted up into a wolf's smile. "Shall I spin for you so that you may inspect my back side as fully as you are my front?"

Lula's heart thudded in her veins. His voice had been low, almost teasing, taunting. *Daring.* His voice and that smile he was giving her had indeed been teasing, softly, *sensuously* teasing. She watched as he spread his arms wide causing the wet shirt to cling to his bulging biceps.

War kept the smile on his face as he turned slowly, giving her a good view of his body in his wet clothes. *Would she faint at what she would indubitably see? Or would the frightened little deer run?*

Lula's eyes widened, but she could not tear her eyes away from the back of him anymore than she had been able to look away from the front of his body. His wet shirt hid nothing from her gaze. She watched as sleet trickled down from the back of his wide, massive shoulders where she could indeed see terribly scarred skin. Still, her eyes were drawn down his beautifully sculpted, broad back and over the wet breeches clinging to his taut, rounded buttocks and then down his muscular thighs.

Her breath turned ragged as her eyes went back to his masculine, battle-hardened hands. Those were not the hands of an aristocrat, nor a coddled member of the *ton*. Her Aunt Eggy would say that those hands were the hands of a warrior.

Those hands.

A brief glimpse of large hands wrapped around her waist, holding her safely, flitted through her mind. A familiar smell drifted from his coat to her nostrils.

Hastily, she shrugged out of his coat, holding it and the memories starting to crowd her mind away from her. She stepped forward and reached up to place it over his shoulders.

"You are wet and cold," she said in a nervous whisper. "This is yours."

The crooked smile dropped from War's lips as he spun around to stare at her. *Had she seen his scars and wanted to hide them from her eyes?*

But then he realized now that she was not wearing his coat, that she was the one who would soon turn wet and cold, clad as she was in a flimsy, white dressing gown with lacy ruffles up to her chin. Already, she was rapidly becoming wet. He noted her wide, blue-green eyes shone in her pale face as she stared back at him as she took fast, shallow breaths. A cloud of burnished brown curls dampened with diamonds of ice curled riotously over her forehead with one small curl tangling in her long eyelashes. Her hair wreathed her face before falling down her body. One curling lock had escaped to embrace one of her breasts, curling around it in perfection, making it apparent to him just by the shape of that breast that this was not a young girl before him.

She was a woman grown.

The rest of those wild curls fell to a tempting, tiny waist, just above the enticingly shapely curve of her hips. His fists clenched. He wondered if his big hands could circle that small waist.

Slowly, he unclenched his fists and narrowed his eyes on her. "You gave me your coat?" he stated with suspicion and some amount of shock. "A lady does not give her coat to a man."

"'Tis yours," she said haltingly as her eyes still clung to his.

"You need it," he stated in a gruff, hesitant voice.

He was suddenly very aware that she was looking at him. She was not averting her eyes. Instead, she was drinking him in. She was of a certainty neither frightened, nor repulsed.

He did not understand the way her open perusal of his body was affecting him. He suddenly felt like a shy, young boy.

An unusual feeling swept over him. He felt something previously unknown to him bloom within his chest. Hope? Longing? Whatever it was, this new feeling made him feel raw and vulnerable.

He could only stare at her. "You need it," he stated once again in a voice made hoarse by his uncertainty of his own reaction to hers.

She waved her hand at him. "It is yours, not mine. You must take it." She swallowed as she hugged her waist tightly, "It smells, you see," she said in a clipped voice. "I mean it smells like you," she said awkwardly as she finally looked away from the wet shirt clinging to his chest.

His shy uneasiness left him in a rush. He raised his chin, looking down his nose at her. "So now tis not only my face but my *smell* that repulses you?" he growled in his baritone.

Her eyes flew to his. "No!" she stuttered with cold and nervousness. "That is not what I meant."

He tilted his head at her. "What did you mean? You said the

coat smells." He took a quick whiff of the coat that lay over his shoulders and then shrugged, looking at her with a question in his narrowed eyes.

Lula nodded once, trying to pull her eyes from his chest but they kept coming back to it, the wide expanse of it. It seemed like he took up the whole width of the battlements. It was as if he took up the very air she was desperately trying to breathe. "It does smell," she said in a quiet murmur. "Of you. Horses, leather. I think perhaps sandalwood with maybe a bit of frankincense," she shrugged. "I do not need the coat. *You do*. You are wet," she said weakly as she went to motion toward his chest with a shaking hand.

One of War's dark eyebrows lifted ever so slightly. She had described exactly the oils he preferred to use in his bath.

Interesting, he thought.

"Now *you* are wet and cold." He spoke in a low voice made thick by her selfless action, but also at her awareness of his scent and, in particular, the look in her eyes. She was looking at him like a grown woman seeing a man and, in particular, *him* for the first time. She was not looking at him as most women did, not as someone to be feared but as a man whose person stirred something within her.

The frightened deer was changing before his eyes. He had been glad to see her become brave when she was angry, but this? This shook him. He was unused to such a look by a female. They gave his great size and gruff countenance a wide birth whenever they came near him.

This, he had secretly hoped for. But as cold reality hit him, *he knew he could not have it.* Not now, not here, not at Graestone.

Not ever.

Love did not last.

Not for him.

The little, frightened deer would do better to turn that blue-green gaze elsewhere. He did not know what to do about such things.

Nor did he deserve such admiration, *or more*, his mind reminded him. How many lives had been lost around him, *because of him?*

He watched as she hugged herself tightly and a great shiver ran through her.

He walked forward, surprised to see that she only took one nervous step back. He opened his coat and started to gather her to his side. "Come. I will walk you back to your tower. You must get out of this weather." He placed his hand on her thin shoulder to gather her under the coat.

Lula hastily shrugged him away. "You are too close." She spoke quickly as she started to panic. Her world began to spin with the increased rhythm of her racing heart.

War quickly took his hand off her shoulder. "You will *not* faint," he ordered her in sudden desperation while still shielding her from the icy rain with his coat.

Lula gasped and raised her eyes up to him before quickly looking away. "You cannot order such a thing," she retorted obstinately as she tightened her arms around her waist and refused to let him see her shiver or the fact that she was struggling to overcome her dizziness. The cold air was a blessed help with that. Though he was not touching her, still, she felt like she was in an intimate cocoon with the big baron as he continued to hold his cloak over her head, shielding her from the icy sleet.

War scowled. "Very well, as long as you do not faint I will not have to make such an order." His voice was curt as he stared down at her. He had heard the tone in his voice. He could not help it, however. He noted that she kept her eyes averted from him again, as she had the evening before. He looked up at the bruised, early morning sky. "The weather is getting worse." He looked down at her, watching her struggle to regain control and giving her the time to do so. He wondered if she had even heard him. "There will be snow soon." He waited but she still remained silent as she looked over the battlements. "Great amounts of snow. It may snow for days."

She glanced up at him then with a question in her great, big, blue-green eyes. "You have no way of knowing that. We have rain and sleet here and some snow, but *great* amounts of snow? I could more easily imagine the sleet will turn to nothing but rain," she mumbled and then shivered as she looked away.

"My word is truth." War spoke in his smooth baritone. In the gray dullness of the morning, her shining blue-green eyes seemed to light the mist. He paused a moment, again watching the inner battle of emotions on her face. Without thinking, he added, "I vow I will get you out of this," he murmured quietly.

Lula stilled as she slowly looked up at him with her eyes growing wider. "What did you say?" she said on an exhale of her breath.

War was quiet. He nodded once, but it was his turn for his cheeks to redden as he looked away from her eyes.

"I should go back to my room and change into my gown." Lula began to quickly chatter away nervously. "I have warmer clothes better suited to the stables, you see, but they are in my trunk at the inn with the carriage. My gown will have to do for I should like to check on Buttercup before I leave today." She lifted her night dress and stared at the icy ground as she began to walk slowly and carefully along the icy battlements walkway.

War grunted as he caught up with her, raising his great coat over her head once again. He frowned. "You cannot make it back to Aldbey Park in this weather. At least not today."

She glanced up at him and then scowled up at the bruised sky as she paused in her slow, careful steps. "You said I must leave today. So, therefore, I shall make haste to do so, *after* I check Buttercup. I trust I can make it back to Aldbey Park for *I believe* you are *incorrect*. It shall *not* snow."

War's frown increased as he kept pace with her smaller steps. "If you do not believe me then I shall have a carriage take you to the inn after your breakfast. The wheel of your carriage should be repaired by now and you may try to return home this very morning. That is, if you are so positive this will be but a brief weather occurrence."

Lula stopped and stared up at him with wide eyes. She struggled silently with warring emotions; the desire to flee back to her home of Aldbey Park versus the need to stay and prove herself. Finally, she shook her head as she looked down at the icy walkway and started carefully walking once again. "I told you that I must see to Buttercup." She slipped slightly on the ice but caught herself. "No one can know how long this storm may last, not even you. However, I should not like to be caught in any snow *or sleet* trying to get home to Aldbey Park, much less having my driver sitting atop the carriage in this weather and I did not bring a post boy rider to help, so I shall wait until this weather passes." She stopped and took a breath as she gingerly walked along. "And then I shall leave as you bid me to. *After* the storm passes." *Or until I convince you I am more than just a girl with a piece of paper,* she thought to herself.

War nodded once with an internal, silent sigh. He did not want to think about his own reaction to her words or what his Uncle Veyril would say if he had found out that War had proposed to send the Darley girl away, out into the storm.

War looked down his nose at her with a deep frown. "We are agreed that you will stay here at Graestone Castle." He added gruffly, "*Only* until the storm passes."

Lula smiled tightly as he continued to guide her back to the tower.

"I will send my men to retrieve your trunk." War looked up at the bruised gray sky again as the freezing rain hit his face. "They should be able to make it to the inn and back before all the snow comes."

"'Tis good news, that," Lula said through her chattering teeth. She added in a wry voice, "We do not get overmuch snow here, but your word is truth, so we must expect a *great* amount of snow. Not rain as is usual."

War frowned and narrowed his eyes at the subtle hint of teasing in her voice. "We will have snow." His voice was firm.

"My word is truth."

Just then, she let out a small squeal as she slipped once again with her arms flailing about as she tried to regain her balance. The walkway along the battlements was rapidly icing over everywhere.

Without hesitating, War scooped her up into his arms.

She immediately froze.

"Put me down." She felt the panic start to envelop her.

War gentled his hold and continued to walk carefully along the battlements. "No."

"Yes," she said through clenched teeth as she tried to stiffen her body so that she would not touch any part of him. "You are no gentleman!"

"No, I am not a gentleman and those yellow boots of yours are useless things," he growled.

"My boots are beautiful. I do not like to be touched. Please put me down," she demanded again as her panic threatened to overtake her.

War stopped as the sleet pelted down around them. It was now starting to mix with snow. He grimaced as he stared into her ashen face so close to his. She was refusing to look at him. Her breathing was fast. She was terrified of being in his arms. "Look at me," he said in a dulcet baritone. "Miss Darley? Look at me," he commanded in a firm voice.

Slowly her eyes rose to his. "Why should I look at you? It does not help," she said tightly as her breathing continued to be fast and panicky.

"Tis sleeting. Ice accumulates easily on these battlements. Tis getting slippery and your boots *will not help*." He stared down his nose at her, watching the panic in her eyes. "You will not faint," he commanded her quietly.

She moaned quietly. "You have the audacity to think you can order people about over anything."

"It is what I must do." He spoke in a low, calm voice as he walked.

"That is highly arrogant. That would take immense trust. Who would allow you to do this?"

"My men. Those that rely on me. Those that I am responsible for. In battle, those that I was trying to keep alive."

Lula stilled and stared up at him. "And did you? Keep your men alive?"

"For the most part, I did, yes. Some, I could not," he said quietly with a frown.

"Because they did not follow your orders, I presume?" she asked curiously.

"Yes," was his short, clipped answer as he stared down into her eyes. He glanced up at the sky again. Snow was definitely mixing with the sleet now.

"If I do not follow your orders, harm could come to me, is that what you are saying? There is no battlefield here, Baron."

He looked back down at her for several moments and spoke softly. "There is always a battlefield."

She stared up at him and suddenly trembled. A chill went through her and not from the weather. She rubbed her arms as she looked away from him.

"I vow I will get you out of this," he rumbled softly in his baritone voice.

He watched as she gulped and stared into his eyes like a person drowning, clinging to their last hope. The look in her eyes reminded him of the young men—boys really—that had become so terrified on the battlefield that they could not think past their fear. "Speak of something else, anything. What do women talk of?"

Slowly, Lula's breathing calmed somewhat and her eyes traveled over his face.

"Very well. Why do you wear a beard?" she asked in a nervous, chatty voice. "'Tis not fashionable. Is it comfortable? It looks rather scratchy."

He began walking slower, gentling his hold of her within his arms. "It is not scratchy at all," he said lightly. He was pleased that she was talking about something else, though he knew it was her nerves talking. "Touch it if you will and see for yourself." He had said it as an offhand comment to distract her from her fear. However, when he glanced down at her, he saw that she was studying his beard as if she *did* want to touch it. With a slight tilt to one corner of his lips, he said, "Go ahead." He watched as her eyes flitted nervously away from his face. He looked back at the icy path before them and, without thinking, he lowered his voice. It became soft and almost mellifluous as it dropped even deeper and quieter. "*I dare you.*"

Lula frowned, she could feel the rumble of his deep, smooth voice right through his chest and into her breasts. It gave her the oddest feeling. Her fingers clenched and unclenched as she stared up at him. She was surprised that she did indeed want to feel his beard. How odd of her. He was not looking at her now. He was watching the path ahead as he strode carefully with her in his arms. It made it easier that he was not staring down at her, for her to lift her fingers up to his jaw and stroke the soft beard there.

War silently gasped at the first gentle touch of her fingers. He stopped and stared down into her eyes. She was staring at his mouth, her fingers trailing over the short hair that grew above and under his lips. His heart started beating faster as he watched her eyes. They were following the stroking movement of her fingers. His whole body went into a state of havoc. This was another feeling new to him, to have a woman touch him, and with such gentleness. Her face seemed to come into sharp focus. Her long lashes, the glittering blue-green of her eyes, the rosy colors of her cheeks, her lush, red lips.

"Bloody hell," he whispered in a voice so deep it vibrated once again through his chest to her breasts. "*You have freckles,*" he said throatily.

She frowned up at him then, with her lips becoming pert in annoyance. "I do. What about my freckles?" she demanded.

War scowled down at her. The anger and fight in her was back. The frightened deer was gone and in its place was the lioness. "The devil confound it," he said tightly as his eyes roved over her face, knowing that he had lost his inward battle. "Why do you captivate me so?"

"What—" Lula started to ask in a surprised voice, but she had no chance to say anything more.

His mouth descended on hers like a sudden storm.

Her world went blank to anything but him.

All of her senses awoke with the feel of his lips hungrily moving over hers. The taste of him was both mysterious and splendid along with the heady, spicy, male scent of him that filled her nostrils. All of this was so new and wondrous that her breasts seemed to fill and ache with want and need. She clutched at his shoulders as she tipped her lips up to him with a soft whimper of surprise and pleasure. She was greedy for more.

War moved his lips over the lush fullness of hers. Hungrily at first, and then lightly, sipping, tasting, reverent. Until a growl grew in his chest when he realized that her lips were chasing his.

She was kissing him back.

He growled again with need and slammed his mouth down fully on hers once again, devouring her lips, gentle no longer. Swallowing her soft whimpers of surprise and need and pleasure. His mouth moved urgently, like a man starved or trying desperately to quench his thirst, fitting his mouth over hers first one way and then slanting it the other way as her lips continued to chase his. He kissed her until he had explored every bit of her lips and, still, it was not enough. He wanted more. He tightened his hold on her and was about to thrust his tongue between her sweet lips when he felt her tremble and shudder.

He pulled his mouth from hers as the sleet made itself known once again. He stared into bright blue-green eyes that were wide with wonder and confusion. He noted that both of them were breathing hard as they stared at the other.

"You kissed me." Her voice had been filled with a hint of surprise, shock and panic as she tried to push against his chest.

"You kissed me back willingly enough," he said indignantly.

"Put me down." She started to struggle once again.

"I will not."

"You are no gentleman!"

"I am not, and I must warn you, nor am I a man to love. Women do not fall in love with me, *nor I them.*"

She froze and stared up at him. "I can assure you that I have *no* intention whatsoever of *those* emotions." She could say no more as she had to clutch his shoulders to steady herself.

He had torn his eyes from hers and was walking again, faster now. He thought he heard her humming under her breath. Or was it singing? He reached her tower and set her quickly on her feet without looking at her.

"Your door." His jaw had gone tight and tense. He stared at the door. Not at the woman he had just had in his arms.

"Oh! Thank you," she said curtly. But still, she stood there.

"You are disheveled and freezing. My word is truth. Go inside," he growled.

He opened the door to the tower and pushed her none too gently inside before stepping back. Only then did he let himself look at her. Her expression had changed instantly. She was looking at him in fear again. He held her eyes for several moments before nodding once and turning away to walk back along the battlements to his tower.

A frown turned down his lips as he walked through the freezing rain.

What had just happened?

He had kissed her!

At least she had not fainted.

She had looked up at him with those wide eyes of hers rimmed in long, curling, black lashes that glittered with the freezing rain. She had tried to conceal her fear even with her sarcasm on his statement about the snow to come, and her comment about ordering people around and the comment about his beard, but fear was there, barely hidden, in her eyes.

Until she had reached up to touch him.

And that simple touch of her fingers had been his undoing.

It had captivated him.

He could not stop himself from kissing her. It was as if his very life depended on him doing so.

But, as soon as he had tightened his hold, her eyes had changed once more.

Fear, dread, trepidation, anxiety, distress, uneasiness—what have you, one of those was always there each time he looked into her eyes.

But that fateful night when he had first met her at the Lansdowne ball, when she had followed him and his uncle through the house as he had pointed out the wondrous architecture to his uncle, the fear had not been there.

No, this young girl had been curious, intelligent and clearly educated in the artwork and architecture and décor of the house. She had walked behind him at first, in her pink gown with a darker pink velvet spencer with fringe and intensely pink dangling pom poms amongst the fringe. The pink pom poms were also dangling at the hem over startling green kid slippers. She had been eavesdropping to assuage her curiosity and thirst for knowledge. She had not been interested in the young bucks of the *ton* or dancing.

It was not until later that evening after the ball, when he had tried to help his friend, the prince. The prince had enemies from his country who had come to kidnap the woman he was to marry. That woman was Lula's sister, and they had taken Lula as well. That was when he had jumped in to help.

It was there, in Hyde Park, when her eyes had become filled with fear and pain. He had tried to, but had never been able to forget them. And all that hair that had come undone and fallen from her artful coiffure. *Oh, yes*, he had *never* forgotten the *annoyingly* chaotic riot of curls that had gotten in his face and blocked his vision when he had pulled her in front of him on his horse that night in Hyde Park. He had not been able to keep an eye on their attackers because of all that hair flying about as she fought. And fought and fought to help her sister until she could no more.

Had he ever met a female with such a chaos of hair or such loyalty to another?

He sobered then as a thought struck him, picturing the fear in her eyes as he had pulled the door shut just now.

Was she beginning to remember that night and his part in it?

He had purposely used the words that he had said to her that fateful night. The very night that she and her sister had been attacked by assassins in Hyde Park. *I vow I will get you out of this,* was one of the vows that he had made to her that dreadful night. He had also vowed that he would not let them hurt her. He had broken that vow and it threatened to destroy him each time he looked into her wide, frightened eyes. Those men had struck her so hard that she carried the scars to this day, on her hand and forehead and in her mind.

It had been difficult, to put it mildly, when men who served under his command had lost a limb, an eye or suffered any other of the number of horrible injuries that occurred in battle. When men under his command had lost the supreme sacrifice of their lives in battle, he carried it with him forever. Too many had been hurt. Too many had died.

The memory of that night, however, when he had not been able to successfully protect this slight, delicate girl who had fought as bravely as any man, had stayed with him.

When she had been injured under his protection, it had infuriated him and haunted him and made him want to rage and shake his fists up to the heavens.

He had always been a man who had protected those who were weaker. He was a military man, a leader, a fighter.

He was a man who took his responsibilities seriously and his responsibilities for others just as seriously.

He was a man whose word was his vow and his truth.

And he was a man that had broken his vow to this girl. For she had been injured.

This annoying, stubborn, irritating girl with a chaos of curls and freckles that drove him wild.

This girl who had taken furtive glances at him with a look in her eyes he had never seen from any woman before. She looked at him as if he were a delicious sweet she wanted to sample, who had kissed him back as hungrily as he had kissed her.

He was surprised to note that his hand trembled as he went to grasp the iron handle of the door into his tower.

Good God and bloody hell and the devil confound it! He swore silently as he held up his shaking hand and stared at it. *She* had done this to him.

What havoc could this girl wreak upon him and his responsibilities to Graestone?

What havoc could she wreak upon this man who had no heart to give? This man who did not deserve a woman like Miss Lula Darley.

This man who was surrounded by death and suffering.

CHAPTER TEN

L ULA SAT ON the window seat in her room staring out onto the white, wintry courtyard as she stroked Courage's warm fur where he lay by her side. She had just returned from having luncheon in the silent, drafty, dining room all by herself. She had eaten breakfast by herself as well. The windows in that room had been shuttered closed. Just like the great hall windows. It appeared that no one opened them during the day.

In between her lonely meals, she had made an attempt to explore the upper hallways in search of whoever was weeping. As she walked along, she noted that the walls were a soft creamy yellow with honey-colored wood wainscoting below. More portraits hung all along these walls of men in short tunics with wide, puffed shoulders and hose on their legs. The women wore tall, conical hats on their heads and long, flowing gowns with narrow, tapered and pointed sleeves on their arms. Lula slowed down to peer up at them all.

The sound of weeping had slowly come to a stop before she realized it and she found herself in a hallway that she had never been in. As she stood there listening for the noise of crying, she swore that she heard the sound of a soft, hauntingly sweet violin. She walked a few steps on the creaking floor as she looked around her. The paint on the walls of this hallway were stained with damp and peeling with chunks of plaster work missing. There was no color visible, only a sad grayness was left. The smell of must and mildew filled the air along with a distinct, damp chill.

She was standing there, thoroughly lost, when Todrick found her. He stopped and stared at her with a bent scowl on his scarred lips.

"I am lost." She shrugged her shoulders innocently.

"I bloody doubt that." He glared at her. "Stay out of the west wing. There is nothing here that is any concern of yours. The bloody floors are falling in, the roof is leaking and the ceilings could come down at any moment. You could be bloody hurt or killed and no one would ever find you in this pile of rocks that is Graestone Castle."

Todrick's lips moved in a painful, unnatural way from the burn scars, Lula noted. She reached into the slit in her skirt to the little pouch hanging there and pulled out her tiny jar of ointment that she used on her own scars. "Todrick, please take this. It will help soothe those scars on your lip," she said as she offered the little jar to him.

Todrick glared at the offering in her hand. He made a sound like a small laugh. "Stay in the east wing where your bedchamber is." His voice was dismissive as he ignored the ointment she had held out to him.

And with just a look and a finger pointing behind her in the direction in which she had come, he had sent her back to her room like a naughty child.

So here she sat, staring out the window, alone with her thoughts and her dog.

The icy rain and sleet had indeed turned to snow.

The baron's word was truth, after all.

At least on the subject of their current weather.

The man had kissed her.

Oh, and he was a man. His kiss had not been the simple peck of the village boy who had given her her very first kiss so long ago. This was so different. He was sure and in command and most demanding.

He was a man. *Not a boy.* And she was not *just a girl.* She had seen that awareness for her in his eyes and felt her own awareness of him within her body.

She had not been afraid. She had not panicked or felt faint.

That is, until his grip had tightened.

She had panicked then. Memories had suddenly flooded her mind. Memories of that awful night in Hyde Park. Memories of startling pain and men trying to attack her.

Yet, something new in those memories was bothering her, there at the back of her mind. She could not put her finger on it. Instead of thinking about it, she wrapped her arms around her knees and thought of his kiss.

She could not stop reliving that kiss.

His wondrous kiss.

She touched her lips for the hundredth time as she replayed every move of his mouth on hers.

As she recalled each of his breaths.

As she closed her eyes and recalled his heady, spicy scent.

She frowned. He had held her too tight. Far too tight. Why had that brought back her memories?

Her heart began to race and she felt panicky. Her stomach suddenly felt wretched.

She did not want to think about that fateful night. Panic threatened to overtake her once again any time she did.

She frowned again and nibbled on her thumbnail, a terrible habit it was, she knew this. She stopped herself. Then she stared at her thumb. She hadn't chewed on her thumbnail since she was a child, and since *that night*, after the attack in Hyde Park. Inwardly, she groaned and willed her stomach to settle.

She must never, ever, let him kiss her again, nor be near enough to try.

The incorrigibly rude man had even said not to fall in love with him, and that he could not love. Then he all but shoved her inside the door to the tower as soon as he set her on her feet. Clearly, he could not be rid of her soon enough—from his arms, or from his castle.

She leaned her cheek on the cold, glass window as she watched some of the baron's footmen tamping down paths in the already accumulating snow with ropes attached to a flat, wooden plank. They made paths to and from the gates and to the stables as the snow continued to fall, obscuring their efforts.

Suddenly, she heard a familiar baritone voice from below.

She sucked in a breath and pulled away from the glass as the baron strode through the courtyard in his tall, black boots and a long great coat. The shoulder cape of the coat made him look even more immense and formidable. His rakish, brown, curling hair was bare of any hat as the snow fell all around him. He pointed this way and that, directing his men where to make paths as they hurried to do his bidding.

Lula could hear the low rumble of his voice through the glass. He must have sensed someone watching him for he turned and glanced up at her window.

Lula gasped and leaned back out of sight behind the long draperies that framed the glass. When he turned and strode out of the courtyard, she let out a breath and then resumed watching the activity in the courtyard until her heartbeat had settled back to normal.

Idly, she combed her fingers through her wild curls and then gathered the length of it all up and secured it in a knot at the top of her head and used a bright green ribbon to hold it off her face, tying it securely behind her head, on the back of her neck. Without thinking, she pulled some of the curls free from the ribbon down over the scar on her forehead.

Her mind went back to days ago and a conversation she'd had with her old Scottish Aunt Egidia. Aunt Eggy, as Lula sometimes called her, had been telling Lula about the position here at Graestone Castle. She had compared Baron Warwick de Walton to the Scottish warriors from her country in the old days. She had not said much about the baron, but she had said that the baron had quite a reputation. Her beloved aunt had then laughed and patted the ever-dwindling, sparse, white curling hairs sticking up from her balding, pink scalp. Bits of her hair were a shocking chartreuse color. Aunt Eggy was currently experimenting with dying her hair. She had attended at least one ball with her hair a startlingly bright pink.

Of course, when Lula pressed her, her wily Aunt Eggy had not told her exactly what the baron's reputation was.

Lula grunted quietly. *A reputation of being feared*, she thought as she pictured the huge man with the name of *War*, of all things. No one was allowed to question him, or disagree with him. According to him, his word was the only truth.

She imagined him trying to have a conversation with her aunt as she had. Aunt Eggy had cleverly changed the subject of what, exactly, the baron's reputation was to the kittens that Aldbey Park's stable cat named Tom had had. Tom obviously was not a male cat, after all. If Aunt Eggy did not want to tell you something or talk about anything she simply would not.

Lula couldn't imagine the baron being comfortable with Lula's unconventional family that lacked the propriety that was expected of the *ton*. Baron War was all about his regimen, rules, control and orders. There was nothing soft about him. There was nothing at all about him that seemed able to enjoy anything of life save war and battles.

Lula began humming quietly as she stared out the window with one arm wrapped around her knees and the other over Courage.

A soft noise from outside in the hallway came to her. Courage lifted his head and let out a soft *"woof"* of alarm. She watched as he jumped off the window seat to scuttle under the bed. And then her door opened. It was two of the house boys. They brought in her trunk and walked over to set it down by the wardrobe.

Her eyes immediately followed the boys. She found herself looking for scars, fingers missing, a limp, something. Sure enough, one boy was missing an ear. The other boy kept his head low. She could not see his face but imagined he was hiding some scar from an injury.

The boys quickly hurried to the door before she could speak to them.

Lula called out a quick thanks to their departing backs.

She waited until they closed the door, then she jumped up and ran to her trunk and threw it open with a sigh of relief.

Warm clothes! Working clothes!

She wasted no time in hanging her things in the wardrobe and folding the rest of her hose and sundries on the shelves there.

She quickly pulled on a fresh pair of thick hose and then her Devonshire brown-dyed leather breeches which reminded her of the dark-colored whisky that her mother's new husband, Lord Alexander Hawke, sipped in front of the fire. She pulled on her black Hessian boots. Her boots were without a tassel at the top, which she was told by the indignant bootmaker was not the fashion. Still, she insisted there be no tassel. She had instead asked the bootmaker to edge the tops of the boots which reached to just under her knees in a vibrant lilac-dyed leather. He was horrified, of course, but she had insisted and since he was keen to acquire a Darley Thoroughbred, he acquiesced to her odd wishes for her boots. In the end, Lula thought them quite delightful.

She then added her warm, quilted spencer that just barely reached her waist. The smart purple mulberry-colored jacket was in the military style with a high collar and epaulettes at the caped shoulders. It had Hussar and Brandenburg pipings and closings and decorations everywhere that the seamstress could put them. Lula thought it a masterpiece.

Lastly, she wrapped a shawl that her Aunt Eggy had given to her around her neck and shoulders that would also serve to cover her hair if need be. The shawl was a cheerful coquelicot color that reminded her of the roses in the garden at Aldbey Park that were a vibrant rose-pink color.

She picked up her favorite pair of Saxon green work gloves, checked that the green ribbon was still holding all her hair and went over to the bed. She knelt down to peer under it.

"Come on, Courage!" she crooned.

The dog thumped its tail once and crawled on his belly out from under the bed.

The two of them went out the door of her bedchamber and paused. The dog looked up at Lula and whined softly as he nudged at her hand with his wet nose.

Lula's hand went to his head and stroked it slowly as she listened to the castle. Silence. This morning, there was no sound of a person crying somewhere in the house. But then it came to her. A soft, achingly sweet melody was being played on a violin.

Lula's breathing stopped as she listened to the violin. She had seen one in the baron's study, but surely it was not him playing such a piece. Only a woman could play such a heart-wrenching, lovely melody as the one she was hearing. She listened for more, but whoever was playing had stopped and silence came to the castle again. No weeping, no beautiful music. Silence.

Lula and the dog continued down the hallway and the main stairs to the great hall.

"Eh! There you are!" came Tuedy Tweedy's high-pitched voice.

Lula looked across the hall to see Tuedy hurrying toward her with his hands raised up as he waggled his fingers at her.

"Did you get some breakfast and some luncheon? I know you did not have any super last night, eh?" he asked as he stopped in front of her with a big smile.

Lula smiled back at him. "I did and both were very good. The eggs and sausage this morning were cooked to perfection." She looked down at the dog and ruffled his fur. "Courage was most happy to get the sausages I brought to him this morning," she said with a cheerful grin for the tall, elegant man.

This morning, Tuedy's black hair was artfully coiffed in a high wave back from his forehead instead of onto his forehead. He bent over and stroked Courage's head.

She asked him, "And do I have you to thank for bathing him

and I am guessing also feeding my dog last evening?"

Tuedy stood up from petting the dog and blushed. "I am responsible for it, but the chore was gladly done by one of the house boys. Please do not tell Toddy, eh?"

Lula gave a mock shiver. "I would not dare tell Todrick. He is most displeased with me for wandering the castle but tis only because I dearly wish to discover who is crying."

Tuedy shook his head quickly. "You must not wander." He noticed what she was wearing and let out a soft screech. Then he leaned closer and whispered, "You are wearing men's pants."

Lula leaned in as well. "I know," she whispered back with a big grin. "Tis safer and easier when working around horses. Skirts get in the way terribly. These are also very warm and comfortable. Who knew?"

Tuedy stood up tall and studied her clothing with one arm across his chest and the other arm resting atop it. He put a finger to his chin as he studied her. "They are most becoming on you. The breeches and even the spencer hide nothing of your figure, eh? I had no idea you were so pleasing." He had his fingers on his chin as he spoke while studying her. He looked at her hair, tilting his head this way and that. "I am not so sure of that coquelicot-colored shawl with that parrot green ribbon holding your hair, Miss Lula. Or those Saxon green gloves." He made a "tsking" sound with his tongue as he continued to look her over with an assessing eye. "I do admire your boots and your bravery in wearing all those colors together, however!" He gave her a secretive wink.

Lula touched her cheerful shawl with her hand and then her fingertips grazed the bright green ribbon in her hair. "I do so love bright colors, Tuedy." She had spoken quietly and there had been a hint of embarrassment in her voice. She looked down at herself and knew she was wearing many colors. She raised her eyes to his. "Sometimes something that is so unusual that would be considered ugly is beautiful to me," she said with another glance down at herself. She gave him a grimacing smile. "I suppose I am guilty of that powerful and merciless enemy of beauty."

Tuedy grinned. "And what is this powerful and merciless enemy of beauty that you are guilty of?"

Lula shrugged her shoulders and grinned back at him. "Bad taste."

The two of them started laughing but then Lula sobered. "Truly, I do not care, Tuedy. I find the colors cheerful. It is not in the stars to say what is beautiful. Each of us finds our own beauty."

Tuedy nodded. "Beauty lives with kindness, Miss Lula. At least you acknowledge the colors you choose are unusual. 'The worst of all deceptions is self-deception.'"

Lula gasped with a smile. "You are quoting Plato!" she said with pleasant surprise. "I would add, 'You will never do anything in this world without courage. It is the greatest quality of the mind next to honor.'"

Tuedy grinned. "And it takes quite a bit of courage to dress as you please, eh?"

Lula stilled with her hand on the dog's head. He was leaning against her legs and looking up at her with his tongue lolling out. "I had never thought of that," she said softly.

Just then, the baron strode through the hall, talking quietly to one of his men beside him. He paused in his conversation as he glanced at Lula where she stood next to Tuedy. He stopped and stared at her. He took a small step toward her and then halted with a scowl on his face. He opened his mouth as if to speak to her but then closed it and abruptly turned about and continued on, resuming the conversation with the man he was walking with.

Lula's eyes widened, and then followed him. Without taking her gaze away from the baron, she murmured to Tuedy, "Such a contrary man. I must wonder at *his* self-deception, for never have I met a man so convinced that he is always correct."

Tuedy turned and looked to see where she was staring. He saw the baron talking to the man walking beside him. "His word is truth?" Tuedy looked back at Lula with a question in his eyes.

"Yes." Lula let out an exasperated sigh. "The man allows no other opinion but his own."

Tuedy fluttered his fingers at her. "Do not confuse opinions with rules. Rules are important, Miss Lula. Particularly here."

Lula turned to him with a frown. "I do not understand."

Tuedy pointed to the house boys that were moving through the dim great hall to the side hallways and up and down the stairs, going about their chores. "What do you see?"

Lula looked around the shadowy, dust mote-filled great hall, studying each of the young house boys and the tasks they were all busily completing. Some were carrying logs for the fireplaces, others carried ash buckets to clean the hearths, while others had linens for the beds or items for the kitchens. "Servants, footmen and house boys working." She turned to Tuedy with a questioning look.

He leaned toward her. "Men. You see *men*. This house is full of men," Tuedy said in his rather high-pitched voice "*Military* men."

Lula was silent for many moments as her eyes continued to look around the dimly lit great hall and the bustling "staff" coming and going through it.

"*Injured* military men...and boys," she whispered with a dawning awakening as she observed a boy walking through the hall with an ash bucket. He was the boy who had hid his face when bringing her trunk into her room. He was missing an eye. A horrible scar covered the place where his eye should have been.

Tuedy smiled and relaxed. "Yes. All of us. Taken in by Captain War. Accepted for whatever we are now, not who we were or who some think we should be." His face pinkened but he quickly hurried on. He kept his voice soft as he continued, "He is a man that knows that work is good for the soul and the body and that work creates value within each person. He also knows that work is necessary to heal wounds both physical and of the mind."

Lula turned her gaze to two men chatting amicably as they

walked through the hall with wood for a fire. One of the men spoke roughly, like a farmer, and the other was speaking in an educated, nasal tone. It was easy to take him for a member of the *ton*. Both had a military bearing in their walk, however.

Tuedy nodded at her. "The baron seems a hard man and I do not know all that he has been through in the war, but he accepts any and all, eh? Even me. Do you understand?" He blushed and looked at her with a question on his face.

She smiled at him with gentle ease. "Yes, I do, Tuedy."

He smiled with relief and then looked off in the direction the baron was walking. He added in a quiet voice as he stared after the baron, "You may be a bluestocking, Miss Darley, and not see it, but *pon rep,* Captain War is one devilishly attractive and pleasing man with his hard looks, eh?" He turned back to Lula with a smile.

Lula's brows furrowed as she, too, turned to stare after the baron. "'Tis most difficult to tell whether he is pleasing under that beard and all that hair. I simply cannot know if he is pleasing or not, though perhaps he may be tolerable in a rough sort of way. To some."

"Ah, Miss Darley, did you not just say it is not in the stars to tell us what is beautiful?" Tuedy continued to stare after the baron. "Beauty does indeed live with kindness. Look beyond what you see, eh?"

"He has scars on his neck and shoulder. He uses the beard to cover those on his neck, I assume?"

Tuedy's eyes came back to her. "Yes. He is a bit of a hero, eh? I heard he carried a cannon off the battlefield. It was a light cannon and the only remaining cannon from an artillery platoon that got decimated in a battle. The platoon was in retreat but he went back." He stared after the baron and then shook himself as if from out of a dream. "One can only imagine the sight of him with a cannon on his shoulder." With those soft words, he sighed and then tore his eyes from the baron's retreating form. "I'll leave you to your work now, Miss Darley! Come along, Courage. I shall have Ned find you something delicious to eat in the kitchens and he can then take you outside and after that he can brush you again." With that, he and the dog walked away, back toward the kitchens.

Lula shook herself from the vision that Tuedy had put in her head. "Tuedy! There is no need, I can do that," she called after him.

Tuedy stopped and turned to her. "Young Ned enjoys the dog. Tis good for him to use his injured hand by learning to manage a brush." He added with a smile, "Your ointment has eased the scar greatly. Besides, I can see how happy Courage makes him. I believe he had his own dog at some time in his past, eh?"

Lula could only nod as she watched them go.

She looked back to see the baron's retreating form striding into the darkness of the side hallway to his study. She was about to leave when she stopped and turned to watch the house boys with renewed interest. She wondered how many of these boys had gone off to war because they had no family, no home. How many had nothing to return to, or were unable or unacceptable to do any work after the war due to their injuries? The baron had made sure they found a home here, at Graestone. He had given them a position and a job that they could do.

Or were they just a source of inexpensive labor, these men and boys who were used to taking orders?

She frowned as she walked toward the doors that led out into the courtyard and to the stables.

She had no idea what the baron's finances were. There were many great houses that could not afford the help they needed. It would make sense if this was the case. The castle was dark, there were limited candles being used, and many of the hearths were left cold. Perhaps the shuttered windows in the great hall and on the first floor were an effort to keep out the cold and save the firewood for the occupied parts of the castle. More evidence was that an entire wing was apparently unused for it was in total disrepair and seemingly left to rot.

On top of that was the baron himself. She thought him opinionated, gruff and snarly. He did not have to give her orders as if she were one of the men.

She huffed out a frustrated breath. *His word is truth. His rules are the only accepted rules.*

The baron was also called *Captain War.*

She paused in her steps. He had been a captain.

Had he not sent these very men into battle?

This was not some magnanimous gesture he was doing by bringing these men and boys to Graestone.

This was guilt.

The baron had brought them here out of guilt to assuage his own part in their injuries from the battles he himself had sent them into.

He had said that he was not a man that women fall in love with nor he with them. So he was a man who had no love to give. Such a man could be no hero.

Not to her. Certainly not to her.

She continued walking again with her face grim.

He was one of those obstinate, opinionated men who knew only one thing—barking orders at those who served under him and thought very little of women's abilities. He also very probably thought women were good for only one thing. She touched her lips and frowned.

She imagined he would have been one of those stubborn men that she and her sisters and her mother had encountered when they had first tried to sell the Aldbey Park Thoroughbreds at Tattersalls auction house. Those men were unbendable in their ways.

He was the very opposite of her mother's wonderful new husband, Lord Alexander Hawke, who had also served his time for king and country in the military like Baron de Walton. Yet Alexander had been kind and thoughtful and accepting of her mother breeding, training and selling Thoroughbreds with the help of Lula and her sisters.

No, Baron Warwick de Walton was certainly not a virtuous, honorable, accepting man.

CHAPTER ELEVEN

L ULA WALKED OUT into the white-blanketed landscape of the courtyard and stopped. The men who she had watched tamping down paths were gone. She stood there alone in the silence of the snowflakes drifting down all around her and on her as she stared at the snowy scene. She turned slowly and looked up. The castle battlements that were normally a severe gray and stained with the dark history of the castle's past were now covered with glistening, pristine, virgin snow. She looked up higher and saw that the tops of the turrets were frosted like icing on individual cakes. Lula smiled and opened her gloved hands to catch the flakes as she inhaled the cold, fresh air. Wonderful smells came from the kitchens off to her right on the first floor. She sighed with pleasure. Tuedy was baking a delicious roast and a pudding, no doubt. A wonderful meal on a cold, snowy day was to be had by all.

Lula frowned slightly. She would be eating alone, however, in that great, big, poorly lit, dark and drafty dining room. Oh, how she missed her sisters, Julia and Birdie, and her Aunt Eggy and her mother, and Pasha and Lord Hawke as well. The family would be gathered around the fire in the drawing room on a day such as this or gathered at the table for a warm, nourishing meal after they had fed all the horses in the large stables at Aldbey Park.

Suddenly, out of the corners of her eyes, she spotted a snowball flying through the air toward her. She quickly ducked just as it sailed past her arm. She grabbed a handful of snow into her hands and patted it into a tight ball as she stood up and looked for her attackers.

"Once again, your aim is off, Machabee," she called out cheerfully.

Machabee, Melchisedec and Jolyon popped up behind a short wall of snow they had piled up. The two older boys had big grins on their faces. Jolyon looked unsure of the situation.

"My aim was fine. My uncle says a man must never hurt a woman." Machabee lifted his little chin. "I meant to miss you on purpose."

Melchisedec frowned at his brother. "Aw, you plain missed her and you know it, Mack! She was too fast for you. She ducked!"

Machabee's eyes went down to Lula's booted legs. "Why are you wearing breeches and boots like a man?"

Lula sighed. "Tis easier to work around the horses and tis much warmer, that is why."

"You ate in the dining room." Machabee's voice had a hint of accusation to it. "Todrick Tweedy says we cannot eat in there because it makes more work for the house boys." Machabee furrowed his brows after he made that statement.

"I see," Lula said quietly. "Then perhaps it makes more sense if you three join me. Why make the house boys do the work of lighting all those candles and bringing food from the kitchens for one person when they can do so for all of us?"

Machabee's face instantly brightened. "We used to eat in there. I should like to again!"

Melchisedec nodded his head adamantly in agreement. "I should as well! The castle has become far too glum since, since—"

Machabee nudged his brother hard with his elbow. "We are not to talk of that, Mel," he whispered.

Lula heard him however. "You cannot talk of what?"

The boys frowned and averted their eyes as Jolyon continued to stare quietly at her.

Lula waited another moment. "Are you boys warm enough?" she asked. It looked as though they had just put on as many pieces of clothing that they could find. She could not even see Jolyon's hands past the sleeves of the several shirts he wore as well as the thick woolen tunic over it all. All fell far below his hands. It appeared that he could barely bend his arms. The collar of his woolen coat obscured almost half of his face, leaving only his curious eyes.

Melchisedec turned to Lula with a grin on his young face. "Of course we are warm enough. We are not babies. We can dress ourselves just fine! We even dressed Joly!" He pointed to their small, younger brother. "Now, are you going to throw that snowball that you have there in your hand or melt it? I bet you can't even reach us! Uncle War is the best snowball thrower. He is game anytime, even at night, for he says he cannot sleep. *Go ahead, throw it!*" He grinned at her as he issued the impish dare.

Lula tossed the snowball up and down in her hand as she thought of what he had said. *The baron could not sleep. Perhaps this is why he was so surly.* She looked at the eager faces on the three boys. Her smile grew. Without a word, she hurled the snowball right at Melchisedec's chest where it exploded into wet snow.

The boy looked down at his chest and started laughing happily. He looked from Lula to his older brother. "Mack! Did you see that? She can throw better than you, I think."

Lula watched Machabee's face. He was staring at her in a calculating way. Suddenly, he bent down and grabbed up an armful of premade snowballs. He stood up with a huge grin on his face as he took one of the snowballs into his hand.

The game was on.

Lula ran, packing up snow into balls as she dodged the snowballs the laughing, giggling boys were throwing at her.

She threw her own back as fast as she could, laughing and dodging and ducking as she made her way across the courtyard to the stable door. She ducked within the door and peered out.

"I have made it safely to the other side of the courtyard and escaped your ambush! Well played, men!" she called out. "Well played! A fine snowy ambush that was!"

She heard them laughing. "Well played to you as well, Miss Lula!" she heard them call back to her. She watched as they began to refill their supply of snowballs for the next person who dared to walk out into the courtyard.

Lula grinned and shook her head as she watched them. She turned away from the scene of the young boys playing in the snow and looked over her shoulder into the stables. She saw that the lanterns had been lit inside. She made her way down the aisle to the sound of horses moving about in their stalls, or standing quietly with their heads down eating the fragrant hay that had been cut and dried from the fields around the castle just this past summer.

The smell of horses reminded her of home.

As she walked down the aisle of the stables, she noticed that every stall was clean and had fresh straw on the floor and hay in each manger and water in all the wooden buckets for each of the horses. She went to Buttercup's stall and greeted the big horse in a soft voice. The old war horse seemed very content and amiably sniffed her proffered hand. She looked around but found no one working in the stables, not Poppy or Bertie. She opened the stall door and entered Buttercup's stall so that she could better check the wound. The horse snorted and backed up a step but Lula kept her hand out to the big animal as she talked softly.

Finally, the old horse sighed and let her approach. She pulled off her gloves and gently prodded around the wound for heat or swelling. Satisfied, she reached up to pat the old war horse's neck.

"You'll be just fine," she crooned. "You'll be back to munching buttercups in the spring grass, I warrant." She laughed softly and gave the horse several pats on his glossy neck.

Buttercup looked down at her and dropped his big head over the top of her hair and down to her shoulder. He snuffled at her hair and pulled at the shawl that was draped around her neck and over her shoulders.

She stood there thinking as she looked around the stables and at the other occupants of all the stalls. She gave the big horse a last pat and then walked out of the horse's stall.

She walked slowly down the aisle, looking at the horses.

Really looking at the horses.

War horses.

Light infantry horses. Heavy infantry horses.

Draft horses that were used to pull artillery wagons.

The entire area was full of military horses. Each and every stall held a war horse.

All with scars, terrible scars.

Horrible scars.

Some scars were fresher than others, like Buttercup, and some had scars that were very old.

There were some horses still in their prime. There were many old and weary horses that stood in their stall with one leg cocked and their heads hanging low. There were some that just seemed to stare inward. It was the quiet ones that broke her heart. She could only imagine the horrors that they had been through to turn so inward.

A small, brown gelding refused to look at her. He kept his head in the corner, staring at nothing, no longer wanting to be a part of this world. She could not blame him, though she cooed and called to him to no avail.

Others came to the stall door to sniff at her hand or accept a bit of oats. These were typically the geldings, still wanting to believe in the goodness of men.

The stallions spun to stare at her in suspicion, as if deciding if she was foe or friend. They raised their necks and watched her every move, still ready for battle if need be. No matter their injury or that gray hairs now showed on their muzzles or above their wise old eyes.

The mares were the proudest. They were standoffish like the

grand queens they were, studying her before approaching, as brave as any of the stallions.

Tears came to Lula's eyes as she looked around at all of their injuries. None were unscathed.

Missing an ear. Missing an eye. Mutilated. Burned fur right down to the hide. Legs that did not work the way they should anymore as those horses took lurching steps forward to the door to greet her. Many, too many, with tails or manes or both burned off to the point of never growing back.

She then came upon the two big draft mares that the baron had needed her for. Both looked heavy with foal. If she was correct, they would be foaling before spring. This was unlike the Aldbey Park Thoroughbreds whose breeding and foaling the Darleys timed so the foals could romp in the warm sun on the fresh spring grass.

Lula stared at the pair of enormous draft horses. Both of their bodies had burn scars; huge, patches of horrid scars, much larger scars than any of the other horses in the stables. Were these the two that the baron had led off the battlefield? The ones that had been left behind that he had gone after?

She could only imagine the horrors that these and all the other loyal war horses had gone through. But then it came to her, *these were the ones that had made it off the battlefields to come home.*

Lula took a gasping sob as she stumbled backward, her legs working stiffly as she backed down the aisle of the stables. She placed a gloved hand to her mouth, stifling her tears as she stared into the stables. Her whole life had been lived in beautiful Aldbey Park, raising and training the exquisite horses there.

But this? She had never seen anything like this. Her heart was breaking at the sight.

How was she to help them?

Suddenly, she heard someone approaching at the other end of the stables. She swiped at her tears and ducked into the nearest stall, standing behind the horse there. It was a smaller horse, though broad enough to carry a man or pull a cart. She ducked and then peeked over the horse's back to see the baron come striding into the barn. He walked down the aisle, looking left and right as he spoke softly to each of the horses. He held his hand out for the horses to sniff and gave several a gentle pat.

Lula moaned silently to herself. Would he find her here, hiding like a ninny with tears on her face?

She watched as he went into the stall beside the one that she was in. It was Buttercup's stall. He began talking in his soft baritone. His voice was a soothing, caressing, low bass as he approached the big, wary war horse.

"She has done an excellent job on your injury, has she not, my boy?" he crooned softly to the horse as his gaze went over the stitches. "I have never seen such fine stitches."

Lula lifted herself slightly onto her toes to peer over the neck of the horse she was hiding behind. The baron was running his fingers gingerly over the stitches, checking for heat or swelling.

She watched and listened as he continued to check over the war horse, using the same gentle voice to coax the big horse into letting him near. If the injured stallion moved or pinned his ears, the baron became firm though gentle and then returned to speaking in his coaxing tone. It occurred to her that Baron Warwick de Walton was using the same voice that he had used at times with her.

Her horse suddenly moved, moving its shoulders into her and almost stepping on her toe. She let out a small yelp and hastily stepped away from it.

"Who is that?" the baron demanded as he moved away from Buttercup.

Lula heaved a sigh and stood up fully from the horse that she had been hiding behind. She stared silently at the baron, knowing her face was pale and possibly still tear-streaked.

"You." His voice was strained. He stared at her frightened face and her fascinating freckles and her wild, chaotic hair. Tiny curls wreathed her face with a bright green ribbon trying to hold the masses of them at bay. She wore a shockingly bright pink shawl around her shoulders that lit up the skin of her face as if it were a sunny day, instead of the bleak, snowy day that it was.

"Do not faint," he added softly.

Lula's heart started beating frantically, though she wasn't sure if it was from fear and panic or from the way his voice had sounded, causing a fluttery feeling within her breasts. Either of these feelings was unacceptable. She would not fear this man, nor let him cause such odd feelings within her.

"I am not frightened of you." She had put voice to her thoughts before she had thought better of it. She remained standing where she was, with the horse between her and the baron.

War walked out of Buttercup's stall to come over to the stall she was in. He rested his arms on the top of the stall door to stare at her. She looked pale. Upset. Angry.

"I would not have that of you." His voice was soft, gentle.

Lula furrowed her brows and crossed her arms over her chest. He was using the same voice as he had with the wary stallion. "Do not talk to me in that voice."

War stared at her disgruntled face as his lips firmed into a scowl. "What voice?" he growled in a deep, dulcet whisper.

"That one. You are doing it right now. The voice you use to calm and win over the horses. You are using it on me."

"Do you prefer me *contrary* and always *assured that I am correct*?" he said quietly with an arched brow.

Lula closed her eyes briefly and dropped her arms. He had overheard her speaking to Tuedy. "You have a propensity to be rude, Baron."

War let out a grunt. "You have a propensity to misunderstand certain things," he said softly.

Lula took a breath as her lips turned down. "You have a propensity to be arrogant in thinking everyone at Graestone will blithely follow your orders."

War narrowed his eyes as his jaw tightened. "Now there, *there* you are very incorrect."

"Only you are correct, of course."

"I am, when it comes to the rules here at Graestone Castle. But you spoke of orders. *You* will not follow my orders, therefore not *everyone* at Graestone follows my orders." He sighed loudly and looked around the stables. "I have told you not to be here in the stables or around the horses alone." He caught her eyes and held them. "Make sure that Popplewell or Bertram Bumstead are here with you, then I will allow it."

"How very kind of you to *allow* me this."

War shook his head as he lowered his eyes to the stall floor. He sighed heavily as his gaze came back to her. He spoke quietly, gently in his deep baritone. "I have no wish to argue with you, Lula," he said in a near whisper.

Lula sucked in a breath. He had said her name in what sounded like a soft caress. He had not called her Miss Darley. She shook her head, she would not let his familiarity affect her. "You have a propensity to think you can 'cure' everyone."

War went still. "And do you presume that you are one of those that I am trying to—as you say—*cure*?"

Lula's gaze flew away from his. "'Twould be another success for you, like the men and boys you have at Graestone," she murmured.

War growled softly at that. "*Success is a collection of failures and hardships overcome and problems solved. But success can only be had by one's own work, not mine.*"

Lula gasped. She knew those words. She had read them in the *Morning Post*. They had been written by a widow who had risen from dire circumstances. Lula had never forgotten those words. She flailed her hand at the baron as tears misted her eyes. She raised her chin. "Very well. You carry some measure of guilt for these injured men. Therefore, you have a propensity to think that you can *help save* people." She looked away from him to the horses. "And save these horses," she added quietly.

War forced himself not to flinch at her statement. He looked down at his hands, resting on the top of the stall door. "If only that were so, that I had the ability to save them, the men *and the horses*." He looked back at her. "I hope I have you to help with the horses." He paused as her face went solemn. "However, what you said was also unkind. Once again, you have a propensity to misunderstand." He added quietly, "And to forget."

Lula's eyes dashed to his. "That is unfair. Now you are the one who is unkind. Have you no compassion? I was injured and it caused me to be unable to remember what happened to me."

War's jaw tightened. "You will not let yourself remember."

Lula raised her chin higher. She opened her mouth and then abruptly closed it as a single tear spilled from her eye and ran down her cheek.

"Devil confound it," he said in a harsh whisper as he stood up to his full height. "Do not cry, Lula, I cannot bear it." He opened the stall door and entered Lula's stall. He started to stride around the horse so that he could pull her into his arms, but she hastily backed away, keeping the horse between them.

She held a trembling hand out to him, palm forward to stop him as she moved further behind the horse. "Do not come any closer, if you please," she said in a tear-choked voice. "You may not kiss me again." She swiped at the tear on her face. "*Ever*. I, I did not enjoy it."

War stepped back away from her. His back and shoulders went rigid. "I was not going to kiss you just then. I wanted only to…to comfort you." He frowned. "*You* kissed me willingly. And you *did* enjoy it." His voice had been a soft growl of indignation.

"I did not." She lifted her chin stubbornly.

"Is your word truth?" he demanded in a tight voice.

She stared at him with her breasts heaving. She would not, could not answer that. Not when she had indeed enjoyed his kiss. *Very much.*

He stared at her, unwilling to let uncertainty overtake him. "You did not faint."

"That is true," she said grudgingly.

"Kiss me again and find out. *I dare you*," he whispered in a voice thick with need. *What was this havoc that had taken over him?* He found himself desperate to prove her wrong. She *had* enjoyed his kiss, he had felt it in every fiber of his being. For a brief moment, it felt like they had been one.

Lula's eyes widened as her breathing increased. *Was she panicking because she wanted to kiss him?* She shook her head, though she could not think if it was at him, or in response to her inner question. *"Why?"* she demanded of the baron. "Why do you *trifle* with me? I am leaving in the next day or so, am I not?" Her breasts heaved as she stared at him and then it dawned on her. "I see. That is it. You are sending me away, thus you are safe from having yet another female fall in love with you like so many assuredly do. And since you do not fall in love with them, therefore you are free to trifle with me as you wish."

He took a step toward her with a scowl on his face. "No, you are entirely wrong."

She shook her head adamantly. "Do not come any closer!"

War's jaw tightened as he studied her face. Her eyes were wide and her breasts were heaving. She looked anything but afraid of him, however. In fact, her eyes had settled on his lips. It appeared his mouth fascinated her. She was not averting her eyes from him as she had before. But she was clearly angry, and possibly unsure or confused and definitely *defensive.*

"Very well," he said quietly as he continued to try to read all the emotions crossing her face.

Before War could say anything more, she fled from behind the horse, out of the stall and was hurrying down the aisle. She was out the door of the stables before he could register what she had been wearing.

He had gotten a glimpse of a very fine, rounded bottom and elegantly curved legs under tight-fitting, brightly colored cloth.

Good God and bloody hell and the devil confound it.

Was she wearing men's breeches?

CHAPTER TWELVE

T HE NEXT MORNING as she was about to leave the castle to go out into the courtyard to the stables, she passed the baron walking through the great hall.

He paused in his great stride and looked back at her. "Miss Lula," he called to her.

Lula turned around but he stood there, silent, staring uncomfortably at her.

"Good morning, Baron," she said and was about to continue on when he spoke again.

He called after her. "The weather today—"

She stopped and turned once again. She waited but he said nothing. "Yes? The weather?"

He continued to stare at her with the cheeks above his beard showing pink. Finally, he ran one big hand over his beard in agitation and took two steps toward her. He stopped abruptly and took a step back, adjusting the space between them. "The weather. It is still bad. I cannot return you home to Aldbey Park today." He ran his hand over his beard again and was about to turn to leave when he abruptly spun back to her. "And I do not trifle. My word is truth."

With that, he spun on his heels and walked away.

LULA SPENT HER days trudging back and forth to the stables through the snow with Courage trotting faithfully beside her.

Once in the stables, the dog would find a comfortable old horse rug to curl up on. Some days, however, Tuedy would intercept her and take Courage to the kitchens for Ned. She and Tuedy would share a knowing look. Sometimes, there were other things that healed the body and the heart and Lula knew one of those was the companionship of an animal.

Lula would remove her simple woolen overgown and work in the breeches she wore underneath it. She felt it best to not walk through the castle with all the men and boys there that may see her wearing her breeches.

Second Lieutenant William Popplewell and Ensign Bertram Bumstead were there to greet her each day. She expected that the baron had reassigned them to daily duties in the barn so they could watch over her. They became a large help to her, however, and entreated her to call them Poppy and Bertie.

Lula took the time to examine each of the war horses and make notes on what could be done for them. Each day, she visited the far too quiet brown gelding first. Grooming and rubbing ointment into his burned hide to soothe and soften it. She spoke softly to him the whole while, entreating him back to this place and this time, waiting for his ears to perk up and for him to "see" her. She was determined that the little gelding would improve.

The most common injury from the battlefield for the horses seemed to be burn scars like the one the small brown gelding had. She went to the kitchens to enlist Tuedy Tweedy's help in creating concoctions and more ointments to soothe the horses' injuries or their scarred hides with some of the dried leaves and roots she had brought with her.

She had little sacks filled with different plants and herbs and roots. The root of the True Love plant for colic, crushed leaves from cleavers to stop bleeding in wounds. There was also bishop wort, wormwood, helenium, red nettle and, of course, white willow bark.

Tuedy helped her make tea from the willow bark or gave her lard to mix some of the crushed powder from the leaves into her ointments. Tuedy was very glad to help and was eager and curious to learn. He watched as Lula added some alkanet; an herb known for easing pain, into an ointment to use on those horses most recently brought to Graestone whose wounds were still far too fresh.

She also made a special ointment just for Tuedy's hand, and then two poultices, one for Poppy, who had a bad knee and another for Bertie's injured shoulder. They sat in the barn while she worked, enjoying the soothing poultices with smiles on their faces.

"Are you happy to rest and get out of work or are you feeling the healing from the poultices I have made you?" she asked the two men.

Poppy's drooping jowls lifted into a smile of pure contentment. "I do not hurt. Tis a wonder this poultice is. I thank you, Miss Lula."

Bertie opened his eyes and grinned at her. "Poppy has it right. My shoulder doesn't hurt. First time in a long time, Miss."

This gave Lula another idea.

She refilled several more small jars with ointment and made more poultice wraps and teas that she began offering to some of the men and boys that she came upon during her days learning her way around the castle.

Many of the men at first had been distrustful and refused what she offered them. As word got out, however, that others had found great relief from her ointments and poultices, they were grateful to receive what she offered. Some of the men sought her out and asked for something to aid their wounds.

She learned their names little by little and asked after their injuries so that she may hopefully mix up something specifically for each one that may ease the pain from their wounds and hasten their healing. She explained what each medicine she was giving them was for and how it may help them and asked after them whenever she saw them.

She spoke daily with Buttercup's owner, who never missed a day visiting the big war horse. This gave her another idea. She began to invite the men and boys who were interested to come and just groom or pet the horses. She vowed they would not have to work. She just wanted attention and gentle company for those horses who needed it the most. Many took her up on this and she assigned each person a particular horse.

She introduced the small brown gelding to the wildlings and twice a day the three little boys spent over an hour in the small gelding's stall brushing him and petting him in between their snowball fights. It was a match that could not have been better for the little gelding or the little boys. Slowly, the brown gelding was beginning to come back. A few days later, she even heard a quiet, soft neigh from the horse when the three little boys came running into the stables.

Lula also did a daily check on the two draft wagon horses that were in foal. She put her ear to their bellies to listen for a strong heartbeat in each of the mares. She ran her hands over their heavy bellies and felt the unborn foals moving within. She still worried that the mares would foal before the snow left the ground and the spring grass came in.

Poppy and Bertie would hold each horse she was examining or bring water when it was needed when they were not resting with their poultice wraps. They were very interested in everything she was doing. The only horse they refused to hold for her was Buttercup. The big war horse continued to be difficult with most anyone and was acting up after being confined to a stall during the snowy days, often kicking the wall of his stall so hard it made the walls shake. Luckily, the stallion's scar was healing nicely and he seemed to calm with a soft voice and touch.

Lula passed the baron often as she came and went in the stables. Each time, she held her breath, waiting for his admonition about the wildlings and the brown gelding or the medicinals she was giving the men and the boys. He never did, however. Each time, he would stop whatever he was saying to the men he was usually speaking with. He would pause slightly in his long-striding walk, making sure that he was not too close to her. Then he would tell her there was still too much snow on the roads for him to return her to her home. He did not seem interested in waiting for her answer but always strode away with his men. That was all he said.

IN THE EVENINGS after Lula had dined, she returned to her chamber and climbed into her big bed. She often heard the heartbreakingly beautiful sound of the violin or the pianoforte being played. Often, she drifted to sleep at night with the music still playing softly in the castle like a loving lullaby.

She began having dinner with the three boys as she had suggested to them. So far, no one but Tuedy and a few house boys were aware of this. Tuedy was delighted that the boys were eating in the dining room with Miss Lula and that she was not eating alone.

The second night that they had dinner together, she had asked about the sound of someone weeping in the house. Machabee and Melchisedec had looked at each other and then at Jolyon before their solemn gazes returned to Lula.

"Tis our Mama, but we are not supposed to speak of her, Miss Lula," Machabee said quietly.

"Your mother? She is here?" Lula asked with surprise. She had assumed their mother had gone away, or was even deceased.

Melchisedec nodded quickly. "Yes. Please do not ask us anything more," he said pleadingly with a glance at little Jolyon.

Lula looked from Machabee to Melchisedec and finally to Jolyon who had stopped with a piece of bread midway to his mouth to stare at her with big eyes.

"Very well then, I shall not press you on this any further," Lula said with a polite smile. She stared at her plate as she pushed her venison tenderloin with a Madeira green peppercorn sauce around with her fork. Tuedy had proved to be a most excellent cook. A thought came to her then of the music of the violin and pianoforte being played. It could only be the boys' mother.

"Can you tell me if little Jolyon ever talked," Lula asked calmly, "or has he never said a word in his young life?"

Melchisedec shoved a fork full of the tender venison into his mouth before he answered her. "Oh, he used to talk all the time!"

Machabee frowned at his younger brother and bumped him with his elbow. "Hush about that!"

Lula pursed her lips and changed the subject. She would seek out their mother and get some answers. Since no one at Graestone was forthcoming on why the poor woman was crying all the time, or why Jolyon had stopped talking, she would find out for herself.

"I was thinking that Jolyon could be called Lyon. So that his name is as strong as his brothers' names. What do you think of that Jolyon? May I call you Lyon?"

Jolyon smiled broadly. His brothers tested the name out and decide they liked having a little brother named Lyon.

Lula smiled. "Excellent, we are agreed! Now then, as we are on the subject of names. How did you come about being called the wildlings?" she asked with an interested grin.

Machabee smiled proudly. "Tis because we are Wildlings. Our father was Lord Wildling. He's dead. He fell off his horse and broke his head open," he said calmly and with the innocence of a child as he shoveled some food into his mouth. "Twas our stepfather that started calling us the name." His smile fell. "But he didn't say it as our name. Now though, the rest of the castle calls us wildlings, too, even though our stepfather is gone." He shrugged his young shoulders and then puffed out his chest. "My brothers and I have decided that *we* will find our mother a nice man to marry this time. A man that would like to be our father."

Lula stopped with her fork midway to her mouth. She slowly put it on her plate. "I see," she said in a near whisper. "Your stepfather was not…er, *pleased* to be a father to you?"

The two older boys shook their heads while Jolyon just stared wide-eyed at her.

"We hid from him," Machabee said.

"Lyon, too?" she asked slowly.

"Yes, all of us. We all hid. We are glad he wasn't here long."

She asked carefully, "And when you say your stepfather is gone, you mean he died?"

This time, it was Melchisedec that answered. He nodded quickly and smiled. "Yes, he's dead! That is when Jolyon, I mean Lyon, stopped talking." His face squished up tightly. "We cannot speak of it, or ask about it, though."

Lula could not help herself. She looked quickly over to little Jolyon. He was staring down at his plate in silence.

She looked back at the older boys. "I see. Very well then, we shall not speak of it." *She would speak to their mother, of a certainty.* "Do you boys have any warm coats to wear out in the snow? Surely you must be cold when you are outside without any proper clothing or even a hat?"

Machabee shrugged. "No one cares what we do, so we do what we want and wear what we want. Though Jolyon, I mean Lyon, does need some new clothes, he has grown so. We give him ours but they do not fit him."

"Goodness. Indeed," Lula said quietly.

"Uncle War takes care of us," Melchisedec said defensively.

Machabee looked at his brother and nodded. "That is true. If it weren't for Uncle War, well—" he stopped and looked at both of his brothers with his eyes coming to rest on Jolyon. "We want to be just like Uncle War one day," he said fervently.

Lula smiled at him and finished her dinner, listening to the two boys chatting on about their hero; their Uncle War who was strong enough to carry men and cannons off the field of battle. All at the same time, evidently. He had taught them to ride, and to fence. He also had taught them how to fish and how to hunt rabbits with a bow and arrows. They were particularly excited to tell her how he taught them to walk like "real men" and how to use their fists correctly in a fight and where to kick a bad man to make him cry. Soon, they said, Uncle War was going to teach them to shoot.

"Goodness," was all that Lula could say.

Machabee shook his head enthusiastically. "We will never have to be afraid of a bad man."

"I see," Lula whispered.

After their meal, Tuedy always made sure there was a delightful pudding to be had. There was their favorite—a gooseberry fool, and then there was also gingerbread cake, sugar biscuits, jam tarts or sometimes a trifle. Each evening, Tuedy made special dishes sure to delight each of the boys. It was as much a delight for Tuedy to present them as for the boys to eat them.

Tuedy had also opened up the small drawing room just a few doors down from the dining room. The elegant sofa, chairs and petite tables had all been covered in dust cloths but Tuedy had them removed and made sure the fireplace was lit each evening. The room was warm and cheerful in all its shades of soft greens and pale blues. There were some books in this room as well and she found that the boys loved having a story read to them in front of the fire. They also were rather adept at cards or opening up the beautiful illustrated book of maps they found in the room and pointing out faraway places on the maps within its pages.

In a corner of the study was an exquisite, painted glass globe sitting on an elegant wooden stand by the small bookcase.

Lula spun the globe until she found Arabia and told the boys of the story of the very first Darley Arabian being purchased in the deserts of Arabia before being shipped all the way back to

Aldbey Park. She then told them about Eclipse who was one of the Darley Arabian's sons. She told them how he won every race he ran and only retired because no one would race him anymore for they knew he could not be beaten.

Lula spun the globe again and told them stories of her sister Julia's new husband, Pasha Darius who had been a Prince of Persia but gave it up because he loved Lula's sister, Julia, so very much. This caused the boys to roll their eyes and make silly faces. She hurried on to tell them all about Pasha's mother, the Supreme Imperial Majesty Bibi Habibeh, who smoked an ornate water pipe called an argila and who blackened her eyebrows so that both of her brows were almost connected over her nose.

The boys tried over and over to say Queen Bibi's name. Lula laughed with them and explained that her Aunt Egidia—who was called Aunt Eggy—was now Queen Bibi Habibeh's very good friend, and even her aunt still could not say her name correctly.

She spun the globe again and pointed to the far north of Scotland. She told them many stories of Great-aunt Egidia Ross, particularly all about the Highlands of Scotland where her aunt was from. She told the boys the ancient tales of the Ross Clan and particularly the sisters who raised Clydesdale horses and rode them into war.

Todrick found them on the third night after they had eaten in the dining room together. "This is not right," he rasped as he stood in the doorway, looking around the bright room and then angrily at Lula where she sat with the boys on the settee, reading them a book.

"Why ever not, Todrick?" Lula asked curiously.

Todrick's scarred lower lip rose to almost cover his top lip in a fierce frown. "It just bloody isn't," he croaked.

"You really ought to try my ointment on your lip, Todrick. I do believe it will help you immensely," she said, keeping a pleasant smile on her face and in her voice.

Todrick glared at her. "Bloody nonsense. I'll not use your potions like the other men. Bloody fools, all of them!" And with those words, he walked away.

Lula looked over at Machabee and Melchisedec just in time to stop them from shooting spitballs at Todrick's back.

Lula feared that Todrick would have the room closed, or worse, tell the baron that she was reading to the boys in the opened-up drawing room and that the baron would, for some reason, say that she could not do this.

One morning, Lula's path crossed with the baron's in the great hall just as she came out of the dining room and he out of the hallway from his study with another well-dressed man. The gentleman was talking about one of the baron's merchant ships that had recently arrived at the docks with a treasure trove of goods. The baron held up his hand to interrupt the man when he saw Lula.

Lula stopped when War asked after her, and as had become usual, he did not wait for an answer but informed her brusquely that she still could not return home due to the weather.

Lula quickly stepped in front of him, blocking his path. She watched as his eyes widened and his high cheekbones blossomed with a trace of pink.

"I am well, Baron, and I understand that I still cannot leave," she sighed in annoyance. "I would speak to you, however, if you please?" she said politely but firmly.

Her eyes went to the man he was with. He was incredibly handsome and had a dimple on his chin. He was dressed like a typical member of the *ton* in an indigo waistcoat with black embroidery all over, a silken white cravat tied neatly *a la Bryon* and a matching indigo frock coat.

The baron had his sleeves rolled up, which only made his muscular forearms more apparent, as did the straining of the seams at his broad shoulders. The top two buttons of his shirt were undone, drawing her eyes to the patch of skin there. His silver waistcoat was unbuttoned as seemed usual for him. The well-fitted waistcoat accentuated the narrowness of his trim hips and flat abdomen. His black breeches were not a fine material like his companion's but appeared workmanlike and his tall boots were well worn with patches of wear on the insides from riding horses.

The two men were quite a contrast. The baron, however, possessed a natural maleness that threatened her normally common sense attitude to the world around her.

She was not her older sister, Julia, who had an ease about her with men, particularly Pasha who was now her husband. Nor was she her younger sister, Birdie, who daydreamed and flirted with all men. Lula had always been a reader and most interested in educating herself. She had not been interested in men or matters of the heart. When she had received the scars on her forehead and on her hand, the scars had only solidified the simple fact that no man would be interested in her any more than she would be interested in them.

Until this man threatened everything she thought she knew that she wanted. And he was a man who had told her he could not love.

The baron stopped at her request with a quick glance at the man standing with him. When the other man stayed beside him showing great interest in whatever it was that Lula had to say, the baron turned his back on him and stared down at Lula with a concerned look.

"What is it you wish to speak to me about, Miss Darley?" he asked quietly. "Are you well? Are any of the men bothering you with unwanted attention or demanding more of your time and medicines?" he asked in a low baritone. "Yes, I know all about that." He leaned closer. "Any fainting?" he asked very quietly.

Lula stared at him a moment, blinking several times to clear her wayward mind. She could not deny the concern she had heard in his deep voice. It made her heart flutter briefly. She managed to pull her eyes from his as she reached up to pull some of her curls down onto her forehead. She saw that his eyes had followed her hand. She stiffened her spine and lifted her chin. "'Tis your nephews, Baron."

War frowned with surprise. "My nephews? What about them?"

Lula glanced quickly next to the baron to the man staring at her with open curiosity. She noted his gaze went from her Pomona green gown, down to her bright jonquil yellow boots. He had an open grin on his face and an obvious look of curiosity. Lula wondered at the baron's rudeness in not introducing the man to her.

"Please excuse my friend's rude manners," War said curtly. He scowled at the man standing there looking at Lula so openly, until the man shrugged his shoulders and just grinned back at War without moving away. War looked back at Lula. "Well?" he asked.

Lula glanced back up at the baron. "Pray forgive me, what did you say?" she asked in confusion as she watched the two men. One was scowling and the other was grinning with open good humor.

War heaved out a sigh and then crossed his arms as he stared down at Lula. He took a step to block his friend who was staring at Lula once again. "You wanted to speak to me about my nephews?" he prompted.

"Oh, yes," Lula said with a start. She wanted to ask him about Jolyon but she hadn't the nerve when he was staring down at her so fiercely. She would not ask him. Not yet, anyway. "Are you aware that the boys play outside without the correct clothing? There is nary a jacket nor hat worn between them all."

War's scowl deepened. "What is that of my concern?"

"Are you not their uncle and the Baron of Graestone?"

His eyes narrowed as he drew back in suspicion. "I am."

Lula nodded once, firmly. "You see? That makes you thusly responsible for them."

The man with the dimple tried and failed to control his grin as he looked back and forth from War to Lula. "Baron Warwick de Walton responsible for the wildlings? You do not say!"

War turned to snarl at the man. "I do *not* say," he said firmly with a glare for the man. He looked back at Lula when she began tapping her foot impatiently. He stared down with an arched brow and narrowed eyes at her bright, yellow, booted toe, tapping away from under her green woolen gown.

"They just layer on clothing," Lula said as she stared up at him. "They cannot be warm enough, surely?" she asked with concern.

"They have a mother," War growled. "And Tuedy, of course," he said quietly as his cheeks pinkened further. He glanced at the man beside him. "You are finding this far too amusing for my liking, Fairfax." War looked back at Lula. "We are done here."

He started to walk away but Lula stopped him by clearing her throat.

She sighed loudly in exasperation when he stopped and turned to her with a frown and an arch of one eyebrow. She walked over to him and stepped right in front of him so that he could not leave again.

War looked down at her. He leaned closer with his lips very close to her ear so that his beard tangled in her hair. "You are standing very close to me, Miss Lula. Are you not worried that I shall 'trifle' with you?" His voice had gone deep and velvet and sensuous, dangerously sensuous.

Lula's breath caught as heat suddenly pooled between her legs. "Stop that." She took a step back. "We are not done here. Tuedy, as you mentioned, has other responsibilities, though I must confess he does remarkably well for the boys. However, their mother is...*is indisposed* from what I can see." She crossed her arms and stared up at him, waiting. He made no move to answer. "Though no one will answer my questions about her, I can only assume she is the one crying." She waited again, but still he did not say anything about the person that could be heard weeping in the house now and then. She sighed long and loudly in exasperation when he continued to stare down at her saying nothing. "Thus the duty falls on *your* shoulders, you see?"

The man with the dimple on his chin continued to watch the two of them as his grin widened. "Yes, War. The wildlings are your responsibility. Can you not at least stop them from shooting those spitballs at my back?"

Lula glared at the man. "This is not something to make jest of, Sir." She looked back up at the baron. "Poor little Lyon must be freezing when they go out into the snow. He has outgrown his clothes and his brothers have lent him theirs. The little boy can barely move for his brothers think tis fitting to just keep piling clothing on him. They clearly feel there is no one to turn to that may find him a proper warm coat and hat so they have taken the matter into their own hands," she finished with a quick breath. "There must be someone responsible besides an eight- and nine-year-old boy for procuring him clothing that fits."

As soon as she had finished with her diatribe, she saw Todrick walking past them. He paused and looked back at her with a severe scowl.

Lula put her hands on her hips and scowled right back at the ill-natured butler who seemed to have such a great dislike for her.

Todrick turned away from her and hurried along with his chin in the air.

Lula could not miss the three small bits of white on the back of his black coat. *Spitballs*. She peered into the dim hallway from which Todrick had come, but saw nothing. It appeared that the *wildlings* had struck again.

War cleared his throat, capturing her attention. "Did you say *lion?*"

Lula faced him with a tight smile. She dropped her hands from her hips and straightened her shoulders in defiance. "Yes, Lyon. Joly is not an appropriate name for a little boy. Particularly one with brothers who are named Machabee and Melchisedec. Lyon is a strong name, for a little boy who appears to need some," she flailed her hand as she tried to come up with the word. "*Confidence*," she said triumphantly as she pointed one finger at him.

War's jaw tightened. He did not think, he took her arm and ushered her over to a dark alcove a few feet away from them, just under the curve of the stairs. Only then did he take his hand from her arm.

Lula had her back to the wall as she stared up at him in the shadowy space. She could see well enough in the dim light to notice that his cheeks had darkened as if he were blushing, but she knew he was angry. "You held me by my arm," she said accusingly.

"You did not faint," he said, watching her with wary eyes. He peered closer at her face. "Are you going to faint from my *touching your arm?*"

"No, I will not faint. But I cannot promise not to in the future. Do not put your hands on me again and I will not faint."

"Giving me orders, are you?" he said with an arched eyebrow.

"In that, I am entitled to." She lifted her chin as she waited with breath held for his answer to her defiant statement.

"Very well. I shall try not to put my hands on you." War nodded once, conceding to her statement. His shoulders lost their tension. He knew he was wrong to handle her as he had done and force her to this private spot. "I vow I will not hurt you, but I cannot vow that I will not touch you." He spoke in a whisper, knowing his all too curious friend was nearby and most likely avidly listening to everything he said.

"And your word is your truth?" Lula repeated what he was known to say.

War gritted his teeth. "It is, in that I will not *hurt* you. Of a certainty not touching you is killing *me.* So *you* are hurting me."

"Not touching me is killing you?" Lula whispered with wide eyes.

"Yes," War growled. He stared down at her, trying to form the words he wanted. He paused and took a breath. "You are *not* entitled to rename my nephew, Miss Darley," he commanded.

Lula placed her hands on the wall on either side of her hips. He was indeed angry. "But—" she squeaked.

War's eyes narrowed as he glanced at a movement to his side. He noticed that his friend had come closer and was eagerly trying to eavesdrop. "I will smash your pretty face in, Fairfax, if you do not walk away and give us some bloody privacy," he said firmly. When his friend finally walked away down the hall, he turned back to Lula.

"You are angry," she announced nervously. Still, she continued on, "You should not be. You should join your nephews in the dining room and have a meal with them." She left out that she would be in the dining room as well.

"I have far too much work to catch up on for me to take the time to sit and have a meal. I have been away from Graestone for too many years and my uncle in his poor health let the management of it go. I eat in my study while I work." He sighed in aggravation and ran a hand down the back of his neck, turning it this way and that to ease the tension there. "I am now responsible for multiple villages and farms in the county as well as the castle and the estate itself."

For the first time, Lula noted the exhaustion on his face and in his eyes. "Your uncle is in poor health?"

"Yes, his heart and his lungs. All his life, they have weakened him. When my father was alive, he ran the estate for Uncle Veyril. He travels to warmer climates when he can, or warmer houses, instead of this cold castle."

"Goodness," she whispered, but his next words stilled her sympathetic thoughts.

"It is not for you to determine what is best for my nephew, much less give him a new name," War said with annoyance.

Lula shook her head once and looked anywhere but at the baron's glowering face. "I did not give him a new name, just a new nickname. He likes it," she added weakly.

"How would you know that? The boy will not talk," War snarled quietly.

"And why *is that*, pray tell me?"

War stilled and stared down at her as his jaw tightened. "That is none of your concern. I am trying to help him—" He abruptly stopped whatever it was that he was going to say. His hands balled into fists at his sides as he clamped his lips shut.

Lula's gaze flew to his as her nervousness disappeared. "So you do notice the poor child!"

War took a deep breath as the tension drained from his face. "Do you truly think so little of me?" he asked softly.

Lula fidgeted with the fabric of her gown as she frowned in annoyance. "I do my utmost to not think of you at all, though you truly vex my mind, *far too often.*"

A slow grin lifted War's lips. A tightness that had been in his chest for days, lightened. Her words had made him happy, ridiculously happy. "That is not what I meant." He leaned closer, placing his hands on the wall on either side of her head, careful not to touch her. "Though it pleases me greatly that you think of me, *far too often.*" He looked down at her perfectly bowed lips as his voice lowered and his eyes took on a slumberous look. "I think of you, *far too often,*" he whispered. "I think of kissing you, *far too often,*" he said in a velvet baritone. "In fact, I am kissing you in my mind, just now," he said in a deep, gentle whisper. His languid gaze traveled up her face, past her adorable freckles, to capture her eyes with his. He gave her a rare, full smile. "I am going to kiss each and every one of the captivating freckles I count on your face." His voice lowered to a deep growl. "And every freckle I find on your body. And I vow that I will kiss each and every scar as well."

Lula sank back against the wall as her knees grew weak and that familiar heat spread throughout her again. The heat that only he could cause. Her breasts rose and fell rapidly. She stared up at him. *Caught in his sensuous gaze.* She was trying to resist the pull of his eyes and the far too magnetic pull of his mouth. She was also afraid, in so many ways. "You are cruel," she whispered hastily. "You are *trying to frighten* me."

His smile gentled on his lips as he shook his head slowly. "No," he said in a dulcet, deep voice. "The men in Hyde Park who attacked you were cruel, and evil as well," he said carefully. "All men are not intrinsically thus. I assure you, Lula," he whispered. "I am not like them. I vow I will never hurt you." His dark eyes traveled to the riot of curls on the top of her head and back down to her blue-green eyes. He ached to touch her, to delve his hands into all that wild, unruly hair of hers. To watch those curls wrap themselves around his fingers. To press his body to hers, thighs to thighs, pelvis to hips, chest to breasts, there against that wall behind her and kiss her thoroughly and leisurely. Until his desire for this woman who captivated him was assuaged. "My word is truth," he murmured in a husky whisper as he leaned down closer.

Lula tilted her chin upwards, leaning toward his lips, captivated by him as the sweet, hot fingers of need spread throughout her body. Her lips fell open as her heart pounded in her breasts. She warred with wanting to kiss this man or run.

He did not give her a chance to think through her dilemma. His lips landed fully on hers, sweetly, hungrily demanding and she met him with a rush of breath and relief that he was kissing her. The soft brush of his beard against her lips and chin only heightened her need. He melded his lips against hers over and over and over again and then when that was not enough for either of them, he slid his tongue between her lips. It felt like liquid fire to Lula as she stilled, her sole focus on the wondrous feel and taste of him as his tongue met hers. Lula was overcome by the velvety yet rough, warm feeling of his tongue as it explored and tangled with hers. Again, he was gentle at first and then as one, their breaths hitched as the kiss became deep and devouring as he growled with need and she whimpered with wanting.

His hands dropped from the wall on either side of her. He grasped her shoulders to pull her against him and she froze.

A boom of a cannon on the battlements above them shook the castle, sending dust motes billowing from the beams above.

Lula's breathing stopped. She was clutching his shirt and had not even realized it. She dropped her hands and blushed. *Had she frozen from his touch, or the sound of the cannon?*

War growled and pulled away from her as his jaw tightened and he sighed heavily with regret.

Footsteps hurried toward them.

"War?" His friend cleared his throat awkwardly from somewhere near the stairs.

War grunted as he looked upward. "I heard it. Todrick is firing the cannons again." He looked down at Lula and his face hardened at the look in her eyes. *Fear.*

"Forgive me, Lula. I must go."

CHAPTER THIRTEEN

"WELL, WELL, WELL. What have we here?" came a loud, brassy voice.

It was early in the morning a few days after she had confronted the baron about his nephews and then they had kissed again when Lula found herself alone in the stables. She had come through the courtyard and the only people that she had seen were the wildling boys. She had thrown some snowballs and won her way across as usual but Poppy and Bertie were nowhere to be found.

She looked behind her with startled eyes to see Mister Womersly and another man. Womersly was standing right outside Buttercup's stall, blocking the stall door.

Lula's heart started pounding. In her mind, she began humming her song. She dared not sing it aloud, not to Womersly.

With a chip chop! Cherry chop! A shark was on the starboard side and sharks no man can stand. For they do gobble up everything, just like the sharks on land. With a chip chop! Cherry chop! Fol de rol riddle-rop! Chip chop! Cherry chop! Fol de rol de ray!

She tugged some curls down onto her forehead with trembling fingers and then quickly put her scarred hand behind her back.

Womersly was smiling at her with those pale eyes of his under long, bushy, white brows. His copious hair was still held back in a short queue but he must have spent a restless night for several strands had come out and stood up untidily around his head. His pale blue eyes were rimmed by even paler lashes protruding from his red-rimmed eyes.

Another man came walking into the stables from the opposite end. He was wearing a navy top hat pulled down low, a fine, navy frock coat with the collar turned up almost to his cheeks and dove-colored gray gloves. He nodded and murmured that he was going to oil his saddle that had gotten wet from the storm when he had ridden in it days ago. He glanced at the two men and then briefly at Lula as he moved past them to go down the aisle into the tack room.

Lula's eyes returned to the second man still standing beside Womersly. He was bald, save for his sideburns. He was the man who had called Tuedy terribly names. She watched as one of his hands reached up to stroke the long, bushy, red sideburns that outlined the sides of his harsh cheekbones all the way down to his chin. Her eyes followed that hand. It was heavily lined with scars and the nails were yellowed and thick with several of those nails broken, cracked or black and blue. Dirt appeared to be crusted under them. He just continued to stare at her in silence, as if assessing her.

"Good morning, Mr. Womersly," Lula tried to say firmly as she looked away from the younger man with the yellow fingernails. "And a good morning to your companion." She took several steps back further into the stall, away from the two men.

Womersly mumbled a greeting and nodded his head toward the man beside him. "This is Cloudsley Shovell," he said as he looked past her at Buttercup's stitches. The other man named Cloudsley ignored her greeting as well while he continued to look her over with his eyes straying to and staying at her hips.

"Wearing breeches, are you?" Cloudsley said in a sly voice. "I believe you said you were a girl, or was it a woman? Right now you just look like a boy with wild hair." He laughed in a cackling voice as his cracked lips tilted up into a grin while he continued to stare at her hips and legs with eyes that were even paler than Womersly's.

"Buttercup is doing very well this morning, Mr. Womersly," she said tightly as she refused to acknowledge the other rude man. "Please mind your distance, both of you. This horse requires it. You are both too close."

Cloudsley's eyes darted to hers and then quickly back to her legs. "I don't care what that horse *requires,*" he laughed. "Now then, as for you, I do not think you are a woman," he said softly in almost a hiss of breath. "I have been at sea too long to be sure. Perhaps we should make sure, eh, Mr. Womersly? An inspection, so to speak?" he asked with another grin from his pale, saltwater-cracked lips.

"What?" Lula asked tensely. She glanced at Womersly who was now staring at her hips in shock as well and then she looked frantically around the stall. Her eyes landed on Buttercup's empty wooden feed bucket, hanging on a hook on the wall. She quickly grabbed it. "You will not come any closer to me nor touch me," she said firmly. *"Either of you."* Her voice rose as she asked, "Where is Second Lieutenant Popplewell, or Ensign Bumstead?"

Womersly narrowed his eyes as he placed his hand on the latch of the door. He did not answer her question right away until he saw her start to lift the bucket. "What's this fuss? Cloudsley Shovell is only funning you, Miss." He let out a loud, barking laugh and thwacked the bald man in the chest before turning back to her. "You are far too young for me, Girl, and besides, I cannot abide all that hair and those colors you wear." He shook his head and grimaced. "Hurts my eyes to look at you. Now then," he demanded loudly, "move aside for we must check the horse's injury." He lifted his hands up in a nonthreatening way when she did not move. "That's a big battle horse behind you. Don't raise a breeze now, or you could get yourself hurt." He put his hand on the latch of the stall door.

Lula stepped to the back of the stall and then watched, keeping the bucket ready as he opened the stall door. The two men slid into the stall which was already crowded with the huge war horse taking up most of the square space. Lula tried to walk forward to leave, for she had nowhere to go with the three of them and the big horse in the stall. Cloudsley stepped in front of her, blocking the door with a leering grin.

Lula stared at him, trying to control her breathing and her panic. Behind her, Lula heard Buttercup snort and paw at the straw on the floor as he shook his head up and down at the men who had entered the stall. Lula backed away from Cloudsley, pressing herself into the corner while Womersly walked straight at Buttercup.

The big war horse let out a short, sharp snort of warning. He raised his head as he stomped one great front hoof at the man trying to come closer. The horse pinned his ears and snorted again, louder and sharper.

"Do not go any closer, Mr. Womersly!" Lula said urgently as she stepped out of the corner. "Buttercup clearly does not want you near him!" Lula called out in warning.

Womersly ignored her, but Cloudsley was furious at her interruption.

"*Shut your mouth, Girl!*" Cloudsley said angrily to her as he turned and swung his arm in her direction in fury. "You know nothing! We have been around horses longer than you, I wager."

Lula closed her mouth and pressed herself back into the corner as she watched the big horse weaving back and forth in agitation. Suddenly, without warning, Buttercup rushed forward, slamming his powerful chest into the men invading his space.

Womersly flew back against the stall door, hitting it hard and then losing his footing as he slid to the floor, landing on his backside.

Cloudsley hit the door as well, but stayed on his feet. He braced his legs apart as he leaned forward, staring at the big horse. "Well, you are a bad-mannered stallion, aren't you? I knew you needed to be taught some manners from the first moment I saw you," he hissed as spittle flew from his lips. He reached over the door and grabbed a rope. He turned to the horse and stood up, gathering the rope in one hand while leaving a long length free in the other as he readied to whip the horse.

Lula ran out of the corner to stand in front of the horse with her arms wide and the bucket hanging from one hand. "You will not strike this horse," she said firmly.

"Get out of my way, Girl!" Cloudsley hissed.

"I will not." Lula stood fast, unmoving in front of the huge horse.

Cloudsley said something unintelligible under his breath.

"Putting manners on a horse is one thing, beating it is another and tis unacceptable!" Lula said tensely as she stood there.

Womersly groaned and began to rise slowly to his feet. His eyes narrowed on her as he rested his hands on his thighs, unable to fully straighten up as he took great gulps of air. "How do you think we managed to have horses below deck on our ships at sea, Girl? They could not act out or the whole ship would be put in danger!" He stood to his full height with a heave of his breath. "They must have some manners!" He grabbed another rope from over the stall door and stood there weaving. He motioned to Cloudsley to continue.

Cloudsley did not need to be told. He lunged toward the horse, shoving Lula aside, snapping the rope at the horse's injured shoulder and the stitches there.

Buttercup snorted sharply as he backed up, slamming his haunches into the back of the stall wall with a loud, resounding crack of the wood and a shaking of the entire stall. He was becoming frantic at having no direction to flee.

Lula did not think. She raised the bucket, slamming it down onto Cloudsley's arm and hand where he held the length of rope and was lifting it to strike the horse again.

Cloudsley howled and then whipped around to face her. He sent the rope snaking at a frightening speed toward her. Lula barely had time to squeeze her eyes shut and try to duck before she felt the hiss and sting of it against her cheek. She swung the bucket at him again and felt it crack against his hand.

Cloudsley backed away from her into the corner of the stall, holding his injured hand and looking at her as if she were crazed.

Lula turned away from him just as Womersly approached the horse with his rope. He lashed it in fury straight at Buttercup's eyes to make him back away just as the horse raised his head in fear. The rope thankfully missed.

Lula darted in front of Womersly just as he was about to strike the horse again. She blocked him from the horse, taking the lash of the rope on her shoulder without a thought of the pain she felt through her quilted spencer. She sent the bucket cracking down on his head before he could send the rope against her or the horse's shoulder one more time.

Womersly let out a howl of pain and dropped to one knee as he glared up at the girl standing over him ready to strike him again with the bucket.

Buttercup snorted from behind Lula. The snort was quieter this time as the huge horse raised his head up and down. He shook his great neck with his mane flying as he eyed the two men.

"Get out of this stall, *both of you*," Lula said in a low voice. "I will be reporting you to the baron," she grated out. "You *and* your man Cloudsley."

Womersly stood up quickly, looking back and forth between the girl with the chaotic hair and the horse with the wild mane as he reached up to touch his head. He visibly swayed on his feet as his face went gray. "You hit me," he said plaintively with surprise in his voice.

"You hit me. And the horse," Lula said firmly. She turned to inspect the horse's injury with gentle fingers. Her stitches were still intact. She turned back to stare at Womersly with anger in her eyes. "The horse's stitches have not reopened, no thanks to you or Cloudsley. Still, the baron will hear of this."

At a blinding motion of speed beside her, she saw too late that Cloudsley was lashing his rope at her face.

A large hand with a gray glove reached out and caught the rope in his fist.

Lula looked over to see that the gentleman in the navy frock coat and navy top hat and gray gloves had caught the rope. With his other hand, the man punched Cloudsley and sent him flying back into the corner where he fell to the straw.

"Are you injured, Miss?" the gentleman asked with great concern.

Lula stared at the sharply handsome man standing outside the door. He had a dimple on his chin. He was the man that she had seen in the hallway with the baron. She shook her head quickly as she took a step back. "I am quite fine. I thank you for coming to my aid, Sir."

The man smiled a devilishly charming smile with perfect white teeth in a face that could have only been sculpted by the heavens. "Ten Adair, at your service, Miss Darley." With an ease that shocked Lula, he reached over the stall and hauled Cloudsley to his feet.

"Out," he ordered the man.

Lula backed up quickly as Cloudsley shuffled past her while rubbing his injured jaw.

"No cause to punch me, Mister," he groused as he hurried out of the stall.

"It is the Earl of Fairfax to you," the gentleman named Ten said coldly.

Lula watched as the man named Ten narrowed his eyes on Cloudsley as Cloudsley sauntered past him. Lula watched Cloudsley as well as he leaned nonchalantly against the stall opposite.

Cloudsley cradled his jaw and glared up at the gentleman. "Don't be looking at me like that. So you're a lord now, are you? Of course you are, standing there all high and mighty." He made a snorting sound and turned his face away.

"You deserved to have someone plant a facer on you." The earl swiped off his top hat and ran his gloved hand through all the waves of thick, glorious hair atop his head.

"Aw, come down off your high horse. You've no cause to interfere in our work. Ringing a peal over my head just because you are some sort of lordship now," he said snidely. "Bugger off, will you?" Cloudsley grumbled.

Lula watched as the gentleman's jaw tightened, straining the dimple there in the center of his perfect chin.

"Do not tell me to bugger off, *you sod*. *You* struck a woman. You know Captain War does not stand for men who hit women, *or* animals, nor do I. He would say you aren't a true man and I must agree," Ten said curtly and then punched him again. Hard.

This time, Cloudsley sunk to the floor and stayed there. He stared up at the man who had hit him. His mouth went slack and his eyes slid closed as his chin fell to his chest.

The gentleman named Ten turned back to Lula as he straightened his frock coat and cravat. "Pardon me." He placed his top hat back on his head with a quick tap of his hand on the top of it to snug it down. "I must apologize that I did not come sooner. I heard the ruckus but did not know it was these two that caused it. I thought a horse was acting up is all."

Lula executed an awkward curtsy in her boots and breeches, which was rather different when one was not wearing a gown. "Lord Fairfax," she said with a bow of her head. She tried to curtsy again, she felt she could do a much better job of it now that she had tried it once in boots and breeches.

Ten stopped her with a lift of his gray-gloved hand before she could drop into another curtsy. "Please, no. I am new at being an earl and I am very much not used to being called *Lord* Fairfax. Please, call me Ten. Everyone does."

Lula clutched her hands together. "That would be most improper."

Ten gave her that charming smile again. "Nevertheless, I wish it so." He looked at Womersly. "Womersly hit you as well, I believe. With the rope he is still holding." He arched an eyebrow at Womersly and looked down meaningfully at the rope still in his hand. "Womersly? What have you to say? Are you aware of what you did this time?"

Lula looked sharply at Ten and then back to Womersly.

Womersly's mouth fell open. He dropped the rope he had been holding. It fell into the straw as he stared aghast at Lula. He took a step toward the stall door and fumbled with the latch as he kept his eye on the girl and the horse in the stall and the man out in the aisle in the top hat. Finally, he managed to unlatch the door as he stumbled out of the stall. He stood there, holding a shaking hand to the top of his head as a trickle of blood seeped down onto his forehead. He wiped it away with a rag hanging near the stall and then threw the rag down as the trembling in his hands increased.

"I hit you with the rope," he breathed out, making it sound almost like a question.

He exhaled deeply as he tried to stop swaying on his feet. He looked at the girl in the stall as he took deep breaths, struggling to get his words out. "You cannot tell the baron." He gulped several times. "Yes, he'll send me packing, *but he will send you away as well.*" He took another breath and continued, "Women have no business in a place such as this. The baron does not want you here. He has made that clear. He knows the problems that women can cause." He narrowed his eyes on her. "You are only one woman in a castle full of men. Think about that." He watched her face for a moment. "You know as well as I do that he doesn't want you here. I can read it on your face. You *and that dog you brought with you.*" He squinted at her as he paused and looked around. "Is that mongrel in here," he asked fearfully.

Lula shook her head. "No, Courage is not here."

Womersly frowned as he looked back at her in surprise. "Courage? Foolish name for that cur. Well then, I say a truce is needed between you and me."

Lula gave a short laugh. "A truce?" she asked incredulously.

Ten started to step forward but Lula ignored him as she turned her body to face the older seaman. "It is important that the baron knows what you did," she said firmly.

Womersly face went from gray to white as his whole body began to tremble violently. His voice became almost pleading. "I do not want to leave Graestone. I have not been here long and I don't know where else I'd go." He became more anxious as he spoke. "I have no one! I have been at sea for more years than I can remember!" He touched his head again as he swayed on his feet, grasping at the edge of the stall door to stabilize himself.

Lula backed away from the door. She felt safer inside this stall with the big war horse than out in the aisle with the three men, one of whom appeared to have been knocked out by the only one who was a gentleman.

Her shoulders lost their tension. Perhaps Womersly was damaged, too, but his scars were all on the inside. She took a breath and then released it. "I will not speak of this to the baron, but there is a way to train a horse so that he respects you when you approach. Neither you nor Cloudsley approached the horse *correctly.*" She pointed to Buttercup. *"That is a stallion and a battle horse.* You went straight at him and struck him with that rope. What did you and Cloudsley expect the horse to do? He is trained for war. *You attacked.* It is a lucky thing you did not strike his eye with the rope and blind him. It is also a lucky thing that the horse did not crush your skull with one of his hooves. That is what he is trained to do in battle, you see?"

Womersly stared at her for a long moment as his white face went totally blank and his mouth went slack. He looked behind her to the now calm war horse standing meekly behind her. His eyes returned to Lula. "What would you know of training war horses, Girl?"

Lula stood up tall and straightened her shoulders. "I am a Darley of Aldbey Park. We train horses, for whatever job they are best suited to do. Not that we train horses for actual battle, you see, but if they seem suitable for it, we do make sure they are brave and bold and fearless."

"A Darley you say?" Womersly squinted at her as if seeing her for the first time. He blinked several times. "Somewhere in all the Seven Seas I think I have heard that name."

Lula furrowed her brows. "I told you my name not so many nights ago, when I stitched up Buttercup's wound."

Womersly shifted on his feet as he coughed and sputtered while staring at her in surprise. "What were you doing on my ship at night?" he demanded.

Lula tilted her head as she studied the man. She stepped up to the stall door with the now broken bucket. She lowered her voice, "We are not on a ship, Mr. Womersly." She added gently, "These are the stables." Lula looked over at Ten who was watching Womersly with concern on his face.

Womersly looked at her and then around to all the horses in the stalls with surprise and some concern on his face. "Yes, yes, of course." He reached up to touch his head. "My head hurts a bit," he said with a confused frown.

Lula grimaced. "I hit you over the head with the bucket."

His eyes flew to hers. "Why would you do that?"

It was Lula's turn to be confused and concerned. "You do not remember whipping Buttercup just now? We were just talking about that very thing." Lula looked again at Ten.

The tall gentleman walked forward to Womersly and cupped his elbow kindly.

Womersly's face crumpled as his color returned. He looked over at the big horse. "Oh, no," he whispered. "It happens sometimes." He looked up at Ten and then turned back to Lula as he folded and unfolded his hands together. "When I hit my head sometimes. The bucket must have done me in." He gently touched his head where the blood had ceased trickling from the cut there. "I was told long ago that a piece of a ship's mast struck me on the head during a sea battle and I didn't wake up for days. I don't remember it though. Last I remember, I was paddling in the dark water, watching my ship burn away in the night." He swallowed. "A head injury can make you act different, they say. Please do not tell the baron this happened, Miss. He'll send me away."

Lula frowned. "True, he may do just that. He is a harsh, unbending man."

Ten turned his head sharply to stare at her.

Womersly shook his head with a confused look. "Perhaps you misunderstand him. He allowed me to come here. He is a man that when he says yes, he means it, and when he says no, he means that as well." He swallowed as he stared fearfully at her.

Lula furrowed her brows. "That may be so. He is unshakable in his belief that only his word is truth."

Womersly stepped away from Ten and laid his big-knuckled hands on the stall door as if to take the weight off his feet. He peered into the stall at Lula. He looked over at Ten. "She doesn't understand."

Ten stepped forward. "A man must feel that his word is taken as truth when he is responsible for others. Particularly when he has the responsibility of sending others into battle when he knows there is the distinct possibility that they may not return."

His gaze went to Womersly and the two of them shared a look. Then Womersly looked off down the aisle before his eyes returned to hers. "I was a ship's master and I had the honor of transporting Captain War and his men and horses *several* times. That man does not take sending his men into battle lightly, I can tell you that. He chose his men personally for their strengths, weighing them against their weaknesses. He placed them in the positions where they could do their best. He listened to the men and what they said they could do. Believe me, there were many more men that vied to serve under him."

Ten nodded solemnly. "Womersly is correct, Miss Darley."

Lula exhaled slowly. It was her turn to be confused. "That is all over. We are at Graestone now, there is no battle here."

Ten Adair shook his head as his eyes became sorrowful. "That is where you are wrong, Miss Darley. For us, the battle is never over. Life is our battle now," he said quietly and then he looked toward the castle. "He knows this."

Lula's heart stilled, remembering the baron saying that there is always a battlefield. Several heartbeats passed. Her gaze went back to Womersly. "Go. You should rest," she said quietly. She looked up at Ten, hoping that he would escort the old seaman back to his room.

"Are you steady now, Womersly?" Ten asked politely.

Womersly stood up straight and squared his shoulders. "Never better," he grumbled. "I do not need any help if that is what you are thinking."

Lula watched the old seaman pull Cloudsley to his feet. Cloudsley hung his head as he followed Womersly as he walked out of the stables with uneven steps of his bowed legs as if he were still on a ship at sea.

She hurried out of the stall as she heard the wildling boys' gleeful cries. She went still, holding her breath as they ambushed the two seamen, pelting them with snowballs. Both she and Ten started toward the stable doors but they stopped when they heard Cloudsley mumble something and Womersly gave a colorful response. They could hear them as they broke into a lumbering run, crunching through the snow to get across the courtyard. Then they heard Womersly make a happy whooping noise. He must have managed to throw a snowball back at the boys and hit his mark.

Lula relaxed further when she heard the boys laughing. She then heard Todrick's raspy, grating voice call out to Womersly and then holler a warning at the wildlings from the door of the castle.

She heard the castle door bang shut.

Cloudsley and Womersly had been saved by Todrick Tweedy.

All was quiet again with only the murmuring voices of the boys outside in the courtyard. Lula imagined they were restocking their arsenal of snowballs for their next victim.

Ten took a step toward her. "Your cheek," he started to say more but Lula quickly backed away, raising her hand in supplication.

"That is close enough, if you please," she tried to say in a light tone.

Ten nodded once, staring at her with curious eyes. "Very well." He bowed his head. "You know I must tell War about this. He would want to know those men hurt you. And the horse."

Lula shook her head adamantly. "Please don't. He will judge me as weak for not handling it. Because I am a woman, you see. If I was a man, it would not have happened. And poor Mr. Womersly doesn't even remember what he did."

Ten smiled tightly and bowed his head. "Cloudsley Shovell knew full well, however. Now, if you will excuse me, Miss Darley? I must return to my task," he said as he touched his fingers to the rim of his top hat. "If you need my assistance you have only to shout." He smiled charmingly and then began to walk down the aisle in the opposite direction than Womersly had.

"Promise me that you will not tell him," she called after him.

He stopped and walked back. He came closer to her this time as he looked down into her face to the mark on her cheek. "That I cannot do."

Lula stared up at him a moment as her heart raced. She did not think she had anything to fear from the devilishly handsome man named Ten, but she could not control the panic that seemed to come over herself nevertheless. Men who got too close had either attacked her, or kissed her.

She took a calming breath as he walked away, and then slowly exhaled as she went back into the stall with Buttercup.

CHAPTER FOURTEEN

SOMETHING COLD AND wet hit Lula right on the side of her head. She heard the boys laughing.

She sighed. She had forgotten they were lying in wait behind their snow wall for anyone crossing the courtyard. She took a big breath and stepped away from the doorway. Bending down, she scooped up some snow and then whirled around as she quickly packed the snow into a ball. She made a mad dash into the courtyard as the boys gleefully pelted her with more snowballs.

Lula kept dodging and making new snowballs to throw back at the boys who were hooting and hollering. She began laughing and screeching as well when their snowballs struck her in a splatter of cold, hard, wet snow. She was slipping and sliding as she ran with her arms flailing wildly to keep her balance when, suddenly, a snowball hit her in the back with a force unlike any of the others. It propelled her straight forward. She slipped once more and then tumbled down onto the snowy, hard-packed path with a bounce of her head.

She stared up at the white sky as snowflakes drifted down around her face. She gingerly reached up to prod the back of her head and winced. The packed snow had offered no cushion for her fall.

There was utter silence and stillness in the courtyard. She slowly moved her head to see three pairs of eyes staring at her in utter fear.

"Are you dead, Miss Lula?" Mel whispered.

Mack nudged his brother hard with his elbow. "Her eyes are open," he said with derision.

"She can be dead and have her eyes open," Mel whispered back. "But she does look as queer as Dick's hatband."

Lula winced and said with a grimace, "Who is this Dick person anyway? My sister, Birdie, likes to say that, too. Makes no sense, none at all."

Mack tilted his head at her. "She isn't dead." He looked down at his littlest brother. "See there, Jolyon, she isn't dead. No need to cry, Joly, no need!"

Lula looked up at the small boy. His collar reached up past his nose but his eyes were indeed filled with tears. "I am quite fine, little Lyon." She looked over at Mack and Mel. "I thought we agreed we will call him Lyon. You have strong names, he should, too," she grumbled as she lay there. "He is Lyon. It's part of his name, after all." She stopped. She was chattering away. She closed her eyes. Her head hurt and she felt dizzy. She gently touched her head and moaned and then, suddenly, there was another figure looming over her when she opened her eyes.

She let out a muffled scream as the dark figure dropped to one knee beside her.

"He's the one that hit you, Miss Lula. Twasn't us!" Mel said in a rush. He nudged his brother, Machabee. "Come on, Lyon!" The two boys hastily grabbed their younger brother by the hand and hurried back to the far side of the courtyard. They ducked behind their snow wall to replenish their supply of snowballs once more.

"Miss Darley?" came a smooth, dulcet baritone.

Lula winced again, keeping her eyes closed. It seemed to help the dizziness. Then she opened her eyes when that deep voice registered in her foggy mind. It was the baron, and he had sounded angry. He was the one who hit her, Mel had just said. *Why was he angry if he was the one to have caused her fall?*

"Why do you sound angry?" she grumbled as she opened her eyes and stared up into his dark, angry eyes. "Why did you throw that snowball at me?" She swallowed and touched her head. "Was it a snowball? It felt like a cannonball." She moaned and closed her eyes again.

"I thought you were one of the house boys playing with my nephews," he gritted out.

Lula opened her eyes again. "I am not a house boy," she said with a disgruntled frown.

"*Obviously*," he said tersely as his eyes ran down her body and legs.

She sat up slowly with another groan. "I will accept your apology," she said with another wince as she touched the back of her head gingerly.

War rested an elbow on his knee and leaned toward her. "Oh, will you? I have nothing to apologize for," he said curtly and distinctly as the cold air formed into a mist as he spoke. "You, however, should apologize to me," he said with barely controlled anger as his eyes raked down her body in the clothing she wore. He did not understand completely his feelings in seeing her dressed like this. Or rather, at others who may see her dressed in this way.

Lula drew back. "Surely, you cannot be serious!"

War narrowed his eyes on the young woman sitting in the snow beside him. As usual, her wild hair had come undone. This time, it was a complete shambles and was falling down all around her shoulders. There were snowflakes caught up in the curls and he was having a hard time pulling his eyes from the beautiful chaos of it. Her cheeks were pink with the cold and her lips looked bright red against the rest of her snowy, white skin. He even noticed that the splash of freckles across her nose that drove him wild stood out even more on her pale, creamy skin. Her bright blue-green eyes were rimmed in long, curling, black lashes that were caught with tiny diamonds of snowflakes. She looked healthy and alive and those glittering blue-green eyes of hers were flashing with anger.

At him.

"Yes," he growled. "I am *very* serious. You owe me an apology, Miss Darley. I gave you the order not to enter the stables without my permission. I then gave in to your wishes and said you must have Popplewell and Bertram Bumstead with you. I know they were not there this morning. They were needed elsewhere," War said with a firm look. His eyes traveled down her long, graceful, lithe legs encased in form-fitting breeches that followed her every womanly curve. He closed his eyes and swallowed tightly as he ran a hand down his face to his beard. He opened his eyes and took a breath as he tried not to stare at her legs. "And you are wearing men's clothing," he said through a tight jaw and gritted teeth. His eyes went to her boots. "I have never seen black boots with that, what color is it, *lavender* trim? And a *military* jacket in such a color." He waved a hand toward the jacket. "And with all those useless fripperies on it." War shook his head. *"Not here,"* he snarled. "You will not wear men's breeches here at Graestone."

"But," Lula started to argue back.

War held up a gloved hand to silence her. *"Not. Here.* I am aware that the Darley ladies wear men's clothing in the Aldbey Park Stables. This," he moved a single finger toward her legs, "is far too distracting for the men. I cannot allow it here at Graestone."

"You will not allow it? Now you are telling me what I am allowed or not allowed *to wear?"* she asked with frustration.

"I said I *cannot* allow it. Not here. Not around the men."

"I usually wear my dress over them. I forgot it today." She frowned at him. He looked immense, kneeling beside her with the collar of his long, dark coat pulled up high around his neck.

He rubbed the back of his neck in aggravation. "You cannot forget. Women do *not* wear breeches, as you very well know," he said in annoyance as his eyes flashed stubbornly at her. "This, *this clothing* will wreak havoc on my men. You can*not* wear it."

"Does my clothing wreak havoc on you?" she asked curiously and in disbelief. Nothing about her had ever incited a man to any type of emotion.

"Surely you must know that it bloody well does," he growled as his eyes returned to her long legs in the breeches. He looked back at her and in a tight voice he said, "You must change into a gown. *At once.* I order you to do so."

Lula stared back at him as anger poured through her. This man was the most obstinate man she thought she could ever meet. She leaned forward with her green-gloved hands placed on either side of her hips in the snow. "You are the most unaccountably rude man I have ever encountered. No," she said into his face in a low and firm voice. And then in an even stronger voice, she said, "No! I am not *one of your men* that you can give *orders* to." The mists around her lips mingled with his as the cold air and snowflakes swirled between them. "You give me an order telling me that I cannot wear clothes that *are appropriate* for what I am doing. You give me an order telling me that I cannot go to *the stables* without your permission or unless Poppy and Bertie are with me, when I work in stables and *around horses every day* at Aldbey Park." Her voice trailed away at the growing look of anger on his face. Her breasts heaved with the outpouring of her frustration. The man looked positively thunderstruck. She took a breath and said with renewed courage, "You say I cannot stay at Graestone then *every* day you say that I cannot return home." She got even angrier as she leaned toward him. "I forgot my dress. Pray forgive me! And do please tell me when you see fit to finally get rid of me and take me home since I am *wreaking such havoc* in your castle."

War leaned even closer. "I will personally take you back to Aldbey Park in my own carriage and then I will open the carriage door and drop you at the front gate."

Undaunted, Lula leaned just as close as she retorted hotly back, "Before the carriage even stops rolling, I imagine."

War looked down his nose at her legs and then back to her

eyes. The corners of his lips barely lifted. "And why not? That should not be a problem in those breeches," he said quietly as he gave her a challenging look.

Lula gasped and leaned away from him. "You are certainly no gentleman!"

War smiled at her outrage. "You keep telling me I am no gentleman and I keep telling you that you are indeed correct." His smile turned wolfish. "I should think you could manage the jump easily enough from a rolling carriage without your skirts to hinder you," he said in a low, provocative tone as he leaned closer, staring into her flashing blue-green eyes. His smile grew, showing even white teeth between his lips. If he leaned any closer, he could rub his lips gently across the tip of her nose, caressing all those freckles that seemed to turn pink with her anger.

Lula could not help it. She leaned back toward him and said indignantly, *"You. Would. Not. Dare!"* Lula huffed out as she stared challengingly back into the depths of his dark, brown eyes. She noticed the faint flecks of green within them. Her gaze drifted down his face. She could not help but to be drawn to his inviting, sinfully sensual-looking mouth.

Her breath caught at her wayward, unladylike thoughts.

What was wrong with her?

"Do not tempt me," War whispered as he leaned so close his nose almost touched hers.

A fleeting thought raced through his mind.

What was wrong with him?

He was in a sparring match with Miss Darley! *And he was thoroughly enjoying it*, he realized. No one had ever riled him as this young woman did. This captivating young woman with her freckles and chaotic hair and oddly bright-colored clothing. This young woman who he wanted to kiss, every time he saw her. He had not felt this alive since his parents had died so many, many years ago.

He stared at Lula in chagrin, until he noticed that her gaze was on his mouth. He watched the change in her as her eyes returned to his, *subtle,* but it was there.

Interest, desire.

For him.

His blood thickened as his heart began to pound in his chest as if he were a young boy new to the feelings brought on by a woman.

Want. Need.

Intense desire.

For her. He wanted to kiss her again, and to have her return his kiss as she had before.

Lula returned his gaze as the snowflakes and cold mists of their breaths mingled together and swirled around them, enveloping them in their own private cloud. Her eyes drifted back down to his lips, drawn to them as if she had no will of her own. Those lips she knew the feel of, the taste of.

"I dare you," he whispered throatily without thinking what he was saying. He could only react.

Lula's eyes flew to his. She watched as his pupils dilated and his nostrils flared as his breathing increased slightly.

"W-what?" she said tremulously.

"You want to kiss me. Kiss me as you did under the stairs and out on the battlements," he said softly. His voice dropped lower. "Go ahead." His lips tilted up into the hint of a rare, teasing grin. "You have courage enough to wear men's breeches. Where's that courage now? Go ahead. *I dare you.*"

"You may not touch me." Even to her ears, her voice had been weak and unsure. Was her panic at his touch lessening? "You are no—"

War's eyes crinkled at the corners as he held her eyes captive within his. "Yes, I know. I am not a gentleman. I think I told you that myself. However, I vow I will not hurt you. Nor shall I touch you if that is your requirement of me." His voice deepened into a velvet baritone as he remembered the feel of her gentle fingers stroking his beard. "But you may touch *me,* if you wish."

He watched as her breath caught and shuddered from between her lips as her eyes widened. "You dare me to kiss you, but you say you will not touch me?" she asked in a trembling voice.

"Yes," he said hoarsely as his eyes drifted down to her lips. "I can kiss you without even touching you," he whispered. *"Even my lips shall not touch you in this kiss,"* he murmured.

Lula trembled again as her eyes clung to his. "I do not understand," she breathed out.

She watched as one corner of his lips tilted up, ever so slightly. He moved closer and Lula's heart caught and then sped up, threatening to fly from her breasts. She froze as his lips came within a breath of hers, hovering just above them. She stared into his eyes as he moved his lips back and forth, slowly, just above her lips. Her breath trembled out of her as her lids slid closed. Still, she was aware, so very aware when his mouth slid toward her cheek, traveling over her cheekbone with the barest brush of his silken beard over her skin. He then moved close to her ear. His lips hovered just above her delicate ear lobe as her curls caught in his beard, tangling and holding tight before he pulled free and his mouth was traveling up, just above her eye and the scar there. Always, his lips were just a mere breath above her skin before he returned once again to her lips.

Indeed, it had felt like he had just thoroughly kissed her lips, and her cheek and her ear and her forehead. She was enchanted, enthralled, as her breath continued to tremble from between her lips.

"Come. Kiss me. *I dare you,*" he said again as his lips hovered just above hers in the barest of whispers.

Once again, she realized that she was clutching him. The thick wool of his heavy coat was in her hands. She had been pulling him toward her. She let go as if she had been burned. "You are too close," she said in a weak voice as she leaned away from him.

"You pulled me toward you," he said in a dulcet baritone.

"I- I should go," she whispered as she looked anywhere but at the big baron on his knee in the snow beside her.

War lifted his hand toward her and then stopped. He grimaced. He knew that he had started to reach for her without even thinking. She had so captivated him that he had lost his control. Yes, he had lost control in such a simple thing as barely kissing this woman.

He moved back as he saw the familiar look of fear return to her eyes. This young woman was making him lose his normal calm. *Good God and bloody hell and the devil confound it,* he had wanted to kiss her again! *Desperately.* He had also wanted her to touch *him,* not just to pull him toward her, but to return his kiss as ardently as she had before. This irritating, yet oh so fascinating young woman with wild hair and freckles had managed to thoroughly drive him mad.

Lula leaned further away. "I want to leave," she said in a panicked rush.

War sat fully back with a scowl, hiding his disappointment as he schooled his face to stare calmly back at her. "As soon as the weather clears, you *will* leave. Just as I told you," he said in a tight voice that hid his desire. His eyes narrowed as his attention went to her cheek. "The devil confound it! What happened to your face?" he roared as he leaned closer once again to look at her cheek as she leaned further away.

Lula reached up to tug a curl over her forehead. She realized however that was not where his gaze rested. She touched her cheek. Had the rope left that much of a mark? How could she explain the mark on her cheek without telling on Mr. Womersly?

She lifted her chin. "My cheek must have hit the snow when I fell." She raised her chin further. "When I said I want to leave, I meant I should return to my room," she said frostily. "Not go home." She furrowed her brows. "Why do you say '*I dare you*' to me? I do not understand."

War answered her with curt impatience. "Because you think you have no courage. I am asking you to reach within yourself and bring forth what I know is there." He huffed out a breath in irritation and looked away from her. He did not want her to see how frustrated he was with himself.

"Miss Darley!" came Ten Adair's voice as he ran up to them. "Are you hurt? Did you fall in the snow?" he asked as he rushed to her other side and knelt down on one knee to grasp her hands. He looked over at the baron and scowled. "Bloody hell, War, why haven't you helped her up?" Ten stood up, pulling Lula solicitously up with him. He kept hold of her hands as he looked down into her face with grave concern.

War stood up slowly as he watched his friend with Lula. His eyes narrowed as he stood there with his shoulders hunched and his arms flexed and his fists tight. He suddenly wanted to slam a fist into his good friend. *What was wrong with him?*

Lula tried to pull her hands free as she stared nervously up into the sharply handsome face of Ten Adair. To be exact, she stared at his dimple. She found that she could not look him in the eyes, not after War's lips had kissed her without even touching her. For that is what he had truly done. She was blushing furiously and she knew it as she tried to pull her hands away. "I am only slightly dizzy. I shall be fine, I assure you," she said quietly with an uncomfortable smile on her face as she continued her efforts to pull her hands free of his hold. She also tried to take a step back so that he would have to let go, but his hold was firm.

War frowned as he watched Ten with Lula. He pushed Ten's hands away from Lula's. "Let go of her hands and step away from her, Ten," he growled. "She doesn't like men close to her, much less touching her. And why are you wearing a top hat and that frock coat and cravat? Are you going to London? One of your clubs perhaps? You can't make it in this weather, Ten, but feel free to try," he snarled as he motioned to the gate. "Please do."

Ten frowned at the big baron. "She is hurt, War. Why are you acting like a snarling, bad-tempered wolf? Why, you are no better than those two men in the stables who put that mark on her cheek earlier."

"What?" roared War. "*What men?* Who did this to you? Give

me their names," he demanded as fury overtook him.

Lula raised her hand to stop War's tirade but Ten interrupted.

"It was that Cloudsley Shovell and Womersly." Ten quickly gave a brief review of the incident in the stables with Buttercup. His voice lowered insistently. "I can see that you wish to kill them but you know that you cannot."

War was staring past them with a storm raging in his eyes. "Then I will order them to leave, *immediately*. Of course, I will notify the Prime Minister of this...*problem*. It was he that asked me to take them on."

Lula spoke up hastily. "Womersly remembers nothing! I believe he does not know what he did," she said forcefully. "He has had a head injury! Let him stay."

War's frigid glance turned on her. "Those men *hurt* you. They also hurt a horse. What would you have me do? Would you so easily have forgiven your attackers in Hyde Park?"

Lula shrunk away from him. "That is not fair," she said hoarsely.

War took a breath and tried to release the tension in his shoulders. "Perhaps that was unkind of me. At the very least, Shovell *must go*. I will think on Womersly. I have a physician friend in London who has been very good about injuries to the head from the war. Perhaps he can help with my decision."

"Thank you," Lula said with a relieved smile.

Ten touched Lula's arm. She jumped and immediately moved closer to War as she glanced at Ten. "Oh! Do forgive me. Your hand on my arm startled me." She rubbed her arms as a shiver overtook her.

Ten bowed his head. "No, please forgive *me*. I did not mean to startle you. You are cold. Would you like my coat, Miss Darley?"

War let out a quiet hiss between his teeth as he narrowed his eyes on Ten and moved closer to Lula. "She doesn't want your coat, Fairfax," he growled.

War was standing so close to her that she could feel the seething anger vibrating off him. He did not offer her *his* coat, however. She shivered again.

Ten grinned over at War and then turned back to Lula. "Very well, but you *are* cold. Please, will you let me escort you inside, Miss Darley?"

Lula nodded with a tight smile. "That would be most gentlemanly of you, Lord Adair." She resisted the strong desire to frown back at the baron.

Ten smiled with his perfect white teeth. "Please, once again I must insist that you call me Ten."

War watched as his friend put one arm around Lula's waist. A small sense of satisfaction hit him when he watched Lula hastily shrug out of Ten's hold and put space between them as they walked.

Still, War stood there as fury bubbled within him, watching the two of them walk away, though he was not sure why he was so angry. Was it because she had said he owed her an apology? Because she let his ridiculously handsome friend get close, close enough to wrap his arm around her small waist, even if for only a brief moment?

Was he angry because he could not take his eyes off of her curving hips and rounded backside or her shapely legs in those breeches? Or that he was entirely captivated by the scattering of freckles across her pert nose on the creamy skin of her face which was surrounded by a riotous chaos of curls?

Or was he simply envious at how quickly and naturally she had become a part of Graestone by her kindness, her easy and open friendliness and a desire to help any and all—the horses and the men and boys here?

Or was he simply angry because she seemed to have no interest in kissing him, as he so desperately had wanted to kiss her? Or *bloody hell,* was he angry because she was so afraid of him and could not abide his touch?

Or could it simply be because he had hurt her once again, this time making her fall and hit her head? Or that she had been hurt by those two fools in the stables and that it had been the dapper Ten Adair that had come to her aid instead of himself?

HE RUBBED HIS jaw as a thought struck him. *She had moved closer to him when Ten had surprised her with a touch on her arm.* And then, *why wasn't she afraid of Ten Adair, who also just happened to be the brand new Earl of Fairfax and a renowned and handsome rake?*

Miss Lula Darley was a problem. There was too much to do here at Graestone. Too many people depended on him. And he, *he knew nothing of love.* Perhaps his altogether too handsome and charming friend would take her off his hands and away from Graestone.

His hands fisted at his sides as his jaw tightened at the thought.

War stood there in the falling snow. He finally realized that his nephews had come back over and were staring up at him. He looked down at the three boys. They were wet from the snow and shivering, particularly his youngest nephew who appeared to be wearing quite a few layers of his two older brothers' clothing, just as Lula had said.

"How many ambushes, men?" he asked them as he managed to quell his anger and his wayward thoughts about his friend and the annoying Miss Lula Darley.

"Lots," Mack said with a grin. "Though Miss Lula has been the best opponent of them all! Each day, she has returned our fire! We will wear the red coat someday, just like you did, Uncle War!"

War's jaw tightened. Of a certainty, he would make sure his nephews never saw the horrors of war. Then he realized what they had said about Lula being the best opponent, returning their snowball fire each day. *Of course she was.*

He shook his head and smiled at the boys in chagrin. He then bent down and scooped up Jolyon carefully in one arm.

Jolyon tensed and his face went white as he looked down at the snowy ground.

"I have you, little Lyon." War spoke gently as he adjusted the little boy in his arms. "You are safe," he added softly. "Do not look down, though you are not so very high off the ground, truly. Why don't you hold tight to me? Put your arms around my neck and hold on like a strong, brave lion would," he said with gentle care for the small boy.

The little boy stared up into his uncle's eyes and then, slowly, a smile came to his face. He wrapped his arms tightly around War's neck.

War smiled at him with some amount of relief. He looked down at the other two boys staring up with concern at their small brother. "Very good, men. Now, how about we get this little man inside and you all can get warm? Before I came outside, I am fairly sure that I smelled some delicious hot scones that Tuedy Tweedy no doubt has waiting for you along with a cup of chocolate."

Machabee and Melchisedec let out a whoop.

War knelt down so that Machabee could jump up onto his back, his arms joining his little brother's around his uncle's neck. Melchisedec was scooped up in his opposite arm.

"Uncle War?" Machabee said from his back.

"Yes?"

"Do not let Lord Ten take our Miss Lula."

"Your Miss Lula is she?" War grunted.

Machabee and Melchisedec said as one, "She is!"

"Of course she is," War grunted.

He stood up and strode through the snowy courtyard with the three boys. Once he was inside the castle, he gently put Jolyon down and then stomped the snow off his boots, making a great show of jostling the two older boys he carried, much to their giggling delight as Jolyon looked on solemnly.

He set them down and watched as Machabee and Melchisedec stomped and strutted around him as they rid themselves of the snow on their little boots and shoulders and hair, mimicking their uncle. Jolyon watched solemnly, though a small smile began to rise on his lips. They were still giggling wildly while War watched them with his hands on his hips, trying not to laugh, when Tuedy and Todrick Tweedy came hurrying into the great hall. The wolf-like dog that Miss Darley had named Courage was trotting beside Tuedy with his tongue lolling out happily. When the dog saw the boys, he bolted forward with a happy yip.

The two older boys let out another holler as they dropped to their knees to pet the dog. Jolyon came forward as well and wrapped his arms around Courage's neck. He laid his head on the dog's warm fur with a smile.

War dropped to his haunches and stroked the dog's head as he studied silent, little Jolyon still clinging to the dog.

Tuedy's hands flew up in the air when he came to a stop in front of the boys. "I thought someone had died what with all the noise you little wildlings were making, eh! You boys look like melting icicles!"

Todrick came along behind his tall, thin brother. He eyed the boys up and down and then the floor around them. "That's not right," he barked in a raspy, annoyed voice. "You've gotten snow all over the clean floors." He pointed to the wet puddles on the floor with a scowl. "More work for someone else to do, cleaning up after you three."

War stood up and shook his head at the Tweedy twins with a rueful smile.

Tuedy made a small, high-pitched sound as he fluttered his fingers at his twin brother. "Never mind the puddles, Toddy, the boys are wet and cold, eh?" He smiled at the three boys and waved his hands. "To the kitchens with you three wildlings and take the dog with you! There is some hot cider or perhaps a cup of chocolate and some warm scones with jam waiting for you in the kitchens. Ned will help you. Now off you go, eh!" He clapped his hands and then paused as he quickly called after them in his high-pitched voice, "Do not play any games on Ned, mind you, eh? No toads in the flour sacks, or a mouse in any of my clean pots! The last house boy you played a trick on when you put that beetle in the soup cast up his accounts all over my floor. Do not do that to Ned, eh!"

War watched the three boys and the dog hurry toward the kitchens. "Are you speaking of Ned from Picklescott? How is he doing for you, Tuedy?"

Tuedy fluttered his fingers. "He manages very well, Baron. Miss Darley gave him some ointment that is helping his hand. He is doing better and better each day in fact." He stared at the baron in a meaningful way. "In fact, she has given many of the men different types of ointments and balms and soaking teas to help their injuries."

War leveled his eyes on Tuedy for several moments. "I am aware of this." He nodded thoughtfully and then tilted his face up to the stairs, listening. "She is crying again."

"Yes," Todrick croaked as he scowled up toward the second floor.

Tuedy folded his hands together as he, too, looked silently up the stairs with his brows furrowed together.

War sighed loudly and looked around the dimly lit great hall. "Where did Ten and Miss Darley go when they came in?"

Todrick scowled. "The only bloody room on the main floor besides the kitchens with a warm fire in this godforsaken ancient pile of stones," he croaked in a grumbling voice. "It's just not right, taking her there," he said in a low rasp.

"My study?" War growled with surprise.

Tuedy made a motion with his fingers. "Yes, in your study. Alone. Together, eh?" He attempted to lower his high voice. "The exquisitely handsome Ten Adair, Earl of Fairfax, is no doubt making sure our Miss Darley gets *warm*." He winked and smiled.

Tuedy's twin brother groaned. "Tudor, stay out of it." Todrick looked up at the baron out of the corners of his eyes and scratched at the side of his scarred lips.

War looked at Tuedy. "*Our* Miss Darley?" he said in a low voice as he put his hands on his hips. He let out an exasperated huff of breath. She had become his nephews' Miss Lula and now she was *our* Miss Darley to Tuedy Tweedy as well.

Tuedy let out a soft squeak at the look on the baron's face. He looked at his twin brother for help.

"Do not look at me," Todrick said with furrowed brows. "You get yourself into these things without me, Tudor. You must bloody get yourself out as well."

War sighed long and loud. "Out with it, Tuedy Tweedy. What's on your mind?"

Tuedy flustered about with his fingers in the air and fidgeting where he stood. "It is just that the earl was looking at Miss Darley in," he looked meaningfully at the baron and his voice rose even higher than normal, *"that way.* He may have bid her a good morning, but his eyes had good night on the mind," he finished dramatically as his eyebrows rose up and down several times. "He does have quite the reputation as a rake, mind you."

War's hands dropped from his hips. He scowled as he looked off toward the hallway to his study. He rubbed a hand down over his beard as his scowl changed to furious anger. "The hell you say. Ten would not dare. Not under my roof!" he thundered.

Todrick Tweedy groaned again as he passed his hand over his eyes and looked up at his twin brother between his fingers.

Tuedy shrugged his thin shoulders. "I can only report on what I saw, Baron." He touched a long finger to the elegantly coiffured curls pushed back from his forehead. "I cannot say what the earl's intentions are. Miss Darley looked most indifferent and was walking several feet from him."

War let out a pent up breath and seemed to relax.

Tuedy spoke up once again. "Though I can only assume that since he is the new Earl of Fairfax after his poor, aggrieved father and brother so recently passed on into the abyss of death that surely he must procure a wife and forthwith secure his line, eh? Wouldn't you say I am correct, Toddy?"

Todrick narrowed his eyes on his brother. *"Forthwith secure his line?"* he rasped incredulously. He turned to the baron and rubbed again at the burn scar on the side of his lips with annoyance as he spoke. "Pay no heed to my brother, Baron. His imagination is—"

"Never mind, Tweedys," War growled as he spun away from the twins. He began walking across the great hall toward the dark hallway that led to the mostly closed off west wing of the castle save for the baron's study.

Tuedy took a few steps after him. "Baron! We must discuss your uncle's ball. When is he returning home, eh? Shall I go ahead with his plans? What should I—"

Tuedy's voice dwindled off. The baron had disappeared down the dark hallway and was out of sight. Tuedy looked at his brother. "His Uncle Veyril already sent the invitations out, Toddy. The ball is scheduled in less than a fortnight, eh? Any of the *ton* that is in town will be coming to Graestone as well as those in the nearby estates! It will be a crush!" He clasped his hands together nervously as his voice rose shrilly. "Oh, this is a problem to be sure! Toddy! What am I to do, eh?"

Todrick stared up at his brother with his eyebrows twitching. "It's a bloody ball, Tudor," he rasped angrily. "What would I know about that?" He pointed up toward the second floor. "She's still crying. Now that's a problem." With those words, he stalked away.

CHAPTER FIFTEEN

L ULA HURRIED PAST Ten to the blazing fire in the large fireplace that warmed the study. She pulled off her bright green gloves and laid them on the ornate mantel. With a sigh, she held her hands out to the warmth of the flames. She looked to her side to stare at Ten Adair, the Earl of Fairfax. He was wandering about the room, looking at this and that. He had taken his top hat off as well as his gloves and frock coat and had lit a wax candle on the desk with a splinter of wood from the fire.

She could not deny that he was a very fine-looking man. The dimple in the center of his chin was intriguing and only added to his fine countenance. She watched as he stopped and was looking at some pages of sheet music on an ornately carved wooden music stand.

"You are not like the others here," she mused quietly as she held her hands flat to the fire. She tilted her head to study him.

He looked up from the sheet of music to the young woman at the fireplace. "Oh, I wore the red uniform for long enough. An officer's uniform it was and foolishly made in a poor and freezing fabric of a ridiculous bright red that could not repel the wet weather, but only absorbed it and was easily seen by the enemy. We English seem to have a preference for how one looks, rather than the usefulness of what we wear." He touched the sheet of music, his fingers tracing the notes absently. "The only thing the red coat is good for is to attract any females in the vicinity. Some women have a predilection for the uniform, assuming that a man wearing scarlet is superior to all other men." He looked over at her. "I must confess that it is most dashing on the male form, *mine in particular,* of course." He gave her a charming smile. Seeing that his statement had not made any impression on this particular young lady, however, he chuckled softly. He then added in a serious voice, "I am not flawed, you mean?"

Lula made a face. "I did not say that. We all have flaws." She raised her pert chin. "I am quite sure that you do as well, Lord Adair. A lack of humility being one, most obviously."

Ten let out a brief and very charming laugh. "Forgive me, I was teasing. You meant that I am not injured. You are somewhat correct in that assumption, though incorrect in assuming I have no humility."

Lula blushed. "Forgive *me.* That was rather rude of me, was it not?" She blushed and quickly turned her head to stare back into the fire, holding her hands out once again. She gave an elegant shrug as she tried again. "It is simply that you are an earl. You have family, I must assume." She glanced at him furtively before staring back into the flames and reveling in the warmth there. "Is Graestone not a haven for those with nowhere to go after being injured in war?"

Ten came strolling over. Not so close to make her uncomfortable, though she took a step to the side, away from him, but close enough to observe her. He looked down at her hands that she held toward the fireplace fire. He noted the horrible scarring on one of them. He had already seen the scar on her forehead that she tried to cover with her curls.

He put his hands behind his back and stared at the lovely profile of this highly unusual young woman. He forced himself to stare only at her face. If he allowed his eyes to drift down to her rounded buttocks and lithe legs in those breeches, he feared his body would betray him. His member was already threatening to thicken. He had a suspicion that his friend, War, would threaten him with bodily harm if he dared even look at Miss Darley inappropriately, particularly in the privacy of the man's own study.

Ten gave her a friendly smile. "Yes, there are orphans here at Graestone, but there are also sons of the aristocracy here, second sons of course."

"Second sons?" Lula asked.

Ten frowned slightly, "One cannot have the first sons of the aristocracy dying off, now can one?" His eyes drifted to the fire as his voice lowered. "The men here are learning to adapt and use their bodies again after their injuries. Before they return home."

Lula's gaze raked over his suddenly solemn face. "Were you injured? You said you were 'somewhat' injured," she asked quietly.

Ten's eyes went to hers. "No one escapes war without being damaged in some way," he said softly as his eyes went back to the fire. "But no, I was not *physically* injured." After several breaths, he added quietly, "I brought my nephew here. He is, or rather was, an architect, before being injured in the war. He is working on architectural plans to restore the old wings of Graestone while he is here."

Lula took that in. She dared not ask what had happened to the Earl of Fairfax's nephew. The earl seemed so sad. His normally cheerful and charming smile was gone. She rubbed her hands together and then stood up from where she had been bending near the fire. She clutched them tightly together as she took another step back from the man with the charming dimple on his chin.

"That is good. I mean, I am glad you were not injured, you see. I mean, I was afraid that you were going to say that you had a brother that was injured. Oh, dear, I am so very sorry. I am making the devil's own scrape of it, I fear."

Ten smiled politely at the blushing young woman. "I understand what you meant, Miss Darley." His smile wavered a mere moment as he looked down at the floor. Just as quickly, he looked back to her and his smile broadened, showing once again all his perfect white teeth and that dimple. He said charmingly, "I have eight sisters. I was the last of ten children. A surprise you see, born after my twin brother. The heir and the spare, they say. Hence my name. My father was vastly relieved to have two sons, *finally*, as you can imagine."

"Goodness! Eight sisters!"

"Yes, eight sisters," he said drolly with a crooked grin for her.

Lula frowned. "But you are a twin, and the earl?"

Ten turned away from her. "My father and twin brother passed recently. They both suffered from breathing problems. Asthma. Particularly difficult in the cold weather. This winter has been brutal as you know. I was pulled from the battlefield to come home." He turned back to her and looked down at his own clothing. His smile faltered. "I could no longer serve in the military once I became the Earl of Fairfax," he said with a hint of bitterness. "I must find another way to serve my king and country." He paused a moment and stared intently into her face. "My nephew is the first born of my eldest sister." He frowned sadly as he gazed into the fire. "He means the world to me. I very much appreciate the ointment you gave him for his wound. You have helped many of the men and boys at Graestone, I hear."

Lula managed to quietly release the breath she had held at the news of the death of his twin and his father. To lose one's twin is like losing half of yourself, if not all of yourself. She could not imagine the pain he must feel. "I am so sorry about your twin brother," she whispered. "And your father, of course," she added quickly.

She watched as he spun from the fire and went to stand by War's desk. He turned and studied some sketches on the wall behind the massive desk.

Lula walked over slowly, her eyes scanning the books on the shelves along the wall. She trailed her finger over them, reading the titles. Shakespeare's *First Folio*. *Common Sense* by Thomas Paine. *The History of the Decline and Fall of the Roman Empire*.

Voltaire's *Candide*. Benjamin Franklin's *Experiments and Observations on Electricity*. *The Federalist Papers*.

Lula's lips dropped open slightly as she studied them and opened a few. There were books written entirely in French and Russian, and books on science, mathematics, history and governments of the worlds.

The leather bindings were all well-worn, cracked, oft-opened she surmised.

Who was this man?

At a movement to her side, she looked over at the earl and then to the black and white sketches that were framed behind the baron's desk that he was staring at.

Ten turned to her with a sad smile. "These were what kept us all going," he said quietly. "At night when we gathered around a fire, when we were all freezing, hungry and many injured, War would sit and draw pictures of home. Pictures of Graestone. We would pass them around." He turned back to the sketches. "Graestone sitting atop a hill, grandly looking over vast rolling hills and trees just as it has for centuries. Unconquered, undamaged by war." His finger moved to another as he traced the scene. "Horses and sheep grazing contentedly in the lush fields." He pointed to another one. "His Uncle Veyril who raised him. His three nephews and his sister." He moved on to the next. "The views from the towers and battlements." His finger moved to another. "The village." His voice had become quieter and quieter until he stopped.

"The baron drew these?" Lula asked with surprise as she leaned closer to inspect his drawings. She studied the picture of his Uncle Veyril. He was smiling as if he had just heard a wonderful story. In the next sketch were the boys with their mischievous grins. All three of them grinning wildly, even little Jolyon who was always so solemn. She looked at the beautiful young woman laughing with the three boys. The baron's sister, who must be the three boys' mother, Lula presumed. "These are very good," she said quietly with shock in her voice. "The boys' mother is the baron's sister? She is the one crying, is she not?" she asked carefully.

Ten looked at the sketch of the laughing woman with the three little boys. "Yes, she is War's sister. Loveday de Walton. She was the diamond of her season. She became Lady Wildling, and then Lady Bland." He shrugged sadly as he stared at the sketch. "She is a widow now."

Lula looked at the drawing of the woman as well. She could see the resemblance to War, the dark, wavy hair, the bright eyes with the long lashes. She looked very happy.

"What happened?" she whispered.

Ten turned to her with a small smile. "'Tis not my story to tell. I will warn you, however, that you should not believe any rumors you hear." He looked around the room and then back to Lula.

"But," Lula started to ask another question about the baron's sister.

Ten was not going to give her time to ask further questions about War's sister, however. He interrupted her. "The baron is a good man." He waved his hand toward the sketches. "He is a man of many talents, Miss Darley. Do not discount his as a stern, rough character. He has had to be. He was thrust into the leadership of his family when both of his parents died suddenly."

"How did they die?" she asked cautiously.

"His father walked into a lake when he lost Graestone's fortune and drowned, and his mother drowned with him, trying to rescue him. He has never been the same since."

"Goodness," Lula whispered.

Ten nodded and continued, "War raised his sister, Loveday, and ran the estate until her betrothal contract came to date." He made a dismissive gesture with his hand. "Yes, his father's older brother, Veyril, who was the Baron of Graestone before War, was here, some of the time. When his health allowed him to be," he said, touching the sketch of Veyril. "But if you have met Veyril you would know that the responsibilities still fell on War's shoulders. When Veyril started having problems with his memory as well as his physical body, he handed it to War when he came home. This time, title and all so that he could travel to a warmer climate for his lungs and heart." He turned fully to her as he spoke in earnest. "When War entered the military, it was the same. He earned his rank because he was a leader there as well. He was always so calm, so brave and so wise beyond his years in his decisions. He was a good leader; confident, assuring. He was so carefully calculating of any and all risks to his men, to his entire unit." His eyes drifted away from her then, recalling the past as his voice softened. "Nothing riled his temper, nothing managed to irritate him under the worst of conditions. He was always solid, reliable. After a battle, he would walk amongst his men, checking on the wounded first. Then he would shake each man's hand and thank them while looking them in the eyes, *really* looking them in the eyes. It was obvious he cared, it was obvious he valued each man as well as their loyalty and dedication and hard work. He always went back to find his men that had not returned from the battleground. And when he lost a man..." He snapped out of his reverie and looked back at her with a smile and a shrug. "Men wanted to fight with him from the very beginning."

Lula glanced behind her shoulder to the door. "And those men and boys that work here at the estate now? They were all his men?"

Ten let out a soft laugh. "No. There are ship's boys here, men from the royal navy like Mr. Womersly and Cloudsley Shovell, artillery men, rocketeers like the Tweedys and dragoon men. Word got out that he could help those injured that were no longer able to fight. They could find a position here, honest work. Acceptance." He looked back at the sketches. "Time to heal."

Lula watched his face. "Tuedy Tweedy told me much the same. 'The baron is a man that knows that work is good for the soul and the body and that work creates value within each person. He also knows that work is necessary to heal wounds both physical and of the mind.' Is this what you mean?"

Ten nodded with a glint in his eyes. "Yes. Do you see? He is not such an arrogant beast as you thought."

Lula gave him a rueful grin and turned away to walk around the study. "Was I so obvious, then?"

Ten wandered back to the fire and stared down into it. "All women are afraid of him."

Lula stared at the incredibly handsome man. "You care about him a great deal."

Ten did not look at her. "Yes. I have many reasons to. He saved my life on the battlefield when my unit was in retreat. They had left me there, but he came back for me. He also went back for the artillery horses. He came out of the smoke of the field carrying a cannon on his shoulder while leading the last two artillery wagon draft horses off the field as well." He did look at her then. "I will never forget the sight. It was snowing, or perhaps the air was just filled with ashes from everything that was burning in that hellish night. Still, it was cold and the night was smoke-filled and here comes this giant of a man, shirtless, carrying a cannon on his shoulder while leading two bleeding, massive draft horses. Our battalion was speechless." He looked away from her for a moment as his voice quieted. "He does not think he deserves happiness, or love even. He blames himself for all of the men he has lost. And the horses as well. I believe he also blames himself for not being able to rescue either of his parents, though he almost drowned himself, diving down over and over into the dark depths of the lake. It took six of us to drag him away from the water." He turned back to her. "He has shut himself away from any happiness in life or any love. Even this castle. You may have noticed that it is not fully opened. It is dark with much of it still under dust cloths and years of neglect," he chuckled sadly. "For him, there is only work and his duty to others. He has made Graestone's fortune back one hundredfold and still he labors on. I am quite sure he works as hard as he does to escape." His eyes stared sharply at her. "I do believe, out of anyone, he has earned his own happiness more than any could ever deserve it."

Lula had to look away from his intense stare. She was stunned. "I had no idea," she whispered. And then she did look back at him. "Why are you telling me all of this?"

Ten leaned one arm against the mantel. "He was very protective of you when I came to your aid in the snow. I have never seen such a look on his face. Definitely not for a woman."

"You are being fanciful," Lula whispered as she looked uncomfortably away, unsure what to make of his comment.

His dimple became more pronounced as he smiled wickedly. "And of course, Todrick Tweedy told me that War kissed you on the battlements, and Tuedy Tweedy told me he saw War kiss you under the stairs."

Lula's fingers flew to her lips. "Goodness. Oh, Lud," she whispered.

"You should be aware that the Tweedy twins miss nothing that occurs in Graestone." Ten's smile turned wry.

"I see. Thank you," she murmured.

Ten momentarily looked down into the fire before turning back to Lula with a stern expression on his face. "I bid you, do not hurt him. I believe he has a growing affection for you, Miss Darley," Ten said quietly.

Lula shook her head. "I cannot agree with you, Lord Adair," she said firmly. "I do not believe he has any affection for me at all. Twas merely a trifle for him."

Lula heard the earl chuckle quietly. She walked over to the music stand standing on a lovely Persian rug. She touched the corner of the page of written music resting there. The page was signed *Warwick de Walton. So he wrote music, too?* Her gaze drifted to the violin leaning against a chair by the music stand and then to the pianoforte where more music in his same elegant writing lay.

"I assure you that War does not *trifle*. With *anyone*."

Lula frowned slightly as she stared at the music notes he had written on the page. *Was the baron the one that she had heard playing so sweetly?* How could a man as hard and gruff as he, play such sweet music? Music that had lulled her to sleep each night? Her finger traced the notes as her frown increased.

"I irritate him. That is all and tis quite clear," she said absently in reply to Ten's comment that the baron did not trifle. She silently hummed the notes as her finger moved over them. The melody was a lovely one. She had not heard this one being played.

"Women are afraid of him and he does not give a tinker's damn about their reaction to him. But you, *you* faint at the sight of him." He chuckled softly. "And it frustrates and irritates the hell out of him," Ten said with another low chuckle. "That is how I know."

Lula glanced up at him and then back to the next piece of sheet music. "You are quite wrong, not in his reaction to my fainting, for it clearly annoys him, but the reason for his annoyance, of course. He has not a single feeling for me other than irritation. And, of course, annoyance."

Ten gave her a secret smile. "Shall we test that?" he said as he strolled like a great, sleek cat toward her.

He spoke so quietly that Lula had barely heard him. She looked up and hastily backed away from his advancing form and the look in his eyes. Instantly, she began to panic as her heart started racing and the room threatened to spin out of control.

Ten glanced at the door just before pulling her into his arms and lowering his mouth to hers.

Lula squeaked and placed her hands on his chest as she pushed at him. She turned her mouth away from his and pulled back as she slapped his face.

"Get your bloody hands off of her!" came a roar from the doorway.

Lula felt large hands pull her away from Ten Adair's hold. She heard his deep voice murmur near her ear, "I vow I will not let him hurt you."

She was held firmly against a warm, solid chest within two

heavily muscled but gentle arms.

She did not struggle.

She did not resist his careful hold.

She knew that it was Warwick de Walton who held her. She knew his scent; horses, leather, frankincense and sandalwood. She knew that deep baritone voice. Heaven help her but she knew the feel of his body against hers. The feel of his arms holding her, protecting her.

Memories flooded her mind. Scenes from that night in Hyde Park raced across her vision, that frightening night when those men had attacked her and her sister. It had been War who had pulled her away from those men, up onto his horse. He, who had fought those men off. It had been War who had saved her. Who had said, "I vow I will not let them hurt you."

Tears came to her eyes and rolled down her cheeks.

"Good God, I could kill you for upsetting her, Ten. *She's crying*," growled War in a threatening, low voice mixed with anguish. "The devil confound it but I would smash my fist into your pretty face if I didn't know that it would upset her further. Touch her or even upset her again and I vow that you will regret it to your dying day if I let you live that long," he added through clenched teeth.

"Regret it to my *dying day* if I *live that long*, you say? Very amusing, my friend. Or perhaps your heart is overtaking your sensible brain." Ten chuckled.

War growled deep and low in his throat.

"Stop, both of you," Lula said firmly. She glanced at Ten and then back up to War. "I believe he heard you coming."

Ten held his hands palm up when War's eyes snared his. "A simple test was all it was, my big friend."

War swore under his breath. "I will wreak such havoc upon you—"

"No," Lula said quietly.

Lula pushed out of War's arms and stared up at him. She knew her face was very likely white and that her eyes were rimmed in tears. She swiped at the tears on her cheeks as she looked first at Ten, who had the audacity to wink at her, and then up at War's ferocious expression.

"Did he cause you to feel faint?" War asked her, ready to reach for her again.

Lula silently shook her head as she stepped well out of his reach and wiped at the tears sliding down her cheeks. "He is harmless, though I am sure he is a rake or a rogue."

Ten looked much taken aback at her statement.

War grunted. "He is all of those things, yes. *He made you cry*," he said in a gruff voice with barely controlled fury.

Lula shook her head. "No, he did not make me cry," she said softly as she stared up at him.

Ten quickly reached inside his waistcoat and brought out a folded, lacy, white handkerchief. He handed it to Lula. "Here, Miss Darley. A gift for you so that you may wipe away your tears. It is a pretty thing I purchased in France."

Lula shook her head and put her hands behind her back as she stepped away from Ten as well.

"She doesn't want that, Ten," War growled as he pushed Ten's hand holding the handkerchief away from Lula. "She likes colors. That is plain and boring and not unique." He scowled. "Give it to one of your eight sisters like you had planned when you purchased it," he said in annoyance.

War looked at Lula and then stalked over to his desk and opened a drawer. He pulled out a long, rolled-up piece of leather. He walked over to Lula and held it out in his hands, silently and almost shyly offering it to her.

Lula looked up at him. The tips of his cheekbones had gone pink. She took the leather roll and slowly unrolled it. Inside was a wooden tube with a small bell shape on one end and a larger bell shape on the other end. She looked up at him.

"Is it a musical pipe?" she asked quietly.

War shook his head nervously. "It is a doctor's listening device. You hold it against the patient's chest or back and listen to his heart or his lungs." His cheeks turned even brighter. "I met a man named Rene Laennec who was selling a medical instruction booklet that I wanted so that I could better help my men." He pointed to the object in her hands. "He made it. Though he is still making improvements on the design. This is one of his first attempts. He called it a chest scope or stethoscope. He gave it to me when I purchased the booklet. He believes every physician will want to have one someday, once he gets the design correct. I have never tried it, but I thought you would know better how to make use of it than I." He shrugged in awkward anticipation of her reaction. "I thought you could use it on the horses."

Lula examined the wooden tube with pleasure. "Thank you. I am most pleased to accept this!"

War's cheeks reddened even more. He chanced a quick glance at Ten who had his arms across his chest and was grinning at him. "What are you looking at?" War growled with embarrassment.

Lula's eyes went back to War. She stared at him wide-eyed, realizing that he was nervous over her reaction to his gift of the stethoscope. Slowly, new tears fell from her eyes as a tremulous smile grew on her face. She hugged the stethoscope to her breasts. "Truly, this is the loveliest and most thoughtful gift anyone has ever given me," she murmured through her tears.

War gave Ten a triumphant look and a quiet grunt of satisfaction.

Ten held up both hands. "I shall take myself and my most boring and un-unique handkerchief and return to my bedchamber." He gave a wry salute to his friend who turned his scowling face at him.

"Leave, Ten," War snarled as he motioned with his head toward the door. "*Now.* Or risk my fist to your face."

"Peace, my lucky friend." With those words, Ten walked to the door of the study, giving his large friend a wide berth. He was closing the door behind himself when he gave the couple a last look. He caught Lula's eye. He grinned at her and nodded reassuringly. Then he winked and quietly shut the door.

Lula stood there staring at the door. "He did it on purpose, didn't he?" she said with shock.

War scowled at the closed door. "I would wager that Ten not only heard me coming, he waited until I was at the door." His head whipped back around to Lula. "Did you enjoy his kiss?" he asked tensely.

It was Lula's turn to blush. She cradled the chest scope tighter to her breast and looked up at War. "Not at all and well you know it." She smiled a small smile. "I did slap him. And I did not faint."

War looked down at the rug beneath their feet. "I saw that." His eyes returned to hers. "I would have killed him if I did not know that he was pushing me."

Lula carefully put the chest scope down on a chair and stepped closer to War. She stared up into his dark eyes. "Why would Ten feel the need to push you, Baron?" she whispered. "Is it because you will not seek nor accept happiness for yourself?"

War sighed silently. He would not tell her that his friend, Ten, had been insistent that War had feelings for Miss Lula Darley since that first, fateful night in Hyde Park. He had been fighting those feelings, particularly because his presence seemed to make her so fearful that she would faint. Seeing Ten kiss Lula had made him realize, however, that his annoying friend was correct. He had been a fool for trying to deny it for so long, and a fool to risk her giving her heart to anyone but himself.

War inhaled slowly. "My name is War. I know you think it a foolish name, but it is mine, nevertheless," he said in a low voice. "I would hear it from your lips," he whispered.

Lula's breath caught. She smiled up at him. "*War*," she whispered on a drawn out breath. "Thank you for saving me."

She watched as the big bear of a man blushed again and looked entirely, uncomfortably, awkward.

"You had already slapped him. You did not need saving. You are stronger and have more courage than most men I know," he said and swallowed tightly as he stared at her.

Lula shook her head slowly. Her voice dropped to a tremulous whisper. "*No*. Thank you for saving me that night in Hyde Park, when those men attacked my sister and me." Her smile faltered and then bloomed. "I have misjudged you so terribly. *I remember*. It was *you* who held me in front of you on your horse. *You* who fought those evil men off."

War suddenly felt a weight off his chest. He exhaled loudly. He started to pull her back to him, but she quickly stepped away.

Lula held her hand up. "I may have remembered what happened but the memory still haunts me," she faltered and stopped as she rubbed at the scar on her hand, unable suddenly to look at him. "I still panic," she whispered with shame as she stared at the scar.

War took a big breath. "Lula—" He whispered her name so that she would look at him. "I understand. Tis no shame or embarrassment in your fear. It lingers from your memory. For now, at least. The memory and fear will lessen over time," he said in a dulcet baritone. He sighed quietly. "I vow I shall not hurt you, and I know that you do not like to be touched, but," he paused, weighing her reaction to his next request, "but I would invite you to touch me, whenever it pleases you to do so."

Lula looked up at him then, surprised at the gentleness in his voice. She felt an easing of the panicky tightness that lived within her. Of course this man understood. Look at the men around him. Men he was giving the chance to heal.

"Are you daring me?" she said pertly.

War gave her a crooked grin, pleased to see her spirit and her courage return. "As a matter of fact, I believe I am," he said in a velvety growl.

CHAPTER SIXTEEN

L ULA TOOK A hesitant step toward War. She was lost in the sensuous look in his eyes and the crooked tilt of a grin on his beautiful lips.

He reached out with his hands toward her once again but she hastily shook her head no. Slowly, he held his large hands up, and then just as slowly, put them behind his back and grinned gently at her.

"I vow I will not hurt you."

His voice had lowered into a velvety, deep whisper that sent a shiver of awareness through Lula from her breasts to the "v" between her thighs.

"My word is truth, Lula," War murmured as he stepped away from her until the backs of his thighs hit his desk. He sat down on the desktop and gripped the edges of it tightly on either side of his hips. "My hands shall not leave this desk," he said quietly.

Lula stared at him as a war began within her. She wanted to touch this big man who had mesmerized her with his surprising gentleness, his sometimes shyness and his oftentimes gruffness, while also possessing a quiet ability to make her feel safe and protected. He had also not made her feel foolish for panicking or for fainting. She tilted her head at him.

"You cannot order me not to faint, War," she said with a smile.

He tilted his head at her in the same way and grinned wolfishly. "I can make you angry enough to forget that you may faint when I order you thusly," he murmured slowly.

Lula had to laugh. "You are incorrigible." Her laughter faded when she saw that hungry look in his eyes. "Why are you looking at me like that?" she whispered nervously.

"Like what?" he asked in a husky growl with a crooked grin.

Lula frowned and flailed one hand in his direction. "Like that," she said.

"I am staring at your freckles," he said softly.

Lula sighed and touched her face with her fingers as she stared back at him. "Ladies should have perfect, creamy complexions. But I ride quite a bit, you see, when I work the horses at Aldbey Park and that means spending time outdoors in the sun." She stopped talking when she realized he was shaking his head at her.

"You misunderstand me. I am captivated by your freckles, Lula," he said sweetly.

"You are?" she breathed out in surprise.

He nodded his head. "I am."

"Truly?" she asked again as she put both hands to her cheeks.

He nodded again, never taking his eyes off of her. "I am thoroughly captivated by your freckles. And your hair, and your lips and your eyes, and your breeches." He grinned. "But mostly, your freckles," he growled softly. "I meant it when I said that I wanted to kiss every freckle on your face." His grin turned wolfish. "And your body," he said huskily. "Every damned time I see you."

Lightning arced through Lula's breasts and spread down to her legs, making her knees weak with the sudden hot longing that raced throughout her body. Her heart started thudding deep in her breasts, in a good way. *Yes, a very good way, and oh, how she wanted to touch this big baron.*

She put her hands on her hips and grinned back at him. "War?" she said sweetly.

"Yes, Lula?" he asked with a grin of his own.

"Hold tight to that desk." Lula was pleased to see that War lost the grin that had tilted up one corner of his sensuous mouth. She watched as his breathing increased and his whole body went still. Waiting for her.

She started walking slowly toward him. She watched as he tried to swallow and then tried once again as his eyes stayed on hers. She walked right up between his legs and stared deeply into his eyes for several heartbeats. "I am going to touch you," she whispered.

War closed his eyes and then opened them again as he whispered in a rough voice, "Good God and bloody hell and the devil confound it, Lula." His breath shuddered out of him. *"Finally,"* he said in a voice thick with need. "Touch me, please."

Lula reached up with a trembling hand and let her fingers lightly trace his cheekbones just above the line of his beard. She ran a featherlight finger over his eyebrows as her breath trembled from between her lips. Then she lifted her hands and plunged them into his hair, dragging her fingers through the silky waves with a sigh.

"You are beautiful, Warwick de Walton," she said in a soft whisper.

War grunted. "No one has ever called me beautiful before," he said with embarrassment.

Lula was charmed to see that his cheeks went pink once again. "I think you are," she repeated shyly.

He stared into her eyes, holding them with nothing but his own gaze. He felt a rawness within him. With it came a new lightness within his chest. "That is all that matters," he said throatily.

She smiled and moved her hands back through his hair, watching the silken waves slide through her fingers. She then lightly trailed her hands over his broad shoulders, down his arms, just to his biceps, where she experimented with a light squeeze. She heard him suck in a breath, but she only had eyes for the parts of his body that her hands were exploring. Next, she moved her hands, palms flat down his chest. Her gaze was riveted there, as she felt the rapid beat of his heart beneath her hands and the rise and fall of each breath he took.

"Lula?" he said hoarsely as his eyes dropped down to her pert breasts outlined in the unusual purple-colored, tight-fitting jacket she wore with the military epaulettes and other frippery. He growled silently as his eyes continued down to her hips, her thighs, and the "v" of her legs in her breeches. He closed his eyes and clenched the desk tighter.

"Hmm?" Lula murmured as her fingers continued to explore his face, his shoulders, and his chest.

"Please kiss me or I vow I will die," he growled. *"Now.* I dare you, *now,"* he croaked as he looked into her eyes.

She stilled and stared at his beautiful mouth. "War," she said tremulously. "I am new to kissing. I am afraid I may not do it right," she whispered.

War closed his eyes. "Anything you do will be right, Lula," he said in a rush of breath. "My word is truth," he whispered and opened his eyes again to see her staring hungrily at his mouth.

Lula lowered her lips to his as she held the sides of his face. She breathed in his sigh as she moved her lips lightly back and forth over his as he had done to her. Her heart fluttered at the small moan that came from within War's chest. She deepened the kiss, experimenting with more pressure and he instantly opened his mouth, covering her lips with his own as he strained toward her. It was her turn to sigh and whimper as he took her top lip between his and then moved on to her bottom lip. Over and over, their lips met and tasted as he whispered her name and she whispered his as one or the other moaned and sighed the other's name.

War whispered her name again on a long drawn out sigh. "Lula…I dare you to take more." He swallowed. "I vow I will not hurt you or frighten you."

"You do not frighten me, War. Show me," she moaned softly against his lips.

War thrust just the tip of his tongue along the seam of her lips, begging entrance. Teaching her that there was more, so much more. He was proceeding much more carefully than he had when he had kissed her this way the first time under the stairs.

This time was different. There was a cherishing, a reverence for this woman that made him shake with the desire to go slowly, to show her he could keep his vows now and in the future.

He touched the tip of his tongue to hers, gently at first and then more assertively as his tongue fully penetrated between her lips.

Lula moaned and leaned into the kiss. Loving the feel and taste of his warm, velvety tongue against hers.

Their tongues entwined as their breaths mingled and their hearts raced. Their mouths moved slower and then slower still as the kiss deepened and sweetened. They explored and savored as tongues moved as one.

Hearts raced.

Blood pounded.

Eyes became clouded with desire.

Minds became numb to nothing but the taste and feel of the other.

Until the kiss was not enough and then it was wild breaths and heaving chests. Tongues twining and lips suckling and teeth biting as they ravaged one another's mouths. Their moans became louder and the names of one another came out in guttural groans of need and desire, *heady,* hot *desire.*

An earsplitting crack split the air in the silence of the study.

They pulled apart and looked down at the desk.

War's face went red.

In his hands was the edge trim of the desk. He had snapped it off. His grip had intensified to the point that his fingers had broken the trim right off the desk's edge.

He looked at Lula and grinned with a small shrug of his broad shoulders. "I did not touch you," he said.

Lula smiled and placed her lips on his again.

CHAPTER SEVENTEEN

L ULA WAS WALKING through the great hall with a soft smile on her face as she recalled the evening before in War's study. This morning, the great hall was dimly lit as usual though it was still very early and no one was about to light any sconces. She wanted to get to the stables particularly early to make sure that Buttercup's stitches had indeed not suffered at the hands of Cloudsley Shovell or Womersly.

She paused to try to peer through the layers of dust to the portraits that were hung along the walls, looking for any of the men that may resemble Warwick de Walton.

"Miss Darley! Miss Darley! There you are! Oh, thank heaven you are up early. A moment of your time please, eh?" came Tuedy's high-pitched voice calling to her.

Lula looked over to see Tuedy rushing toward her with his hands in the air, looking to be in a state of panic.

Lula turned to give him her full attention. "What is it, Tuedy?" she asked in alarm.

Tuedy stopped in front of her and placed a hand to his chest as he bent his head down, gasping for air. "Tis a *very* important matter." He stilled as he looked down at her. He tried valiantly to stop the grin that was spreading on his face. "You spent a long time in the study with the baron yesterday."

"Tuedy Tweedy!" she said in admonishment with her hands

on her hips. "Now then, what is this very important matter you hailed me for?"

"Eh? Oh! I have to plan *the* ball!" he squeaked. "It is in less than a fortnight."

"Goodness," Lula said as she folded her hands in front of her and tried to control her smile.

"I need your help!" Tuedy said in desperation.

"I see," Lula said and then she did smile. "I am happy to, of course," she said calmly.

Tuedy let out a sigh of relief and clapped his hands together. "Excellent. *What should I do?*"

"Oh!" Lula's smile faded. She asked slowly, "Well then, what have you done so far?"

"Nothing," Tuedy squeaked with a panicky look on his face.

Todrick came walking up with a sneer on his face. "What are you bloody bothering her for?" he asked with a sideways glance for Lula.

"I need help, Toddy," Tuedy said in exasperation.

Todrick scowled with a cynical bend on his scarred lips. "'Tis bloody much ado all for nothing. A *ball*," he rasped with disgust. "A waste of bloody time, I wager." He threw a quick scowl at Lula. "She'll be of no help. What would she know of such things? You are asking her for help? That's not right," he said in his painful, croaking voice.

"Todrick," Lula said as she dug her little ointment jar out of the satchel in her skirt. "My ointment really would soothe the tightness in your lips." She held her hand out, offering the ointment to him once again.

Todrick shook his head adamantly. "I have heard of all the medicines you have been giving the men here. I'll not use anything you make, so stop bloody offering." He walked away shaking his head.

"Goodness, he does not care for me at all," Lula whispered as she watched Tuedy's twin brother walk away from them. She stood up straighter, resolved to try to help Tuedy, if only a little.

"Well, I can tell you that the menu must be planned well in advance, Tuedy, and the musicians must be hired of course." She looked around the hall. "You must also have the great hall thoroughly cleaned. And the dining room and the ballroom." She looked around and then back at Tuedy. "Have you a ballroom here at Graestone?"

He nodded quickly. "Yes," he answered, although it was more of a question. With growing dismay on his face, he clutched his fingers together tightly. He turned this way and that as if a ballroom would materialize before him in the murky shadows of the great hall. "Somewhere. Most of the rooms have been closed down." He pulled a pristine, white handkerchief from his black waistcoat and wiped at his brow and his upper lip and then flapped the handkerchief wildly in the air. "I shall have to open hundreds and hundreds of doors to find it, eh? Perhaps Toddy will know where it is. He has wandered every bit of Graestone." He stuffed the handkerchief back into his waistcoat with a frown.

Lula bit her lip to stop from grinning. "You or Toddy will have to find it. I am sure a castle such as this would have a ballroom." She paused as she gazed at his tense face. "Can the baron not help you with what must be done, or his sister perhaps?"

Tuedy groaned. "I have tried and tried. The baron is a soldier, eh? He does not plan balls, or so he growled at me."

"And his sister?" Lula asked carefully. "The one who is crying, upstairs?"

Tuedy flitted his fingers and shook his head. "I cannot, or rather no one is to disturb, I mean—it is just that, well, I can't, eh?" He raised his hands, palms up, as he fumbled haltingly into a nervous and embarrassed silence.

"I see." Lula furrowed her brows and looked away from the red-faced cook, up to the second floor. The soft, whispery sound of weeping was apparent, though no one but her seemed to want to speak of it. She looked back at the distraught man. "It is not my place, Tuedy," she said gently.

Tuedy's face fell as a look of misery took over. "I can think of no one else to ask that may know what planning a ball entails! I am at a loss for what to do, eh!"

Lula frowned and chose her words carefully. "It should be Lady Loveday planning this ball, should it not?"

Tuedy shook his head frantically. "This was *Veyril* de Walton's grand ball, eh? But Lord Veyril is not here!"

Lula drew back with surprise. After a moment of thought, she arched one eyebrow. "And Uncle Veyril just happens to be visiting my sick, Great-aunt Eggy." She sighed and with her hands on her hips, she started tapping the toe of one booted foot as she looked around the dark and colorless great hall. She lifted her hand and started rapidly ticking off a list on her fingers. "Very well then, the staff needs to be divided into various tasks," she stated briskly. "You should select the extra staff that you will need to help you in the kitchens preparing the food. Others need to be assigned to cleaning." She thought a moment. "Make that *several* others." She looked around and said softly, "I fear the cleaning will be the most enormous task." She smiled suddenly as a thought came to her. "Perhaps you could send to the village for help. I am sure there are women and girls there that would be eager at the chance to come up to the castle to help."

Tuedy put a finger to his chin and pursed his lips. "The men will be embarrassed or uncomfortable with their injuries being seen by strangers. I am not sure in particular that they would appreciate the assuredly curious eyes of females."

Lula stared at him with her eyes sparkling at her plan. "Nevertheless, please send someone down to spread the word that help is needed immediately, and then we shall see what we shall see." She beamed consolingly at the doubt she could read on his face and touched his hand briefly with reassurance.

"Now then, what else?" She continued to gaze around the massive hall. After a moment, she looked upwards to the high, vaulted ceiling and the shadowy hulk of the immense, dust-covered chandelier. Her little sister, Birdie, would delight in dramatically saying that it reminded her of a giant, hovering spider, hanging there ready to pounce on unsuspecting prey below. That it had been waiting there so long that the poor thing was gray with a thick coat of dust and cobwebs amongst its once elegant arching arms. Even the dust cloth draped over it was in dark dust-covered tatters.

Lula sighed loudly as she stared up at it.

"What is it, Miss Lula?" Tuedy asked with dread.

She pointed upwards. "The chandelier needs to be carefully cleaned of all that dust and fresh candles put in it and lit."

Tuedy groaned. "We have intentionally left it alone. That chandelier is a leviathan," he whispered. "The house boys are terrified of lowering it, much less touching all that fragile crystal," he murmured as he arched his head back to stare at the gray shape of the crystal chandelier with its hundreds of fragile, hanging, crystal droplets all covered in dust as well.

Lula stared upwards. "So it is glass? One cannot even tell. Still, it needs to be done."

Tuedy nodded in resignation as the two of them stood there with their heads back, silently staring up at the massive thing.

Lula sighed and then looked around the hall again. "The window there." She pointed to the three, arched, tall windows on the landing where the two stairs joined. "The shutters need to be opened and the glass needs to be cleaned. I fear it is so dirty that barely any light can get through it and we need light in here. Tis so dark. The other shuttered windows need to be opened and cleaned as well." She turned to the walls. "The portraits should be carefully dusted." She swept a hand toward the dust cloths covering what must be furniture along the wall. "All the dust covers must be pulled from the furniture." She tapped her chin as she turned in a slow circle, looking all around. "And the great fireplace. The mantel is black with soot. When was the last time a fire was lit in it? The chimney must be checked first, of course, and then a small trial fire should be done. Perhaps ask after a chimney sweep in the village," she murmured. She then looked down at her feet. "The gray stones of this floor must be scrubbed until they are clean."

"Tis marble, Miss Lula," Tuedy murmured as he, too, stared at the floor.

Lula made a startled noise as she looked down at the floor she was standing on. "Are you quite sure? I assumed because this is an old castle that it was perhaps stone."

Tuedy shook his head. "No. I believe it was updated to marble at the same time that other areas of the house were updated." He flitted his fingers near his head. "The entire castle was left mostly uncared for while Lord Veyril came and went. That was while Lord Warwick was away in the military. So, years it's been, eh. That was before any of us were here, of course. I imagine there was just a limited staff to do everything so only certain rooms were maintained. Of course, I have no idea what particular shape the castle was in before that," he said musingly. "I should not say, but I did hear from someone in the village that it was in very poor shape while Lord Veyril was here. So, eh, I do not know when the floors were done."

Lula made a humming noise. "I see. Well, really I cannot see," she murmured as she rubbed the toe of her boot on the floor. "We can only guess at the color of the marble," she said to herself. "Well, we shall leave its color a surprise. Now then, we definitely must have more light. We simply cannot inspect anything well enough. Can you have the house boys light every sconce they can find on these walls so that we can better see what needs to be done here? This will be the initial gathering place, of course, you see." Lula tapped her chin with one finger. "I fear what we may find once we discover the location of the ballroom. Old castle or no, everything must look clean and presentable." She turned to him with a great smile. "I do know that whatever you prepare for the guests to eat will of a certainty be *most* delicious."

Tuedy was nodding his head in agreement with everything she said as his face became calmer.

"Yes, yes, I do see!" He clasped his hands together in excitement. "I shall come up with an impressive menu at the very least! I shall make marchpane war horses in honor of the baron and a tower of cakes with sugar plate!"

Lula smiled at him and then looked up to the second floor as a thought struck her. She nibbled at her bottom lip and looked back at him.

"What is it?" Tuedy asked with dread.

Lula winced. "I hate to bring more work on you or any of the staff, but I would suppose some of the guests are staying?"

Tuedy let out a muffled shriek and covered his mouth. "I have no idea!" he said from behind his fingers as he stared at her in growing horror.

Lula pursed her lips. "You must ascertain the number so that you know how many bedchambers to prepare. Todrick could help with that as well as the other tasks. You needn't take this all on your shoulders, Tuedy."

Tuedy shrieked and turned to hurry toward the kitchens with his hands flailing. "I shall have to make an order for extra foodstuffs, and make sure the linens are fresh and, and pull the men away from their work restoring the northwest wing to help and some may have to give up their bedchambers, and oh, *bollocks*! Toddy? *Toddy!*" he shrieked in his high voice "Come at once! At once, eh!"

Lula watched him scurry away with a small smile of pity on her face.

She tilted her head. Of course War was restoring the old wings of his castle. Her smile slowly faded. She looked up to the second floor.

Lula took a deep breath, paused and then strode up the stairs with determination.

LULA FOLLOWED THE soft sound of weeping undeterred. She sang softly to herself as she walked cautiously along, looking out for Todrick just in case Tuedy had not found him. Hopefully, however, he was below stairs getting an earful from Tuedy about what needed to be done for the ball.

"They threw him out some tackling
To give his life a hope
But as the shark bit off his head
He couldn't see the rope.

With a chip, chop! Cherry chop!
Fol de rol, riddle-rop!
Chip, chop! Cherry chop!
Fol de rol ray!
With a chip, chop! Cherry chop!
Fol de rol, riddle-rop!
Chip, chop! Cherry chop!
Fol de rol ray!"

This time, she walked down the second floor east wing hallway after stopping to put one of her woolen sleeveless gowns on over her breeches and linen blouse. She would not meet Lady Loveday in her breeches.

SHE KNEW THE sound of weeping was coming from somewhere toward the back of the castle. She thought she might try to follow the sound somewhere near the tower south of hers. As she walked down the long hallway listening for the sound in between her song verses, she looked out of the windows that were spaced on the outer wall down the length of the hall. These windows were clean, lighting up the hall with a muted white light from the snowy day outside.

She walked over to one of them and looked out and then down. The windows on this hall looked out onto another large walled courtyard, not very much smaller than the immense front courtyard with its rows of stables. Looking down, she could see the shapes of hedges and paths that wove throughout. All were covered in snow.

It is a walled garden, Lula thought with pleased surprise. There was another area that had several straight rows. *And there is a kitchens garden space as well.* She could also make out benches circling what looked like a round fountain. All were covered in a pristine blanket of fresh snow.

It appeared that each of the four sides of the square castle had a large area surrounded by stone walls, each being used for something different. There were wrought iron gates in the walls connecting each of the courtyards or gardens to one another.

How lovely!

Lula continued down the hallway but came to an abrupt wall which forced her to turn a corner. This led into the center of the castle with doors all along the hallway on her left and right. All was silent here. She quieted her singing to a whisper as she tiptoed carefully over the broken floorboards and pieces of fallen plaster, looking all around.

"At twelve o'clock his ghost appeared
Upon the quarter decks.
"Ho, pipe all hands ahoy" it cried,
"From me a warning take."

With a chip, chop! Cherry chop!
Fol de rol, riddle-rop!
Chip, chop! Cherry chop!
Fol de rol ray!
With a chip, chop! Cherry chop!
Fol de rol, riddle-rop!
Chip, chop! Cherry chop!
Fol de rol ray!"

She rubbed at her arms to ward off the chill as her singing let out small puffs of air. The floors creaked loudly and the walls showed their age with the dust-covered paint cracked and peeling. Where there was wallpaper, it was hanging off in sad, mildew-covered sheets, even the ceiling plaster was missing in several areas with its dusty remnants lying in piles on the floor. The once beautiful paneling on the lower half of the wall was falling off, or rotting.

Lula was happy to turn another corner. This hall led back the way she had come, until finally she was stopped by a set of double doors. These doors appeared to shut off the back section of the castle. She pushed the huge wooden doors open and sighed with relief. This part of the castle was in good repair. She continued down another shorter, much more cheerful hall than the last.

She sang quietly as she walked. "With a chip chop, cherry chop, fol de rol, riddle-rop! Chip, chop, cherry chop, fol de rol ray!"

She came to another door recessed ever so slightly, there on the right side of the hall, just before the hallway turned a corner. *This has to be the tower,* she thought, for it looked the same as hers. It was here that the sound of weeping was clearly coming from.

She rapped lightly on the door, but the weeping only continued with no answer.

She rapped harder, hesitant to just open the door.

"Go away," came a muffled sob from within.

"Lady Loveday?" Lula called with her face close to the door.

The weeping suddenly stopped.

"Who is that? Are you the one that has been singing in the hallway?"

Lula put a firm smile on her face. "Yes, that was me. I am Miss Lula Darley, come to see you, Lady Loveday."

"You should leave as soon as possible, Miss Darley!"

These foreboding words were followed by another wrenching sob.

"I should dearly love to visit with you," Lula called through the door.

She listened with her ear to the door. Silence.

"Lady Loveday?" Lula called out hesitantly.

Another sob.

"Leave, Miss Darley! *Leave Graestone*, before my brother destroys your life as he did mine!" Lady Loveday cried.

CHAPTER EIGHTEEN

L ULA DREW BACK from the door and stared at it in horror.

How had War destroyed his sister's life?

She put her hand on the door knob and took a breath as she pushed it open, just enough to step inside.

Lula stopped and stared at the sight before her.

Lady Loveday was sprawled on a gold velvet-covered settee. Her face looked like a painting that had been left out in the rain before it had dried. It appeared that she wore quite a bit of cosmetics; white face cream, rouge on her cheeks and lips, and charcoal paste to line her brows, upper eyelid and lashes. Her tears were washing it all down her face. The high neckline of her gown, also all in gold, was beginning to stain from her tears.

"Lady Loveday?" Lula asked hesitantly.

Loveday sat up abruptly, wiping at her face with both hands as she looked away. "Please go. I am not presentable, nor am I accepting visitors."

Lula huffed out a breath and walked forward into the room. This bedchamber was awash in soft golden colors. It was also neat as a pin.

Lula walked straight to the settee and, without a care, knelt on the golden Persian carpet in a puddle of skirts and stared at War's sister. "Why do you cry?" Her voice was quiet and gentle. Something horrid must have happened to this woman.

Loveday worried at the handkerchief in her hands. It was stained with rouge and the black charcoal.

Lula tilted her head and waited. She noted that Loveday's cheeks and lips were still covered in some of the rouge and the white face paint, though the black charcoal was smeared all down her cheeks. Her face was unusually pale underneath the blurry colors. Her hair was as black as a raven and pulled back into a severe plated bun at the base of her neck.

"I must look a fright," Loveday said as she stared at the stained handkerchief in her hands. "I keep trying to cover up my red, blotchy face but then I just cry again and it runs everywhere," she said in a shaking voice. "You see?" she said and held up the once white handkerchief edged in delicate lace. She laughed sadly which turned into another small sob.

"But why do you cry? I hear you almost daily, it seems."

Lady Loveday dabbed at her face and did not answer Lula's question. "I have been told that you are one of the Darley daughters. I have read in the *Morning Post* all about your mother and the Duke of Leids, and the prince and of course you and your sisters." She looked up and peered at Lula as she sniffled. "How *very brave* of you all. To go to Tattersalls, I mean. To make them let you sell your horses." She sniffled and wiped her nose. "You trained them all yourselves? Truly?"

Lula gave her a genuine smile. "We did train them, my mother and my sisters and me."

"You are here to take care of my brother's horses." It was a statement, not a question.

"I am, if he will let me."

"I believe he will," Loveday said with a soft smile.

Lula did not speak. She waited while Loveday stared at her with eyes similar to War's until she began to feel uncomfortable. Loveday was intently studying her face, her nose, (*very probably the freckles there*, Lula thought) and of course her hair. Everyone stared at the messy curls on her head. And the scar on her forehead above her brow and the one on the back of her hand.

Finally, Loveday looked back down at the stained handkerchief and then nervously back at Lula.

"I should offer you something, perhaps give you tea, shouldn't I?" Loveday asked in an anxious voice.

"No, that is not necessary," Lula said pleasantly.

"Well then," Loveday said as she looked around the room in agitation. "I must fix my face." Loveday abruptly stood up from the settee and straightened the extraordinary gown of golden satin she wore. It was trimmed in lace dyed gold and had enormous puffed sleeves and a huge ruffled flounce on the hem. The neckline that rose high to her throat was trimmed in golden lace as were the sleeves. She walked over to a small table with a mirror. She sat down in a swish of golden skirts and began repairing her face. "Would you like to put some powder on your scar, or your nose perchance? A smooth complexion is most desired. Or repair your hair?" Her hand stilled on her cheek and shook as her eyes stared stricken at Lula in the mirror. "Oh, dear! How rude of me! Please, please forgive my poor manners! My boys think your scars are quite the mark of bravery. As do I! Truly, I meant no insult about your freckles or your hair, or, or the scar." Her eyes flitted around the room, looking anywhere but at Lula. Her shoulders fell as she frowned anxiously and sniffed at the fresh tears on her face. "I do not know how to talk to anyone," she murmured.

Lula stood up with a broad smile. "I took no insult, Lady Loveday."

Loveday stared at her in surprise. A smile emerged, trembling on her lips. She began slowly patting some white cream on her face with a shaking hand. "I must confess that I have not conversed with another woman in quite some time," she said awkwardly as she tried to steady her fingers to apply the cream. Her eyes flitted back to Lula's in the mirror and then away. "Conversation is not easy for me." She patted more cream on her face. "Oh! I know, I read an exemplary piece in the *Morning Post* just last month that may interest you." Her voice was apprehensive and her movements were jerky. She recited rapidly, "'You will not do well to let your hair embarrass you when you ride. The hair should be plaited; or, so neatly arranged and secured that it may not blow into the eyes, nor, become unruly from exercise, or the effect of humid weather, nor be liable to be so discomposed, as to become embarrassing.'"

Lula grinned. "Yes, I read that as well. It was written for lady equestrians." She shook her head as she remembered parts of the article, written by a man, of course.

Loveday nodded without noticing Lula's bemused expression. "I thought it a most excellent article. You would appreciate it even more, perchance. Did you read the second installment? It said, 'A gentleman looks for a lady that sits just so and is easy, but not slovenly in the saddle. Nothing can be more disappointing to the grace of a lady's appearance upon a horse's back to a gentleman, than a bad position. It is a sight that would mar even the loveliest landscape in the world.'" She smiled at Lula as she continued to repaint her face. "And it went on to state: 'A lady must never beat her horse—it is ungraceful and uncouth. Ladies certainly ought not to ride upon horses which require frequent correction for these horses have not been trained by a gentleman. Also, a lady ought never to be seen in the act of flogging her steed. It would bely her grace, her sweetness and her gentleness.'" She nodded again. "Do you not agree with the writer of this piece, Miss Darley?"

Lula bit her lip. "Well, of course one should not *flog* one's horse."

"The writer states a most important rule. 'A lady must always ride with a man, particularly he is useful to shield her if in case her petticoats start to show or be blown about.' I thought that was an especially pertinent point."

Lula furrowed her brows. "Yes, well—"

"The *Morning Post* writer also stated, 'A gentleman must ride on the left of a lady, therefore, by having his right hand toward her, in case of her needing assistance, he might, the more readily and efficiently, be enabled to afford it, than if he were on the opposite side; and, should any disarrangement occur in the skirt of her habit, he might screen it until remedied.'"

"Goodness," Lula breathed. "Well, I suppose if a lady does not have her skirts attached to her stirrup to stop them blowing—"

Loveday continued to layer on thick swabs of the white creamy paint to her face. "The writer also states, 'No lady of taste ever gallops. She must say no when asked. Even if she is with her husband or has the approval of her husband to do so, she must still abstain from such an undesirable and ungraceful exertion as galloping, that will of a certainty, cause her breasts to do the most unladylike and unthinkable of all things; *to heave*.'" She nodded as she turned her face this way and that as she looked into the mirror, checking that she was covering the entirety of her face in white. "'Most of all, do not ride a horse who is anything less than perfect. The beau ideal of this kind of horse is superlatively elegant in form, exquisitely fine in coat and exceptionally beautiful in color; of a height, in the nicest degree appropriate to the figure of the rider; graceful, accurate, well-united, and thoroughly safe in every pace; light as a feather in the hand, though not at all painfully sensitive to a proper action of the bit; bold in the extreme, yet superlatively docile; free, in every respect, from what is technically denominated 'vice', excellent in temper, but still though gentle, yet not dull; rarely, if ever requiring the stimulus of the whip, yet submitting temperately to its occasional suggestions as only a horse trained by a skilled gentleman could be.' Much like a lady trained by her husband to be a docile and perfect wife." She leaned toward the mirror and applied a harsh red rouge to her cheeks and lips and then picked up a small bone pin with one end carved into a ball and the other somewhat pointed. She poked it into a tiny glass jar of black powder and applied it to her top eyelashes. "Would you not agree?" She then picked up some small tweezers and set about plucking her eyebrows which appeared to be almost gone from over-plucking. Once that was done, she applied some thin charcoal paste to make a curved line over her eyes where her eyebrows used to be.

Lula grimaced as she watched. "Er, Lady Loveday I cannot agree with the writer of the *Morning Post*. It begs the question; how would a gentleman train a horse to accept skirts billowing or flapping around a horse's back or legs unless he himself wears such clothing in this training? Much less, I must question the gentleman having to sit off center on the back of a horse and therefore off balance on a side saddle? Which, of course, ladies are expected to use. And I certainly cannot compare a horse trained away of its vices who submits to a bit or the whip, with a perfect wife trained by her husband. The union between man and wife should be one of partnership, friendship, harmony and love, not submitting to proper and perfect training with the intent that she become docile to his every command. I shudder at the thought."

Loveday went still as her harsh red mouth dropped open. "I have offended you again!" She put her face in her hands and started crying. "Please do not be angry with me," she cried into her fingers. "I was only reciting the paper. I do not remember how to converse politely as I should. I have only that which is in my head from all the reading I do of the *Morning Post*. Twas silly of me to have committed it to memory. Silliness, all of it!"

Lula hurried to Loveday and dragged another chair over and sat down. She pulled Loveday's hands gently away from her face. "Do not cry, you will ruin all your—your efforts to repair your face from your last bout of crying." She watched some of the white paint and the black charcoal drip with her tears. A murky, gray-white droplet fell on her golden gown. "You have gotten some of your cosmetic paint on your beautiful ball gown," she murmured. "Were you trying it on for the ball?"

Loveday looked down at her dress. "No. It is just that my husband said that one must endeavor to always look one's best." She limply wiped at the stain on her bodice and shrugged. "Tis silly to wear a ball gown, I know. Tis out of fashion but it still fits me." She looked away from Lula as another tear dripped down her white face.

"It is very beautiful."

Loveday looked back at Lula as she twisted her hanky in her lap again. "Do you forgive me for making you angry? About the lady equestrians? Of course, you and your sisters and mother know more than that silly writer! I, I just thought it was a topic we could converse on."

Lula nodded. "Of course, I forgive you." She paused and thought a moment. "Do you ride, Lady Loveday?"

She shook her head quickly. "I did when I was a young girl. War taught me. We rode all over the countryside. It was most wonderful and freeing!" She looked at her hands. "That was so very long ago. Neither of my husbands allowed me to ride, however. Actually, Lord Wildling, my first husband who was the father of my three boys, may have allowed it, but he said my duty was to my children, not to my pleasures. He fell from his horse and perished. My second husband Lord Bland, forbid me to ride." Her voice droned into awkward and uneasy silence.

"I see," Lula murmured.

"I have spoken too openly," Lady Loveday said with embarrassment.

"No," Lula said gently. She studied Lady Loveday. She was not that much older than her sister, Julia. She must have married quite young. She was still startling pretty, and she was also very curvaceous. Her hair, from what Lula could see of it in the severe style she wore, still looked lustrous and her eyelashes, like War's, were long and black and currently mostly smeared with the charcoal paste she used on her lashes and brows. "The ball I mentioned will be held here, at Graestone. Please tell me that you will help with the preparations."

Loveday looked back at her with a startled expression. Her eyes flicked around her bedchamber. "I, I am not sure that I can. I feel most comfortable when I stay here in my chamber."

Lula frowned and sat back as she stared at the woman in front of her. In a compassionate whisper, she asked, "What happened? Why do you spend your days crying?"

Loveday shook her head and would not look at Lula. She stared at her hands in her lap.

Lula leaned closer and placed her hand over Loveday's hands to still her fretting with the handkerchief. "You said your brother destroyed your life. How?" she asked in a whisper. "I must know."

Loveday still did not look up. "He killed him." It was a whisper. "That is why you must leave Graestone at once."

Lula sat back. "Who killed whom?"

Loveday raised her eyes from her lap. "War. War killed my second husband. He killed Lord Bland."

Lula could not breathe. "Why?" she said in a rush of breath. "How?"

"War said that Bland fell from the battlements. I believe War pushed him, or threw him, for tis a certainty that War could have picked Bland up and thrown him over the battlements. Bland was of a short and delicate stature. War hated Bland, he wanted him gone. I assume they argued and things got out of hand."

Lula tried to stay calm, yet her whole body was vibrating with dread. "Why would War hate your husband so much that he would want him gone and what did they argue over that it would result in War pushing him over the battlements?"

Loveday looked anywhere but at Lula. "Bland had a temper," she said quietly as she fidgeted with the handkerchief again.

"I see." Lula's voice was sympathetic. She continued to watch Loveday's stricken expression. In a quiet voice she asked, "Did Lord Bland ever hurt you or the boys?"

Loveday did not answer. She stood up abruptly in a loud swish and rustle of her golden skirts. She walked across the room to stare pensively out of the window. "Jolyon saw it happen. He has not talked since though daily I try to get him to speak to me."

Lula stood up as well and faced Lady Loveday. "I cannot believe it of War." Her voice was a tight whisper. "Someone must have seen—"

Loveday whirled to face Lula. "No one else was there but War and Bland and my poor little Jolyon."

Lula shook her head adamantly. "It is quite clear that Jolyon loves his Uncle War. Surely Jolyon would be afraid of his uncle now, if indeed it were true that War," she struggled even saying the word, "...killed his stepfather?"

Loveday turned back to the window. "I cannot speak to that. Jolyon will not tell me anything. He will not speak at all," she said with her voice choked with tears.

Lula's full lips thinned. She walked determinedly toward Loveday. "You cannot speak to it because you pay no attention to your own sons." She spoke quietly but calmly, in a firm but gentle tone. "You spend your days crying in this room. Do you miss your husband so very much that you ignore your duties as a mother? Your duty to your youngest child who has suffered some sort of distress and now no longer speaks?" She knew she was being unkind but the words were out before she had thought that she had best not say them.

Loveday whirled around to face her with her mouth open in shock. She started to form words, but then stopped. She turned slowly back to the window. "I love my boys. They are everything to me. I have tried and tried to get Jolyon to tell me what happened, or just to speak to me! I long to hear his precious voice!"

"Did you love Lord Bland?" Lula demanded. "Did you love him so much that you have forgotten to love those who live? Have you simply told Jolyon you love him and miss his voice? Instead of demanding that he tell you what happened when he clearly does not want to remember!" She groaned inwardly. She had spoken without thinking first once again.

Loveday choked back a sob and went to sit back down at the dressing table. She pressed her hands to her face as she shook her head. "I have told Jolyon I love him, *over and over*! As for Bland, *no*." She put her fingers to her lips. "I am so ashamed. *No*," she said again in a whisper. "I, I disliked him. It has been an immense relief of a sort. He was cruel and a, a tyrant. He was always angry and, and yelling." Her voice had lowered to a whisper.

Lula frowned. "Then why do you miss him?" she demanded earnestly.

"I suppose that I do not. I am just, *I am afraid*. I do not know why! I suppose I do not know who I am anymore." Her shoulders fell as she swallowed tightly. "Two husbands," she said in a tight voice. "I have had *two* horrid husbands and I have three sons. My wonderful little Wildlings. The only good that came of any of it." Her lips lifted up into a soft smile when she spoke of her sons. Her expression changed as she looked back at Lula. "It changes you, Miss Darley." She wiped at a tear and continued, "War says I must marry again. He says he will find me a more suitable man than my last two husbands. Of course, he has had no luck." She glanced into the mirror and away again. "A penniless woman twice widowed with three children and a useless title. Or perhaps tis that my brother frightens them all away because they know he will kill them like he did Bland if he disapproves of how they may treat me or my sons."

Lula's fists clenched at her sides. "I do not believe that War killed Lord Bland. There is more to this, I am sure." *She would speak to War as soon as possible.* She took a deep breath and blew it out. "Though it sounds to me that you should be grateful that you have a brother that watches over you." She picked up the handkerchief from Loveday's dressing table and lightly dabbed at the tears on her face. "War did *not* kill Bland," she said as she continued to blot the tears that had run into the white paint on Loveday's face. "Cease that thinking this moment for I will not believe it nor have you saying such." She gentled her voice as she lifted Loveday's chin. "He is your brother and I am sure he loves you. I have seen the drawing he did of you and the boys in his study. That is not a man that would kill his beloved sister's husband."

Loveday fidgeted and took the handkerchief from Lula. "I do

not know how else Bland could have died. War insists that he did not throw Bland over the battlements, yet he says he is responsible. *What does that mean?*" She added quietly, "War visits me every day though I refuse to speak to him now. He has not told me what happened! I need to know! How can I pretend all is well? How can I help my Jolyon when I do not know what he saw to make him lose his voice?" She flapped her handkerchief in frustration. "My brother tries to encourage me to leave this room." She added with doubt in her voice, "He has that infuriating saying of his where one cannot argue with him. Even if I *was* speaking to him, there is no use." She crumpled the hanky in her hands. *"His word is truth."*

"But, you see? You must take heart in that. You *must* believe your brother. His word *is* truth after all. And give Jolyon time, his voice will return." Lula grinned determinedly. "Don't you see? You have another chance at love." She made a fist and raised it in the air. *"Seize it!"* She smiled at Lady Loveday's stunned face. "First, however, you will cease locking yourself away from the world. You will help Tuedy Tweedy with the ball. You will secure new clothing for your boys. It is cold out and they have not the proper clothing to keep them warm. You will care for your sons as a mother should," she said forcibly.

Lady Loveday sniffled. "Are you always so plainly spoken?" She sniffled again. "They do sleep in here with me," she said defensively. She pointed to the pile of blankets neatly folded beside the fireplace with three pillows atop them. "We sit in front of the fire and I read to them until they fall asleep. It is our own cozy nest, we say. I am teaching them math, and reading and writing and history, of course. They tell me of their progress in playing the pianoforte. My brother is teaching them to play." She looked down at her hands and fussed with the handkerchief held far too tightly there. She looked up suddenly. "We have dinner in here together as well, and our breakfast." She looked away and then back to Lula. "Though they tell me that lately they have been having dinner with you." She tilted her head as she studied

230

Lula. "They tell me a lot of what happens downstairs."

Lula could not help the blush she felt blooming on her cheeks. "War plays many instruments?"

Loveday nodded. "The violin is his favorite. He plays at night to soothe me and the boys to sleep, though lately his music has changed. It is not for me or the boys. It is very different, romantic I think." She studied Lula's blushing face.

Lula nervously looked down and picked some horsehair off of her sleeve. "The music he writes is indeed beautiful."

"Yes. It has been a very long time since he has written his own music. But lately, well, I believe he has been inspired by something. Or someone."

"Goodness," Lula whispered as she looked up from her sleeve. She could feel her cheeks turning pink.

Loveday smiled softly at her. "I do thank you for having my boys in the dining room for dinner. However, please do not think me so remiss. I will see to their clothing, though I fear I have burdened my brother enough with our needs. Bland used up what monies I had from my first marriage, and more. He pressed War to let us move back here to Graestone. He promised War that he would oversee the upkeep and repairs of the castle until War came home."

"Did he?" Lula asked. "Manage the upkeep and repairs to the castle for your brother?"

Loveday shook her head sadly. "I do not think he spent any money on the castle. It is only these last months since War returned that I have heard the sound of hammers and other repair work happening." She looked around her room nervously. "Bland is dead and he has left us with nothing. Even my own pin money and jointure is gone." She added in a whisper, "*Nothing.* I dare not tell War this. He has had such a burden on his shoulders and still has now that he is home, yet I think perhaps he knows." She dropped her hands to her lap and clutched at her skirts. "I, I just cannot seem to force myself to leave this room. I do not know what is wrong with me, really."

Lula took a deep breath and released it. "You are sad and unsure of your future." She walked forward and knelt down by Loveday. She placed a hand over Loveday's tense fingers. "All will be well."

"How can you be so sure?" Loveday sniffled.

"Because I was attacked in Hyde Park, you see. It left me scarred and terrified and with no memory of the night. When I came here, I blamed War because I remembered just enough to know that he was there in Hyde Park that fateful evening, but not why he was there. My memory, it has finally returned," she said softly. "War was there to rescue me." She took a breath and smiled reassuringly. "Jolyon's voice will return. I know this."

Loveday smiled tremulously.

Lula took another deep breath and leaned closer, squeezing Loveday's hand gently. Her voice was still caring but stronger. "I can tell you that sitting in here will not help. You must find your courage." Lula motioned to the dressing table as she stood up. "Wipe your tears. Fix your face. And no more plucking your brows!" She smiled to gentle that last order. "Then you must change into a dress that is not a ball gown and, please, come down to the great hall with me." She smiled as she nodded to Loveday's gown. She quietly clapped her hands together. "We have a ball to plan! Your Uncle Veyril is away and right now there is no one to do it save poor Tuedy Tweedy."

Loveday slowly stood up and looked down at herself. She clutched her golden skirts in each hand as she stared down at the satin fabric in her fingers. "Even if I could make myself leave my bedchamber, I cannot. I have nothing that fits." She dropped her skirt and wrapped her arms around her waist as if she had a bellyache. "Bland said as much. He said I must stay in my chambers until I looked more pleasing and presentable. He is the one who insisted I pluck my eyebrows. He said they were ugly. He also said that my face and figure was displeasing. Now, I suppose I am just too afraid to leave."

Lula's mouth dropped open. She collected herself however.

"Oh pish to anything that he thought. You are beautiful! As for being afraid? You should sing a merry ditty, as I do, when you feel afraid. It works a treat for me!" Lula strode over to the wardrobe and pulled it open. She looked through the many sumptuous gowns hanging there in every pastel color one could imagine. All were as elegant as the ball gown that Loveday was wearing, however most were outdated or overly wrought with large ruffles and flounces and laces, each with high, prim necklines and full sleeves that covered one's arms from shoulder to wrist.

Lula pulled out one gown after another and showed them each to Loveday who shook her head adamantly, pointing to her hips for one dress, or her breasts for another, or her stomach for others.

"Tis impolite to speak of it, I know, but I have had three rather large babies, Miss Darley," she said with resignation as she spread her hands wide and looked down at herself.

"You are beautiful, Lady Loveday, and your figure is most attractive! Never doubt that." Lula rifled through the gowns again. "These are all evening dresses. Have you no day dresses?"

Loveday shook her head. "Bland insisted I look my best at all times. He chose all of those." She shook her head. "If only I had known the cost. Twas such a waste of money."

Lula pursed her lips at that as she continued to look through the wardrobe. She made a triumphant noise as she pulled one last dress out and looked it up and down. It was in a soft, warm, woolen fabric of Turkey red with long, only semi-fitted sleeves and a full skirt. The bodice was neither too low, nor too high. It looked perfect and it was not an evening gown. "How about this one?"

Loveday frowned. "Tis very old. I cannot remember how long ago it has been since I have worn that," Loveday mused as she studied the gown. "Bland would not allow me to wear it. He said it showed an indecent amount of my bosom. I cannot leave this room in that."

"He is no longer here to tell you what you may or may not

wear," Lula said firmly and then bit her lip. "You could add a lace fichu to cover yourself if you feel it is immodest. Do you think you could walk with me out of this room, but only as far as *my* bedchamber for now? I am sure I have a fichu that you may borrow." She watched as Lady Loveday frowned in indecision. Lula delicately added, "We do not have to go any further than my chamber. Come with me. You must admit the red dress is better than wearing a golden ball gown just to walk down the hall to my bedchamber." She grinned with a questioning look at Lady Loveday.

CHAPTER NINETEEN

S EVERAL HOURS LATER after trying on most of the gowns to prove to Lula that they would not fit, Lula and Lady Loveday were walking arm in arm down the hallway. Or rather, Lula was pulling a nervous and reluctant Loveday along.

Loveday still wore the gold satin gown. The Turkey red woolen dress would only fit after a few adjustments to let out the waist slightly and the bosom and the hips quite a bit, and then several stitches of a needle and thread. They had determined the same for several others that would need similar alterations. Lula carried these gowns over her other arm, making sure to hold tightly to Loveday.

Loveday was walking slowly and nervously. Lula feared that War's sister would turn around at any moment and run back to her bedchamber in the tower. Before Lula had managed to get her to leave her chamber, Loveday had put on a fresh coating of the white cream, more bright red rouge on her cheeks and lips and a thin line of the charcoal paste onto her upper lashes, brows and eyelids.

Lula said nothing. She felt the cosmetics were a sort of mask for Lady Loveday to hide behind.

Lula decided to teach her the ditty she liked to sing as they walked down the hallway.

Loveday was starting to relax little by little as she repeated the words of the song along with Lula. *"With a chip chop, cherry chop, fol de rol riddle-rop."*

"Very good, Lady Loveday!" Lula said with happy pleasure as she hugged Loveday's arm with her own.

Loveday smiled tentatively. "Please, call me Loveday. If we are going to sing a sea ditty together without any proper ladylike decorum, why bother with appellations that are only meaningful to the *ton*?"

Lula grinned at her. "And since we are walking down empty hallways with peeling paint and paper?"

Loveday awkwardly laughed. "Most certainly. Still, I would be pleased for you to call me simply Loveday, if you will?" When Lula nodded with a big smile, the lady who had been weeping daily actually laughed. And then she began trying to sing the chorus again, on her own.

Lula led her to her own bedchamber and while Loveday walked around her room, she found a fichu amongst her things.

They spent hours there working on the red dress and the other dresses as well. Loveday was fascinated by Lula's breeches that she had on under her woolen dress. Lula showed Loveday her jonquil yellow boots and her Pomona green cloak and gloves and her pink-red coquelicot shawl.

Lula had dinner with Loveday and the boys in Loveday's bedchamber that evening. The next day, Lula met Loveday at her chamber and walked her back to her own bedchamber where they continued sewing the alterations on the gowns for the rest of the day.

"Miss Darley? Miss Darley!" came a highly excited voice outside the door.

Lula hurried to open the door and found Tuedy there, looking positively flustered. He looked over Lula's shoulder and stared at Loveday in astonishment until Lula cleared her voice.

"Eh? Oh! You must come at once, at once, eh?" he declared with a flourish of his hands in the air. He did not wait for her but turned around and, with his long legs, he took hurried short steps back the way he had come.

Lula looked over at Loveday who had ducked out of sight. She was staring at Lula with a wide-eyed, stricken look.

"We must go see what all the commotion is about," Lula said. "Come along!"

Loveday shook her head "no" in adamant nervousness. "I simply cannot make myself. Even if I could, I do not wish to see nor talk to my brother." Her voice was filled with distress.

Lula let out a silent breath. "Very well. But I must go see what has gotten Tuedy into such a tizzy. You may wait here and continue to work on the dresses if you wish. I can walk you back to your chamber when I return."

With those words, Lula hurried out of the room to catch up to Tuedy Tweedy.

He was already down the stairs and standing in the middle of the great hall by the time she caught up with him. As she came down the curving staircase, her steps slowed, and then slowed further as she looked around.

The great hall was *filled* with men and boys. There were also several women and girls from the village. All were diligently working at a task. The women were intermixed with the men, chatting happily away with no care for any of the men's injuries. There was a general buzz of happy chatter as everyone worked to bring the great hall back to what it once was.

There were ladders set up everywhere it seemed, and buckets and rags were being carried by boys back and forth at the instruction of several older men who sounded like they were once commanding officers of some rank in the military.

But what had caught Lula's attention was the hall itself. It was bright. She whirled around to look at the huge window on the top landing where the two curved stairs met on a balcony. She had hurried right past it. The shutters were open! It was clean, with bright, late afternoon sunlight pouring in through the glass. She looked back at the great hall. The other windows' shutters were also open. And there were indeed sconces all down the long length of the hall, just as she had thought there must be. Now, however, each held multiple lit candles that gave off a warm, illuminating light enhanced and reflected by the decorative, newly washed mirrored glass behind each of them.

She turned slowly as she took in the great hall that had been so enshrouded in darkness since she had arrived that she had not been able to clearly see what it looked like.

The walls were a pleasant green color while below the chair rail there was elaborate paneled oak wainscot being freshly waxed by several men and women to a warm glow.

All down the length of those walls were portrait after portrait after portrait of various barons and baronesses of the de Walton family through the centuries. Men were busily dusting portraits of men in ruffs and women in elegant, bejeweled French hoods. There were also men wearing chest plates sitting upon valiant war horses who had proudly arched necks, looking ready to charge into battle or triumphant from their last battle.

Here and there placed between some of those portraits were fifteenth and sixteenth century swords arranged in a circle with their points all meeting in the center. There were also old shields and lances, also arranged in an artful manner, even old muskets.

Freshly polished suits of armor from various centuries were still being cleaned and sheets had been pulled away, revealing Chippendale side tables and chairs along the walls. Huge porcelain vases of blue and white Chinoiserie and large trans-ferware bowls sat empty awaiting fresh bouquets of flowers and displays of fruits.

Two men on a ladder were cleaning a massively wide and tall mirror with an elaborate, gilded baroque frame that hung above a long, narrow Chippendale table across from the hearth. Two young women stood below them, handing them up freshly rinsed cloths from buckets on the floor.

Many others were busily sweeping and scrubbing the floors.

She spotted Todrick amongst them. He was directing some men to unroll a large Persian rug that had been rolled up against a wall. A large woman from the village stood next to him, speaking away to him and calling out her own directions to the men much to Todrick's annoyance. As the rug was unrolled, it revealed rich colors of greens and golds. It was being unrolled upon a large swath of newly cleaned floor.

The scrubbed floor revealed large squares of a lovely dark green and cream marble.

Todrick directed the men to adjust the placement of the rug in front of the massive hearth while the woman next to him was pointing and correcting the placement in a different way. Todrick and the woman began arguing.

Lula smiled and looked away from them to the mantel and hearth itself.

The mantel was beginning to show the same honey waxed shine as the wainscot along the walls. The paneled wainscot surrounding the hearth continued all the way up to the high ceiling. It was impressive and marked a focal point of the huge hall. Six men were working on cleaning the mantel of years and years of soot.

Lula stilled and glanced at Tuedy with a huge smile and then she continued to look all around the hall again. "I had no idea this hall was so lovely," she said with awe in her voice. She turned fully to beam at him. "You have accomplished so much in so little time!"

Tuedy was vibrating with eagerness. "I had no idea it would look like this either. We left everything as it was when we arrived, eh? It is good to see what was under all that dust and dirt and those dust covers when we finally had more light!" He clasped his hands together as he fidgeted from foot to foot. "With an army of men putting all their efforts into this hall, we did indeed accomplish even more than I anticipated, though we are far from finished!" He pointed to one of the men coming their way. "This is Mr. Smyth. He coordinated the men cleaning the suits of armor."

"Ah, yes," Lula said. "And how is your foot, Mr. Smyth?"

"Oh, much improved, Miss Darley, thanks to you!"

Tuedy pointed to another man. "And there is Mr. Penterbirthy. He is leading the group wiping down the walls and portraits." Tuedy pointed out several more men, telling her what tasks they were each responsible for.

Each time Tuedy announced a name, Lula called to them, remembering what injury they had sustained and asking after them.

Each man stopped and came forward to thank her for whatever ointment or poultice she had given them until Lula was surrounded by smiling men and boys.

She was not nervous, nor afraid, nor panicky.

She knew these men.

She had given many of them ointments and poultices and asked after their injuries when she came upon them in the castle and answered any of their questions about how to care for their wounds. She had tried to help them.

Lula walked over to each man and shook his hand and thanked him, much to their surprise. She then turned to all of the men and boys as well as the village women who had been working so hard. "I commend you all and I thank you *so very much!*" Lula said loudly with a happy smile on her face.

An older man who had severely burned his leg from a cannon blast hobbled forward. "We were pleased to do this, Miss Darley, for all you have done for us."

The heavy woman who had been arguing with Todrick spoke up. "We are happy to be a help in bringing dear Graestone Castle back to what it was. Tis a big part of the village and the county. You have no idea what this means to us." She smiled and nodded.

Another woman also spoke up. "I knew things would change when you walked into my father's inn and said you were coming up here to the castle. I knew you would make a difference."

Poppy and Bertie stood there at the front of all the men, smiling and nodding. "You have, Miss Darley. You have made a difference to the castle and all our lives. Twas happy we were to do this for you."

Lula's breath caught as tears formed in her eyes.

A murmur of *"For you"* ran through the crowd of men standing before her.

Lula looked around at the men. She had learned all of their names and she knew of their injuries.

"You are the ones that have brought this castle back to life with *your* efforts," she said through her tears. "It is your home." She smiled through her tears. "Now then, I am sure that Tuedy will be pleased to give you all a grand supper this evening for today's hard work!"

She looked over at Tuedy who nodded his head and smiled back at her. Her eyes went back to the people in the hall whose attention she had. "Do not forget, tomorrow there shall be more work to do in the ballroom, but I am quite confident that you are all up to it! Am I correct?"

Someone loudly called out, "Yes!" Another let out a cheer and this was quickly joined by several of the others.

The chorus of cheers spread to each man and woman and a "hear! hear!" rose up into the great hall.

Lula laughed and clapped her hands as she smiled at the men and women gathered there. "Thank you," she called out. "Thank you so very much!"

The men clapped each other on the backs and the woman beamed as they all went back to work with renewed vigor.

Tuedy leaned toward her with bubbling excitement. "That was unexpected and well done, Miss Darley! The men have developed a great affection for you, eh? And it has spread to the village! But that is not all they accomplished in their work today!" He pointed up as he watched her face in anticipation. "We started first, hours ago, *with that."*

Lula turned and looked up to the ceiling. Her mouth dropped open.

She was staring at the massive crystal chandelier. It was now cleaned and twinkling with hundreds and hundreds of lit candles.

However, the chandelier was not made up of all clear crystals. This chandelier was of Murano glass. It had colored flowers and petals of greens and blues and yellow and pink interwoven along the graceful, curving glass arms.

It was exquisite.

"Goodness," Lula whispered as she stared up at the chandelier that had been so completely dust-covered that they had all considered it a monstrosity. "'Tis the most beautiful chandelier I believe I have ever seen!"

The spicy scent of sandalwood and frankincense came to her as someone spoke from behind them. "Is that what all the commotion I just heard was about? My grandfather commissioned that chandelier for an exorbitant cost. It must have wreaked havoc on the castle's funds. A flagrant show of his wealth as it were. He thought it may help to attract him a new wife after his first wife died."

Lula turned and smiled up at War. "And did it?"

War lips turned up into a seductive, secretive grin as he stared down into her face. His gaze lingered on her lips. "My grandmother fell in love first with the chandelier, and my grandfather second," he said in a deep rumble as his eyes became slumberous with desire.

Lula's heart fluttered within her breasts. She could guess what War was thinking for she could not help but to think the same thing when he was near her.

The kiss they had shared in his study.

She could still feel his lips on hers. She could feel the rough silk of his tongue tangling with hers, still hear the low groans of desire that had rumbled through his chest and into her breasts. The heady taste of him caused lightning to sizzle through her again, at this very moment, just looking into his eyes.

They had kissed deeply, softly, playfully, demandingly until, finally, he had reluctantly pulled his mouth from hers. He had declared that they must stop or he would be carrying her over to the Chesterfield sofa where he would indeed be *touching* her.

Lula stared up at him, intoxicated by the sensual look in his eyes and on his lips. "I must wonder at such a woman that would fall in love with the lord of the castle because of a chandelier," Lula said softly.

War's breath caught as hope bloomed hesitantly within him. He took one step closer as his eyes caressed her face. He whispered hoarsely, "I would ask then, what would it take, Miss Darley, for a woman to fall in love with the lord of the castle?"

Lula was caught by the hunger and need in his eyes, but there was also a hint of tension there. Her breath trembled from her lips. His wide shoulders and broad chest seemed to engulf her, making her feel safe, protected. Heat raced through her, for he had used that deep, velvet voice of his that made her heart race and her mind go numb until she felt, heard and saw nothing but him.

War's cheeks pinkened and his shoulders stiffened when she did not answer. He added in a gruff whisper, "What would it take when that lord is a man that cannot love?"

Lula shook her head slowly, seeing the hidden longing within his tense stance. This man could love, of a certainty. It was evident everywhere she looked in this castle. The men and boys that he gave hope to. The horses he saved. His nephews, who adored him. *Cannot love? No*, she thought. *He was afraid to love, afraid his love would not be returned.*

"I do not believe that your word is truth, not on this of which you speak. Love is evident everywhere in this castle." Her lips lifted up into a soft smile. "I do not need a chandelier to fall in love with—" she whispered just as the doors to the great hall were pushed open.

"We are here!" announced Uncle Veyril.

"Och, but I need a wee sip of some warm whisky. My bum is numb and I am fairly puggled out!"

Lula whirled around. "Aunt Eggy?" She stared at her great-aunt with astonishment. She watched as the tiny, little, old, Scottish woman pulled off her bonnet as she walked into the great hall as calmly as she pleased. Her thin white hair was sticking up in short, wispy strands all around the tiny little bun that was sliding away from the center of her balding, pink head.

Lula smiled with delight and hurried to her. She wrapped her tiny, great-aunt in her arms. The dear old woman felt like a delicate and fragile bony bird. Lula knew, however, that her great-aunt was anything but fragile or delicate.

Lula stepped back and studied her great-aunt with an arched eyebrow and a wry grin. "Are you feeling better, Aunt Eggy?"

Veyril laughed heartily. "She is fine! Fine!"

Aunt Eggy scowled at the short, white-haired man next to her as she rapped his arm with her bonnet. "Dinnae be a wee clipe, Veyril." She turned back to Lula with a forced smile. She clutched her chest as she let out a small cough. Her voice suddenly turned weak. "Yer poor mither was vera worried aboot me for a while, but I am much better now, lass." She turned to Veyril with a scowl and said firmly in a strong voice, "Isnae that correct, Veyril?"

Veyril's mouth dropped open. "Oh, yes, my, my! She is well now! Near death she was—"

Aunt Eggy rapped him with her bonnet again as she kept a smile fixed on her face. "I was never near death, Veyril. Dinnae overdo it now." She turned back to Lula, "It was just a bout of the sniffles. I mean, er, a small cough. I am quite well, however. Highlander strong ye know."

Lula grinned. "I am quite sure you are *very* well, Aunt Eggy." She watched Veyril de Walton walk hastily away to speak to Todrick. She heard him ask for some men to be sent out to bring their bags in from the carriage. Lula frowned. "Aunt Eggy, you came here in a *carriage*? I thought you vowed you would never ride in a carriage?"

Aunt Eggy waved her hand negligently in the air. "I wasnae going tae. Ye know I willnae sit behind a horse's arse in a wooden box. Horses are meant tae be ridden! These glaikit contraptions ye ride inside these days are deadly." She patted her tiny bun and then with a dignified shove, she pushed it from where it had slid to rest on the top of her ear back to the center of her head. "However, my dear friend, the Supreme Imperial Majesty Bibi Habibeh, gifted me with one of her water pipes, those lovely vases with pipes that she calls an argila."

Lula's lips dropped open. "Aunt Eggy, are you telling me you smoked some hashish before you traveled?"

"Before and during," Aunt Eggy declared. "Then I had a lovely nap. It made the journey tolerable." She raised her chin, much like Supreme Imperial Majesty Bibi Habibeh had a habit of doing. "I am nae blootered if that is what ye are implying."

Lula was about to question how often her great-aunt made use of the argila when another thought struck her. "How on earth did you make it to Graestone with all the snow? The roads are impassable."

Aunt Eggy tilted her head and frowned. "Impassable? No. They were guid and clear of snow. Wet and muddy in places but the horses didnae have any problems. Mr. Smith returned last week and reported the same."

Lula's mouth fell open. *"Last week?"* She put her hands on her hips and turned slowly to look at War who had walked forward to stand beside her. "The roads are not impassable, Baron. What do you make of that?"

War's lips tightened. He looked at Aunt Eggy and bowed his head. "I am glad to find that you are feeling better, Lady Ross." He raised his head and stared down at the tiny lady with one of his brows arched in warning to her. It was clear that Aunt Eggy knew not what he was warning her about.

"The *roads are fine*, War," Lula repeated firmly, but when War only stared at her great-aunt, she turned her scowl back to her Aunt Eggy.

Aunt Eggy became confused and curious as she looked from her great-niece to the big baron standing there looking stubbornly silent, *and,* she was pleased to see, very guilty over something. *How very interesting,* Aunt Eggy thought with delight. *The baron* had obviously told her great-niece the roads were impassable. She hastily added, "What was I saying? Och, the snow *was* vera deep, aye, vera deep as we got *closer* tae the castle! I thought we were going tae have tae stay in the inn, but alas, we made it." She let out a breath when she noticed the slight release of tension that had been held in the baron's shoulders.

War's face turned red as he looked from Lula, who was staring at him with her brows furrowed and her arms across her breasts, to her Aunt Eggy. He cleared his throat. "I would not risk Miss Darley on the journey, Lady Ross. We received a great deal of snow *here* as you saw when you arrived. As her great-aunt I am sure you can appreciate that it would have been far too dangerous to travel." His cheeks flushed darker as he cleared his throat again.

Aunt Eggy reached up and patted War's broad chest. She gave a little sigh as her eyes roved over the expanse of him. "Of course ye are correct and tis guid tae see ye, Baron. Ye look even more like a warrior of auld standing here in this castle, my large friend. When I first met ye at the Lansdowne ball I thought ye looked oot of place. A warrior ye looked. Here in this auld castle is where ye belong." She patted his chest again and let out another little sigh as she stared at his wide shoulders. She gave him one last pat and clapped her hands once. "Now then, tis glad I am tae know that ye took such guid care of Lula and would nae risk bringing her home in the terrible, terrible snow here at Graestone. Tis guid she stayed here in yer care, of course."

Aunt Eggy gave War a quick wink and turned back to Lula who was still frowning doubtfully at her. Aunt Eggy gave her a pleasant smile.

"Ye dinnae seem tae be singing, or worse fainting at the sight of this big warrior anymore, lassie," Aunt Eggy said with great curiosity.

Lula's frown fell from her lips as she turned to look up at War. "I have remembered that it was War who rescued me from the assassins, Aunt Eggy. Particularly since the snow was so deep that it made the roads impassable and therefore I could *not* leave, which gave me time to help his horses, even though I am naught but a girl with a piece of paper." She crossed her arms over her breasts again as she stared cheekily up at him. "A piece of paper that deems me competent to practice the veterinary arts by the Odiham Agricultural Society and the Veterinary College of Lyons France."

War groaned. "Lula—" He started to say more but was interrupted by Aunt Eggy patting his chest again.

"Och, she is vera competent as *I am sure ye have had time* tae see, but," Aunt Eggy stared speculatively back and forth from the big baron to her great-niece. She made a satisfied humming sound as she patted her top knot again. "*Lula* and *War,* is it? Nae Baron de Walton or Miss Lula? Ye two seem tae have gotten quite familiar," Aunt Eggy crowed as she tilted her head up to study the big baron's bemused expression and then she looked over at her great-niece again. Lula was blushing. *So he didn't want to let Lula leave and he hadn't accepted her skills as an animal doctor? And Lula wasn't fainting?* Aunt Eggy stifled her grin. "Perhaps I left ye two alone tae long?" Aunt Eggy turned back to War with an expectant look on her face.

War cleared his throat loudly as his cheeks went pink once more. His throat clearing turned to another groan when Ten Adair walked up to them.

"Oh, they have been alone, quite right you are!" Ten's voice was jovial. He walked past War and gave his big friend a sly wink as he ignored War's growl of warning and went straight to Aunt Eggy. "As I live and breathe! Who is this beautiful creature?" In a gallant gesture, he took her hand and bowed his head to the tiny woman and kissed the back of her gloved fingers. "Lady Egidia Ross! Last time I saw you, your hair was an unusual shade of rather bright pink." He smiled charmingly at her. "I do so hope you are feeling better. I heard that you were unwell and could not accompany your great-niece here to Graestone."

Aunt Eggy's cheeks turned pink as she fluttered her eyelashes and swatted at the handsome man bowing over her hand. "Dinnae haver so, young Ten, I have known ye since ye were a wee lad. Ye are still a gallus cheeky mon, arnae ye? And the Earl of Fairfax now, I hear?"

Ten released her thin, bony hand. "Yes, I am an earl, though I cannot get used to it."

Aunt Eggy laid her hand over his where he still held her other hand. "Yer father was a guid mon, the best of mon, in fact. I was sorry tae hear of his passing." She patted his hand. "Ye will do right by the title, I am sure."

Ten bowed his head again over her hand. He was unaccustomedly wordless. His throat had tightened at the mention of doing right by his father's title.

"And yer sisters? Will they be coming to the ball?" Aunt Eggy asked with eager relish.

Ten gave her a wry grin and let go of her hand. "Tis like herding wild cats with them, so who knows. But they did say they were planning to come."

Aunt Eggy bounced up on her toes with excitement. "Vera guid, vera guid that is!"

Lula narrowed her eyes on her great-aunt. "Aunt Eggy, I know that look. What are you up to?"

Aunt Eggy shoved her thin bun of hair back to the center of her head and looked away from Lula toward the front doors expectantly. "Why would ye think I am up tae some mischief, lassie? Tis just refreshing tae have some new, young faces at Veyril's ball."

CHAPTER TWENTY

"LULA! LULA! TARE an' hounds and thunder an' turf but it is good to see you, Sister! I hope you do not mind, I have brought along a family friend!"

Birdie hurried into the great hall pulling along a tall, blond man in a bright red officer's uniform.

"Birdie!" Lula exclaimed. "Is that *Freddie* Rockingham?"

"Yes, I brought the duke with me! Isn't it exciting! We shall have such a merry ball and Freddie has promised to dance every dance even if the soles of his best boots are thin and wearing away and his feet are bloody and painful from all the ladies dancing on his poor, poor toes!"

"Birdie," Lula groaned as she held up a hand to stop her little sister. She knew Birdie delighted in her dramatic rants.

"Freddie's words, not mine, truly!" Birdie sang out happily with her bright blue eyes flashing gaily. She pulled off her pale blue velvet bonnet to reveal her raven hair. She twirled around in her matching pale blue gown and perfectly fitted chintz jacket all in cream with blue swirling vines and a darker blue satin brocade down the front as she looked wide-eyed all around the great hall. "Tis a true castle you have here, Baron de Walton!" she said with excitement as she stopped and pulled off her blue gloves while continuing to stare all around. "Do you have any ghosts? I do believe those suits of armor could come to life at any moment to protect the castle from attack! *Oh!* Look at all those swords—I expect some still have blood on them from ancient battles! I can just imagine they chopped many a limb or a head quite off! And there are battle axes and shields as well! May I touch them?"

Lula shook her head quickly. "No, you may *not touch them,* Birdie!" Lula noted that the young men in the hall had all stopped what they were doing to stare at her pretty little sister with her midnight hair and vivid blue eyes and always smiling lips. She looked over at War to see if he, too, was as enraptured with her sister as other men always seemed to be.

He was not staring at Birdie, his eyes were on her. He looked hungry.

"War," she whispered as she blushed and lowered her eyes.

He came closer to her side and bent his head until his lips just barely grazed her ear. "I am patiently awaiting the day that I may touch *you,* my captivating Lula."

Lula's eye's rose to his. She swallowed as her breath trembled from her lips. A strand of her curly hair had been caught in War's beard near his lips. She pulled it free, letting her fingers graze his sensuous lips. She noted that his nostrils flared at her touch. She felt a rush of pleasure shoot through her body and marveled at the effect she could elicit from him with just her simple touch. "Admit it. You did not *want* me to leave," she said in an attempt to be teasing, but her breath trembled from between her lips as she stared up into his eyes.

"Baron de Walton, I do hope it is not an inconvenience that I have accompanied Lady Ross and Miss Birdie?" Freddie Rockingham's voice interrupted them.

War pulled his eyes from Lula's and looked over at the dashing blond man that Birdie had pulled forward into their circle. She had linked her arm through his and was smiling cheekily up at him. Frederick Rockingham, the new Duke of Trenton looked very uncomfortable as he stared down at Birdie's arm, firmly linked through his with her fingers clutching the red fabric of his uniform.

"Why *did* you come, Rockingham?" War asked with thinly veiled hostility as he studied the man in the scarlet coat of an officer.

Lula looked sharply up at him. "War!" she whispered hastily. "He is a duke. You must call him *Your Grace*."

War kept his eyes on the young duke and smiled a wolf's smile as he answered Lula. "When he wears the red coat he has no social rank. Though I am quite sure that his father or one of his *older* brothers purchased his Commission, *before they died*," he added in a deadly quiet voice. "Rockingham did not earn it before fortuitously inheriting the title of duke." He paused, watching Rockingham's reaction with sharp eyes. It was clear that he was correct when the man shifted on his feet. War's lips thinned. "Last I saw of you, Rockingham, you were leaving the battlefield in that scarlet coat you wear. *Without* your men."

War watched as Freddie Rockingham's eyes narrowed and he straightened his shoulders and raised his chin, no longer looking like a fresh, inexperienced member of the aristocracy.

"I was on an errand for the king at the time," Freddie stated firmly. "It is because of my king that I still wear the red coat. He bids me stay in the military, though I am now a duke."

War grunted at the change in the man's countenance. "A spy are you?" He looked him up and down, noting that this man with the artfully pomaded blond hair could appear harmless one moment, and then have the ability to look masculine and soldierly in the next moment. This man in the red coat staring back at him just now looked rather like a hardened man of great experience. War thought he would reserve his judgment, however. "Of a certainty, I would have said that you had not the nerve, Rockingham. Nor should you be giving that bit of knowledge away."

The two men stared at one another. Neither showed any sign of emotion on their hard faces.

"How *did* your father and your older brothers die, Rockingham?" War asked in a silky, almost threatening voice.

Freddie's expression changed then. His face went white and then taut with strain. "How dare you?" he hissed.

"Oh I dare, *Your Grace*, I dare," War growled.

War turned away before Freddie could respond. "Tweedys!" he bellowed into the hall. When Todrick looked at him, he jerked his head toward their guests. "Please have some of my men show our guests to their chambers and bring along their trunks. And find *His Grace* a room befitting his title and rank, will you?"

"War," Lula hissed in warning. "Where are you putting him?" She felt his big hand lightly touch hers in reassurance and then it moved away.

War did not answer her beyond the quick touch of his hand on hers. He had gone still for he was staring up to the top of the stairs.

Lula glanced in that direction and made a happy sound as she moved forward to stand at the bottom of the stairs.

Loveday was standing at the top of the stairs in her golden gown with all her white paint covering her face and the rouge on her cheeks and lips. She was staring down at them nervously.

"Lady Loveday!" Lula said in a pleasant and calm voice. "Won't you come down and meet my younger sister, Birdie, and Aunt Eggy? I was just telling you about them today, if you recall? How lovely that they are here now to meet you!"

She felt War come to stand at her side. He was silent a moment as he stared up at his sister. "Loveday?" He paused, unsure what to say, so surprised was he to see his sister out of her room. He took a breath. "Please, do come meet Lady Ross and Miss Birdie Darley. And the Duke of Trenton as well," he added begrudgingly. He leaned slightly toward Lula. "I am not sure how you did it, but I think you had something to do with my sister's appearance outside of her bedchamber today, much like the miracle you have wrought to my men and here in the great hall."

Lula smiled up at him. "Your sister and I had a lovely visit." She looked back up the stairs to Loveday as she whispered to him, "She told me you are responsible for her husband's death.

But, of course, I know she is wrong."

War turned and looked down at her. His face was tight. His mouth was firm and scowling. He looked away from her to stare back up at his sister. "She is not wrong."

Lula gasped softly as she whirled to face him. "You killed him?" she whispered in astonishment. "Oh, I cannot and *most certainly* will not believe that of you," she scoffed.

War shook his head once as he glanced at her and then back to his sister who was slowly descending the stairs. "I am responsible for his death, yes. There can be no doubt of that. Trust me not to question the matter further."

Lula stepped back from him, her face set stubbornly. "I am quite sure that I have nothing *but* doubt in what you say. I do not believe your word is truth on this. Until you trust *me* enough to give me the truth, I have nothing more to say."

War could see the determination, even anger on her face.

He leaned toward her, "Lula, you must—"

"Must what? Believe you are a murderer?" she demanded before he could finish his sentence.

He looked down at her with starkness in his eyes. "Yes."

Just then, Loveday took the final step down from the stairs. Lula gave War one last look and hurried over to Loveday. She took her arm and led her over to Aunt Eggy and her younger sister and Freddie Rockingham.

War could only stare after them. His sister had turned her face away from him, still refusing to speak to him.

He clenched his fists and turned around. He found himself staring at the great hall, all of it. *How had this one woman accomplished in such a short time what he had not been able to face since he had returned home?* And his men had cheered at her pretty speech thanking them. He had heard it all. His chest had filled with pride, hearing their cheers.

This was his home. For the first time in a very long time, it looked just how he remembered it—in the good times. He had been gone for so long. Too long.

His gaze went over to Lula and his sister, Loveday. Both had turned their backs to him.

Suddenly, his home felt as empty as the day he had left it. All those many years ago when he was left to himself after his father had walked into the lake unable to cope with the fact that he had finally gambled away the last of Graestone's funds. His mother had gone with him, or rather, he preferred to think she died trying to save his father, though he knew, deep down, it was not true. His mother had loved his father desperately and could not, would not, live without him.

The castle had already been sinking into ruin and desperate disrepair long before their deaths. Most of the staff had been let go, also long before by his father's orders. The place had gone untended for far too long.

Loveday had been married off to her first husband before their parents' deaths and Uncle Veyril was out somewhere in the world, looking for a place where his health would improve and abdicating all of the responsibility of Graestone to his father.

War had been left alone. His parents dead, his uncle gone. His sister married and gone as well.

The house had seemed so empty then. Devoid of love.

It had been an easy choice to simply flee the pain of it all. He joined the military and, in a short time, was approached to work for the crown in other, secret ways. He had moved like a ghost, unseen on the battlefields and seas first between England and France and then in other countries, other battles. He had made more money than Croesus in doing so. First for William Henry Cavendish-Bentinck, the third Duke of Portland when he was Prime Minister. Warwick de Walton was already a legend by the time Spencer Perceval became Prime Minister in 1809. He, like Cavendish-Bentinck, had also paid War well to risk his life for the information that was needed for success on the battlefields.

It was a well-kept secret that both of these prime ministers had also bid him to keep safe certain second sons of the aristocracy that had donned the red coat. His duty had been to guide them, to train them, and ultimately to make sure they returned to their fathers' estates—alive. War did not separate the safety or training of his men from those that were aristocratic or those that were poor farm boys. He wanted them all to return alive and preferably in one piece.

Two of those young men moved across the great hall chatting amicably as they shared the weight of the ladder they carried. One was a young man that had been raised on an estate with every luxury possible. He walked with a limp now as he carried the ladder with one arm. Where the other arm should have been, the sleeve hung empty. The other young man was an orphan. He came from nowhere and no one. Where his right leg should have been was a wooden post. Still, he shouldered the burden of the ladder as he moved in awkward, stilted steps, talking away to his companion.

War's jaw tightened as his eyes fell away from the young men to the floor at his feet. He had brought them home alive, but not always in one piece, he thought with aching, painful guilt.

He had not deserved the prime ministers' faith in his abilities. It had cost too many men their lives or limbs. The evidence was all around him in the men and boys here at Graestone.

His eyes lifted to gaze at Lula's stiff back. He thought that she had been about to tell him that she loved him when they were discussing the chandelier in the great hall. How foolish of him to hope such a thing could happen to him.

He did not deserve her love.

She stubbornly believed he could not be a murderer.

He did not deserve her loyalty.

War knew, *knew* with every beat of his heart, that he would have indeed killed Bland for what he had tried to do.

War's guilt was not in *killing* his sister's husband, but rather, for not trying to *save* him.

Instead, he had gladly watched him die.

CHAPTER TWENTY-ONE

"**W**HAT IS IT, dearling?" Aunt Eggy leaned away from the grand dining table toward Lula and peered into her face.

Lula shook her head, poking her spoon into the gooseberry fool in the lovely little glass bowl set in front of her. The pudding was a delicious dessert that Tuedy had made but she found she could not eat even one spoonful of it. She put her spoon down and folded her hands in her lap on top of her skirts. She had changed out of her breeches and into a proper gown for dinner. A green gown with little pom poms around the tips of the sleeves and the hem. They were a perky bright daffodil color and she thought them a lovely touch.

Aunt Eggy decided to wait for Lula to be ready to talk about whatever it was that she seemed so quiet about. She settled her bottom further on the two cushions that gave her a boost up on her chair as she looked down the long, candlelit dining room table to study the other guests as she spooned the delicious pudding into her mouth.

Aunt Eggy's eyes went to Birdie who was chattering away with Freddie Rockingham about the latest sale of Aldbey Park's Thoroughbreds at Tattersalls. Freddie appeared uninterested but resigned to her company. He was nodding at the right moments in the conversation without looking at pretty Birdie, sitting next to him and talking away.

Aunt Eggy glanced to the baron's sister. She stared at her as she took another spoonful of the gooseberry fool. She tilted her head and studied Lady Loveday's face with her heavily applied cosmetics. The baron's sister was watching Birdie silently but listening to her speak to Freddie in fascination. The widow seemed nervous, awkward. Uncomfortable. Aunt Eggy made a humming sound as she savored another bite of the sweet pudding while watching Lady Loveday with great interest.

She pulled her gaze from the sad widow and next stared at the handsome and very large Baron Warwick de Walton who was sitting at the head of the table. He was speaking with his Uncle Veyril who sat on his right and Ten Adair on his left who was simply wickedly dashing and had a dent in his chin. The baron was discussing a man name Cloudsley Shovell that he had ordered gone from Graestone.

"Are you done studying everyone, Aunt Eggy? I thought the cushions would give you a better view of the table so you could do just that very thing," came Lula's soft voice beside her.

Aunt Eggy turned back to Lula and grinned. "Och, I thank ye for providing the cushions lass, ye are so vera thoughtful, as always." She noted where Lula's gaze kept going. "Dinnae ye usually sit next tae him for supper?" She had also seen that the baron's gaze went to Lula whenever he thought she was not looking at him.

Lula hastily pulled her eyes away from War. She frowned and looked back down at her pudding. "There is no 'usually' about it, Aunt Eggy. This is the first time I have *not* eaten in this dining room *alone*, well, save for the last few days when the little wildlings ate with me. They are the baron's nephews and Lady Loveday's children, you see. The baron never once took a meal with me."

Aunt Eggy pursed her lips at that. She scraped every bit of the last of the pudding from her bowl with her spoon as she thought about what her great-niece had just said. She did not like to think that Lula had eaten alone in this big dining room for the length of time she had been here. She reached over and stuck her spoon in Lula's pudding and scooped up some of the gooseberry fool as she thought a moment. "I had a niggling suspicion that ye and the big baron were smitten. Are ye going tae tell me what has changed?" She put the spoonful into her mouth and closed her eyes, humming with satisfaction. "I think I may be keeping that man named Tuedy Tweedy that made this delicious pudding," she mumbled over the mouthful. "I dinnae know that English food could be this guid. Mr. Drunkbird and Mrs. Plotkin need tae take some examples from this Tuedy Tweedy."

Lula looked at her great-aunt then. A smile lifted her lips. She pushed her pudding toward her great-aunt. "Take mine." She shook her head. "You mean you want to hire him, Aunt Eggy, or secure him a position at Aldbey Park. You cannot just announce that you are *keeping* someone, Aunt Eggy, and the Aldbey Park butler is Mr. *Druckbert*, not Drunkbird, and well you know it."

"Och, he is of course nae a drunken bird and the farthest thing from it because he is a pompous, stuffed shirt of an English butler. But I do enjoy teasing him, just as he likes to rile and insult my Scottish self. However, as for Tuedy Tweedy. I *can* keep him if he agrees and it's time ye know that people do choose tae keep someone. Tis an auld Scottish tradition. Yer mither chose tae keep Lord Alexander Hawke. Julia chose to keep Pasha, or he chose tae keep her, I dinnae remember," she said over another mouthful. "I suspected ye had chosen tae keep that big warrior of yers. Ye no longer faint at the sight of him. Instead, ye sigh and yer eyes turn funny."

Lula stared down at her tiny great-aunt sitting beside her at the dining room table. "My eyes turn funny?"

"Aye," Aunt Eggy said with her mouth overly full and a knowing grin on her face. "Ye want tae keep him."

Lula watched as her tiny great-aunt smacked her lips and looked around the table, presumably for another bowl of the gooseberry fool that someone else had not finished. "You are as tiny as a hummingbird yet you eat so very much, Aunt Eggy. How is that?"

Aunt Eggy shrugged, causing the little knot of white hair at the top of her head to slip down toward her forehead. She absentmindedly shoved it back to the top while licking her spoon of any remaining pudding while she eyed Freddie Rockingham's untouched bowl of gooseberry fool. "Dinnae change the subject, lass. I saw the way ye and the baron were looking at each other. Enough tae make an auld lady blush it was." She looked at Lula and smiled. "Nae this auld lady, however. Freddie!' she called out. "If ye havenae eaten that pudding yet, I dinnae think ye are going tae. Pass it here, if ye please, and thank ye."

"Aunt Eggy, where are your manners!" Lula whispered as she watched Freddie hastily pass his gooseberry fool down to her great-aunt.

Aunt Eggy glanced at her niece as she pulled Freddie's bowl of pudding in front of her. "If ye want something, ye must work tae get it." She pointed her spoon in War's direction. "Perhaps ye havenae told him ye are keeping him." She put a large spoonful of pudding into her mouth while she watched Lula's face.

Lula looked down at the empty bowl in front of her. "I cannot," she whispered quietly. "It is not that simple, Aunt Eggy." Her voice quieted further. "He, he *killed* Lady Loveday's husband."

Aunt Eggy sniffed in dismissal. "He didnae," she said calmly and with assurance.

Lula looked at her. She nodded her head adamantly. "Loveday says he did, and War said as much to me, too. I do not believe it, of course, but still—"

Aunt Eggy stared sharply at her great-niece. "Ye know he would do no such thing. There is more tae this than what he told you. Dinnae let doubt fill yer mind." When Lula started to object again, she put her spoon down and touched the base of Lula's neck and then her forehead. "In here and here. Ye know in yer *heart* and in that *wise mind* of yers that this couldnae be so." She smiled gently at her great-niece. "Ye wouldnae fall in love with a man that could do such a thing." She shook her head as her smile fell and she pursed her lips at Lula. "I know ye are in love with him. I can see it on yer face. However, now that I think on it, if he is a bampot, ill whilly murderer, we must leave as soon as possible." She looked at her great-niece out of the corners of her eyes.

Lula's eyes flew to her great-aunt. "I am not leaving until I find answers. I cannot believe it of him, Aunt Eggy. You are correct, I cannot let doubt cloud my judgment."

"No, I think it best we leave. We dinnae want tae be murdered in our beds." She patted her hair as she surreptitiously watched Lula's reaction. "I cannae die with my hair like this. The pink color is gone and I had a lovely blue dye I wanted tae try next on it. I must look beautiful when death comes for me."

"Aunt Eggy! You cannot be serious. You are concerned with how your hair looks if you are murdered?" Lula hissed. She narrowed her eyes on her great-aunt. "He did not murder anyone and he certainly is not going to murder you," she whispered curtly. "Though *I* may. You are trying your machinations on me, aren't you, Aunt Eggy? Just like you did Mother and Julia."

Aunt Eggy grunted as her eyes widened in innocence. "And look how it worked oot for them. Now then, I am only saying if that big warrior is a murderer, we mustnae trust him. We must leave, now! With those excellent, er, large hands of his, he could strangle us so easily with just one hand. What do ye really know aboot him? He could be the worst of men. Leaving a trail of poor, weeping and wailing widows behind him."

Lula leaned her chin on her hand as she stared down at her tiny great-aunt sitting beside her. A small smile lifted her lips. "I see what you are doing, Aunt Eggy." She leaned closer. "You are correct in that I do love him. *I do.* And I believe in him as well. I am not leaving unless he tells me to."

Aunt Eggy made a soft crooning noise of triumph as she patted her hair again and preened. "Of course, I knew it. I knew ye wouldnae fall in love with a bampot scoundrel. Nae my great-niece who can see beyond all those odd colors she wears tae the beauty that can be." She picked up her spoon and scooped up another bite of pudding. "Besides, ye are a Darley. The Darley girls arenae fools and wouldnae let themselves fall in love with a bad mon." She glanced down the table at Birdie. "Except for maybe Birdie." She shook her head. "I think I must find her a man tae keep as well, and quickly. She thinks it will be all roses and rainbows with that Freddie."

Lula looked down the table to her younger sister. "Only a duke will do for Birdie. She has been sighing after Freddie for some time now."

Aunt Eggy snorted. "Freddie is a naft, numpty, glaikit idjut."

"Aunt Eggy!" Lula whispered. "Perhaps one could say that he was an idiot when he was a boy and trying to court Julia, however he is not an idiot any longer." She sighed. "And do I dare ask what naft, numpty and glaikit mean?"

Aunt Eggy shoved a spoonful of the gooseberry fool into her mouth and talked around the delicious dessert. "Naft and numpty mean empty-headed." She jammed the spoon into the air to make her point. "Glaikit means foolish and not very clever."

"Goodness, Aunt Eggy. I cannot say that I agree."

"No matter. That Freddie isnae for our Birdie," Aunt Eggy said with a stubborn grunt.

"Freddie gave you his pudding, Aunt Eggy."

Aunt Eggy paused and then she patted her hair as she lifted her chin. She spoke in a disgruntled voice. "There is that wee tidbit of kindness he showed, I suppose."

Lula studied her wily, little great-aunt. "Aunt Eggy, you said you must find Birdie a man to keep *as well*. What did you mean by that?"

Aunt Eggy turned to level shrewd eyes on Lula. She leaned close and whispered, "That warrior who has been staring at ye like a hungry wolf down at the end of the table *is for ye tae keep*. Why do ye think I sent ye here alone?"

"*Aunt Eggy*! I knew you sent me alone on purpose! I just knew you were not sick."

Aunt Eggy chuckled quietly and then flapped her hand at Lula. "Never ye mind that. Ye fell in love with him and he loves ye, just as I knew it would happen. Dinnae fash, dearling. It will all work oot as it's meant tae." She looked down the table to the baron who was staring at Lula with a brooding look, while the charming and dashing Ten Adair with the dimple in his chin continued talking to him.

"You men go off tae yer port and cigars," Aunt Eggy called down the table. "We ladies must plan what else may need tae be done for Veyril's ball. That is, whatever my dearling Lula has nae already thought of! Off ye go now!"

THE LADIES ADJOURNED to the small drawing room that Lula had been using after dinner with the three little boys. The fire was lit and it was cozy and warm. Aunt Eggy settled herself onto a tufted chair by the fire and gratefully accepted the blanket that Lula wrapped around her shoulders. Aunt Eggy made quick work of insisting that Lady Loveday stay to discuss and plan the ball. When Aunt Eggy asked, no one could ever deny her, not even a reluctant and nervous Lady Loveday.

Lula had also asked Tuedy to join them and her great-aunt and Birdie were discussing selections of food for the ball with him.

Loveday sat in silence, looking uncomfortable and awkward.

Birdie turned to Loveday, leaving the menu to Aunt Eggy, Lula and Tuedy. "Lady Loveday?" Birdie asked as she leaned closer, studying Loveday's face in open fascination. "What do you have on your face?"

Loveday immediately froze. "Tis a cream I wear."

Birdie leaned even closer. "Your skin looks as if you have

painted it. Tis as white and fine as a porcelain doll. And your eyes look very mysterious. You are wearing kohl, yes? Like a princess. Like Bibi Habibeh. She is a Supreme Imperial Majesty. That is higher than a queen, which is why she can smoke hashish at an English ball, of course. She wears kohl on her eyes and across her eyebrows. You also have something red on your cheeks and lips. Though may I ask why? I think that you are exceptionally beautiful. I should think you need none of that. Perhaps you are hiding some terrible scar or deformity? Or perhaps your beauty is so very great that you must cover your face so that men do not flock to you in droves and droves and fight over you? Instead, you bide your time and wait for the only man you could ever possibly love and who loves you with a love never before felt by any woman because it is so great and true and so very romantic." She sighed dramatically as she clasped her hands together under her chin and closed her eyes. "And the two of you shall live together, for ever after, in the most perfect of happiness." Birdie opened her eyes and smiled at the widow.

Loveday raised her brows as she looked at the pretty young woman with the striking blue eyes and jet black hair. She opted for honesty. "I have three young sons. My chance at a happily ever after is long gone. Also, my husband thought my looks disagreeable. I also cannot seem to help that I cry a lot. The cream covers my blotchy face."

Birdie started to say something else to Lady Loveday but Lula stopped her.

"Goodness, Birdie," Lula said hastily. "Leave Lady Loveday alone, please." Lula also knew that Aunt Eggy's sharp eyes and ears were watching and listening to everything for Aunt Eggy had been studying Loveday with great interest.

When Birdie turned to Lula with a question on her face, Lula just frowned sadly and stood up.

She excused herself and left the room. Loveday quickly joined her outside of the door.

"You cannot leave me," Loveday pleaded with Lula.

Lula looked away from her, touching her fingers to her forehead. "I have a headache. I should like to retire early, I think. Do please make my excuses to my great-aunt and sister." She turned and began walking through the great hall. She had only gone a few steps when Loveday caught up to her with her hand on her sleeve.

"War told you something of Bland's death. I saw it on your face. What did he say? You must tell me," she said in a desperate whisper.

Lula heaved out a great sigh. She shook her head and could not meet Loveday's eyes. She could not tell her what War had said.

"My brother did indeed kill him. He did not deny it to you." Loveday's shoulders sank as she read Lula's thoughts. Her voice was quiet, lacking any emotion. "I had so hoped I was wrong," she murmured as she clutched at her golden skirts. "You had me starting to believe."

Lula touched Loveday's hand in solace. "You must believe in your brother. Jolyon believes in him. Something else made your son stop talking that fateful day. You love War and part of loving someone means giving them your trust. His word is truth, remember that." She looked away and touched her forehead again. "Please make my excuses to my great-aunt and sister," and then she hurried away.

CHAPTER TWENTY-TWO

T HE BIG WAR horse was fractious. He was throwing his head and trotting in place, eager to run after being locked up in a stall for so long. Lula sat upon his back, holding the reins in one hand while she crooned to him and stroked his neck with the other.

She was staring at the snowy landscape from just inside the courtyard gates. White snow blanketed everything before her. Between the full moon and the snow-covered rolling hills and stone walls, there was an ethereal silver-blue quality to the moonlit night on the land.

Buttercup wanted to run. She could feel the massive energy collected up underneath her seat and between her legs encased in her breeches and boots as well as in the pulling of the reins within her hands. Instead of giving the reins out and letting the big horse run, she ruled for safety first. She was staring down a snowy hill. Slowly she gave slightly on the reins, just enough to let the horse go forward in his massive trot, but not enough to let him run full out down the hill through the snow. She needed first to see how deep or slippery the snow was. Running, if they were able, would come later, for she was as eager as the horse to run. She was trying so hard to not question the truth of War telling her he was indeed responsible for the death of his sister's husband. Why would he not tell her more? It weighed heavily on her mind. Her blind trust and love for him, versus what was behind his words.

She squeezed her heels and nudged with her seat, giving the horse the signals to go more forward as they went down the hill.

Buttercup's trot was slow and dramatic with his knees raising high above the snow as he lowered his haunches, lifted his shoulders and arched his neck like the proud stallion he was. Lula expertly held the war horse lightly in check with her hands giving and squeezing on the reins, lifting him with her seat, her abdomen and heels into the slow, rhythmical trot called a passage. She was surprised at the massive movement underneath her, for this was no elegant, Aldbey Park Thoroughbred, but a massive war horse, used to carrying a man and his bevy of weaponry or pulling an artillery wagon.

Buttercup's shoulder did not seem to be painful anymore for the war horse moved with fluid grace. *Massive,* fluid grace, she thought with an excited smile as she managed to move along with the huge horse. Riding this big war horse was almost enough to make her forget why she had come out to the stables.

"Easy, Buttercup, easy," she crooned to the horse as he threw his head about, chaffing at the bit in his desire to run. She could not help the smile on her face at using the huge war horse's name, for if ever a horse was so obviously misnamed twas this one. He was anything but a tiny, yellow, dainty flower. This was a massive horse with massive movement, and a massive temper.

Once they were safely at the bottom of the snowy hill, the white, snow-covered landscape stretched out before her. She gave on the reins at the same time that she nudged the big horse more forward with her seat and spoke to him again. Asking for more.

Buttercup snorted with eagerness and, in one lunging movement, he had leapt into a canter at her asking. Lula laughed out loud as the huge war horse at first cantered and then stretched his neck out into a gallop through the knee-deep snow.

"Go, Buttercup! Go, you big horse!" She leaned forward and shook her head, freeing her hair from its orange ribbon. The riotous mass flew out behind her in spiraling curls. She looked ahead and steered the horse toward a hill where a single large tree stood sentinel on the hill opposite the castle.

Once they had reached the top, Lula brought Buttercup down to a trot and then a walk. She turned the horse around and halted as they both caught their breath. Buttercup blew out through his nose, pleased with himself and the ability to just run after being cooped up in his stall.

Lula stared at the scene before her. This place and the castle in the center of it all was timeless. She could be staring at a scene from centuries long ago. The gray castle built all of stone with the tall walls surrounding and protecting it. The large, heavy iron gates, the towers, reaching up into the night sky.

A pristine blanket of snow covered everything with the moonlight shining bright on the crystal surface of the silvery almost pale blue snow. She sighed as a tremulous smile formed on her lips.

She loved him.

But how could she give her heart to such a man that would not deny that he killed his sister's husband? *For she knew he had not.* Jolyon would not love him so if he had. Yet something had happened that made the little boy unable to speak.

Buttercup let out a small whinny. The horse's ears pricked forward as he looked away off to the right. Lula turned to see what had caught Buttercup's attention. She saw a rider on a large, muscular, dark horse. The horse was galloping full on, dashing through the snow as the rider leaned low over the horse's neck.

And the horse and rider were coming this way.

Lula tensed, but Buttercup remained calm. This was no stranger.

It was War.

The black horse came lunging up the hill with its rider sitting effortlessly on its back.

Lula could not tear her eyes away from the big man in his great coat with his roguish, dark hair blowing back from his face, sitting on the massive black horse with the proudly arching neck and long, long mane. The man and the horse were well paired.

War must have been an extremely intimidating sight to behold in battle.

She watched as he expertly spun the horse in a circle and halted beside her.

"Lula," War said quietly as he studied her face in the silvery moonlight with his breath coming out as misty, white puffs in the cold air.

"War," she answered calmly. She gave him no time to speak. "Graestone is magnificent."

"Lula," he said again. "I am sorry I am not the man you wished me to be. I am a heartless—"

Lula shook her head quickly, interrupting him by nodding to a group of horses, off in the distance in a large, snow-covered field. "Are they yours?"

He looked at her face, watching the emotions she was struggling with, to the horses out in the snow. "Yes," he said softly.

"Why are they out in the snow? Your other horses are not."

War looked down at her hands on the reins. She was tense, holding the reins tightly.

"Like the other horses in the stables, they came back from the battlefield with injuries. They healed and were ready to simply be horses again. They earned that right."

Lula looked at him and then to the horses, gathered near a wooden shelter built near a copse of trees. "I, I am surprised I have not seen worse injuries on the horses." She was trying not to cry. Her eyes were filling with tears, as much for the horses as for this man that she had fallen in love with. "I expected bullets and shrapnel injuries," she said in a whisper.

War looked over at her where she sat so perfectly on the huge war horse. "Those did not make it back," he murmured tensely.

"I see, of course," she said hoarsely with a tear-clogged voice.

"Lula, you must know that the battlefield is a hellish place. Men die, horses die," he said quietly.

He continued to stare at her but she did not look at him. He turned and stared off to Graestone, his home. An ancient pile of rocks that had survived for centuries. A place that his father had almost lost and that he had worked and bled in order to bring back to life. "I am not a good man, Lula." He looked at her then, though she was still staring out at the horses. "I am not the man of a young woman's dreams. I have told you that I am not an easy man to know and I have warned you that I cannot love for I have no love to give. I have had many men die under my leadership on the battlefield. I have also killed many men there, men whose names I do not know and whose faces I had never seen before but will remember forever. In living that life, my heart is gone. It died within me long ago. I have nothing to give."

Still she did not look at him. Dread and deep, deep sorrow and despair filled him. He wanted to be the man she deserved. He wanted to be worthy of her, her loyalty, her love, her belief in him. Yet he had failed to save his father and his mother, he had failed his sister. He had failed to save too many of his men. He had failed his nephews. He should never have let himself hope that he could have more. That he could have her.

He studied her face as his eyes narrowed. A silent moan rose in his chest.

"You are crying," he whispered gruffly. "I cannot..." He swallowed. "I cannot bear your tears, Lula."

She whirled to face him then with tears streaming down her cheeks. "Why can you not bear my tears, War?" Her voice was ragged, demanding.

"What?" he asked in confusion.

"You said you cannot bear my tears. *Why?*"

"I do not understand what you are asking me," he said in frustration.

"*Why* can you not bear my tears?" she asked emphatically again. "Why?" She whispered the question through her tears. "Tell me? *Please?*"

War ran his hand over his beard in agitation. "It pains me," he finally said in a low voice as he looked away from her.

"It pains a man who claims to be heartless to see a woman cry?" She stared at him, waiting for him to look at her. He turned to stare at her after several moments. His eyes were bleak as his breath came out in great heaving puffs of white clouds into the silvery-blue of the night. His face was filled with anguish.

"I let Bland *die*, Lula. *My sister's husband*. Only a man with no heart could do such a thing. A man who has killed *many* men."

Lula bit back a sob. "You *let him die*? Is that not different than killing him?" She held up one hand to thwart his reply. "I do not believe that you would let him die unless he did something horrible, *terrible*. I cannot believe it of you. *What did he do?*" she demanded in a choked voice.

War's face hardened. He bit out, "Letting a man die is *no* different than killing him. You deserve better than a man such as me, Lula. *Leave it.*"

"I will not leave it!" she said forcibly. "Tell me what happened, and if you cannot or will not tell me, then *tell your sister* the truth of it for I know there must be more and it *involves Jolyon!*"

"I cannot," he growled angrily. "I told you, *leave it.*"

"I cannot leave it," she said achingly. "Surely," she swallowed her tears, "surely you must know that I—" She choked on a sob and tried again. *"Can you not see that I am in love with you?"* she said firmly. And then when he did not look at her, she spoke again, quieter, *"I love you, Warwick de Walton."*

He gulped and turned to stare at her. "I cannot love. I am damaged, *scarred*. Inside and out. You deserve more, Lula," he said in an aching, deep, dark baritone. "My word is truth," he said quietly.

She shook her head, squeezing her eyes shut as the tears spilled forth.

"You ridiculous man," she whispered tremulously and closed her eyes against the stark pain on his face and the stabbing pain in her heart. "I know you have scars. How can you not? I also know

that you have scars under that beard you wear. I am scarred, too, inside and out and *you*," she opened her eyes to stare into his, "you have *sweetly*, *gently* and with a *huge heart* brought me back." She wiped at her eyes and looked at him with all the love within her pouring out for this big, fierce warrior of a man. "Only a fool would say that you have no heart." She waved the hand that had just wiped the tears off her cheek toward the castle. "One only has to look around Graestone to see all the men you have saved. All the horses." A sob broke free. "You have the largest heart of any man I know."

She stared at him as tears poured down her cheeks, waiting, waiting for something, *anything*.

He did not react. He only stared ahead with his lips in a firm line and that bleak look of anguish still on his face.

"I love you and I am *keeping you*," she said through her tears.

He shook his head without turning to her.

"Do you wish me to leave then?" she asked tightly.

He spoke in a dead, emotionless voice. "I do not deserve you, Lula. Only death and darkness surrounds me. Forgive me for ever kissing you. You may return to Aldbey Park as planned with your great-aunt and your sister. Stay for the ball if you like. But after that, you should leave. I have nothing to offer you. My word is truth." He gathered up his reins and urged his black horse away from her and away from Graestone, through the snow.

Lula stared after him. "I love you," she whispered into the night. "My word is truth on that." After several long moments when she could no longer see him or his horse, she picked up her reins and rode Buttercup at a walk back to the castle and through the gates.

CHAPTER TWENTY-THREE

LULA PUT BUTTERCUP away and was slowly walking through the courtyard as she tapped her riding crop on her thigh. She was deep in thought when she heard some loud voices above her on the battlements. She stopped and looked upwards to see what looked like two figures struggling near one of the cannons protruding from a crenellation within the wall of the battlements.

"Todrick?" she called out urgently. "Is that you?"

Her attention was caught just then by a child's voice calling out her name. She saw a small figure running down the stone stairs from the battlements and then across the courtyard toward her.

"Jolyon!" she said in surprise as she ran forward and then knelt down, dropping her crop as she opened her arms to catch the small boy hurtling toward her. He ran straight into her arms. "Why are you crying, dearling? *What has happened?*" She stood up, holding him gently as she wiped the tears from his face.

He sniffled and then squirmed down out of her arms. He grabbed her hand and pulled urgently. *"Come!"*

Lula's mouth dropped open in shock. He had called her name, he had demanded she come! Jolyon had spoken! "Where are your brothers?" she said fearfully.

He pointed up to the battlements. "Come, please?" he said in a fearful voice as he tugged at her hand. "Toddy is in trouble.

There's a bad man."

A bad man, Lula thought with alarm. She recalled Machabee saying that their uncle was teaching them how to fight so they would never have to be afraid of a *bad man*.

Suddenly, she heard Machabee and Melchisedec yelling and then the loud snarling and frantic barking of Courage. They were there, up on the battlements with Toddy and the "bad man", whoever that was.

Quickly, she knelt down and gently held Jolyon's arms as she looked him in the eyes. "Brave Lyon, you must get more help. Find some of the men. Find Tuedy! Go into the castle and *yell!* Yell as loud as you can! If your uncle returns back to the castle on his horse, *tell him.* Just like you did me, you brave boy!"

He nodded his head silently as his lower lip trembled.

Lula grabbed her riding crop, stood up and began to run toward the stone stairs leading up to the battlements. She began singing softly to herself.

"Through drinking grog,
he lost his life,
his anger woe to meet!

So never mix your grog too strong,
But always take it neat!

With a chip, chop! Cherry chop!
Fol de rol, riddle-rop!
Chip, chop! Cherry chop!
Fol de rol ray!"

Lula rounded the last bend of the stairs and slowed as she listened. Courage's frantic barking suddenly rose followed by a sharp whimper of pain. She stilled, her breath held in fear for the dog. But then Courage resumed his snarling and barking and the boys' angry yelling intensified. She came around the wall, moving quickly but carefully as she surveyed the scene before her.

The boys were beating their small fists against a man wrestling and punching Todrick. Blood was streaming into Todrick's eyes from a gash on his forehead. It was evident that he could not see his opponent well. The man flung Todrick against one of the cannons. Then he grabbed him and punched him as Todrick tried to wrestle his way out of the man's hold. They spun and twisted until they were at the opening of a crenellation not blocked by a cannon.

Courage was barking furiously and snapping at the man's legs.

Lula tightened her fist as she looked at the man hitting Todrick. He had white, long hair tied in a queue at the back of his neck and bushy white sideburns down to his chin along with thick straggly, white eyebrows.

It was Mr. Womersly.

"Machabee! Melchisedec! Get away from them!" she called out loudly.

Just then, Womersly viciously kicked out at Courage and sent his elbow into the two boys hitting him with their little fists. He kicked again, his foot brutally striking the dog who was biting at him.

Courage skidded across the ground and slammed into the stone wall at the opposite side of the battlements.

"Boys! Leave him and go to Courage!" Lula shouted.

Both boys turned to her in surprise and relief and scurried to the dog who was lying far too still against the wall. They scooped Courage up into their arms and huddled there as they stared at Lula with wide eyes.

Lula's breath shuddered out of her at the sight of the dog and the frightened boys. She tightened her fist on the crop in her hand. It was all she had.

She ran forward with her arm raised and brought the crop down as hard as she could on Womersly's head.

Visions of that night in Hyde Park when she had been attacked kept rushing through her mind. She and her sister, Julia, had fought with the only thing they had, their riding crops. Just as she was now.

"Let go of Todrick! Let go of him!" she screamed as she brought the crop down on the top and sides of Womersly's head, over and over.

Womersly ducked his head from the stinging lashes of her crop. "I am sick of this one and his cannons! I cannot sleep for the booming!" He barred his teeth at her in anger and then he hit Todrick one last time before flinging him away. Todrick hit the stone wall opposite and sank down onto his back. He stared at Lula in shock and confusion and then his eyes slid closed. Blood seeped from the several cuts on his face.

With unusual speed, Womersly turned on Lula and grabbed her around the neck. The strong stench of alcohol fumes hit her in the face.

"I told you to get off my ship, *Girl!*" Womersly raged at her with spittle spewing from his lips. "I'll throw you over the side myself!"

In a twist of his body, he pushed her back and then back some more, until the heels of her boots hit the low crenellation. She could go no further and had to step up onto the narrow stone in the opening. If she lost her footing and fell backward, only his hands around her neck would keep her from falling over the side to the ground far, far below.

She dropped her crop and grabbed both of Womersly's wrists and hung on as she struggled to kick out at him with her booted feet.

"Mr. Wo-," she gasped. "Mr. Womersly! Tis I!"

Womersly's face was turning bright red as he stared at her with gleeful, crazed, pale blue eyes.

"I know who you are," he sneered in a hissing whisper. "You are the girl who made a fool of me. Because of you, I may have to leave. Shovell is already packing his things. And you brought that mongrel here. He was mine but he turned on me so I beat him again but he never learned," he whispered and then laughed wickedly. "I tied him out in the woods when I came here. I am surprised he survived. I should have thrown you both over the ship."

"No, he, he is not a killer! Let go of me!" She gasped out the words as she struggled to pull his hands from her neck. "You are not...not on *a ship!*"

Womersly slowly smiled at her. His eyes were clear. "I know," he hissed in a taunting whisper. He cackled once and then tilted his head as if confused. "Or do I?" He smiled suddenly, leaning into her face as he leered at her with gleeful anticipation.

Lula turned her face away from the evil in his eyes and his fetid breath. Fear and dread raced through her.

Suddenly, she heard Courage barking and snarling somewhere near her legs. She knew he was biting at Womersly's legs again, but all she could think about was that the dog was unhurt. Then she heard Machabee and Melchisedec nearby as well, yelling and punching away at Womersly.

"Get away or I'll let go of her," snarled Womersly. *"I'll let the sharks have her!"*

She thought she heard Todrick's rasping voice, telling her to hang on, but she was getting dizzy. And then came Tuedy's high-pitched voice shrieking at Womersly and several more voices joined in and then more and more.

One of the voices was Loveday's voice, speaking loudly in a worried panic.

Aunt Eggy was there as well, swearing in Gaelic, calling Womersly a blaegeard and a mac na galla.

Lula pressed her fingernails into Womersly's hands but it was to no avail. She brought her arms down hard on his as she tried to kick at him. The man's strength was frightening. However, still she kept trying to break his hands free of her neck.

And then she heard Jolyon sobbing. Something about his father or perhaps he had said stepfather.

Womersly pushed her backward, threatening to send her over the edge. "Get back!" he screeched to all the people gathered there behind him. "Get back, *all of you*, or I'll push her into the sea!"

Lula was able to turn her head, just barely, and look down into the courtyard. *How far down will I fall?* she thought fleetingly.

A movement caught her eye, there, down in the snow-covered courtyard.

It was War, moving to stand just underneath her.

"Lula," he called calmly up to her in his dulcet, deep voice. "Hang on my courageous, captivating, freckle-faced girl. *I vow I will get you out of this.*"

Lula tried to smile. "I know, I know you will," she said in a ragged gasp of breath. "Your word is truth," she said hoarsely, though she doubted that he could hear her weak voice. She wanted to tell him she loved him, but she had no air left to speak.

"Womersly!" roared War's voice. It was filled with fury and warning. "Good God and bloody hell and the devil confound it! I vow if you do not pull her from that ledge I will wreak such havoc on you! I will kill you in ways *you cannot imagine!*" he thundered.

"War?" came Ten's calm voice. "Rockingham and I are here, just give us the order."

"*No!*" War roared.

"Keep them away from me, Captain!" Womersly spit out.

"*Hold*, Ten," War commanded.

"He is mad," shouted Cloudsley Shovell as he ran onto the battlements. He moved to stand at Womersly's back. "He does not know what he is doing! I swear it!"

Several voices rose up to drown out Cloudsley's defense of Womersly, namely the Tweedy twins who both shouted him down.

Cloudsley nervously looked around at the people surrounding and shouting at him. He grabbed the two closest bodies that he could reach.

"War?" Ten called out over the clamor. "There is a man here with a lovely bald head and rather unfashionable, long, red, terribly uncouth, bushy sideburns. He is the one I told you about, the, er, *incident* in the stables. Cloudsley Shovell."

Cloudsley snarled and started to say something but Ten held up one finger. "Tut, tut, tut. One moment, if you please, I am speaking. And shouldn't you be gone by now?"

Cloudsley's eyes widened as his mouth went slack. "What? Er, yes. But I came back for Mr. Womersly. We have been together a long time."

Ten nodded. "How interesting." He glanced toward the crenellation where Womersly held Lula and where War was standing on the ground below. He called out, "Shovell says he has returned for Womersly." He paused as he narrowed his eyes back on Cloudsley. He spoke again, loud enough for War to hear. "He is holding a knife to Lady Egidia Ross' throat, though she is quite serene. In fact, she seems to be rather relishing it."

"Aunt Egidia?" War thundered. "Is Birdie there with her?"

Ten eyed the petite young woman with the bright blue eyes and jet black hair staring menacingly at Cloudsley Shovell who held her arm in a viselike grip. If he didn't know better, he thought that Cloudsley was about to meet his match in the two tiny women.

"Yes, there is a small, very menacing-looking, young lady with Lady Ross. I'd say both of the women look quite calm. I believe Cloudsley Shovell has prejudged them most incorrectly."

Ten heard War let out a short bark of laughter.

"Och," Aunt Eggy said loudly and very calmly, "that warrior knows ye dinnae need tae fash over me or Birdie, Lord Fairfax." She pursed her lips and looked at Cloudsley with disdain. "Lula's warrior knows we can handle this ill whilly, mockit, manky, mingin, mauchit, blaegeard vera easily!"

"Ten?" War bellowed up to the battlements.

Ten Adair calmly called back. "Yes, I know. I do believe I am relishing this as well." He stared at Cloudsley Shovell as a threatening grin rose on his lips.

Birdie leaned closer to her great-aunt, ignoring the knife the bald man held to her great-aunt, or his snarling face. "What do all those words mean again, Aunt Eggy?" Birdie asked with interest.

"Nae now, dearling, I need tae speak tae the baron," Aunt

Eggy said calmly. "Warrior?" she shouted. "Are ye going tae save my Lula or no? She looks to be fair puckled. She'll be fainting any moment with that mac na galla's hands around her neck."

"Lula!" thundered War's voice as he ran to the stone staircase that led to the battlements.

Lula could hear that the direction of War's voice had changed. She tried to gasp out his name but nothing came out of her mouth.

"Hold on, Lula!" War called out as his heart thudded in his chest with absolute panic.

War ran up the stone steps knowing Lula's life depended on it.

What a fool he had been, hoping that he could have what everyone else had.

Lula *believed* in him.

And now she was in danger of losing her life like everyone else around him had.

This unusual, freckle-faced girl with a piece of paper, no, *a certificate*, who loved healing animals and helping anyone she met and wore oddly bright, mismatched colors. She was the most kind and loving woman he knew.

But he had put Lula in danger, *and she could be hurt again. Or even killed.*

He took the steps two and three at a time until he reached the top of the battlements. He did not pause but strode directly toward the man holding the woman he loved. His fists were clenched at his sides and his mouth was set in a thin, hard line. He dared not glace at Lula. The woman he could not, would not lose. His eyes were narrowed on Womersly.

"Womersly, I vow *this is your last warning*," War growled.

Lula heard the chorus of voices coming from behind Womersly rise, drawing closer, getting louder.

Her world grew dim.

The last thing she thought she heard was Womersly screaming, "Get back! Get away from me!"

And then she was falling.

CHAPTER TWENTY-FOUR

I T ALL HAPPENED at once. Lula fainted, causing Womersly to tip forward as he was holding her full weight. He let go of her as she crumpled down onto the edge. He then teetered there on the edge himself, trying not to follow her as she slid over the side.

War roared and ran toward them, launching himself at Lula. He landed on his stomach, reaching down over the crenellation.

He grabbed Lula's wrist as she went over the side. He lay there, holding her wrist in both hands as he took great heaving breaths.

"No!" Womersly screamed. He kicked at War's head and hands. "Let her go!"

War looked up at Womersly trying to dodge the man's kicks to his head. "What are you doing?" he thundered.

More screams came from behind War. Out of the corners of his eyes, he saw Jolyon and then several of his men led by the Tweedy twins rush at Womersly.

In the blink of an eye, it happened.

Womersly went over the edge, his arms flailing like a child's puppet.

War heard a loud grunt and there came a sudden hard tug to his hands.

He looked over the edge. "Lula," he called urgently.

Lula's body hurt. She opened her eyes slowly and gasped for

air as she dangled, striking against the hard, uneven stones of the wall.

She moaned painfully as she stared at the stone wall in front of her face and then she glanced down. There was a painful, heavy weight on her ankles. Her heart started thudding heavily in her breasts.

Womersly was clinging to her ankles.

She peeked down beyond him to the ground far below and immediately started singing quietly in a shaky, hoarse voice.

"They threw him out some tackling
To give his life a hope

But as his fear did blind the boy
He could not see the rope!
With a chip, chop! Cherry chop!
Fol de rol, riddle-rop!
Chip, chop! Cherry chop!
Fol de rol ray!"

"Lula, Lula! Stop singing. I have you, my courageous girl," War said firmly as he leaned over the edge of the crenellation, holding tightly to her wrist. He said a quick prayer of thanks that she was breathing.

Lula looked up. She was dizzy and stunned. "War?" she breathed out as she stared up at him. She glanced down to the ground far below. She swallowed past the fear rising in her throat. She looked up to War's face staring down at her. "Womersly is hanging on to me."

War smiled down into her eyes. "I see that. Can you give me your other hand?"

Lula tried to raise her other hand to grasp War's but with the pull of Womersly on her body, she could not find the strength. "I, I cannot!" she groaned. She looked up to him with fear on her face. "Please do not let me go," she whispered hoarsely.

"Never. I will never let you go. *My word is truth.*" War's voice was firm as he adjusted his position to take up the weight of the two people.

Aunt Eggy's face appeared over the side. "Is he saying that he is keeping ye, dearling?"

War scowled and looked over to the crenellation where Aunt Eggy was staring at him from. "No," he growled as he breathed heavily at the weight on his arms. His biceps flexed and his shoulders strained. Womersly was not a small man. "Not now, Aunt Egidia," he groaned.

Then Birdie's face appeared over the edge from another crenellation. She was obviously laying on her stomach. She had her chin resting in both hands. She looked very pleased with herself. "All the villains have been vanquished, Lula! Tare an' hounds but it was exciting! The entire castle is up here! You should see it! The bald man with the knife is being held by my darling Freddie right now! Thunder an' turf but Freddie was wonderful! Freddie caught the mockit, manky, mingin, mauchit bald man before he could hurt anyone." She looked over War's back to Aunt Eggy. "Did I get all the words correct, Aunt Eggy?"

Aunt Eggy smiled proudly. "Aye, Birdie, ye did!" She looked at the baron with a frown. "What are ye waiting for, Warrior? Pull her up now! I hear ye carried a cannon off the battlefield on yer shoulder, this should be easy! Pull her up!"

War groaned quietly as he held Lula's eyes and shifted his position once again to take the weight. "Aunt Egidia," he groaned.

Lula closed her eyes briefly in a grimace as she stifled a moan, concentrating all her energy in holding on to War's hand.

"Freddie was so marvelous, Lula! You should have seen him!" Birdie huffed out an angry breath when someone grumbled something behind her. "Oh, and I suppose that man named Ten helped stop the bald man as well." She looked behind her and frowned at the person grumbling.

Ten's exacerbated voice spoke up. "I have Shovell, War. I

thought it best to rescue him from Aunt Egidia." He added dryly, "And the vicious one, the little Bird. I also took his knife away from Aunt Egidia."

Aunt Eggy grinned over the edge at Lula. "Aye, twas vera exhilarating, dearling! Why are ye nae pulling my Lula up, Baron?"

Birdie stopped scowling behind her at Ten and smiled down at Lula as well. "He had no idea how capable we were, Lu! In one moment, we had him bent over and then down on the ground. Aunt Eggy says that he may never father children. I do not understand why, but is that not fascinating?" Birdie leaned farther over the edge. "Why isn't the baron pulling you up? Where is that man that was strangling you? I do not see him on the ground. I should be able to see him, cracked open like an egg!" She leaned over the edge further and was looking all around the ground at the bottom of the wall.

"Och!" screeched Aunt Eggy as she, too, leaned over a bit more. "He's hanging ontae my Lula!"

"What?" roared Ten.

"Help the baron! Quickly now!" Aunt Eggy called out to the men behind her on the battlements.

War groaned.

"Och, his arms have gone numb! The two of them are tae heavy!" Aunt Eggy said fearfully. She turned her head to the crowd of people on the battlements. "He's going tae need some extra hands! Dinnae dither, now! Help him pull my Lula up! Quickly!"

Lula watched as Ten and Tuedy and Todrick and Poppy and Bertie and Alton Ditchburn and a crowd of people rushed to look over the edge, lending their hands to War's hands.

Lula was back up on the battlements before she could catch her breath and Womersly pulled away from her.

Suddenly, she was surrounded by a large group of the men, all crouching around her, touching her, trying to help her where she was sitting in the midst of them all.

Tuedy and Todrick were kneeling on either side of her, looking worriedly into her face while each held one of her hands and was patting it.

"I am fine, I am fine," she breathed out as she smiled up at all the men around her. She was not frightened at being surrounded by these men, not in the least. "Thank you, all of you," she said in a hoarse voice. She leaned over and kissed Tuedy on the cheek and then much to Todrick's surprise, she kissed his cheek as well.

Todrick was stunned but then he beamed with pleasure.

Aunt Eggy pushed the men aside and dropped to her knees in front of her great-niece. "Och! I thought ye were going tae fall when I saw that glaikit scunner hanging ontae ye! But the baron and all his men rescued ye and all is well. The baron will be keeping ye for sure now! He loves ye, tis clear tae see!"

Lula let Tuedy and Todrick help her to her feet, then she reached down and helped her great-aunt to her feet. "No, Aunt Eggy. I do not think that is in the stars for me. Hush about that now, if you please?"

Aunt Eggy frowned worriedly at her great-niece. She glanced around. "Where is that big warrior? He should have been at your side as soon as you were brought up from over the edge!"

Tuedy hovered near Lula with great concern. "The baron is, eh...*speaking* to Womersly, I believe, Lady Ross. Over there, eh." He pointed to where War had Womersly and Shovell up against the stone battlements with one of his large hands on each of their necks while he spoke to them. His words were so low and quiet that they could not be heard, but his face was pure fury. Tuedy could just imagine all manner of things the baron was threatening them with.

Lula did not look at War. She could not. He had not come to her, just as her great-aunt had said. His men had, and they were still all solicitously gathered around her. She looked back at Todrick and let out a small gasp. Quickly, she pulled a lovely orange handkerchief from inside her jacket. "Todrick! You are bleeding! Here, please let me," she said as she proceeded to gently blot the blood from his face.

"That's not right," he mumbled as he closed his eyes and allowed her ministrations. "You almost died, you need not see to me, Miss Lula."

"Hush. You are hurt, Todrick," she whispered with a teary smile.

"You saved me, Miss," Todrick rasped bashfully.

Lula let out a teary laugh. "I did an abhorrent job of it, I fear. You still were injured. Quite badly."

"Why is she crying?" came War's bellow as he pushed through the men.

War was suddenly, *finally* there. "Get back!" he thundered at them all. "Do not touch her!" he commanded.

The sound of a muffled, sobbing laugh from Lula tore at his heart.

War instantly scooped her into his arms and dropped to one knee as relief overwhelmed him. He held her there against his chest, placing soft kisses all over her face.

"I am holding you, Lula, forgive me, but I must. Please do not faint. Let me hold you."

Lula smiled weakly and pulled back, just enough to look into his eyes. "I will not faint. Hold me, please."

War pulled her back against him and stared down into her eyes, reading the pain and the fear there. He sighed with relief at having her safely in his arms. He closed his eyes and leaned his forehead against hers. "I need to kiss you, Lula," he whispered.

Lula kept her eyes closed. Letting herself revel in the safety and warmth of his arms, at the scent of him surrounding her, the sound of his deep and gentle voice. "Why?" she whispered in the barest breath. "Why do you need to kiss me, War?"

"Because I have never been so terrified in my life."

She opened her eyes and placed her hands on either side of his face. "Because you care about me," she whispered against his lips. "You do not trifle."

He took her lips and kissed her hungrily. She wrapped her

arms around his neck and held on tightly, returning his kiss as eagerly with kisses of her own. It was her tongue that delved between his lips, seeking to dance with his, sighing at the velvety roughness of it and the secret, spicy taste of this man she loved. He groaned and tangled his tongue with hers, deepening the kiss as he pulled her against his chest.

War kissed her over and over, thoroughly, with everyone watching them until he realized where they were and pulled back. He raised one eyebrow at his men, particularly at Ten who was standing there with his arms across his chest, grinning down at him.

"What are you looking at?" War growled wryly.

Courage ran up to Lula just then, whining frantically as he began licking her face. She laughed softly and hugged the dog to her with one arm.

The little wildlings walked forward as well and knelt down, facing Lula and War. They stared at Lula in worried silence. Loveday walked forward to stand behind them. She was wringing her hands together, smiling down at her brother and the woman in his arms.

"Where does it hurt, besides your neck, my courageous, freckle-faced girl?" War asked in a deep, low voice. He had eyes only for Lula. His fingers lightly traced the marks on her neck. They would be black and blue soon and she would have a painful throat for days.

"I am fine, truly."

Jolyon was bouncing up and down. "Uncle War, Uncle War!"

War looked over at the small boy in astonishment. "You are speaking!"

Lula nodded against War's chest. "He came to get me and the others. He told me what was happening."

Tuedy raised both of his hands. "He was screaming down the castle! Imagine our shock!"

"Well done," War said in a tired voice as he ruffled the hair on Jolyon's head.

Jolyon nodded in excitement. "And then I helped you. Just like the other time."

War's hand stilled on his nephew's head. He drew his hand slowly back as he stared at Jolyon.

Loveday's eyes widened. "The other time?" she asked softly.

Jolyon looked up at his mother. "Yes, when Stepfather was holding me out over the edge by the back of my shirt. I was very frightened, Mama."

Loveday tensed as she gasped. "Yes, I am sure you were," she whispered breathlessly as her body filled with dread.

"Uncle War came running, just like he did for our Miss Lula. He grabbed me away from Stepfather."

Loveday went very still. "And then what happened, my dearest?"

"I asked Uncle War to put me down. I was afraid of being lifted off the ground because of Stepfather doing that so many times. Uncle War and Stepfather were arguing so neither were paying attention to me. I was afraid that he would hurt Uncle War. I ran and I pushed Stepfather over the side so he couldn't do that to me anymore. Stepfather thought it funny every time he did it, but I did not like it. I knew one day he would really let go just as he threatened to."

Loveday froze as she stared at her youngest son. Her heart broke in two for him at what he must have endured at Bland's hands. She sank to her knees with a moan and held her arms out to him.

Jolyon smiled and ran into his mama's arms.

"I did not know," she whispered against his hair. "I did not know."

"Goodness," Lula breathed out.

Loveday's eyes found her brother. "It was not you that killed Bland," she whispered in a broken voice.

War swallowed and shook his head, once. "I take full responsibility. I should have stopped Jolyon or reached for Bland."

Loveday shook her head. "No," she said in a cold voice. "I

would have killed Bland myself. For what he did to my children."

Machabee and Melchisedec were staring at their little brother in awe. "Jolyon! You *are* a lion!"

Loveday gathered Jolyon tightly against her breast and then opened her arms to hug her other sons. She stood up and began walking with them down the battlements toward one of the towers, murmuring quietly to them. Jolyon looked over his mother's shoulder and called to Courage who quickly hurried after them with his tail wagging and his tongue hanging out the side of his mouth in happiness.

Lula watched them go with a thoughtful look on her face. She tipped her head up to look at War. "You could not tell her the truth. That it was her son that had killed her husband."

War stared after his sister and then down into Lula's eyes. "No, I could not," he whispered.

Aunt Eggy and Birdie came forward and watched Lady Loveday and her children as well.

"I think one must be careful of standing near any open crenellations when Jolyon is around," Birdie whispered to her great-aunt.

"Birdie!" Lula said.

Birdie shrugged innocently and looked around at the men. "Were we not all thinking the same?"

Ten rolled his eyes. "One does not say it though." He shook his head at the petite girl.

She rolled her eyes back at him. "So you *were* thinking it as well!" she said as she shook a finger at him.

Freddie Rockingham, who was standing next to Ten, said loftily, "I was surely thinking no such thing."

Ten scowled at Freddie. "Surely you were."

"Captain," Todrick rasped from where he stood next to his twin brother, Tuedy.

Tuedy began nodding in agitation as he waved Lula's blood-stained handkerchief in the air. "Womersly and Shovell are gone! Disappeared, escaped, eh!"

War stood up slowly and set Lula gently on her feet, keeping his arm around her. "I am not surprised by that. They knew what their fates would be after this." He looked away from Todrick and Tuedy but then quickly turned back to stare at the handkerchief in Tuedy's hands to Todrick's face. "What happened to your face, Todrick? In fact, what started this?"

Todrick took a step away from his brother as he faced Lula and then he looked back to the baron. "Womersly attacked me. He saw me about to light the cannon and grew enraged. Miss Lula came to my aid," he rasped out painfully. His eyes returned to Lula. "I am in your debt, Miss Lula, and the dog. Courage was as relentless as you in fighting Womersly off me."

Both of Tuedy's hands flew in the air. "You see, Toddy? Our Miss Lula and her dog are a benefit to Graestone, eh? You must admit it now!"

War scowled and ran a hand over the back of his neck. "I want to kill him, yet I cannot discount that the cannons may have a part in setting off his war memories," he said quietly. *And it was the prime minister's decision, not his, unfortunately.*

Lula looked up at him. "I am not so sure. Womersly told me himself that Courage was his dog. He was the one that tied the poor creature out in the woods. He said that the dog had turned on him and that beating him had not worked." She looked around at all the men and boys crowded on the battlements listening. "He did not want to bring the dog here. I suppose all would know the man's true nature then."

Aunt Eggy nodded with an affirming look on her face. "Och tae be sure then he was a scunner."

Birdie's eyes flooded with tears. "How horrible, to beat the dog and tie him up in the woods to be left to die in the cold and the snow. Tare an' hounds, I cannot bear it!" She turned to Freddie Rockingham and cried into his red-coated chest while Freddie looked quite discomfited.

Ten put a finger to his lips as he tried not to laugh at young Rockingham's embarrassment.

War ignored them all and looked down at Lula with a question in his eyes.

Lula smiled. "My mother has always said, 'tis the truth that a man that is neither kind nor gentle to an animal is not a man you should desire for a husband, or even an acquaintance for that matter.' I believe that to be true. How a man treats those weaker than he shines a light on his true soul."

"War?" Ten's voice was curt. He had moved to stand at the wall. He was looking over the battlements. "I see them. Cresting the hill."

Tuedy made an excited exclamation and ran to the wall. Aunt Eggy and Birdie and the other men followed.

War's lips thinned into a hard line. He looked at Todrick. One of his eyes was beginning to swell shut.

"That's farther than you've aimed and shot before. And that was with two eyes."

"I believe I can bloody well make it, Captain," Todrick rasped as he rubbed his hands together with eager anticipation.

Tuedy came forward with Poppy, Bertie and five other men to help Todrick move and re-aim the cannon from where Todrick had previously been shooting at the stone walls in the field.

Lula had her arm around Aunt Eggy. She looked back and forth between War and Todrick. "Surely you cannot mean to shoot them?"

War turned to look down at her where she stood beside him on the battlements. "No, but we can give them a bit of a fright to hasten them on their way, and make sure in doing so, that they do not return."

"Ready, Captain," Todrick said.

There was a buzz of excitement from the men.

"Cover your ears, Aunt Eggy!" Lula said hastily.

"*Light it.*" War's deep growl rang out over the battlements.

CHAPTER TWENTY-FIVE

A LOUD BOOM ripped through the air.

The cannonball landed just yards from the two men, sending a massive spray of snow and dirt, rocks and clumps of earth at them.

The men on the battlements cheered as the two scoundrels covered their heads and began to run away from Graestone.

War tipped his head back and laughed.

At a harsh smack on his chest, he looked down.

Aunt Eggy was glaring up at him. "That's it?"

"What?" he asked her in confusion.

Aunt Eggy pointed over the battlements. "That bampot scunner almost killed Lula and ye are laughing because ye shot an auld cannon at him?"

War scowled. "I cannot kill him, Aunt Egidia.

Lula pulled Aunt Eggy back to her side. "He is correct. He cannot kill them, Aunt Eggy. Those men have been damaged by events from the war."

"Och!" spat Aunt Eggy.

War smiled ruthlessly. "I cannot kill them because there are four men from the prime minister's office on their way to Graestone. They are traveling on that very road. They have the men's names and descriptions. The court will decide the outcome."

Aunt Eggy grunted. "In my day, a warrior would defend the honor of the woman he loves and means tae keep." She made a grand jabbing motion with her arm. "He would have run his sword through the scunners." She eyed War. "Ye are keeping my Lula, are ye nae?"

War stood up straight. His face became cold. "Though I cannot pretend to know what *keeping* her means, I assume you mean as my wife. In this I cannot. Duty and circumstances will not allow it."

Aunt Eggy narrowed her eyes up at him. "What circumstances? What duty stops ye? Such havering and blethering ye speak."

Lula bit her lip and tugged at Aunt Eggy's arm. "Aunt Eggy," she said quickly and in a low voice. "He does not wish to marry me. Please, can we speak of this later, just you and me?"

Aunt Eggy looked back and forth between Lula and War. "Ye love him, this I know. And I believe he loves ye, Lula." She turned to War. "Ye love her, dinnae ye?" she demanded loudly.

War stood there like a soldier, looking straight ahead, refusing to answer.

Aunt Eggy rammed her tiny bun of hair back to the center of her head. "We all saw how ye kissed her!" She looked around at the men on the battlements who were staring back at them. They all nodded their heads. She turned back to War. "Ye dinnae kiss a lass like that unless ye mean tae marry her, Warrior!"

Still War stood fast, his lips in a hard line as the tops of his cheeks turned bright red.

"Aunt Eggy," Lula said softly. "Please, you are embarrassing me."

"Och, tis this big warrior that should be embarrassed. And ashamed, I am thinking." She looked up at her great-niece with fiery eyes. "Ye should be mad, dearling! Dinnae defend him!"

"Aunt Eggy," Lula said in a low, beseeching voice. "He does not want me," she said in a tight voice. "Can you not understand that? I can." She sighed in exasperation. "I am not my sister, Julia, blonde and blue-eyed and beautiful. Nor am I Birdie with raven hair and striking eyes that can talk and flirt with any man." She ignored Birdie's gasp. "I am no great beauty! A happily ever after was never in the stars for me. I knew this! I am odd and have always been odd. I am also scarred. I knew no one would want me. I, I just wanted a position to help horses. I am good at that. I have studied hard to be the best animal practitioner that I can be. That is what I want of life. Please do not embarrass me further. Please, just let it go!" she said in a choked voice as the tears threatened to come, for her heart was indeed breaking.

"But dearling, ye love him!" Aunt Eggy whispered.

Lula managed to stand up straight and lift her chin. "I will not demand someone tell me they love me just because I told them that I love them. Not when they clearly do not love me in return. Nor will I *argue* with them if they say *they do not want me*."

With those words, she lifted her chin even higher as she walked past War. She continued to walk along the battlements and away from the watching crowd and into her tower.

Aunt Eggy stared at her great-niece as she walked away. She turned back to War with her head tilted. "Ye better fix that, Warrior. If ye dinnae fix it, ye will regret it for the rest of yer life. Ye will find no better woman who could love ye more than that one right there." She jabbed a bony finger in Lula's direction. "*That one* that just walked away *from ye*." Then she jabbed her finger once in War's chest.

Aunt Eggy was about to walk away when War said her name in a hoarse, pain-filled voice.

"You don't understand, Egidia."

She stopped and turned back to him. "Make me understand then. Ye didnae kill yer brother-in-law so what could be yer difficulty?"

He made a slashing motion toward his men. "This castle and those I am responsible for," he said curtly. "'Tis no place for a wife. Look around you, Aunt Egidia."

Aunt Eggy peered up at him for several long moments. She took a step closer and craned her neck up at him. "I dinnae take ye for a glaikit mon, Warrior. I did look around yer castle. *All around* when I arrived and I asked many questions. Who has helped ye return the castle tae what it once was? Who has helped these men with their injuries? Who brought yer sister out of her room? Who has helped yer horses, *ye daft mon*?" She put her hands on her hips and waited. And waited some more.

"Lula," he said gruffly.

Aunt Eggy nodded her head. "Aye, Lula. But nae *just* Lula. Yer men, ye, and aye, Lula. It takes *all of ye*. Cannae ye see this? Ye cannae do any of this *alone*. A man needs a help mate. Ye couldnae have asked for a better one than that young lady whose heart ye just broke. The one ye just let walk away from ye. Ye need tae keep her!"

War rubbed his hand over the back of his neck. "I watched my parents die. I have watched more men die than I care to try to count. These men that are here, well, tis not always a safe place. I almost lost Lula, just now! And besides all that, I am scarred," he said softly. "You have no idea what is under this beard."

Aunt Eggy scoffed. "I *can* imagine, and I dinnae care about yer scars any more than Lula does. What do ye take her for? Some fluff-minded member of the *ton*?" She scoffed again. "We have all lost people we loved and those we were responsible for in one way or another." She jabbed her thin, bony finger at him again. "But ye cannae stop living, Warrior." She tilted her head up at him. "I didnae take ye for a mon that quits," she added quietly. "Sounds tae me like that is what ye are doing. Ye are afraid, I think. Ye are afraid of losing her, so ye reject her, instead of keeping her as yers forever, by yer side and in yer heart." She made a tsking noise. She looked over at the men, listening avidly to her conversation with their baron. She narrowed her eyes on them. "Seems tae me, they may have a say in keeping my Lula here at Graestone, but if ye all want tae send her away then so be it. I'll gladly take her home, *away from the bunch of ye foolish men*."

She made a sharp humming noise between her lips, shoved her bun off her ear back to the top of her head, called Birdie away from Freddie Rockingham, and off the two of them went in the same direction that Lula had gone.

I<small>T WAS EASY</small> for Lula to stay so busy that she did not see War for the next few days. The planning of the ball took all her time even with the help of Aunt Eggy, Birdie and Loveday. Loveday also offered for Lula to pick out one of her gowns. Lula found one that she thought would be agreeable to wear. It was different than her usual gowns. It was a pale green concoction with simple, plain, short sleeves, an empire waist and a full diaphanous skirt of more of the pale green fabric. It also had matching green slippers and a green ribbon for her hair.

Lula thought it all looked bland and very boring with the gown matching the slippers. There was a distinct lack of any other colors or interesting embellishments to give the gown or the slippers interest. *Perhaps dressing this way would make her less odd and hopefully more attractive to War?*

Her hair was another matter. She asked Loveday and Birdie to tame her curls to assemble it all in a smooth knot at the back of her neck.

Perhaps War would prefer her typically chaotic curls this way, she thought.

Secretly she could hope, but she knew there really was no hope to be had. The man simply did not love her or want her in his castle full of men. Her bags were packed and she would be ready to leave in the morning after the ball.

The night of the ball came and all was ready. The ballroom had been cleaned and it was as impressive as the great hall in all its splendor. It was lit with hundreds of candles in the shining sconces along the walls as well as in the row of gold and crystal chandeliers that hung down the center of the room.

Uncle Veyril was in his element as he welcomed each guest upon their arrival in the great hall. Aunt Eggy was at his side, though wandering off frequently when someone or something caught her attention. This evening, her thin, white hair was dyed an astonishing purple which made the pink of her balding scalp even brighter. Still, she was very proud of her hair as usual in its tiny bun and with her black, crisp, bombazine gown, the astonishing purple of her hair could not be missed.

The elegantly dressed couples that entered the great hall all stopped and stared at the beautiful space and, of course, the massive chandelier hanging above them. Once their awe and curiosity had been satisfied, they were drawn to the open doors of the ballroom where a small orchestra was playing and couples were milling around talking with drinks in their hands.

Lula had her hands full stopping the wildlings from shooting spitballs at anyone they deemed a fair target.

Ten was there with his eight sisters. They were following him everywhere he went like a flock of ducks, all moving in unison. Each of the Adair girls was lovely.

War was nowhere to be seen.

There were red-coated uniforms everywhere, as well, mixing with some of the villagers dressed in their finest. All had been made welcome to the reopening of Graestone.

Uncle Veyril opened the ball and the dancing, with Aunt Eggy proudly joining him in a slow, sedate dance. Soon, the dance floor was full of couples.

Birdie buzzed amongst the redcoats looking for Freddie Rockingham so she could dance as well. She was dressed in a lovely gown of royal blue velvet with dainty puffed shoulders and long, tightly fitting sleeves and a high waist. The gown looked striking with her bright blue eyes and raven-colored hair piled atop her head in a mass of midnight curls.

Tuedy had outdone himself with the menu. His marchpane sugar chess pieces were so beautiful no one dared touch them much less take a bite of one.

Loveday wore her gold gown, of course. Her hair was in a severe bun at the back of her neck and her face was covered in the white cream she preferred to use. She stood at the back of the room, hovering near a potted plant, watching the couples dance.

A hush came over the room at the late arrival of two couples.

A tall man with ebony hair dressed in a black tunic and black pants with a curved, ornamental Persian knife in a decorative sheath on his belt stood at the entrance to the ballroom. On his arm was a regal-looking, lovely blonde woman in a pale, blue-green gown fit for a princess. Beside them was another couple holding a baby boy. The woman had black hair and bright blue eyes and the man had dark hair with a hint of gray at his temples. He had the bearing of a soldier, or an intimidating duke.

Birdie let out an excited scream which caught Lula's attention, and then she, too, was hurrying toward the two couples. Their oldest sister, Julia, and Julia's husband, Pasha, had arrived as had Lula and Birdie's mother, Lady Amelia, along with her husband, Lord Alexander Hawke, the Duke of Leids and their new baby brother, Alex.

Birdie was holding her baby brother and cooing away to him when Lula walked over. Instantly, her mother's eyes were alert.

"Lula, dearling, what is it?" Lady Amelia asked quietly.

Lula did not answer her mother right away. Instead, she held her hands out for her new little brother. The chubby baby gurgled out a bubble and Lula smiled as she scooped him into her arms.

"Lula's heart is broken, Mother," Birdie answered for her. "She is sad, morose, and despondent!"

"What?" Hawke snarled. "Who broke her heart?" he demanded as he looked around the ballroom as if the heartbreaker would appear with his hand raised declaring that it was he.

Julia stared with wide blue eyes at her sister. "You fell in love, Lula? I cannot believe that of you, and why are you dressed in one simple color and your hair is painfully neat and, well, it is not curly? What has happened to you?"

"Lula?" her mother repeated quietly. "Are you sad and despondent and morose?"

Lula stared over the baby's dark, curly head at her mother. "I can assure you that I am not sad, nor morose, nor am I despondent. I shall not let myself have those emotions over a man who does not want me. I can be happy alone just as I always planned I would be. Happily ever afters are not meant for everyone." She frowned and rubbed her cheek over the baby's silken hair. "Only the lucky, I suppose," she added in a whisper.

"Oh, dear," Amelia whispered and looked at her husband.

"Who is this man that does not want you?" Hawke said angrily. "He must be a fool."

"She even told him that she loved him, Mother," Birdie announced. "She is surely sad and morose and despondent. How can she not be when she has been so cruelly rejected?"

Pasha was staring quietly at Lula. He knew her well. She was intelligent and a great reader. She was not prone to emotions or passions like her sparkling sister, Julia, or to flirtations and dreams of fairy tales like Birdie. Lula had always been steady and the calm in the storm. If she had fallen in love and decided she was better off alone—well, he could not fathom this for her.

"To be alone, without someone to love, is a waste of the body. To be not alone, without one to love, is a waste of the soul," Pasha said quietly.

Lula looked over at him. "It cannot truly be love I felt, Pasha. I only knew him for a week or so. I shall return home and all will be as it was."

Pasha tilted his head at her. "Sometimes, a stranger known to us for mere moments can spark our souls to a kinship we will have for eternity."

"*Azizam*—my darling," Julia whispered. "I do not think you are helping."

Lula shook her head. "Pasha, he does not love me. That is all the answer I need to know to make the decision that I should leave this place."

"Sometimes, one must not seek answers, but rather to understand the question," Pasha stated with eyes only for his lovely but very sad sister-in-law.

Birdie crossed her arms over her breasts and began tapping her foot in irritation. "She is heartbroken. What question could there be, Pasha?"

Pasha calmly turned his head to his youngest sister-in-law. "What is stopping this man from loving her? For how can he not?"

"Would someone tell me who is this man we are speaking of?" demanded Hawke once again as he looked back and forth from Lula to his wife and the others.

Birdie spoke to her mother. "They shared some very lovely kisses, right in front of all the men up on the battlements. That was after he saved her from being strangled and thrown over the edge of the crenellation by a madman. He saved her, for a *second* time! It was so romantic! And then he ordered the cannon to be shot at the escaping villains! Terribly exciting!"

"What?" roared Hawke. "*Who strangled you, Lula? Who was going to throw you over the edge? And this man kissed you? He must marry you then. I shall demand it!"*

Pasha began to speak. "To force—"

Hawke held up his hand. "Stop. I cannot hear your wise platitudes at the moment, my friend. Whoever this man is, he compromised my stepdaughter!"

Lula's mouth fell open. "He most certainly did not! He is ever the gentleman! He did not lay his hands on me. He knew I would faint if he did. No, he kissed me without touching me. It was wondrous," she added in a whisper.

"This gets worse and worse," Amelia said with a concerned look on her face for her middle child. "Where is Aunt Eggy?"

"She is on the dance floor, Mother," Lula said calmly as she kissed her baby brother's fingers and rocked him back and forth.

Lady Amelia bit her bottom lip as she stared meaningfully at her daughter. "So, are we to assume that you are no longer fainting at the sight of Baron de Walton?"

Lula stilled her rocking of her baby brother. "Oh, Mother!"

Lady Amelia smiled softly with a knowing look.

"You knew it was him all along, didn't you? Just like Aunt Eggy," Lula said. "You two planned this, didn't you? You knew I would fall in love with him once I realized that it was he that had saved me from those assassins."

Hawke studied his stepdaughter. "You fell in love *with the baron*? I was told he was a big, angry, rough-looking man that terrified you into a faint when you last saw him. That is the man we have been speaking of?"

Lula frowned. "He is only a little angry and I rather like his rough looks. But he is so gentle with the injured war horses and he has given the injured soldiers a second chance. He is well read and writes music and plays the violin and pianoforte, and, well, he is not the man I thought he was, truly."

Hawke scowled. "But this paragon of a man says he does not love you?" he said curtly. "I judged him wrong. He sounds like a typical aristocratic member of the *ton*. A prig and a dandy, no doubt." He looked around the ballroom. "Where is he?"

Pasha hid a smile. "I believe that is him, coming this way. The *dandy* with all those soldiers behind him."

Hawke turned to look where Pasha had motioned.

He went still. It was rare that he found himself looking up at another man. This one was a giant, both wide in the chest and shoulders as well as tall. His eyes narrowed on the man coming toward him.

"You did not tell me that Baron de Walton is the man *better known as Captain War*. The man that carried a damned cannon off the battlefield for God's sake. He is no dandy. The opposite, in fact."

Amelia whispered as she, too, kept her eyes on the large, angry-looking man coming their way. "Lula? Are you sure about this man?" Her voice lowered. "He looks different than when we last saw him at Julia and Pasha's wedding. I do not remember all those scars," she murmured.

Just then, Aunt Eggy walked up behind Amelia. "Och, he has

shaved off his beard! And trimmed his hair tae. It is still long but what a guid-looking man he is! Have ye ever seen such muscles on a warrior?" She clasped her hand over her heart as she watched War come to a stop in front of Hawke.

"Your Grace," War said with a sharp, single nod to Hawke. He turned slightly toward Amelia. "My lady, welcome to Graestone."

Aunt Eggy stepped forward. "May I present the Baron Warwick de Walton tae ye both?"

Hawke found his voice as he stared up at the man in awe. "Captain War. You are a legend. You carried a cannon off the battlefield."

War turned back to Hawke. "A small cannon." He pointed to the scars visible on the side of his neck and lower cheek. "Left a mark, however. You are a legend as well, Lord Hawke."

Lula scoffed. "*That* is the scar you have been hiding? That is *a trifle*." She gave the baby to Birdie. "If you men are done mutually admiring one another, will you all excuse me? I have a few things left to pack and then I shall be ready to return to Aldbey Park with you. At once." She spun around and was about to walk away when War's voice stopped her.

"I would speak to you, Lula."

Hawke shook himself. "No, you will speak to me, her stepfather. And it is *Miss* Lula to you."

War's shoulders straightened and his chin rose as his cheeks pinkened.

"We can discuss this ourselves," Hawke said sharply. "You can dismiss your men. I will not kill you. *Yet*."

"Kill me?" War grumbled. He looked over at Pasha. "Prince," he said with a nod.

Pasha stood there with his arms crossed. He could not help grinning. "War," he nodded.

"What manner of havoc is this, Prince?" War asked in confusion. "He wants to kill me?"

"Dismiss your men," Hawke growled again.

"Good God and bloody hell and the devil take it, what are you asking?" War glared at Hawke.

Another tall man stepped forward beside War. "Allow me. Ten Adair, Earl of Fairfax, at your service."

"Oh, my," Julia whispered as she stared at the handsome earl with the charming dimple in his chin.

Pasha frowned and dropped one arm to curl it around his wife's waist and pull her close.

Ten smiled charmingly. "My big friend here is not overtly loquacious. The matter at hand that must be spoken is this: the men of Graestone wish to keep Miss Lula," he stated calmly.

Silence came.

"What?" Hawke snarled.

Tuedy and Todrick Tweedy stepped up beside Ten Adair. "We want to keep her, eh?" Tuedy said in a high voice as he fluttered the fingers of one hand in the air. "Lady Ross said it is a Scottish tradition. We are invoking it."

Todrick nodded. "She saved my life. I am bloody keeping her, too," he rasped in his hoarse voice. He shrugged. "She has grown on me. Plus, her salve is bloody working so it would not be right if she left," he nodded several times.

"She saved my Buttercup's life," Alton Ditchburn said firmly as he stepped to the front of the crowd of men. "I am keeping her."

"No one can handle the horses like she can," Poppy said quickly. "I am keeping her."

Bertie shouldered his way forward. "She made the castle a home. It is filled with light and life now. I am keeping her."

"We want to continue to hear her sing her songs," Ned said. "So I am keeping her."

"Even though it is bloody strange that she sings sea ditties," Todrick said with a frown. "That's not right, she needs a new song."

Birdie clapped her hands and let out a joyful laugh. "She only sings when she is nervous."

The men nodded and shook their heads as they smiled and, one by one, continued to speak their wishes to keep Lula.

A woman in gold with far too much paint on her face, holding the hands of three little boys, came slowly and nervously forward. "We are keeping her as well," she said with a shy smile. "I would still be hiding in my room if it were not for Lula."

One of the little boys nodded his head emphatically. "She is *our* Miss Lula. She throws the best snowballs and does not mind when we shoot our spitballs at people. Mostly she doesn't mind, anyway. So, we are keeping her."

Hawke looked around at the crowd of people. He then looked over at Lula who was standing there behind him with her hands on her cheeks and tears in her eyes as she stared back at all those saying they wanted to keep her.

Slowly, he arched a brow and turned to stare at the big warrior who had eyes only for Lula.

Aunt Eggy looked up at War as well. "Warrior? Are ye going tae say something? If so, now would be a guid time tae do so."

War's cheeks turned red. He swallowed tightly as he stared at Lula.

CHAPTER TWENTY-SIX

LULA'S EYES WERE caught by War's. She waited for him to speak. Breathless and full of hope.

When he said nothing, she let go of a deep breath and turned to her family.

"He does not want me. I am odd, scarred and freckle-faced with incorrigible, untamed hair and I wear discordant colors that he does not approve of. Please, can you take me home now?"

"I am thoroughly captivated by your hair, *and your freckles*. Have I not told you this countless times?" War asked in a hoarse, gruff rumble. He pointed to her gown. "Why are you dressed this way? Where are all your colors that you said others would deem to be ugly but you think are beautiful?"

Lula looked down at her gown. "I was trying to please you," she said with a lift of her chin.

War took a step toward her. "You please me just as you were, not this way. I love all the colors you wear. I love the riot of curls that are always wreaking havoc around your face." He swallowed tightly as his cheeks pinkened further. "My word is truth when I say that I am captivated by your freckles, Lula, and your scars mean nothing to me, nothing except for a reminder of my failure to protect you that night long ago in Hyde Park." His voice was quiet. He saw no one but Lula. "Just as I almost lost you on the battlements." He rubbed at the back of his neck as he looked at the marble floor and then back to her. "Lula, my love. It is not that I do not love you. It is that I love you so much it terrifies me," he whispered in a thick, deep voice. "I have faced entire armies of enemies and I have never been so terrified as at the thought of losing you." His voice was a hoarse whisper, aching with tension and love.

Lula's heart started racing within her chest. "Oh, War," she whispered as she clutched her hands together under her chin and stared at him.

"I cut my hair and shaved my beard for you," he added nervously.

"I see that," Lula whispered. "You are very handsome with or without the beard, Baron. You did not need to do that for me," she offered with a small smile.

"I am scarred." His voice was tight, wretched, *nervous*.

"So am I," she whispered brokenly.

"I play the violin or the pianoforte at night because I cannot sleep. When I close my eyes, I see every battle I have fought and every man I have lost. Until you came. My music has changed now. It is for you. It is what is in my heart. *You* have become my music."

A tear spilled from Lula's eye and trickled down her cheek. She could only nod. "I love to hear you play," she whispered and took a step toward him.

"Will you keep me, Lula? My men and me?" he said in a soft, low baritone. "I love you," he whispered hoarsely. *"My word is truth* when I say that I love you, every bit of you. *You have thoroughly captivated me, Lula my love.* Keep me?"

Lula put her hand to her mouth to stifle the sob that was threatening to overtake her. She nodded several times as more tears came.

Lula could not hold herself back. She flew into his arms. Instantly, he scooped her off her toes and held her tightly as he swung her around, burying his face in her sweet neck and then covering her face in kisses.

Lula laughed with joy until she caught his face between her hands and put her lips to his.

War growled and carried her out of the ballroom.

"Best tae get those two married quickly," Aunt Eggy said as she watched Lula and War walk out into the great hall. "I knew they would fall in love, aye, I did! It all happened just as I planned." Her eyes went to Birdie who was looking over at Freddie Rockingham. Freddie was surrounded by a group of young ladies vying for his attention. "I havenae found Birdie a husband who deserves her yet," she tsked to herself.

Birdie looked over at her great-aunt. "Aunt Eggy, don't say that. Come, let me bring you over to Freddie and you may talk to him."

Aunt Eggy pursed her lips. "I'd rather have a vera long needle stuck in my eye," she mumbled under her breath.

Birdie turned away from staring at Freddie to look at her great-aunt. "What did you say, Aunt Eggy?"

Aunt Eggy waved her bony fingers. "Och, I said I have something in my eye. I will stay here. Ye go. Off with ye now."

Just then, Ten and his eight sisters walked past her. One of his sisters suddenly let out a "Woops!" as one of her slippered feet slid out from under her on the marble floor. The dainty shoe went flying up in the air as the young lady landed on her backside with her mouth open. She started laughing as she stared up at the people looking at her. She rose to her feet and collected her slipper and calmly put it on, raised her chin and then hurried to catch up with her sisters with a grin on her blushing face.

Aunt Eggy nodded and grinned back to her as she caught her eye.

A tap on her shoulder had her turning to look up at Lady Loveday's white-painted face. "I heard what you said, about Lula and Birdie. Can you find *me* a husband, Lady Ross?" she asked shyly. "A good man. A man who will love my boys?"

Aunt Eggy grinned a big, broad grin as she rubbed her hands together. "Och, aye, I can do that! I can find ye a guid man that will love ye *and* yer wildlings! I must think on it for a wee bit."

>>><<<

WAR ROLLED OVER on his back in the huge bed and pulled his wife against his side. The two of them were out of breath and sweat glistened on their hot skin.

Lula cuddled up against her husband's magnificent chest with a satisfied smile that was also full of wonder.

Her husband did not seem to be having any trouble sleeping these nights since they had been married. But, of course, she imagined he must be tired out from their lovemaking. Lula had no idea she would enjoy it so much, nor that she would be demanding her husband to make love to her each night, several times a night and during the day as well. They snuck off often to find time together. Lula loved her husband's body, she loved his kisses. She loved joining their two bodies together.

"You are carrying my son," War whispered in the dark lit only by one candle beside their bed.

Lula could hear the pride in his voice. "You cannot know that. It is too soon."

"I *know*," War grumbled sleepily. "It is a son."

"It could be a daughter," she said and yawned mightily. She felt War go still beside her.

"Good God and bloody hell and the devil confound it! I shall wreak havoc on the man that hurts my daughter," he growled. He was fully awake now.

"It could be a son," Lula said as she patted his chest to calm him.

War sighed loudly. "This having children is hard."

"Easier for you than me," Lula said with a grin and kissed his shoulder. She rolled over onto her husband's chest and stared into his brown eyes. "I love you, War. *My word is truth.*"

He pulled her down to him and kissed her thoroughly, hungrily and with so much love it made Lula's heart thud in her chest.

"I give you my vow that I love you, Lula my love. I love your freckles, and your chaotic curls. And the odd colors you wear. Even those breeches that mold to your perfectly shaped bottom. My word is truth," War said in a sweet, dulcet baritone. "You *thoroughly captivate me.*"

The end...or rather, the beginning of War and Lula's life together...

This story is for all the men and women who have been through hell and back, whatever that hell may be.

May you find your courage to go after your own happily ever afters.

Never let go of the reins that guide your dreams…

Chantry

About Lula's song

"Ben Backstay" was written by Charles Dibdin. He was the eighteenth son of a poor silver maker. He was born in Southampton in 1740 and died in London in 1814. In 1778, he became resident composer at Covent Garden. In 1803, the British government paid him to write a series of songs to "keep alive the national feelings against the French."

Dibdin's songs were said to be worth ten thousand sailors to the cause of England. His songs were also popular in Canada and America before and during the American Revolution and during the War of 1812.

Ben Backstay was a bos'n
He was a jolly boy,
And none as he so merrily
Could pipe all hands ahoy;
Could pipe all hands ahoy;
Could pipe all hands ahoy.
With a chip, chop! cherry chop!
Fol de rol, riddle-rop!
Chip, chop! cherry chop!
Fol de rol ray!
With a chip, chop! cherry chop!
Fol de rol, riddle-rop!
Chip, chop! cherry chop!
Fol de rol ray!

Once sailing with a captain,
Who was a jolly dog,

Our Ben and all his messmates got
A double share of grog;
A double share of grog;
A double share of grog.
With a chip, chop! cherry chop!
Fol de rol, riddle-rop!
Chip, chop! cherry chop!
Fol de rol ray!
With a chip, chop! cherry chop!
Fol de rol, riddle-rop!
Chip, chop! cherry chop!
Fol de rol ray!

So Benny he got tipsy.
Quite to his heart's content,
And leaning o'er the starboard side
Right overboard he went;
Right overboard he went;
Right overboard he went.
With a chip, chop! cherry chop!
Fol de rol, riddle-rop!
Chip, chop! cherry chop!
Fol de rol ray!
With a chip, chop! cherry chop!
Fol de rol, riddle-rop!
Chip, chop! cherry chop!
Fol de rol ray!

A shark was on the starboard side
And sharks no man can stand,
For they do gobble up everything
Just like the sharks on land;
Just like the sharks on land;

Just like the sharks on land.
With a chip, chop! cherry chop!
Fol de rol, riddle-rop!
Chip, chop! cherry chop!
Fol de rol ray!
With a chip, chop! cherry chop!
Fol de rol, riddle-rop!
Chip, chop! cherry chop!
Fol de rol ray!

They threw out some tackling
To give his life a hope
But as the shark bit off his head
He couldn't see the rope;
He couldn't see the rope;
He couldn't see the rope.
With a chip, chop! cherry chop!
Fol de rol, riddle-rop!
Chip, chop! cherry chop!
Fol de rol ray!
With a chip, chop! cherry chop!
Fol de rol, riddle-rop!
Chip, chop! cherry chop!
Fol de rol ray!

At twelve o'clock his ghost appeared
Upon the quarter decks
"Ho, pipe all hands ahoy" it cried,
"From me a warning take;"
"From me a warning take;"
"From me a warning take."
With a chip, chop! cherry chop!
Fol de rol, riddle-rop!

Chip, chop! cherry chop!
Fol de rol ray!
With a chip, chop! cherry chop!
Fol de rol, riddle-rop!
Chip, chop! cherry chop!
Fol de rol ray!

"Through drinking grog I lost my life,
The same fate you may meet
So never mix your grog too strong,
But always take it neat!"
But always take it neat!"
But always take it neat!"
With a chip, chop! cherry chop!
Fol de rol, riddle-rop!
Chip, chop! cherry chop!
Fol de rol ray!
With a chip, chop! cherry chop!
Fol de rol, riddle-rop!
Chip, chop! cherry chop!
Fol de rol ray!

About the Author

Chantry Dawes lives on her horse farm in the south east where she raised her four sons and wrote historical romance in her spare time. She has two dogs, a cat and several horses. Once her four boys were grown up and gone, she turned to writing full time.

Chantry's stories always have strong women, oftentimes a horse or two, and men who very often think they are coming to their ladies' rescue, only to find out that it was themselves who were *blissfully* rescued by their lady. A self proclaimed history nerd, she is fascinated by the massive part that horses have played all throughout history. She believes that no tale is complete without that sigh worthy hero who comes riding up to his lady on an equally swoon worthy horse.

Step into her new Aldbey Park series and see for yourself... beginning with *Thoroughly in Love*.

CPSIA information can be obtained
at www.ICGtesting.com
Printed in the USA
LVHW051301200422
716609LV00014B/1193

9 781956 003987